out

of

love

out

of

love

A NOVEL

hazel hayes

DUTTON

DUTTON

An imprint of Penguin Random House LLC
penguinrandomhouse.com

First published in 2020 in the UK by Unbound

LIBRARY OF CONGRESS CATALOGING-IN-PUBLICATION DATA
has been applied for.

ISBN 9780593184523 (paperback)
ISBN 9780593184530 (ebook)

Printed in the United States of America
1st Printing

BOOK DESIGN BY ALISON CNOCKAERT

out

of

love

prologue

THERE IS A MOMENT every writer knows; long before they ever put pen to paper, there is a point of inception, inspiration, imagination—call it what you will—a magic hour of the mind made beautiful, like most things are, by its transience. It won't last. You can't keep it. No more than you could keep the spark that lights a flame. But you remember it with every ending; that moment, before it all began, before your perfect creation was made imperfect by logistics and limitations. That moment is what I love most about creating something new: the idea, the spark, the beginning, when what might have been was still what might be.

muscle memory

"CUP OF TEA?"

I've asked him this a hundred times before. I ask it now, casually, as though nothing has changed. As though this time is the same as all the others. But before the words have even left my mouth I think, *That's the last time you'll ever ask him that question.*

I know it's true too. Because all this "let's be friends" stuff is bullshit. Theo has no intention of being my friend; that's just something he's been saying to make it easier—not for me, of course, but for him.

He asked if we could have a break but what he meant was a breakup. He moved most of his stuff out of our apartment while I was home in Dublin, crying on my mother's sofa. He stopped loving me a long time ago but wasn't brave enough to tell me. And so our relationship kept trundling forward like a wagon down a dirt road, with me tied to the back like a rag doll. I imagine myself bouncing about in the dust, with a stitched-on smile and vacant eyes, just happy the rope is holding. The image is so morbidly funny that I have to conceal a grin.

"Sure. Thanks," says Theo.

Go fuck yourself, I think, in response to his perfectly reasonable answer to my question. This is going to be interesting.

As I fill the kettle I can sense him start to notice his surroundings.

"The place looks great," he says. He's not being facetious. It does. I redecorated.

In the two months since he left, I've found it increasingly easy to accept that this is no longer *our* apartment; it is *my* apartment. The things that once served as comforting reminders of him have now grown alien and unwanted, which is why I want them all gone.

The first thing I did was dismantle the photo wall—dozens of pictures of us hung from rows of twine with miniature wooden pegs—my first and only attempt at being the kind of woman who is crafty around the house. As I took the pictures down and placed them in a shoebox (I wasn't quite ready to throw them away), I noted how smug we seemed in each one: big, stupid smiles, cheeks pressed together, arms around waists. Here we were at a music festival. And here, outside the gates of Buckingham Palace. In one photo we were lying half-naked on a beach with the Pacific Ocean stretching out behind us. I remember how Theo splashed me with the icy water, bringing my skin out in goose pimples and making me shriek with laughter.

None of the photos were recent; most were taken early on in our relationship, when Theo would capture me in random, mundane moments—snuggled up on the sofa or laughing with friends. I used to love how he would take my picture unprompted, and not just on special occasions, like this candid of me, standing on the Ha'penny Bridge in the snow, looking back over my shoulder at him.

The last photo I took down was a Polaroid Theo took of me just a few days into what would become our five years together. In it, I'm lying in his bed half-asleep, my body tangled in his bedsheets, back exposed, one leg jutting out, and a mass of auburn hair spilling out across the pillow like warm honey.

He kept those sheets, the ones with the big green, red, and black circles on. They came with us from home to home over the years, and on the night Theo left, as he stuffed some clothes into black plastic bags, he held them in his hands and wondered whether to take those sheets or a different set.

He was going to stay with a friend, he said. Steve, he said. Who the fuck is Steve? I asked, but that was neither here nor there. He would just stay with Steve for a couple of weeks, he said, get his head straight, he said, take a little break and then maybe we could go on a holiday and reevaluate, he said.

"But Steve only has a blow-up mattress, so I'll need to bring sheets."

It struck me as odd how, in the midst of what was a seemingly out-of-the-blue breakup, Theo already knew where he was going and what the situation regarding bedsheets would be when he arrived. And as he stood there, like a child asking his mother which towel to bring to swimming practice, it dawned on me what was happening.

I say that like the information came to me and stayed with me. It didn't. It was more like a gap in the clouds than a dawning, really. Just a glimmer of clarity that would soon pass, returning at odd intervals and increasing in length until eventually the clouds cleared completely and my brain fully accepted that it was over. The clouds wouldn't clear for some time, but in that moment, in that gap, I said, "You're leaving me, Theo, take both fucking sets of sheets." He said nothing. He packed them both.

After I'd placed the last photo in the shoebox, I stood, hands on hips, and stared for a while at the blank space I'd created on the wall. The little wooden pegs hung there, gripping onto nothing, but they didn't stay that way for long; the next day I filled that empty space with pictures of friends and family, covering it in memories independent of Theo, ones that existed in a different part of my mind, a part that didn't hurt to access.

When the wall was full, I looked at the remaining stacks of photos I had printed out and decided to keep going. I stuck them all over the fridge, but still there were more. So I stuck them to the kitchen cabinets too. I had to run to the shop to get more Blu Tack and by the end of the evening my entire kitchen was covered in photos. When I finished, I chuckled to myself at the sheer number of pictures, then realized how much like a psychopath I would seem to the casual observer and erupted into a proper belly laugh at my own expense. My laughter sounded odd in the empty apartment.

I had a cleansing of sorts, boxing up Theo's things and removing everything that reminded me of him. I bought new bedsheets; crisp white with orange embroidery across the bottom. I sold the leather sofa I'd always hated and got a comfy second-hand one instead, scattering yellow cushions on it and adding a knitted throw and a brightly colored rug. I hung new artwork on the walls. I even lit scented candles every night, so that the smell would be different. Everyone who comes to visit now remarks at how much cozier the place feels, and I wonder why I didn't do this before.

I've welcomed the onset of winter and the increasingly long evenings, which provide the perfect excuse to settle into my snug new space and read all the books I'd been meaning to get to. I curl up on the sofa with Norah Ephron or Joan Didion or some other former heartbreakee who's been there and done that and lived to tell the tale. Sometimes I stop to contemplate a particularly relatable passage, relishing the silence as I stare at the bare treetops just outside my window, their skinny black branches quivering in the breeze, blindly searching for something just out of reach.

And when I get cold, I put the heating on, choosing to ignore Theo's voice in my head telling me to turn it off and put more clothes on instead. If anything, the place is a bit too warm.

The hardest and most worthwhile change I made was to replace the framed *Star Wars* posters in what had been our bedroom. I first saw them in Theo's apartment—the one he lived in when we met—and after that they hung in every home we ever shared. Our mutual love for *Star Wars* was one of the first things we talked about, and during our honeymoon days, snuggled up in his flat, we binged the original trilogy on a regular basis.

It wasn't the emotional attachment that made taking down the posters difficult. The fact is, I was absolutely terrified that somehow this breakup would ruin *Star Wars* for me; the physical act of removing those pictures from what was now my bedroom felt like a tiny defeat, and while I could accept that there were songs I'd no longer be able to listen to, places I would have to avoid for a while, and even people I would never see again, the idea that it might now be difficult for me to watch *Star Wars*—that I would forever associate those films with this shit show of a relationship—that stung.

But I did take them down and I immediately replaced them with three new posters of three powerful women; now Ellen Ripley, Sarah Connor, and the Bride hang side by side above my bed and I sleep a little better with them there. By the way, I've since watched all three *Star Wars* films and I'm happy to report that I still felt a childlike glee throughout.

Theo's here today to collect the rest of his stuff—the stuff he didn't shove in a black bag that first night or sneak out of the apartment when I wasn't home—but he hasn't seen the bedroom yet. I'm looking forward to that. In fact, I had to resist the urge to laugh out loud when he walked in and was met by the un-missable display of photos in the kitchen. I could see the cogs turning, his brain offering up to him the possibility that I had entirely lost it, and this, coupled with my chirpy demeanor in what I'm sure he was expecting would be an altogether more somber scene, must be confusing him greatly. It wasn't my inten-tion to confuse him, only to show him that I'm just fine without him. Any other negative feelings on his part are a bonus.

I flick the switch on the kettle while Theo grapples with the new decor. I see him spot a pair of red heels by the sofa—the pair I kicked off after a night out and chose not to put away in the hopes that he'd notice them. It's not pretty, but it's true; I wanted him to see them. I wanted him to wonder where I'd been. What kind of night I'd had. If I got drunk. Or flirted with anyone. Maybe brought someone back here. Had sex with that someone in our bed. I wanted those heels to remind him of the time I wore them for him with red lingerie. And now I want him to imagine me wearing them for someone else. And I want that thought to cut him.

I haven't been with anyone else, as it happens. That night—like most nights lately—I got into bed and cried, partly from loneliness, and partly from a sense of relief at having made it through another day. Truth be told, the thought of anyone touching me right now feels deeply wrong. I did go on a date, but that was just an attempt to convince myself that I'm okay, which is ironic, really, because it only served to prove that I'm very much not.

The date wasn't planned as such. Last week I was having tapas with a friend when I spotted a very attractive guy at the table behind us. I was genuinely taken aback by how good-looking this man was. I say man—I mean boy; he was a boy. At least to me he was; I'm thirty and I guessed he was about twenty-three. He was having dinner with his parents, so to avoid feeling entirely predatory, I wrote my number on a napkin and asked the waiter to give it to him when I left.

It was one of those "fuck it" moments you get in the throes of grief.

An hour later I got a text. I saved him in my phone as "The

Guy from the Tapas Place." We chatted for a few days. Then we went on a date. It was awful.

Now, I'm sure people have been on much worse dates than this one. The Guy from the Tapas Place wasn't sleazy or obnoxious or mean. He was just vapid; a beautiful, empty vessel of a man who taught me that making conversation with someone who has no ambitions in life and no real interest in anything can be quite difficult.

We went to a cocktail bar in Shoreditch with a sort of eighties nostalgia vibe—the wallpaper looks like hundreds of little cassette tapes and the menus come in flimsy cassette-tape holders. Novelty menus become decidedly less novel when your world is falling apart, though, so all of this was lost on me. Still, we ordered cocktails and chatted as best we could for a few short, endless hours.

He's a model—of course he's a model—but he's "not actually that interested in modeling"; he was just eager to earn some extra cash because, as it turns out, working at his mate's brewery didn't pay very well. He was approached on the street one day and offered a modeling gig by an attractive older woman.

"Not unlike you," he said.

I'll take that.

When it felt like an appropriate amount of time had passed, I suggested we call it a night. The waiter came over with a bill for sixty pounds and the Guy from the Tapas Place made no move to get his wallet out. I'm usually happy to split the bill—I don't expect a man to pay the whole thing—but I definitely do expect him to not expect me to pay it just because he's gorgeous, which is what I began to suspect was happening here. Also, the cocktails were ten pounds each, and he'd had four; I'd had two. So we kept talking, but now there was an elephant in the form of a bill, sitting on the table in front of us.

The tension was finally broken when the waiter, half-bent forward in an apologetic fashion, announced that the bar would soon be closing. At this point, my date, having definitely already seen the amount we owed, leaned over, looked at the bill, and inhaled sharply through his teeth.

"That's a lot!"

"Yeah," I said, resisting the urge to explain basic math.

He kept looking at it in puzzlement until finally I caved and we split the bill fifty-fifty.

As we walked toward the train station, he took my hand in his. An oddly tender move for a first date, I thought. When he put his arm around my waist I broke, giggling uncontrollably. I assured him that everything was fine—I was just a bit tipsy, you know, from the two cocktails—but the truth is I found this all incredibly awkward, and I find awkward situations incredibly funny. I don't know why. Maybe it's a physical reaction, like how people laugh on roller coasters. Either way, I was done.

I stopped and announced that I'd rather get a taxi. I said good night and told him I'd had fun, and I really felt like I was doing a good job of ending things there, but somehow he managed to mooch about until a cab arrived and the next thing I knew he was in it with me. Since we both lived in the same direction, he said, we might as well share a cab. I made a big point of telling the driver there'd be two stops.

When we pulled up outside his house, the Guy from the Tapas Place leaned across the back seat for what I thought was going to be a hug. It wasn't. As I put my arms halfheartedly around him he kissed me, but given my assumption that we were hugging, the trajectory was off and his mouth caught the corner of mine. My entire body cringed. He probably felt it. But not one to be discouraged, he looked at me and in the most dramatically Hollywood fashion said, "I can do better than that."

That was it. There was no way I was getting away without kissing this fool. So I let him kiss me. I even kind of kissed him back—nobody wants to be remembered as a bad kisser—and then it was over and he gazed adoringly at me for a moment before finally pissing off into the night, never to be seen again. Incidentally, he didn't offer me any money for the cab.

I looked him up when I got home and found photos of him in Calvin Klein underwear. I imagined waking up next to him, shafts of sunlight pouring across a body that shouldn't rightly exist in nature, carved specifically with moments like this in mind. Then I imagined him smiling up at me, and I shuddered.

I texted him a few days later to tell him the truth: that I thought I was ready to date again but it turns out I wasn't. I left out the part about him being a beautiful, empty vessel of a man, even though he probably would have taken it as a compliment.

Theo looks at the high heels, then at me, then immediately averts his gaze. I can't tell what he's thinking, but his face seems to be locked in a permanent state of semi-anguish. He looks terrible. His longish almond hair, which he always styles into a messy quiff, now lies limp and frizzy on his forehead. His whole body, usually poised in an athletic stance, seems sort of sunken somehow, and his skin is paler than usual, with dark puffy circles under his eyes.

I wonder if he's been crying. If he regrets leaving. Part of me hopes he does. Part of me hopes that being back here reminds him how good he had it, and that seeing me looking intentionally, effortlessly gorgeous will make him realize he made a mistake. I want him to drop to his knees and beg to be allowed back into my life. Not because I want him back, mind you—I'm through the worst of it now and I know that getting back together would be an insult to all I've been through—I just want to know that he knows he won't survive without me. I think that would make me feel better.

"How's your mother?" he asks. I make a mental note that we've arrived at chitchat.

"Great."

"Yeah?"

"No, Theo. She's upset, obviously."

"Oh."

The kettle begins to boil, its steady crescendo adding some much-needed tension to the situation.

"So, are we going to talk about all the women you've been seeing?" I ask.

"Fucking hell!"

That's not a denial.

"Because one of the main reasons you cited for ending our relationship," I go on, "was a desperate need to 'focus on yourself' and 'spend some time alone,' and now I hear you're making every effort to avoid being alone."

"How did you find out?" he asks, and his nonchalance actually hurts a little, but I don't let that show.

"Oh please," I say. "You've spent weeks coming on to every woman in every bar this side of the Thames. We have a lot of mutual friends, Theo. Word gets around."

That's not entirely true; I read his text messages using an old phone he left behind. But I can't tell him that.

"Well, I've been grieving," says Theo. "I'm a fucking mess. It doesn't mean anything, I just needed an outlet."

"I hope you opened with that."

"Piss off."

"No, really, did you tell them they meant nothing up front or as they were collecting their knickers off your floor?" I ask.

"Oh God," I say, suddenly realizing, "have you been fucking women on a blow-up mattress?"

"I've got a real bed now," he retorts, and I exhale involuntarily as his words land like a punch to the gut.

"Well," I say, "who's a big boy, then?"

He regrets saying that. I can tell. But he won't say so.

"Look, can we not do this please?" he says. "I'm not feeling great."

"Not do what, Theo? Argue or break up or move your things out? Because the first is optional but the latter two are definitely happening."

"Well, I'm not the one who's been lording it about all over the internet!"

Two things strike me about this sentence. Firstly, yes, I have dramatically increased both the quality and quantity of my

Instagram posts. They have followed the exact same pattern as that of every other recently dumped woman: beginning with inspirational quotes and pictures of sunsets, shortly followed by photos of the family pet, and then graduating to nights out with friends and overly filtered, uncharacteristically hot selfies. I've been taking a lot of gratuitous selfies lately, because I've dropped more than a stone and I look fucking great. That said, I can't eat when I'm upset and I'd do anything to have my appetite back. But silver linings, eh?

Secondly, did he just say "lording it about"? I should really be focusing on the matter at hand but my brain can't seem to get past this hilarious choice of phrasing.

"Lording it about?" I repeat, but saying the words out loud makes me laugh. Theo looks on, incredulous.

I'm not doing well to dispel the notion that I've lost it.

"I'm sorry," I say, composing myself, "I should have been more considerate. I should have thought about how my actions might affect you. I should have had more respect for you." His eyes narrow at me.

"You're not talking about Instagram, are you?" he asks.

"No."

"You're talking about me getting with other women."

"I am, yes."

"Great!" he says. "When am I gonna hear the end of this?"

I sometimes wish I could record these gems to play back for him.

"Well, I brought it up twenty seconds ago, so . . ."

"Christ, what do you want to know?" he asks indignantly, like he hasn't been behaving like an utter prick. I pull back my shoulders and lift my chin and without a hint of emotion I ask the question I've wanted to ask for months.

"Did you cheat on me?"

"No," he says, a little too quickly.

"I don't believe you."

"Then why ask?"

"You might have said yes," I say. "Or not answered at all, which counts as a yes."

"I didn't cheat on you."

"But you did start hitting on women a few days after you walked out on me," I say.

He doesn't answer.

The kettle reaches its climax and switches itself off. Theo turns and walks back down the hallway toward the bedroom.

Interestingly, I didn't look through Theo's messages to find out if he'd cheated on me; I just wanted to know who'd written the last email I received from him, because I could tell that he hadn't.

Three weeks into our "break" we met for dinner, as planned, to discuss the future of our relationship. I was aware, far back in some shadowy corner of my mind, that said future did not exist, but I wanted to see him. He hadn't spoken to me since he walked out; I had only received emails from him, all purely logistical. One asked if he could swing by the apartment to "pick up a few things," so in an effort to be accommodating, I told him I was in Ireland with my mother but he could of course let himself in to get them. When I returned to London, I asked my friend Maya to meet me at my apartment because I knew, without knowing, what I would find.

Theo's half of the wardrobe was empty save for a bunch of clothes hangers, which jangled together noisily when I opened the door; his underwear and sock drawers had been emptied too, and in the bathroom, my shelf remained untouched—full of jauntily colored nail varnishes, shampoos, and face creams—while beneath it, his shelf was completely bare save for a few rings of dust around vacant circular spots, which at least confirmed that I hadn't just imagined him.

I pictured Theo stuffing his belongings into a suitcase, frantically and unceremoniously, and now—the counterpoint to his frenzied evacuation—I moved through each room as though through tar, tentatively opening doors and pulling out drawers, conducting my morbid inventory. Maya stayed a step behind me. She said nothing. Sometimes our eyes met and we shook our heads in disbelief.

I had moments of panic about random missing items.

"Where's the iron? Did he take the iron? Check that cupboard."

Maya did so, dutifully.

"It's not in here."

"Right," I said. "Okay. I can get a new iron."

"You can get a new iron," she echoed.

"I don't really iron things anyway. I suppose it was more his iron."

"Yeah. It's fine," she agreed. "It's just an iron." I was nodding constantly and involuntarily.

"It's just an iron."

It's just an iron. It's just stuff. I'm just heartbroken. It's just my heart.

I sat down on the bed and called my mother. Maya sat next to me and heard only my side of the conversation:

"Hey. I got back okay . . . Fine. Bit of turbulence, but fine . . . Listen, I think he's gone for good . . . Well, he took his stuff . . . No, not all of it, but, more than 'a few fucking things,' anyway . . . Clothes and toiletries . . . And the iron . . . Yeah, I can get a new one . . . I know I don't, that's what I said . . . No, Maya's here . . . My mam says hi, Maya . . . She's gonna stay the night, Mam . . . Yeah, I'm okay . . . No, of course I'm not . . . He took his shirts . . ."

I will never know why, but it was the shirts that broke me. It's the shirts that have become an in-joke among my friends, one of whom even suggested that I write a novel about him and call it *He Took His Shirts*. It's a good title, but I feel it somewhat undersells the depth of the subject matter.

Tears came then and my voice failed me. I held out the phone to Maya and she took it, rubbing my back as she talked to my mother, reiterating what I'd already said and adding her own opinion of Theo to the mix. Maya is a soft soul who hates no one, and while she's prone to a good rant—usually about everyday injustices like people skipping queues or refusing to recycle—I have never seen her as angry as she was that night. It was a muted, determined sort of anger, far more conservative than the one I knew would soon consume me. While Maya assured my mother she'd stay with me, and, yes, she'd be sure to make me eat something, I went to the wardrobe and slid my clothes along the rail to fill the gap.

Straight after the call, she ordered pizza and watched me eat two slices of it. Then she called her husband, Darren, to let him know she wouldn't be home and to say good night to their daughter for her. Maya and Darren had been our friends for years and had seen us at our best, before things started to fall apart. I could tell they were genuinely disappointed that Theo and I were breaking up, and I knew it would change the dynamic between us all forever.

That's the problem with breakups, though. It's not just two people saying good-bye and going their separate ways; it's the excruciating process of untangling two lives, picking them apart like some sad surgical procedure, trying to detach this thing from that while causing as little lasting damage as possible.

I heard Maya tell Darren what Theo had done, and I heard the long silence on the other end of the line before he finally said, "Fuck's sake, Theo."

That was all he said. That was all he needed to say.

Finally, Maya put me to bed and crawled in beside me. I asked her to tell me stories, silly ones, fairy tales, like "Goldilocks." I knew it sounded childish but I was desperate for simple, familiar things. She happily obliged and even kept talking until she was sure I'd fallen asleep.

So this is how I knew, when I met Theo for dinner, that it was already over. Not only had he taken enough essentials for a new life without me; he hadn't even prepared me for it. My mother had flown to London to be there for me when I got home from seeing him that evening, because—although she wouldn't ex- plicitly say it—she knew it was over too.

While I was getting ready, she asked what I would do if Theo wanted to work things out, and I told her I'd be open to it, because there was a part of me that still hoped we could. But the thought of getting back together also created a quiet unease within me, which I realize now is why she asked; it forced me to imagine both possible outcomes instead of feeling—as I did— that I had no choice in the matter. I began to hope and fear in equal amounts that he would officially end it; I didn't want to have to make a decision and I was terrified that, given the chance, I'd make the wrong one. So I went in accepting my fate, but still I agonized over what to wear and what to say. I almost didn't go. I almost called to cancel. I almost wish I had.

When I arrived too early at the restaurant, in the pretty orange dress and navy coat I'd eventually picked out, I sat outside and waited. It was a mild October evening. Autumn leaves swirled idly around my feet and on the street in front of me, a foot-wide shaft of light thinned to a sliver as the sun moved behind a building. The air cooled and I breathed, conscious of each breath.

My anxiety had flared up since Theo left, and I'd been seeing my therapist twice a week just to manage the almost daily panic attacks I was having. But on that night, I remember feeling oddly calm. Truth be told, I was excited to see Theo; throughout our weeks of forced separation the prospect of even a few hours with him was all that had kept me going. The part of me that still held hope of reconciliation swelled in size, and I decided, then and there, that if he wanted to try again, I would. Even if that meant taking things slow, living apart a little longer, having more space, more time. Whatever he needed, I would give it to him. Because I loved him. And I wanted to make this work.

He turned up in his gym gear.

I tell people that and they need to pause to process the information. Then I repeat myself and, as their faces change from shock to pity, I am humiliated all over again. I feel as foolish now, telling it, as I did then. In fact, of all the things that happened that night and in the weeks and months surrounding it, of all the unimaginably low moments I've endured, the thing I'm most ashamed of is that I sat in a fancy restaurant opposite a man who until recently I thought might one day father my children, while he ended our relationship in a pair of trainers and grass-stained shorts. He said he'd come straight from training, and he hadn't had time to shower or change, but I'd spent three weeks waiting for this. I had lived those weeks. I had sat inside each minute and felt the weight of it pressing in on me. And he didn't even bother to wash himself, or put some fucking trousers on.

Theo told me it was over before the food even arrived; two servings of some sort of chicken in some sort of sauce. He devoured his meal, then asked if I was going to eat mine. I said no, I felt a bit sick, so he ate mine too.

A lot was said and all of it seemed of the utmost significance then, but I struggle to remember it now. Bits stand out. At one point he cried into a napkin. This was after I told him that I'd taken a pregnancy test on the morning he broke up with me and that it was positive.

"I wanted to tell you that night, when you got home," I said, "but I guess on some level I knew you were going to leave me and I didn't want you sticking around out of some misguided sense of obligation."

"Okay."

I can see him trying to compute all this.

"So that's why I didn't tell you. And then you just happened to break up with me. And leave. And the next day I took another two tests and they were both negative."

"Right," he said, staring down at his plate.

"Maybe the first test was broken," I offered.

"So, you're saying it was my fault?" he asked, tears filling his eyes.

"What?"

"That you lost the baby because I broke up with you."

"No! That's not . . ."

I couldn't think straight. Did he honestly think I was accusing him of causing a miscarriage by leaving me?

"I didn't 'lose a baby,' Theo. Like I said, the test was probably broken or something. I just wanted to explain why I was acting weird that day. Why I was so out of it when you were leaving. Why I didn't fight to figure it out. I should have fought harder. But I was scared. And exhausted. And I don't think I was coping very well."

Theo wasn't listening anymore. He had pushed back his chair and dropped his head into a napkin and was now crying heavy, globular tears.

Initially, almost a reflex, I put a hand on his arm and tried to comfort him. I apologized for telling him about the pregnancy test, for burdening him with this information. Then I looked around at the other diners, who were glancing at us over forkfuls of food, and I saw myself as they must see me: a pretty girl in a pretty dress, consoling this man in a pair of shorts.

Something inside me changed in that moment. I'd spent most of the night listening to Theo tell me what I did wrong in our relationship. How me quitting my job to pursue writing had been stressful for him. How my anxiety and depression were bringing him down. How he'd been "miserable" with me. Miserable. I remember that word distinctly. It's quite a severe word. Theo basically made it clear that I was the cause of all his unhappiness; his floundering career, his turbulent relationship with his mother, even his own emotional instability could be traced back to me. As though his life before me had been completely pain-free.

And I had just sat there, so weak and dejected that I believed him when he said I was the only thing holding him back. That if he could just be alone, to focus on himself and his career, he would finally be happy.

Here I was, keeping it together despite feeling like I might at any minute fall apart. Supporting him when I needed support. Being made to feel responsible for all his problems. It was a microcosm of our entire relationship. And seeing him there, with his head between his knees, sobbing, I felt something shift.

I let go, withdrew my hand, pulled my shoulders back, and took a long, deep breath. *That's enough now*, I thought. *That's enough.*

I spent the rest of our time together in a strange, detached state, as we dealt with the peculiar logistics of a breakup. Theo said he'd be in touch about collecting the rest of his stuff. He offered to pay his half of the rent for a couple of months until I figured things out. And he assured me he was not seeing anyone else, that he couldn't even think about that right now. This brought me some comfort, I'll admit.

He also said he wanted to remain friends. That, in particular, stands out, because even though I was hurt and angry, and had just now decided that I didn't want to try again, I still loved him, and I didn't want him to be gone from my life completely.

Afterward, he saw me to a taxi, and just before I got in the car, he took my hands in his and told me to call him if I needed anything. "Anything at all," he said.

We kissed. And I left. And that was it. I felt at once lighter and infinitely heavier.

A few days later, my mother flew home to Ireland and I picked my life up where I'd left off. First item on my agenda was coffee with my boss, Ciara.

I used to work for Ciara when I still lived in Dublin, writing mostly made-up holiday reviews for a magazine called *Taisteal*, which is Gaelic for "travel." She called me early last year, completely out of the blue, to say she was launching her own health-and-wellness magazine here in London and she wanted to give me my own column on mental health. I immediately quit my shit-but-stable full-time job to work for her, because she is a formidable woman who I had no doubt would be successful. And I was right.

Once the magazine took off, Ciara launched a website too, and now I supplement my column with a weekly agony-aunt-style blog. I'm increasingly unsure what qualifies me to give life advice, but people seem to like it.

Ciara always insists on meeting at one of those shabby-chic cafés in Mayfair, where a coffee costs upwards of eight pounds. But she also insists on paying for it, so I can't really complain.

I found her at a table outside, wrapped in a camel-colored coat and a massive cashmere scarf. I was wearing all black—not because I was mourning but because I found any amount of color coordination too exhausting at the time.

"You're looking well," she said when I sat down.

"Thanks. It's this new thing I'm trying where I don't eat or sleep or think about anything other than the fact that I'm a struggling writer on the cusp of thirty with no partner, no kids, and no fucking clue what I'm doing."

"Well, I must say, it suits you."

Ciara's humor is as dry as a bone on a hot day. I imagine you either learn this the first time you meet her or you come away from every interaction feeling deeply offended.

"Besides," she went on, "kids are overrated. As are partners, for that matter."

"How are you and Kate?"

"Oh, you know," she said, with a wave of one hand, "every day with me is like a waking nightmare. But she's too fond of my money. And too tired to divorce me."

"Fair enough."

Suddenly, Ciara's brow furrowed.

"Stop calling yourself a struggling fucking writer, by the way. It's a very romantic notion, darling, but in actual fact you've got a monthly column, a weekly blog, and an as-yet-unwritten bestseller in you."

Her face lit up at this. "Which you've got time for now that what's his face has fucked off!"

"I know you know his name is Theo," I said.

"Whatever. He's an idiot, darling. I've always said so."

"You have."

"And now he's gone and proved me right!" she said with her signature Cheshire grin. The waiter arrived then with two lattes, which Ciara presumably ordered before I got there. She flashed him a sweet smile, then subtly checked out his ass as he left.

"Lovely," she said to herself. "Now, dare I ask how the writing's going?"

"Best not."

"I see."

I had fallen behind on a few deadlines and was expecting a grade-A bollocking. But Ciara just nodded thoughtfully and stirred sugar into her coffee.

"And work aside," she said, "how are you holding up?"

"Well," I said, "I made two cups of tea this morning."

She just stared at me, confused.

"As in, Theo's been gone over a month," I went on, "but this morning I got up, went to the kitchen, made myself a cup of tea, left it brewing, and then came back to find I had in fact poured two cups of tea."

Ciara winced at this.

"Ow," she said.

"Ow," I agreed.

"Some habits are hard to break," she said, and with that she produced a pack of cigarettes from her ridiculously large leather handbag. "Speaking of which . . ."

She offered one to me and I shook my head.

"I don't smoke," I said.

"Neither do I," said Ciara, smirking as she lit one up.

She then took what looked like a very satisfying drag.

"So, you're not doing very well, then?"

"Not really." I sighed. "I just sort of float about the apartment like a banshee, sniffing his old Christmas jumpers and wailing at the walls."

Ciara laughed as she tapped her cigarette on an ashtray.

"It's not funny," I said.

"It is, actually. It's very funny . . ." And then, as if an idea had just come to her: "In fact—"

"Don't you dare!" I said, cutting her off, "don't you dare tell me to 'use it,' Ciara, or so help me God . . ."

Ciara raised her hands in the air and with mock innocence said, "I wouldn't dream of it, darling."

"Good," I said, sipping my coffee.

"All I'm saying," she said, and I rolled my eyes, knowing she had no intention of dropping it, "is that you write constantly, and very well I might add, about how to cope with all the shite life throws at you. And, as it would happen, life has just thrown you a rather large piece of shite, darling. I mean, call me crazy, but it's *almost* like you should be smearing your bleeding heart all over the fucking page instead of sitting here whining at me about it."

Well. There it was. The bollocking had come, just in a slightly different package than I was expecting. I sat there, gobsmacked, as Ciara pointedly stubbed out her cigarette.

"What was it Nora Ephron used to say?" she asked.

"Everything is copy."

"Exactly!" she said. "That's basically what I'm saying."

"Though admittedly Nora did put it a bit more succinctly than you."

Ciara glared at me and I suppressed a smile.

"Point is," she said, "you should thank Theo for the copy and tell him to go fuck himself."

She wasn't wrong. She rarely is. I went straight home, cleared all the crap off my desk, and got to work. For weeks I did nothing but eat and sleep and write. And see my therapist. She insisted that I add some exercise to my routine, which I did, in the form of a yoga class I'd stopped attending when Theo left. In hindsight, I can see that most healthy aspects of my life stopped when Theo left.

A few days after our coffee, I got a text from Ciara asking how I was doing. I didn't reply. I was too caught up in writing to reply to anyone, except for Maya and my mother, who checked on me almost daily and only ever got a thumbs-up in response.

By the end of the first week of radio silence, Ciara messaged again: "Just making sure you haven't gone full Plath on me," she said. An hour later she asked what kind of oven I had, at which point I let her know I was just busy writing and would have something for her soon. The next day I handed in the first of many raw, honest articles about coping with heartbreak.

I kept the details of the breakup vague and focused mainly on my grieving process, something I'd never really done before; I'd written countless pieces on mental health but never *my* mental health. As soon as the first blog went live, I panicked. I had that same sinking dread you get after drunk-texting your ex, or sleeping with someone you shouldn't have. What was I thinking!? Vulnerability is the one thing I fear most, yet here I was, exposing my soft underbelly to the internet! The cruel, hateful, horrible internet.

And then, a miracle. Instead of cruelty and hatred I received hundreds of comments and emails and even handwritten letters from people who had been through what I'd been through in some form or other, people who'd been to the depths of grief and back and who could tell you exactly what the bottom looked like. They said they found comfort in my words, that I'd made them feel less alone, but the truth was they did exactly the same for me; I can't count how many boxes of tissues I went through as I read their messages of hope and support. With each new post, the comments flooded in faster, and week after week my little community grew.

Ciara was delighted, of course; she's offered to help me adapt the articles into a book and has even promised to find me a publisher.

"I told you there was a bestseller in there," she said when we next met for coffee. She clinked her coffee cup with mine in celebration and added, "Sad sells."

This might sound sadistic but it's true; people want to see their sadness reflected back at them because it makes them feel connected to something and connection is the best salve for sadness. The irony is we're usually at our most disconnected when we're grieving, either because we've lost the person we felt closest to or because we've withdrawn from others in order to protect ourselves from future pain, or to protect them from our "brokenness." Sometimes, we even disconnect from ourselves, our bodies becoming battlegrounds as we wage silent wars upon ourselves. That's the hardest thing to come back from and the main thing I've been working on with my therapist lately. Coming back to myself, to my body, feels like coming home, only to no home I've ever known.

That day in the café, I was happy. More than that, I was content. Beginning inside me and radiating outward was an overwhelming sense of wholeness, and fullness, and joy. It was as if I could feel my heart knitting back together, strand by strand, and the sensation was at once odd and painful and deeply satisfying; a healing pain.

Then came Theo's birthday. It had been well over a month since our dinner, and I was feeling ready to speak and eager to sort out the last of the logistics. I decided to extend an olive branch and send a text to wish him happy birthday.

He didn't reply.

A few days later I texted again to ask if he was okay.

No reply.

When another day passed with no word from Theo, I sent him an email asking where we stood. I told him I'd accepted it was over and I didn't want to try again, but after five years together it would be a shame to just cut one another out completely. I also reminded him how keen he'd seemed to stay friends and expressed how hurtful and confusing it was to just be ignored after that. Finally, I asked if he could at least come and get the rest of his things.

Two days later I received an email so bizarre that it's difficult to describe without quoting the whole thing directly. Suffice to say it sounded like a canned response, the likes of which you would expect to receive in reply to a complaint about a faulty refrigerator, not a heartfelt message to your former partner.

There is an unmistakably "almost human" tone to such emails, a sort of faux-empathetic sentiment with a cold, corporate undertone; the uncanny valley of language. It began with a decidedly formal greeting, included something about him "appreciating my patience in these difficult circumstances," and ended with the line, "I do hope this correspondence has not caused you any further concern."

Another mini revelation. Another gap in the clouds. This time I realized two things: one, he lied about wanting to be friends and was continuing to lie because he was too cowardly to just tell me he never wanted to see me again, and two, he did not write that email.

Among the belongings Theo left behind was his old mobile phone. He had only recently upgraded and left the old one in his desk drawer—now my desk drawer—and for weeks I had resisted the urge to turn it on and find out what he'd been saying about me to his friends; that would, of course, be a massive breach of privacy and no good would come of it. But at four a.m. on this particular night his right to privacy seemed suddenly unimportant. I had to know who wrote that email. So I charged his phone, switched it on, and typed in his PIN; there had been no secrets between us, after all.

I found a conversation between him and two of his female coworkers, Lesley and Victoria, in which he had sent them my email and asked them to draft a reply. I should mention at this point that I used to work at the same company as Theo—he in the accounting department and I writing press releases—so I had met these two women quite a few times at conferences and Christmas parties and such. We weren't exactly close friends, but I knew them well enough to be absolutely mortified by this. Not to mention I'd been aware for some time of a flirtation between Theo and Lesley.

There was a lot to take in, but one part that stood out was Victoria suggesting that Theo avoid the phrase "I've moved on."

"It sounds too much like you're seeing another person," she said.

"Oh really, Vicky?" he asked. "Then how do I make it clear I'm seeing multiple people!?"

He then wrote the word LOL, in all caps, several times. "I'm moving in several different directions?" she suggested.

An excessive number of LOLs followed.

After this they spoke at length about what a crazy bitch I am. He said that I'd been messaging him, acting weird, and that he was "terrified" I would show up at his office unannounced. For the record, I had no intention of doing anything of the sort, but I took some joy in the fact that he was afraid I might. Theo said he needed to send this ASAP to "get me off his back"; then they joked about my email to him, and I crumbled.

Suddenly, the faces of every one of his exes flashed through my mind; women I'd met at parties or weddings or school reunions, each one of them a "crazy bitch," according to him. He never spoke to any of them; he had cut them out immediately following their breakups. He confided this to me, joked with me about it, just as he was now joking with these other women about me. I got angry then, not at him but at myself. I had known he was capable of doing this. I was just too naive and too arrogant to believe he would do it to me. We all think we'll be different, don't we?

I opened his messages and the first conversation I found was with Darren. Scrolling back to the date of the breakup, I found the usual supportive messages you'd expect from a friend: Darren saying it was the right thing to do, assuring him we'd both be okay, suggesting they go out for a pint to talk it over. Theo never seemed to take him up on this offer, though, and instead struck up a conversation with an old uni mate named Isaac.

Just four days into what Theo was then calling our "break," Theo started telling Isaac about the women he'd been pursuing. He said he'd "gone back to that club last night and got another girl's number." He talked about a woman he'd met online who he was going on a date with (he took her out for breakfast on his birthday, as it transpires). And he seemed particularly keen on a girl named Natalie, whom he'd been introduced to at a friend's party.

Isaac and I had never really got along—his sole purpose in life was to get laid—so I was surprised when he suggested that Theo slow down a bit and process what he was going through. He also pointed out that Natalie had just gone through a breakup too and might need to be alone for a while, something Theo should maybe consider himself. It had been a long time since I'd seen Isaac. Apparently he'd gone and done some growing up. But Theo was having none of it. He said that Natalie being unavailable only made her more appealing, and then he went on to describe in great detail the kinds of things he'd "like to do to her."

Through a deluge of tears and with shaking hands I continued. I wasn't proud of myself, nor did I feel one iota of guilt. Perhaps I should have—these were his private messages, after all—but I didn't have the capacity to care.

What followed was a blurry montage of conversations with other male friends—some lewder than others—as well as messages to the women themselves. Each time, Theo opened with a similar comment about how he'd enjoyed meeting the girl in question, then followed up with a funny quip specific to their interaction (the tailored touch, nice) and ended with an invitation to grab a coffee or go for a drink, or a run, depending on her interests. It was all so measured, so strategic, that it gave me chills. One conversation got pretty filthy pretty quickly, including pictures from both parties, and I couldn't close it fast enough.

By five a.m. I had come undone. All the wholeness and fullness I felt were gone, replaced by a feeling of desolation.

I called Maya. She answered the phone and was met with the sound of my raspy breaths.

"All right," she said. "Are you choking?" I managed to croak a "no" at her.

"Have you hurt yourself?"

"No."

"Do you need me to call an ambulance?"

"No."

"Do you need me to call the police?"

"No."

"Are you just having a mental breakdown relating to your recent breakup?"

"Yes. That one."

"Well, I'm here. And I'll stay on the line. And you can just talk when you're ready."

God bless this woman.

Once I'd regained something akin to normal breathing, I told her what I'd found. She listened quietly for a long time, and then, finally, she spoke. "Right. Well. He's a cunt," she said.

Maya never used that word.

"I know you're upset, and you have every right to be, because what you've just seen is both disgusting and heartbreaking. But I think we can all agree that you are better off without that sociopathic twat in your life. Also, for what it's worth, he's not okay. This is him acting out because he's incapable of processing his emotions. You'll deal with this. You'll bounce back. He won't."

How does she always know exactly what to say?

"Also he has stupid hair. It's very generic."

"That's fair," I said.

"And his family are all racists."

As a woman of color, Maya had long since struggled with Theo's far-right family, and she wasn't the only one.

"It's a miracle he's just a cunt, really," I said, "and not a racist, homophobic misogynist as well."

"I suppose it is," she said, then: "That mother of his always had her claws in too deep. You should be glad to be rid of her."

"Don't get me started on his fucking mother, Maya."

We laughed at this but the laughter didn't feel right. There was a hollow sort of ache in my chest.

"I failed," I said finally.

"At what?"

"The relationship."

"Don't be ridiculous," said Maya. "You can't fail at a relationship. That's like getting off a roller coaster and saying you failed because the ride is over. Things end. That doesn't mean the experience wasn't worth it."

"I'm not sure it was worth it, Maya. What did I get out of it?"

"You got what you needed," she said. "And then one day it wasn't what you needed anymore."

"I don't even know when that day was."

"I think it was a while ago, my love," said Maya, sadly.

"Were we ever happy? I'm not being dramatic—I genuinely can't remember."

"You were happy," Maya assured me. "You were fucking delirious. I saw it with my own two eyes. And things being shit now doesn't erase all the good stuff. It still happened. Pain is just an inevitable part of life."

"It feels like I'm getting more than my fair share of it sometimes, that's all."

"You've not exactly been lucky, no," said Maya, "but everyone has their shit. And I know there'll be more shit for me down the line. Even if Darren and I don't get divorced, one of us will get sick and die and I'll feel my pain then. It's just a matter of when."

"This isn't your best pep talk ever."

Maya laughed. "My point is, the only way not to feel pain is to never love anyone."

"That's beginning to feel like a real option," I said.

By six a.m., Maya needed to get up and make breakfast for her baby, and I apologized profusely for making her day that bit harder. She of course told me it was fine, but as soon as I hung up, I ordered her a bunch of flowers anyway. Then I went to the shop to buy some boxes because I had decided during our phone call that today was the day I would pack Theo's things.

I had a video call with my mam that lasted roughly eight hours; she went about her business in the background, tidying the house and making phone calls and cooking dinner, while I separated our record and DVD collections, stuffed Theo's clothes into bags, packed boxes full of books, and stacked all of our framed pictures up against one wall. I sifted through our "memory box," the general detritus of a five-year relationship, which I had collected from the start. There were hundreds of photographs and postcards and ticket stubs, but the birthday cards were the worst part; his handwriting, his promises of loyalty and love, even our silly little in-jokes. My mother told me to rip them up, but I couldn't. I felt sorry for myself then. It wasn't fair. Why should I have to do this alone? How come he got to just move out and move on? He would never have to look at this stuff again or sit, like I am now, sorting through it all. I was sinking, fast, when my delightfully dark mind offered me a solution.

I took a drawer full of important documents and files—his

bank statements, tax records, letters pertaining to stocks and shares, even his birth certificate—and I emptied it into a massive cardboard box. On top of all these things he would absolutely need to find at some point, I poured the contents of our memory box and a bunch of funny-looking stuffed animals we'd collected from zoos around the world. I added his collection of 1977 mint-condition stormtrooper figurines for good measure. Then I picked it up, shook it really hard for about thirty seconds, put it down, and sealed it. There, I thought, if he wanted the things that mattered to him, he'd have to go through the things that mattered to me first. I called it "The Box of Doom." Maya suggested I cover all his clothes in glitter too, but I felt that was a step too far.

By that evening, one half of my bedroom was stacked full of boxes and I had officially moved from sadness into anger, a far more productive phase of the grieving process.

I didn't reply to the email Theo didn't write. Nor did I contact him about the messages I shouldn't have seen. I spent the following week writing, exercising, seeing friends, and redecorating the apartment. Then, when I was ready, I called him to say I had boxed up his stuff and would appreciate if he could come collect it as soon as possible. He seemed thrown by my matter-of-fact tone. I enjoyed that. But much more than that, I enjoyed his suggestion that he "drop by in a cab" to pick it all up; he seemed genuinely taken aback when I explained that he had actually been living with me for quite some time and during that time he had amassed a lot of belongings. When I told him to hire a removal van, he let out a long, unnecessarily loud sigh to indicate just how much of an inconvenience this was. I pictured him there, phone in one hand, rubbing his forehead with the other, eyes scrunched up, and in that moment I was glad to be rid of him and his stupid, stressed-out face.

He's standing in the hallway now, looking into the bedroom, processing the new decor and the number of boxes I've stacked from floor to ceiling.

"There's so many."

"I did say," I call back from the kitchen. As I reach into the cupboard for some mugs, he speaks again, quieter this time.

"Thanks for packing it all for me."

He glances toward me, all doe eyes and guilt, and for a moment he is my Theo again.

"You're welcome," I say.

Theo goes into the bedroom, and as I pour hot water over a tea bag, I'm distracted. I look back at the spot where he stood and remember the night he left. Just before he walked out the door I stopped him and grabbed him, and we stood holding one another for what felt like far too long and not nearly long enough. I tried, right there on that very spot, to commit the feel of him to my memory: the weight of his arms, the exact pressure they exerted on my body, the concave dip of his chest where my head rested neatly, how my right hipbone pressed against his left, and how my shoulders folded, birdlike, as he pulled me into him. When he took a step back I remained motionless. He kissed me. Said he loved me. And with that he was gone.

There was a silence then. More than a silence: a vacuum. I felt like all the air had been sucked out of the room and I now stood inside a void so dense that my skull might implode from the pressure. The door seemed to bend impossibly toward me, then away, and I reeled, turning toward the kitchen and stepping onto nothing, as though my legs had disappeared. Before I could check if they were still there, a convulsion seized me, and I grabbed on to a doorframe, leaned over, and retched. Nothing came up. I hadn't eaten that day. I lowered myself to the floor and lay facedown, with my cheek against the cool wood, and somewhere in the distance I could hear a whistling sound.

I don't know how long I stayed that way. Hours, maybe—or it might have just seemed like hours—but at some point I flashed on the pregnancy test I'd taken that morning: a blue cross forming in a tiny window. I saw it materialize, over and over, then pushed it away. *I can't think about that now,* I thought. *I'll think about it tomorrow.* Those weren't my words, though. They were Scarlett O'Hara's. And suddenly her voice was in my head and I was twelve years old again, lying in my mother's bed watching *Gone with the Wind. My mother. I should call my mother.* I'd been recovering from a particularly horrendous bout of food poisoning. I'd had a fever for two days. And when she thought I was better she gave me apple juice and I vomited it back up, hot and thick. I haven't drunk apple juice since. *I should eat something. I need to eat. I need to call my mother. What will I tell her? What the hell is that whistling sound?*

It was me. I was sucking air through what felt like a tiny hole in my throat, and my long, labored breaths were producing a sound not unlike nails on a chalkboard. I probably would have passed out had my stomach not growled so loudly that the sound actually startled me. I told myself, out loud, to get off the floor;

then I scrambled back up the doorframe and eventually wobbled my way to the kitchen like some dazed infant on the hunt for food. I managed a piece of dry toast before staggering to my room and collapsing on my bed, where I lay howling till I fell asleep. I had never cried like that before. The sounds were guttural and animalistic, and I let them come.

The next morning, I went to the office for an editorial meeting. I excused myself several times so that I could go vomit in the toilet; then I got back to work. The day after that I got my hair cut and went to the post office and the bank. I was in shock and I knew it. But I decided that as long as I was still functioning, I should get as much done as possible. It was like I'd been stabbed, and at any moment the knife might be pulled out, sending blood gushing everywhere and forcing me to deal with my injuries. Until then, though, I would continue about my business—knife and all.

The third day was the charm. I actually felt myself go. People talk about hearts breaking all the time, but I don't know how many of them have felt their brain break. It's an interesting sensation.

I packed a bag and got a taxi to the airport, where I marched up to the check-in desk in a headscarf and sunglasses and asked for a one-way ticket on the next flight to Ireland. I'd become a scarf-clad cliché.

By the time I landed in Dublin I was a jittery mess. I knew I couldn't keep going for much longer, so the hour-long wait at passport control was a real fucking treat. When I got through the arrival gates and saw my mother waiting there for me, it took every shred of strength I had left not to collapse into her arms and allow myself to fall apart. As she approached me, I held one hand out in front of me and looked at her with a face that I hoped said, "I love you dearly, but please, do not show me affection right now." She took my suitcase and walked me to her car in complete silence.

I stayed in Dublin for a week, where I spent every day on the sofa, with her next to me in an armchair. We talked endlessly about my breakup and what would happen next. I refused to simply wait and let things unfold, and I insisted on speculating incessantly about every single aspect of it: why he left, whether he'd come back, if he was seeing someone else, if maybe we could be friends. She nodded at me and cried with me, and, most important, she prevented me from calling him.

I couldn't eat. I was hungry, but the physical act of swallowing food made me gag. My mother fed me tiny portions: segments of sausage on my niece's pink plastic plate, sandwiches cut into four triangles—the deal was she'd eat two if I ate two. I was a child again. She even put sugar in my tea, something I gave up years ago. Anything to get calories into me.

Phone calls were made. Family members were notified. Condolences were offered. A breakup is like a death without a funeral.

At night I took sleeping pills, which had been prescribed to my mother after surgery last winter to remove one of her kidneys. I remember the night she called me; I was standing in the frozen-food aisle of a Tesco Metro with a packet of peas in one hand and my phone in the other. She rambled on at length about hospitals and positive thinking and whether or not she'd be fit to cook Christmas dinner, and all I had actually heard were the words "tumor" and "malignant."

"Are we talking about the C-word here?" I asked.

"What!?" she bellowed. She thought I meant cunt. She hates that word.

"The other C-word," I said.

"Oh," she replied, much more quietly. "Yes, love. We are."

After we hung up I stood a while longer, till I could no longer feel my hand; then I put back the bag of frozen peas, abandoned the basket of food by my feet, and had wine for dinner instead.

The surgery was a success, but it took more of a toll on my mother than any of us expected—she retired soon after, leaving her younger sister in charge of the interior design business she'd set up shortly after my father left. She hadn't planned on retiring so young—she was only fifty-eight at the time, and after a string of failed relationships, she used to joke that she was married to her company—but the wind had been well and truly knocked out of her sails.

My sister and brother had been there for her through the operation, but they had their own families to take care of and jobs to get back to, and since I can do my job from anywhere, I decided to go home for a few weeks to help nurse my mother better. In an odd way I was thankful I'd had the chance to do that, to preemptively make up for the care she was giving me now.

I probably shouldn't have taken those pills—not least because they were out of date—but sleep would not come without them and I was desperate for it. Every time I closed my eyes I was met with a flurry of memories that seemed to lash against the inside of my head. They came to me unbidden—the good and the bad ones, the significant and the banal—and among the debris I saw fragments of a life I might have lived. If I'd just done this. If I'd just said that. I played out every scenario, every what-if a hundred times and more, and I never reached a solution. Because there was none. Every morning, somewhere between dreaming and waking, the blurry memory of what had happened slid into focus and I cried anew for what I'd lost.

One night, my emotions became so intense that they manifested as real, physical pain. I lay in bed, hands on my chest in some sort of weird attempt to grab on to my own heart and hold it together—I was sure it was literally ripping apart inside me. My mind, too, felt torn. Pieces of it were coming away and I wondered if I would ever get them back. My body moved about as though independent of me, fists clenching, feet scraping against the sheets, all of me, every inch, agitated and incapable of rest.

Somewhere, deep in that night, the pain consumed me. The thought of being happy again was inconceivable. And even though all I wanted was to sleep, the idea of waking up, still here, still feeling this way, was torturous.

I thought about the pills then, in my mother's room; there was a whole bottle of them in her dresser drawer. I thought about sneaking in there, returning to my bed with them, and swallowing every last one. I walked through it in my mind again and again. And then I realized I'd been here before. A long time ago, I'd been here, I'd felt this hopeless, and I'd found happiness again.

I couldn't remember how I came back from the brink but I knew it was possible and in that moment that's all I needed to know.

And so I prayed. Not to God—I don't believe in God. I prayed to the only thing I knew I could rely on: myself. I begged myself to just get me through this night. I told myself that I would be good, I would be strong, and I would never let this happen again if I could just get through this night.

Sleep found me. And in the morning the fever had broken.

In the days that followed I thought about grief, how nothing and nobody can prepare you for it. People tell you their stories, but until you experience it for yourself you can't possibly understand. There's no going around it. Or under or over it. You've got to go through it. It will hit you in waves so enormous that you are smacked against the shore. It will permeate the very fabric of your life, so that everything you do is stained by it; every moment, good or bad, is steeped in sadness for a while. Even the nice moments, the achievements and successes, are tinged with the knowledge that someone or something is missing. And the first time that you smile or laugh, you catch yourself, because happiness feels so unfamiliar.

I thought, too, how like an addict I had been, how similar this was to some kind of detox. I wondered how much of the feeling of love is chemicals and cravings and dependency, and how much of the act of love is habit.

Eventually, loving someone becomes muscle memory. You don't even notice it happening. One day you realize you've stopped living together and started existing near to one another.

The path you once walked side by side has become two paths, which twist and wind their way around one another, occasionally intersecting long enough for a conversation full of clunky exposition that reveals nothing about the characters. You ask what time the other will be home from work, what they fancy for dinner, if they've remembered so-and-so's birthday tomorrow. They tell you about their day with no humor or anecdotes, just a list of events in chronological order. You cook for two, buy toilet roll for two, book train tickets, sign cards, and RSVP for two. Your autopilot gets set to two.

I don't think there's anything wrong with that; in fact, I think there's something kind of beautiful about it; your mind and body adapting so deftly to the presence of another person that the mingling of two lives, two stories, two sets of thoughts and beliefs, feels effortless. It's possible for someone to occupy a space in your life for so long and in such a specific way that their absence creates a very real sense that a part of you is missing. It is indeed beautiful. But when that's all there is, it's not enough.

I'd like to tell you there was an inciting incident, a reason we ceased to function as a couple, but it was more like a slow, creeping disdain. In the end, habit was all we had left, and I came to realize that what I'd lost was lost a long time ago. For almost two years our relationship had been the romantic equivalent of a zombie—a walking, talking, undead imitation of us—and it was finally being put to rest.

I snap back when Theo calls my name, and I follow him into the bedroom, where he asks me what he should take; he wasn't expecting me to remove the artwork from the walls or hand over our record collection. I tell him the truth, that I don't want anything here that reminds me of him. I tell him it's been too hard seeing it every day, and I need it gone. My throat tightens and I falter over these last few words. I think Theo notices because he doesn't argue; he just starts taking the boxes to the lift.

I feel sorry for him all of a sudden. His actions haven't been malicious; he just hasn't got a clue how to do this. So I offer to help, and, standing next to him in the lift, I see him catch his own reflection and deflate.

"I look like shit," he says, leaning his head against the mirror and closing his eyes.

"You've looked better."

"I need a new job," he says. "I need to move. I need a new life. And a new fucking family." He pauses, and then with an off-kilter smirk he adds, "I suppose I need a new girlfriend now too." It's the oddest, most telling thing he's ever said, and while I know none of those things will fill the space in his heart, I also know he needs to figure that out for himself.

Once the last of the boxes is loaded in the van, we say our final good-bye. When he hugs me, my strength fails and I cry.

"I wanted to thank you," I blubber into his ear.

"For what?"

I pull back so I can look him in the eyes.

"When we met," I say, "I was so lost. So completely unsure of myself. Of my worth. And then you came along. And you made me feel strong and special and worthy of love."

"Oh, angel," says Theo, tears filling his eyes as he reaches out to touch my cheek, "you're all of those things all by yourself. You always were."

He pulls me toward him for another hug and we cry into one another's necks, oblivious of the world around us or the people passing by, going about their ordinary days.

"I really did love you, you know."

I think it's my use of the past tense that gets him, because I feel his body jolt slightly in my arms and I know that's it, the final straw, we're done. He wipes his cheeks with the back of his hand, looks at me one last time, and walks away.

As I step into the lift, my hand moves to my cheek and finds the spot where Theo touched me just moments before.

Catching my own reflection in the mirror, I notice a hint of a smile. The face looking back at me is sad but resolute, maybe even hopeful.

When I get back upstairs I close the door behind me, and this time I don't allow myself to crumble. I walk straight to the kitchen, prepared to throw away the tea I made for us, and then I see it there, on the counter: I only made one cup of tea.

pissing on sticks

THIS MORNING I WOKE up, got in the shower, and vomited. I didn't feel nauseous. I didn't anticipate it at all. One second I was scrubbing shampoo into my hair, the next I was—involuntarily and rather violently—vomiting. It would have only happened once, I think, but the sight of last night's lasagna mixed with foamy water as it swirled round the drain made my stomach turn and I threw up again.

Afterward, I sat on the edge of my bed, wrapped in a towel, not shivering or shaking, showing no other signs of illness whatsoever. I checked my calendar to see when my next period was due. Three days ago.

Right.

I considered calling someone to talk it through. But who? My mother would get on the next plane to London, and I wasn't quite ready for that; my friend Maya was at home with her six-month-old baby, Kayla, so discussing my options with her felt wrong somehow; and Theo was at a wedding in Devon, presumably nursing a fairly severe hangover since I hadn't heard from him in almost twenty-four hours. Besides, even if I could call Theo, he wasn't the person I wanted to talk to.

I took a long, deep breath. *This could be any number of things,* I told myself. And yet . . .

I got dressed, shoved a tenner in my back pocket, and headed to the pharmacy. The nearest one was shut—in my haste I'd forgotten they're closed on a Sunday—so I kept walking for about fifteen minutes until I found another. I spent most of the brisk walk wondering how much a pregnancy test cost these days and whether or not ten pounds would cover it. Thankfully, it did.

I approached the cashier with the same affected nonchalance of everyone who has ever bought a pregnancy test, condoms, or lube and wondered why, as a thirty-year-old woman, this was still the case. It's the same feeling I get every time I walk through US border control; the last time I was asked about the reason for my visit to the States, I said, "Just for the craic, like." The customs officer scowled at me and waved me through. Presumably, if one does intend to buy or sell crack cocaine, one does not announce that upon arrival.

The variety of pregnancy tests on offer was a bit overwhelming. I had chosen one with minimum bells and whistles—I wanted to keep this as simple as possible—and as I placed the blue-and-white box down on the counter, the cashier smiled an excited little smile at me. I gave her a half smile in return, then looked away, hoping to avoid as much of whatever this was as possible. Finally she handed me my change, but just as I turned to go she said, "Good luck." I pretended not to hear her.

• • •

Outside the pharmacy a young girl and her mother were sat eating ice creams. She wore a white cotton dress, her hair was caught up in a pile of wispy blond curls, and her little legs dangled lazily off the edge of the bench. She was so engrossed in her ice cream that she didn't even notice her mother's ongoing efforts to catch the dollops of it dripping into her lap. She was lovely, I thought.

That's the problem with kids, though . . . they're everywhere, and they're designed to be lovely. Literally. Their big eyes, cherub noses, chubby cheeks, and huge, round heads are all just an evolutionary tactic to make them appear cute, and this in turn makes us want to take care of them. Because, let's be honest, why else would we keep them around? Babies are absolutely useless and incredibly gross—all that shit and piss and puke and crying—it's no wonder nature had to trick us into loving them. In fact, the cuter we find them, the more we want to protect them, and this is even truer for women of childbearing age; after menopause, we become less susceptible to this biological bullshit.

So the instinct to love a baby is hardwired into our neural networks. And on top of that we're all hardwired to want one of our own. I'm fully aware that my purpose on this planet is to make a child, that I'm programmed to procreate, that I am effectively just an incubator on legs, with a built-in milk machine. This may sound flippant, but really I'm rather in awe of it all. A woman can manufacture inside of her another whole human being, with its own thoughts and fears and tiny toenails. I have the ability to create life, and from a young age, my body has been preparing itself for that eventuality; my boobs, my hips, my monthly mood swings, they're all just part of The Plan. Capital T. Capital P.

Unfortunately, The Plan is not my plan. My plan involves a prosperous career, weekly trips to the cinema, impromptu holidays, dinner parties with friends, and lots and lots of sex. Oh, and regular lie-ins—a luxury reserved for the rich, the old, and the unfertilized. I'd also like to keep all the other things I'd lose upon becoming a parent, including, but not limited to, my sanity.

I'm not sure I definitely don't want children, I'm just not sure I definitely do want children, and I think that anything short of a deep desire in your mind, body, and soul to have one is not a good enough reason to do it. Right now, what I most want to do is write a book, but I know I will never be celebrated for doing so in the same way I would be for having a child. One wonders whether, if one were to push said book out one's vagina, it might be received with greater fanfare. One wonders this quietly to oneself, of course, and never out loud.

I find it's best to avoid expressing my opinions on offspring, especially to other women. The phrase "I don't want children" is met with everything from confusion to hostility, and there usually follows a sermon on the wonders of motherhood. I loathe the assumption that I will "come to my senses" someday or—worse still—that my status as non-mother means I'm somehow lacking in emotional range; I was once accused, by another woman, no less, of being incapable of empathy because I don't have kids. Clearly, that particular lady has a piss-poor grasp of human psychology, but it still stings a little to be seen as somehow impaired because I haven't given birth.

And let me be clear, my body wants a baby. I've cradled my newborn nieces in my arms, looked down at their tiny bodies—skulls still soft from birth—and craved a child of my own. It's a craving more intense than any I've ever known, born from hundreds of thousands of years of evolution, and it intensifies as my window of opportunity grows shorter. To make matters worse, successfully resisting this craving does not bring with it the sense of pride or achievement you get from, say, resisting the urge to cheat on your partner or smoke another joint. Instead of feeling good about avoiding it, you are punished with feelings of guilt and failure. And these feelings are reinforced by all the stupid cunts out there who claim you can't feel feelings without bearing babies.

Obviously not every woman treats me that way; I've noticed more and more lately (perhaps because I've hit my thirties) a willingness among friends, colleagues, and even complete strangers to reveal to me the true horrors of motherhood, from the pregnancy itself to the complications of birth, to the effects on a marriage, to the effects on a life. I was introduced to a lady at a party last year. She was on her eighth vodka when I arrived and within minutes of meeting me she literally grabbed me by the arm, nails gripping flesh, and said, "Don't do it."

"Don't do what?" I asked.

"Kids," she said. "Don't do it."

I hadn't mentioned kids.

"Okay," I said, half laughing.

"I love my sons," she added. "God help me, I love the little bastards with all my fucking heart. But I haven't slept in three years . . ."

She loosened her grip and I thought that was it until her

hand squeezed even tighter and she suddenly announced, "My vagina is ruined!"

Her equally drunk friend overheard this and casually chimed in.

"Mine ripped all the way to my arse!"

This is the shit they don't tell you.

Then came the relentless worrying, they said, the blood in their breast milk, the death of their sex lives, and their newfound appreciation for being able to take a shit without being watched. And yes, they also mentioned the boundless love felt by a parent for their child and the daily moments of pure joy they would otherwise have never felt, but I found it all quite hard to process following the ripped-vagina revelation.

All the way to her arse? Fuck.

As I arrive back from the pharmacy and raise my key to the lock, I realize I don't remember a single step of my walk home. I let myself in, head straight to the bathroom, read the instructions on the box twice, then follow them exactly; I remove the foil packaging, take off the white cap, urinate on the stick, and put the cap back on (making sure not to hold the stick upside down). I'm now on point number five, "wait ninety seconds."

I set a timer on my phone, close my eyes, and try to think about anything else. My thoughts drift to this day last week.

I was on the balcony watering the plants, and Theo had just returned from his morning run. He started exercising again after his grandmother's funeral—a fairly typical response to a brush with mortality—but lately he'd been hitting the gym several times a day, working out to the point of obsession. He even bought a blender and started juicing—something we had always made fun of together.

I watched as water trickled onto a cluster of colorful pots, all full of wilting plants.

"They're dead," said Theo. He was standing in the doorway, drinking some lumpy green concoction he'd just made.

"Not completely," I said.

"But they're basically dead, though."

"Theo, my flowers are not dead."

"Flowers!?" he barked, before leaning over my shoulder, squinting, and pretending to get a better look. There were clearly no flowers, only dry stalks and crisp, brown leaves that crumbled to the touch.

"They just need some water," I said. "Now, kindly piss off."

I elbowed him playfully in the ribs, almost knocking the glass out of his hand, then burst into laughter as he grappled to catch it and splashed juice in his own face. There was a moment of uncertainty, like those few seconds after a toddler falls down when you're not quite sure how they'll react, but then he started laughing too.

"Serves you right," I said, and I went back inside to finish packing for our flight to Ireland that day. Theo shouted after me to hurry up as he dried himself off.

A few hours later we had landed in Dublin and were driving down the M50 in my mother's car. The sun hung like a hot, white pan, cooling against the sky, and heat rose steadily off every car bonnet. It was an uncharacteristically hot Sunday in September and all around us drivers waited impatiently in long lines of traffic—all presumably headed to the already packed beaches. Elbows poked out of open windows, and as we passed we caught snippets of songs blaring from radios.

My mother never used to pick me up from the airport, but now that I live abroad, she insists. She even parks the car so she can meet me at the arrival gate. Sometimes, especially around Christmas, we stay awhile and watch as other families are re-united. It's maybe the least cynical thing I've ever done.

I was yapping to my mam in the front seat. Theo was on his phone in the back, complaining about Ireland's shitty internet. He was looking at pictures of suits.

"What's that for?" I asked.

"Tom's wedding next weekend."

"Oh. You're getting a new suit?"

"It's Tom's wedding," he replied, like he hadn't been wearing the same two suits on rotation since the day I met him: one plain black, the other brown and thinning at the elbows.

"Can I see?"

He handed me the phone and I scrolled through the images. My first thought was that all of these suits looked great, but none of them looked like something Theo would wear. Something was off. I knew this man. This was not a man who cared about what he was going to wear to a colleague's wedding down the country. I chalked it up to insecurity; his teammates were all quite well-to-do, so he might have felt like he needed to up his game.

When we pulled into the driveway, we were met with the sight of all five of my nieces in the throes of a water fight. The girls were running around on the grass, feet muddy, clothes soaked through, and hair stuck to their faces and necks in wet, stringy clumps. Some were armed with massive plastic water guns in neon pink and orange; some carried buckets of water balloons, which they hurled with gusto at one another, screaming laughter all the while. The youngest, only a year old, was sitting by herself, squirting water from a small pistol onto her own bare foot. She seemed happy enough with this arrangement. The others let her be.

As soon as they saw the car, the girls stopped, heads whipping round almost in unison, like a pack of crazed meerkats; a new target had been acquired. My hand moved to the button on the door and a little motor whirred as my window rose slowly upward. My mother realized what was happening. Her eyes widened.

"No," she shouted, shaking her head violently, "no, no, no, no . . ."

They advanced on the car, guns raised, and she threw them a look so severe I was sure it would stop them in their tracks—I don't know at exactly what point during pregnancy a woman is imbued with this new skill, but every mother is somehow capable of the kind of look that would "put the fear of God in you," as my nana would have said. I saw them hesitate. They were on the brink of surrender when four-year-old Sally, the second youngest but somehow leader of the pack, raised a comically large Super Soaker above her head and roared, "GET THE CAR!"

They charged, pelting the car with tiny water bombs and gleefully spraying the windows. I heard Theo jump in the back seat. He must not have noticed any of this up till now.

My mother's head fell to her hands. "I just had it washed," she grumbled.

I leaned over and hit the lever for the windscreen wipers. They swished apathetically back and forth and we broke into laughter.

After a pretty mild telling off—my mother could barely keep a straight face—we left the girls to their game and went inside to get dinner ready. She has the whole family round for dinner every time I go home: my sister, Una, my brother, Donal, their partners and kids, my aunt, and my granddad. We were never a particularly big family, but these last few years it's grown a lot—my brother now has two young girls and my sister's got three. I get back as often as I can, every two or three months, and each time the kids have sprouted up another inch. There is no more obvious indicator of the passage of time than children growing in your absence.

I said as much to Donal as he passed through the kitchen to refill his beer.

"I know," he replied. "Apparently if you keep feeding them, they keep growing."

"Maybe stop feeding them," I suggested.

"Can't," he said, "they complain." And off he went.

Theo had parked himself at the kitchen table and opened his laptop, avoiding eye contact with everyone who passed him by.

I knew why he was off; his mother had called him late the night before, and while I don't know exactly what she said, I can only assume that some of it was anti-me propaganda, because after the call, Theo mumbled something about how he never sees his mum anymore. When I tried to remind him why *he'd* made that decision, he accused me of causing the rift between them. These were her fears coming out of his mouth.

"I thought we were past this." I sighed.

"Past what?" He bristled, and I almost snapped at him but managed to catch myself just in time.

"I'm not sure it's a good idea for us to get into this again," I said, as calmly as I could. "I think maybe you should speak to a therapist about it."

"I don't need to see a therapist."

"Okay."

"I don't," said Theo. "I'm fine."

"Well, you're the one who suggested it."

"When?"

I sighed again. I could feel weariness setting in.

"Nearly a year ago," I said. "The night your mother . . . the night we had to look after her."

"I was upset. That's all," said Theo. "Just because you need therapy doesn't mean everyone else does."

"All right," I said.

I shut down then to avoid further conflict, but Theo of course took this to mean I was giving him the silent treatment. He made some comment about my mood swings, at which point I, ironically I suppose, went off the fucking handle. He slept on the sofa for the third time in as many weeks.

I don't mean to get so upset about things, but lately it feels like my emotions are all just whirling about under a paper-thin surface, and one tiny scratch could rip the whole thing wide open, releasing them screaming into the world. Sometimes it goes the other way, though—the feelings all vanish completely and I'm left wandering about like an empty husk.

I know these are symptoms of depression—my new therapist was quick to point this out to me—but I still can't quite figure out if the problems in our relationship are causing my depression or if my depression is causing the problems in our relationship. Maybe both can be true.

We'd been struggling for some time when Theo lost his gran, but miraculously that experience brought us closer together. Soon afterward, I quit my job to pursue writing full-time, and for a few brief weeks the fog fully lifted. I was proud of myself for making the leap, for taking a risk, for choosing the road less traveled and so on. And Theo was proud of me too, which manifested in him being more present and playful and at ease around me.

I envisioned myself spending sunny afternoons on the balcony, drinking tea and tip-tapping away on my keyboard, blissfully bashing out some brilliant novel, then telling Theo all about it every evening over dinner and a well-earned glass of wine. But the reality was long, lonely days, a severe case of writer's block, and a dwindling savings account; my monthly column wasn't enough to pay my half of the rent and I had far fewer side jobs coming in than I'd hoped.

I found myself awake most nights, exhausted and afraid, with nothing but the voices in my head to keep me company. They told me I was just another fraud who fancies herself a writer, that eventually I would have to admit defeat and admit to the world that I simply wasn't good enough. I felt insecure and isolated, and in the midst of all this—perhaps even in response to this—Theo pulled away again. To make matters worse, I get anxious about plans changing—I need structure and routine to feel safe—and having just lost the stability of a full-time job, I was now faced with uncertainty about my partner too, both in the grand scheme and on a day-to-day basis; Theo started going to work earlier, coming home later, and suddenly spending all his spare time working out. He never seemed to know what time he'd be home or whether he'd be free to hang out on the weekend, so I was left in a permanent state of limbo, always waiting for him to confirm plans. He knows how much that affects me too, so his thoughtlessness made me resent him on top of everything else.

It was like he wanted to be anywhere but with me, and since all I needed was some comfort and company, his absence only made me feel worse. Unfortunately, me being worse made him want to be with me less, so around and around we went, not knowing which was the chicken or which was the egg or whether it even mattered anymore.

I let this be our rhythm for a while until one day the monotony of being in my own brain with my own disturbing thoughts was too much to bear. I found a therapist and started seeing her straightaway; I took up yoga again, joined a book club, and went out with friends more often. I said yes to every available writing job, no matter how big or small or "beneath me" it seemed. I even worked for free for a while, until finally, my writing started to pay the bills.

I'm ashamed to admit that this new, can-do attitude was based entirely on a desire to make Theo love me again, but the outcome is that I now feel stronger and healthier and ready to tackle the relationship together. The only problem is I can't do that alone.

My mother tried to chat to Theo as she pottered about the kitchen. She asked how work was, how his family were keeping, that sort of thing. He was only half responding, engrossed in whatever he was doing, and it bothered me—that a screen so often took precedence over other humans in the room—but I couldn't face another argument, so I pushed my anger aside and decided to take an interest in whatever he was doing instead. I brought him a cup of tea and saw that he was now shopping for green ties.

"Green?" I said.

He opened another tab and showed me a photo of an impossibly handsome male model in a gray suit with a white shirt and green tie.

"I'm trying to replicate this look," he said, then flicked back to the page full of ties and asked which one I liked best. They all looked the same so I arbitrarily pointed at one.

"Yeah, that one's nice, but I wanted more of a knitted texture. It's so hard to tell from the pictures."

It was getting harder for me to take this as seriously as he was.

"Why not order a couple and send back the ones you don't want?" I suggested.

"I have ordered one, but it's coming from China so it might not get here on time."

I laughed. Because obviously that was a joke. But Theo didn't join in. He just looked up at me in puzzlement. I opened my mouth to speak, and just then my mother, who had been watching this entire exchange, called me over to help her with the dinner.

I joined her at the kitchen sink and we stood side by side peeling potatoes, her hands flitting deftly from spud to spud like a bumblebee on flowers. Long, thin strips of rusty-pink potato skin fell from her knife, while I clunkily chopped off large, uneven chunks.

"Jesus, love. Go easy. There'll be nothing left to cook."

"Sorry," I said. "You know I'm useless at this."

"Well, I'm only good because I had to be," she said. "You don't have much choice when you've got three mouths to feed."

I'm never sure what to say to these self-pitiful remarks—That sucks? Well done? Sorry?—so I said nothing.

"You'll understand one day," she added, but I wasn't sure I would.

Outside the window, the kids were still running and throwing and ducking and shrieking with delight as the sun set behind the house and the heat seeped out of the afternoon. My mam opened the window and shouted to them to come in soon, "before they caught a chill," she said. None of them listened.

We continued peeling.

Scrape. Scrape. Scrape.

"Have you two talked about kids?" she asked.

I glanced over at Theo, who had by now put his headphones in.

"Not in a while, no."

She nodded, fair enough.

"Look," she said, emptying a bowl of potatoes into a pot of water. "The writing's going well for you at the moment. Yeah?"

"Yeah."

"So keep at it," she said. "You're good at that." Scrape.

"I've started seeing a therapist again," I said.

"Oh?"

"Yeah. I just felt bad brain creeping in a bit."

This is what I call my depression around people who don't understand it, because it separates me from the illness, like a broken leg or a wobbly tummy. "Just a bad brain day," I'll say, and in doing so I remove any expectation that I could magically think the problem away.

"I thought you were better now," she said.

Scrape. Scrape.

What most people don't seem to get is that when it comes to mental illness; better doesn't actually mean "better." It's a scale. And with enough hard work you can slide yourself all the way up from suicidal to functioning human to fucking fantastic. But it works both ways. And if you don't stay on top of it you can slide straight back down.

Years ago, when I still lived in Dublin, I saw a therapist named Nadia for almost a year. I adored Nadia. She helped pull me out of a very rough patch, and by the time I stopped seeing her I felt more mentally stable than ever before. It was like I'd just been handed a map that I should have had all along. And suddenly it made sense, why the world seemed so confusing to me and so clear to everyone else; they all had a map. The point is that for a time, I was better, but I wasn't "better." We really need a better word for better.

Nadia always said that healing isn't linear. She told me there'd
be relapses. And that they were part of the process. She even
made me promise, when I left Ireland, that I'd see another therapist in London if I ever needed to. Now I was finally making
good on that promise, and already starting to feel stronger for it.
I probably should have done this a long time ago. I wish I had in
fact, but relapses don't turn up one day and announce themselves
in front of you; they creep up slowly on your blind side.

"I was just struggling a bit," I said. "Having anxiety attacks
again."

"Well, we all get a bit anxious sometimes, love. Sure I got
anxious in Dunnes Stores yesterday trying to get all the groceries
packed."

Scrape. Scrape. Scrape.

"Have you thought about taking a holiday?"

"Yeah," I said. "Maybe that'd help."

I love my mother with all my heart. She's the woman you call
when your heart's been broken or your car's been stolen or you've
accidentally killed someone and you need help burying the body,
no questions asked. Once, when I was twelve years old, a teacher
grabbed me by the hair and shouted in my face. My mother had
her fired. When I was sixteen, I missed a flight to Kerry for my
school trip and my mother drove for six straight hours to get me
there. And a few years ago, when my shithead ex turned up on
her doorstep, begging to see me, she had the bastard arrested.
Actually arrested. He spent the night in Coolock Garda
Station.

My mother is great in a crisis, but if there are no extenuating
circumstances—if you have a nice job and a nice boyfriend and

a nice house—she struggles to understand how you could possibly be sad.

"Do you need some money? For the therapy?"

"No, I'm all right," I said, "but thanks."

She tries.

We hugged one another then, both of us careful to keep our hands, now sticky with starch, out to either side.

"Are you two all right?" she whispered, glancing over at Theo.

"Not really."

She held me a bit tighter.

"We'll talk later," she said. But we never did. The day took over, as days tend to do.

I added my measly pile of potatoes to the pot and went to the bathroom, but when I opened the door I found Sally leaning over the toilet with her water gun dipped right into the bowl.

"Hi," said Sally.

"Hi."

She carried on what she was doing, pulling back a plastic lever that sucked water up from the toilet bowl and into the gun.

"Sal," I said.

Sally looked up, casual as fuck, as though I hadn't just discovered she'd been soaking the other kids in toilet water all day.

"Yeah?"

"Put the gun down."

Dinner was postponed until every child was bathed and changed into whatever dry clothes we could find. Some settled for old, baggy T-shirts, but a few chose items from the dress-up box. Lily,

Sally's older sister, insisted on squeezing into her pumpkin costume from last Halloween, and once Sally saw this, she demanded to be allowed to wear the Batman outfit. I couldn't say which was funnier, but they were equally impractical for dining purposes: one unable to move her arms and the other unable to see. Their parents didn't care because the kids were quiet and content. This, I've discovered, is the nirvana every parent seeks: a happy, quiet child.

The usual chatter ensued and the topic seemed to find its way, as it so often does, back to the children. I don't mind, I like to hear about them, but I've never felt fully part of the conversation. I can't understand the middle-of-the-night feeds, or bitch about school fees, or offer my advice on sterilizing bottles or the teething process. I have no hilarious anecdotes about putrid nappies exploding in public or school plays gone disastrously wrong. If anything, I feel ashamed, listening to all this, about the fact that I get plenty of sleep and my vagina is as tight as ever. So I try to steer the conversation toward film—a topic we all used to have in common—but these same people who introduced me to *Star Wars* and Spielberg and Hollywood musicals, who shaped my love of storytelling and in doing so inadvertently determined my career, now laugh when I ask if they've seen a new release. When you have kids, they tell me, you don't go to the cinema anymore. This makes me feel both sad and selfish. Sad that they've given it up. Selfish that I don't think I could.

When they asked, once again, about me leaving my stable office job—with its pension and maternity leave and on-site gym facilities—to pursue something that to most people must seem like a hobby, I felt the need to explain myself. Yes, I work from home, and yes, I sit on my arse all day and write, but it's not that easy, I tell them, to be creative. It's exhausting, pouring your heart out onto a page, building entire worlds and people to inhabit them, motivating yourself to write every day, running a business alone, worrying where your next paycheck will come from, pitching your precious ideas to people who probably won't remember you . . . And then I heard myself, describing my life as exhausting, and I stopped talking because I know that anything short of being responsible for the physical and emotional well-being of nonfictional human beings who are entirely dependent on you does not classify as exhausting in this room.

Know your audience.

After dinner we collapsed on sofas and chatted a while longer. Theo played Legos with the kids and they each presented their new truck or spaceship to the group for inspection. When they grew tired of building things they laid Theo down, covered him in Lego bricks, and laughed when he rolled over and they all fell off. They repeated this several times and never found it any less funny. He was good with them, I thought, he always had been.

Soon after, hugs were given, good-byes were said, and kids were carted into the backs of cars, all tired eyes and heavy heads nodding toward sleep. Sally and Lily didn't want to leave. They clung to my legs and begged to stay for a sleepover. They'd go to bed early, they insisted, and wouldn't drink any more Coke. They'd be good, they promised, they'd be the very, very best.

The pair of them looked up at me, oozing cuteness, and I found myself laughing at their ability to master the basics of manipulation with absolutely none of the subtlety required. I caught

Donal's eye and he smiled a smile that said he'd seen this routine many times before.

"Is that all right with you?" I asked.

"Is it all right if you take care of my kids for the night?"

"Fair point," I said. "See you in the morning."

"See ya!" said Donal, laughing as he took off to tell his wife about their night off. The girls ran straight to the sofa to fight over which movie to watch. They settled on *Toy Story* and fell asleep halfway through.

Theo helped me carry them to their bed in the spare room. My mother set it up the way they like it—with fairy lights on instead of the bedside lamp, and their favorite teddies peeping out of the covers—and I felt guilty for not knowing all this, for being the kind of aunt who visits every other month, who sees all the milestones but misses the minutiae of their little lives.

But being their aunt was a responsibility I hadn't asked for, I told myself; I didn't choose to have five extra humans in my life to love, and miss, and worry about, yet here they were. And even though they had all just recently come into being, I'd give my left lung to any one of them who needed it. I would kill for them. I would take a bullet for them. And let me be clear, there are very few people I would jump in front of a bullet for; it's a shockingly short list, which takes a very long time to get on. But by merely existing, by doing no more than being born, these kids automatically get a spot on that list, along with my unwavering, unconditional, oftentimes totally irrational devotion. Once kids come along, loving them is not a choice; it's an inevitability.

And these aren't even my kids!

Sally had refused to get out of the Batman costume, so I knelt in front of her now, clumsily trying to remove it. Her body flopped against mine as I peeled black Lycra from her limp little arms. Sally is my goddaughter as well as my niece. On paper that means I'm supposed to teach her about a bunch of Catholic nonsense I don't believe in, but in reality it means I find myself looking out for her that little bit more. There's an affinity there too, and when she tells me that the Hulk is her favorite superhero, that she quit ballet and has decided to do karate instead, that she doesn't ever want to get married because she's "too independent"—her actual words—I see a wildness, an ambition, and a disregard for the established order that are rare in someone so young. She reminds me of me, there's no easier way to put it, and I suppose I'm drawn to her because nurturing her feels a little bit like nurturing myself. Which is all very Freudian, I know.

I managed to slip a nightdress over her head and pull her arms through the sleeves; then I helped her climb sleepily into bed next to Lily, who was already snoring a soft, child's snore. Lily is the water to Sally's wildfire; her gentle nature tames Sally in the best way, and I'm glad that they have one another to lean on in this life. I kissed them both on the forehead and before I stood to go, Sally looked up at me and muttered, "I love you."

My phone beeps. I look down and see a blue cross materializing in the window on the stick. I know what it means but I check the instructions again just to be sure. Then I check them again.

I'm pregnant.

How unceremonious this all is: a world full of women, alone on toilets, pissing on sticks. Each new life heralded by a piece of urine-soaked plastic.

What am I supposed to do now?

What does *she* do now, I wonder, the woman who wants this? I suppose she cries, a giddy little cry. Then she gets ready to tell the father. Maybe she cooks him a nice meal, and wears a nice dress, and sits across the table from him, beaming. He leans over to pour her some wine and she says, "None for me," and at first he doesn't understand but then recognition dawns and he kisses her and holds her hand and they laugh and embrace and make plans late into the night. And she worries she's not ready but he tells her that she is. And he worries they don't earn enough but she tells him they'll make do. And they share their hopes and fears about the family they'll become.

Maybe it's fucking magical. I wouldn't know.

Theo left early for Tom's wedding yesterday morning. I was just waking up as he placed a cup of tea on the bedside table for me. I mumbled my thanks, then reached for the cup and noticed he was already dressed in his new suit.

"I have to go soon," he said, as I took in the sight of him.

"You look great!"

He gave me a little twirl.

"You think?"

"Honestly," I said, "you look really good."

He smiled then, a proper ear-to-ear smile that I hadn't even realized I'd been missing.

"I wish I could come with you," I said.

"I'll be back tomorrow night."

He made one last hair check in the mirror, delicately tousling his dark blond locks with one hand as he pouted at his own reflection. Finally, he was satisfied.

"Gotta go or I'll miss the train."

"Okay. Text me when you get there."

"I'll try, but I might not have signal in the country, so don't worry if you don't hear from me. Enjoy your tea!"

"I will, thanks. I love you."

"You too," said Theo, as he disappeared out the door.

I get up and throw the pregnancy test in the bin, as though doing so will make this go away. Then I check my phone; I sent Theo a message last night to say I hoped he'd arrived in one piece and was having a good time. Still no reply. I wonder if I should call him, what I would say if he picked up. Panic grips me. I feel my chest tighten. Suddenly, I can hear my therapist's voice in my head, reminding me to "stay in the observer role," to stop and notice my feelings instead of being overwhelmed by them.

I notice I am feeling anxious.

Good.

I take a few mindful breaths, relax my body; then I scroll idly through Facebook while I plan what to say.

I'm about to stop scrolling and call Theo when I see a colleague of his has posted photos of the wedding: the bride, the cake, the speeches, and several shots of their team huddled together in a garden at twilight, drinks in hand and toothy smiles all round. There's Theo, still in his suit but with his top button open and his green tie loosened slightly. And in every photo, right beside him, under his arm in fact, is Lesley.

Lesley sits opposite Theo at work. I've met her several times, and she's always seemed quite pleasant, if a little stuck-up. Most worryingly, though, she is exactly his type.

I suppose I should be his type, but I'm not. When we met he told me there were three types of women he disliked: women who smoke, women who vote Labour, and women who have tattoos. I don't smoke, but I do vote Labour, and a few months into our relationship I got my first tattoo, which just so happened to be the topic of our first fight.

Theo's type is what I like to call a Horse Woman. Horse Women are not women who look like horses, but rather women who look like they grew up around horses. They are plain but pretty. They wear very little makeup. They never dye their hair. And they always order salads in restaurants. Horse Women come from money. They vote Conservative. They study at prestigious universities. And then they settle down with a nice Tory boy and throw their degree out the window in favor of raising his bratty Tory children. Basically, a Horse Woman is everything I'm not, and Lesley is one of them.

I've noticed the frequency with which Theo mentions Lesley has increased lately. This is a tactic, I've learned, that men employ in order to make their inappropriate feelings for someone else feel more appropriate. Hiding in plain sight, as it were. They've also been going for lunch and to the gym together more often. *That's not cheating,* I tell myself, *you're being paranoid.* But here she is, hair down, tits out, under my boyfriend's arm. And here I am with his unwanted, unborn child inside me. I see that he's commented on one photo. "BEST DAY EVER!!" it says.

All caps. Two exclamation marks.

I notice I am feeling incandescent rage.

My mother picks up after two rings.

"Sally said she loves me," I blurt out.

"She does," replies my mother. Then: "Hi."

"Hi," I say. "But I'm never there."

"Kids don't care about that stuff. Are you okay?"

"I don't want them," I say.

"Want what?"

"Kids. I don't want them."

"Okay," she says. "What's—"

"I'm pregnant."

A pause.

"Fuck," she says. "I mean. Sorry. I didn't mean—"

"It's fine," I say. "'Fuck' is the correct response."

"I'll get on a plane—"

"Don't get on a plane," I say, at the exact same time.

I sit on my balcony with the phone to my ear and, as the sun makes its way slowly across the sky, I tell her everything. Not just about the pregnancy test. I tell her all the things we're afraid to tell our mothers about our partners in case they tell us what we don't want to hear but already know: that we should leave them.

I tell her that Theo seems almost incapable of being in a room with me anymore. That I look forward to him taking a bath so I can sit next to him on the floor and chat, knowing he won't be distracted by a phone or a laptop or anything that isn't me. I try to laugh at how pathetic it is that I sometimes make my own boyfriend a captive audience, but I end up crying instead. Then I stop myself because there is nothing I hate more than the sound of my own voice strangled by sobs. I catch my breath before I speak again.

"The other night we were sat in bed," I say, "and I asked him how his day had been. So he opened his laptop and showed me his calendar for the day. The meetings he had, where he went for lunch, what class he took at the gym. It was as if he needed visual cues in order to speak to me.

"You know, for a while there I actually thought Theo might have lost the ability to conduct a normal, human conversation. But I've since realized that he just loathes every second we spend together, which, to be fair, seems a lot more plausible than someone suddenly forgetting the art of social interaction.

"And all this stuff about him 'having no signal' is bullshit, by the way. He's got enough bloody signal to leave a comment on Lesley's fucking Facebook photo. It's the same shit. He just doesn't want to talk to me."

She lets me get it all out, listening as I recount all the times he's hurt me: the night I wore lingerie for him and he looked at me and sighed like making love to me was a chore; the time he completely forgot we had tickets to a show and I had to go alone; and my personal favorite, the night of my thirtieth birthday, when he said he'd be home late from a rugby match and asked me to put the dinner on—after we'd eaten the birthday meal I'd cooked for myself, he told me there was a cake in the fridge if I wanted it. It was one of those supermarket caterpillar cakes, still in the box.

I tell her how crazy I feel. That there's a disparity between his actions and his words I can't make sense of: he says he loves me and he wants to be with me, but he seems uncomfortable in my presence. He gets up earlier and earlier to go to the gym. He stays later and later after work. He never smiles around me anymore.

She already knows all this, not the details, but the broad strokes; the things we think we're hiding from people, we're only really hiding from ourselves.

"I thought that stuff with the tie was a bit weird, all right," she says, and this actually makes me laugh.

He spent almost the entire trip to Ireland obsessing over the green tie. He'd managed to get a suit and shirt easily enough, but getting a tie with the exact woolen texture he wanted, in the perfect shade of green, had proven difficult. We went to four different shops trying to find one. My mother asks me now if I think it was all to impress "that tramp"—there is no actual evidence to suggest that Lesley is a tramp, but I appreciate my mother getting on board.

"I don't know," I say, "I hope not. But maybe it'd make things easier. It'd certainly make me feel less crazy."

"I understand," she says, and the next words to come out of her mouth will stay with me for the rest of my life . . .

"Crazy is the space between what they tell you and what you know is true."

I'm still reeling from this reality check when I spot something in my periphery: there, in one of the plant pots in the corner of the balcony, in among the brown, dying leaves, is a sliver of green. I go to it and find a fresh stalk has emerged from the soil, small but strong. Suddenly, salvaging this plant seems immensely important.

I ask my mother what to do and she tells me to start by removing the dead leaves.

"Do the same with all the others. Cut them right back," she says. "It'll feel like you're killing them but you're not. You're just getting rid of what they don't need to help them grow."

I tell her I'll call her back when I'm done; the sun's going down and I don't want to be out here gardening in the dark. We've reached no conclusions but that's okay; my problems are, unfortunately, not going anywhere.

With a task to focus on, my thoughts seem to focus too, and as I kneel here, gently tending to each delicate plant, my mind wanders again to Sally. Me helping her into bed that night. Her tiny, heart-shaped lips forming that enormous statement. She loves me. For no other reason than she does. And there's something heart-wrenchingly pure about that. There's no bullshit, no games, no complications; she just felt something, so she said it.

Maybe I do want it. Maybe I would be a good mother. Maybe I could do it; raise a child, help them to be a good person, protect them from the evils of this world. Maybe I could write too. Maybe I could do both. Maybe the pregnancy would be gentle and the birth would be easy and my child would be the kind who sleeps through the night.

Maybe Theo and I will be okay, I think. Maybe it's just a rough patch. Maybe I'll talk to him, tell him everything, and we'll sort things out. Maybe he'll be kind and understanding. Maybe this will make him fall in love with me again. Maybe it will change everything. Maybe I'll look back and wonder how I ever dreamed of a life without him, without this. Maybe.

And for a few short moments, alone on the balcony, with an aching back, sore knees, and dirt under my fingernails, it all seems possible.

I have just thrown all the dead leaves in the bin and I'm watering the stalks I've saved when Theo comes through the door and sees me outside with the watering can.

"Are you still at that?" he asks. "I told you they're dead."

Later on, we're sitting on the sofa watching a movie, but he's not actually watching it, he's checking his emails, and I ask him to put away the laptop so we can talk. He says he will in a minute.

Twenty minutes pass.

I can't concentrate on the film so I turn it off.

"What's wrong with you?" he asks.

"This doesn't feel right," I say.

"What doesn't?"

"Us," I say. "Something's wrong. We need to talk."

He sighs, closes the laptop, and runs his fingers through his hair the way he does when he's stressed out, dragging it backward off his face. He looks at me, and my heart aches at the memory of his dark eyes staring down at me the first time we made love. It's not that he can't see me now, it's more like he can see me, but I'm spoiling his view.

I want to tell him what's going on, that I'm worried he cheated on me—or that he's going to—that I know he doesn't love me and we're just flogging a dead horse. Mostly I want to tell him that I'm pregnant. But I suddenly realize two things. Firstly, I'll never know if he was going to leave me and only stayed out of a sense of obligation. And secondly, he won't be strong. He'll need me to be strong for us both and I don't think I can do that right now. Before I can decide what to say, Theo speaks.

"I think we should call it a day."

Just like that.

In the morning, I'll wake up alone and find a package outside the door with Chinese writing on the envelope. I will open it to find a green tie, which I'll throw straight in the bin. Soon after that, I'll go to the bathroom and see blood in the toilet bowl. I'll take two more pregnancy tests, just to be sure. They'll both be negative. I'll call my mother and tell her Theo's gone. She'll offer to get on a plane. I'll refuse.

"I'm not pregnant, by the way," I'll say, and I'll hear a quiet intake of breath on the other end of the line.

"Are you sure?" she'll ask.

"I'm sure."

A moment will pass. When she speaks, her voice will be clear and certain.

"Probably for the best," she'll say.

the last good day

THEO'S ABOUT TO LEAVE for work when his phone rings. It's one of his colleagues, calling to let him know that she got to the office early and was sent home. I can just about make out what she's saying. Something about a burst pipe. She tells Theo he may as well stay home, and he thanks her and walks back into the bedroom.

"Looks like I'm staying put."

"I heard," I say, trying to conceal a smile.

"I'm supposed to work from home," says Theo, "but I don't really have much to do."

I pull back the duvet and lightly pat the patch of bed next to me.

"I'll give you something to do."

Theo laughs in spite of himself.

"You're actually ridiculous," he says, but he's already unbuttoning his shirt.

* * *

The day is warm but overcast and the odd rain shower patters by outside. We finally roll out of bed around eleven a.m. and Theo whips up a batch of fluffy, American-style pancakes. I make us a big pot of tea and a heap of bacon, fried to a crisp; then we smother our food in maple syrup and sit to the table to eat. I can't remember the last time we had breakfast together like this; I started working from home around six months ago, and despite being here more I've seen Theo less. He's been busy. I get it. But I've missed him. Truth be told, I've not been doing very well on my own, so having him here today is a welcome change.

We stay at the table a while, picking over the last scraps of food as we talk and laugh and catch up like old friends who haven't seen one another in ages. After that we retire to the sofa, pull the blinds, and squabble over which movie to watch until finally we settle on *500 Days of Summer*. It's been years since either of us has seen it.

I'm beginning to doze a little, all curled up with my head resting on Theo's chest, when I'm woken by him muttering angrily at the telly.

"Fuck's sake, Tom," he says.

I'm only half-awake.

"Hmm?"

"Well, he's making a right tit of himself, isn't he?"

"Mmm."

"She's not into you, mate—get over it!" says Theo to the TV. I'm smiling to myself as I drift off to sleep.

When I wake up, the room is quiet. Theo's gone and there's

a blanket over me. I have no idea how long I've been out for, but my body feels better rested than it has in a long while. I stretch and yawn and I'm nuzzling back into a cozy position when Theo arrives home with two big bags of shopping.

"Hello, angel."

"Hello," I purr from the sofa.

He looks at me and smiles; then he walks over and crouches down in front of me.

"I love you," he says, and I'm a little taken aback.

"I love you too," I say.

"I really do," he adds.

There's a surreal, almost dreamlike quality to this moment. A sense of surfacing. But from where I'm not sure.

Theo kisses me gently on the forehead and again on the lips. He strokes my hair and I press my head against his hand, smiling.

"You're like a big cat," he says, laughing as he goes to put away the groceries.

We cook dinner together, dancing around one another from counter to cooker to sink as music blares—we even slow dance while the broccoli boils—then we eat at the table again, this time by candlelight with a bottle of wine.

After dinner we watch another movie; then I go to bed and read while Theo potters about, getting his things ready for the next day—he got an email from his boss to say the pipe's been fixed and everyone's expected back in the office tomorrow.

He takes a shower before climbing into bed and pulling me

in toward him for a cuddle. His hair is still dark with damp, and I run my fingers through it as we talk.

"Theo?"

"Yes, angel."

"I had a really nice day."

He doesn't open his eyes. But a soft smile forms on his lips.

"Me too."

"Can we have another one just like it soon, please?" I ask.

"Of course we can."

I'm not sure what it is I liked so much; there was nothing special about today, except that it was perfect.

between the sheets

THOUGHTS. EATING INTO DAYS. Gobbling them whole. The light fades. And suddenly you're home. And here I am. In the same spot you left me almost twelve hours ago. Same pink flannel robe. Hair uncombed.

"Have you had dinner, babe? 'Cause I grabbed food with so-and-so. I'll make you something if you like. How'd the writing go?"

"Fine."

Always fine.

Regardless what transpired in the day. Regardless of the mark I made (or didn't make) upon the page. Regardless of this fog inside my brain. Which light and life can't seem to penetrate. Or is it brine? Are all my thoughts just pickling inside my mind? Floating there, preserved. Forever frozen in the moment of deciding if you're still mine.

Are you?

I can't tell.

This is hell, I think, on a basis more than daily now.

I love you. Is the thing. The verb, not the noun. But like some pointless clown performing for a birthday boy who doesn't give a shit, who only wants to sit and play with his new toys, I might as well take off the flaking makeup and fake smile. Pathetic. Unfunny. Futile. God, I wish I could laugh.

I love you. Is the thing. But that joke isn't funny anymore.

I wonder what you think of me when you come through the door. Sickened by the sight of me, no doubt. That must be why you stay out every night. And go to work before it's even light most days. It's okay. I wouldn't be here if I didn't have to be. But I don't have a choice in how far I can get from me.

Maybe I need help or—

"Pass me the remote, babe."

"Okay."

I can't remember what we're watching on TV.

Nor can I remember how it felt, before it didn't feel this way.

You go and I go crazier with every passing day.

How'd the writing go?

It didn't.

It never does.

And without words I don't know what I am. Organs crammed inside a cage of bones. Limbs and skin and teeth and hair and toes.

Beating heart. Moving parts. A flesh sack that I drag from place to place. A creature made up not of matter but of space.

A vacant automaton lacking in the lexicon to decode what this blinking, twinkling flash of life is for.

Unable to think. Afraid to drink. My mother swapped her blood for wine so I swapped mine for ink and now the bloody ink won't pour.

I can't take much more of this.

It's been two months since we so much as kissed. Or touched. And look, I understand. I'm hardly at my peak. I feel like a failure between both sets of sheets. But I think we'd be all right if we could just speak—

"I'm tired, babe. Not now. It's been a long week."

Thoughts. Eating into days. Gobbling them whole. The light fades and I wonder, *Where was I just now?* With you, two years ago. *Or was it three?* It hardly matters anyhow, but something catches. Snags. Like wool. On some frayed edge inside of me. I feel the pull. The sharp snap back. To some point in our history. Poignant or mundane. Always the same. Unchangeable regardless of how many nights I spend trying to rewrite or mend the things we said or did or that we failed to do or see.

All of my extremities are ragged to the touch. And tired fingers work incessantly to unclutch what has caught there.

Memories.

Like swathes of silver fish they gasp at air. Scales catching in the light as they fight to escape. I wish that I could take a file. And scrape.

Scrape.

Scrape.

Until there's nothing left of me. But soft edges. With rounded corners.

At night we lie, silent as orbits. You unconscious. Me awake. Staring at your dreaming face. Your ghostly skin. And the charcoal smudge above your top lip. We stay this way for hours as the shadows creep.

I'd be all right, I think, *if I could only get some sleep.*

bodies

I'M LYING AWAKE IN bed when the phone rings. It's Theo. I
don't pick up. Two minutes later I call him back.

"Are you drunk?" I ask when he answers.

"No."

"Are you done ignoring me, then?"

"I wasn't ignoring you," he says.

"Well, it sure fucking felt like it." There's a pause.

"My gran died," says Theo. His voice cracks slightly. He sniffs.
I sit up in bed and switch the light on.

"Oh, honey, I'm so sorry."

The last time we spoke was in Paris—he's working there temporarily and I decided to surprise him with a visit. To say it ended
badly would be an understatement; as it stands I'm not actually
sure if we're still together. I flew home more than two weeks ago
and he hasn't answered my calls since; he just texts me every few
days to say he needs more time. For what, I'm not entirely sure.

To calm down? To decide if he still loves me? To work up the courage to leave me?

Meanwhile, I've been trying to carry on life as usual, which is proving more difficult than I'd expected; emotional stress aside, the logistics are a nightmare—our friend Trinny is waiting for us to RSVP to her wedding, there are several outstanding bills in Theo's name, and I can't find the number for the pest-control guy. Last night I accidentally left a packet of Jacob's Cream Crackers on the table and the mice burrowed a hole clean through it.

"Okay," I say to Theo, switching into crisis mode. "How can I help? Do you need me to book you a flight home?"

"I'm already home," he says.

"Oh. When did you get back?" I ask, thinking he might be calling from the airport.

"Three days ago."

"Oh."

"My mum called and I came home and . . ." He trails off, then comes back. "She says my gran died peacefully, in her sleep." Sniff.

To be perfectly honest, I couldn't care less how she died. Theo's grandmother Augusta was a cruel, carping, racist old bitch who spoke with great fondness of a postwar Britain, where "people knew their place." From what I could glean, Augusta had never been particularly kind to Theo—and she grew even meaner when he brought home an Irish girl—but he loved her in the same way he loves his mother, with naivety and a selective blindness.

Theo's still talking but I can't focus on what he's saying. He's been back in the country for three days and he didn't even tell me? I've been over here climbing the fucking walls. I almost got a flight to Paris yesterday. What if I had? What then?

"When's the funeral?" I ask.

"Tomorrow."

Tomorrow!?

"Right," I say.

"Will you come with me?" asks Theo. Another sniff. Followed by him blowing his nose directly into the phone.

"Of course I will."

"Thanks," he says. "I'll be over first thing to get my suit. Then we'll drive down."

"In whose car?" I ask.

"I've rented one."

"Right," I say, and then, unable to restrain myself, I ask him what he's told his mother about us.

"There's nothing to tell," says Theo. "We had a fight, that's all."

"Well, that's not all. You haven't spoken to me in two weeks. And you've been back for three days without telling me."

"Please don't make this about you," he says, and I bite my lip hard while he continues. "I didn't want to see anyone, okay? I just wanted to be with family."

"Of course. I'm sorry. See you in the morning."

I hang up before the part where we'd usually say "I love you," knowing somehow that he won't.

The next morning, I'm in our bedroom deciding what to wear when I hear Theo's key in the door. It's just gone eight a.m. I've barely slept.

I tiptoe down the hall in a black dress and bare feet and find him standing in the middle of the living room, head down, shoulders hunched, like a child who's been forgotten at the school gates. I notice he's brought his suitcase home, which puts me at ease a little. I wonder how long he'll stay before he goes back to Paris.

"Nothing's changed," Theo says, glancing around the room.

"Why would it?" I ask.

"When will you be ready?"

"Ten minutes," I tell him.

"Cool. Just gonna grab my suit if that's okay?"

"Of course," I say, and he moves toward the bedroom. As he passes me I catch his right hand with my left and he stops.

"Hey," I say.

"Hey," says Theo, looking at the floor now.

I tilt my face to find his, and finally I catch his gaze and hold it.

"Hi," I say again, and instantly Theo's energy softens. I squeeze his hand, he squeezes back, and with that he lets out a long, shuddering breath, like he hasn't exhaled in days. He drops his forehead to my shoulder and instinctively my free hand rises to stroke his hair. We stay this way a while, facing in opposite directions, his breath coming and going in little stops and starts. I can feel his tears running down my arm and collecting in the crevices of our interlaced fingers.

After a few minutes he rights himself and goes to our bedroom. I've hung his suit on the wardrobe door and placed his shoes beneath it for him. He thanks me, and as he begins to pull his suit off the hanger I see him notice the pile of black dresses discarded on the bed.

"I couldn't decide what to wear," I explain.

"Well, luckily we're going to a funeral, not a fashion show."

He says this with a quick flippancy, but the anger behind it is palpable. My stomach clenches.

"I'm sorry," he says; then he looks me up and down. "The one you have on is nice. Want me to zip you up?"

"Sure," I say, and I turn around and gather my hair up out of the way. But as Theo steps behind me, I feel as vulnerable as if I were facing the edge of a cliff. He zips me up and, without hesitation, returns to his suit. This in itself is of course unremarkable, except that for the past few years, every time Theo zips me into or out of a dress, he stops to kiss me on the back of the neck. I used to think the only way a man could hurt you was by lashing out, but it turns out the absence of action can cause just as much pain.

"I wanted to wear something your mother would like," I say; then, with my back still turned, I pick up my shoes and go, knowing he'll read the subtext.

It's no secret that Theo's mother and I don't like each other; Jocelyn is a difficult person for anyone to get along with, but being the object of Theo's affection makes me the competition in her eyes, and so she treats me like a scorned wife might treat the other woman, with unabashed jealousy and contempt. I learned a long time ago that it's best to keep my head down, let her have all of Theo's attention, and give her absolutely no ammunition to throw at me. That's why I tried on twelve different dresses today, and that's why, instead of choosing the one that I liked best, I chose the one that's not too short, not too low-cut, not too figure-hugging, not too cheap, not too extravagant, and indeed not too plain. I'm keen to see how Jocelyn manages to find fault with it anyway.

A few minutes later Theo emerges from the bedroom in his suit. I'm absentmindedly thinking how handsome he looks when he asks where my overnight bag is.

"I didn't know we were staying," I say.

"My mum's booked us all into a B&B for the night. Didn't I tell you?"

"No," I say, pushing down a wave of anxiety about the plans changing. "But that's fine, I'll grab a few things."

He mumbles an apology as I clack back toward the bedroom in a pair of high heels, which I rethink and swap for flats, partly because they'll be more practical in a graveyard and partly because I don't want to appear "too tall." As I zip up my bag I realize that Theo probably brought his suitcase for the stay tonight. *Silly girl*, I think, *he's not coming home.*

We hardly speak the whole way to the funeral and I'm glad to be behind the wheel; the road is a welcome distraction from the noise in my head and the silence in the car. It's a gray, blustery day. Rain spits sideways at us and a pair of balding windscreen wipers scrape doggedly back and forth across the glass. I ask Theo several times if he's all right; he says he's fine and continues staring out the window. At one point he turns on the radio, scans through the stations, and, unsatisfied, turns it back off. I offer him a cable to play music from his phone but he just shakes his head.

I'm beginning to wonder if Theo's being intentionally vague and erratic to throw me off guard—calling me at the last second, withholding information and affection as a form of emotional manipulation—when I realize that while his actions may seem cruel, it wouldn't occur to him to be cunning. This is just how Theo fights: he doesn't attack; he avoids.

I, on the other hand, become a detective in the midst of an argument, desperately searching for clues as to his feelings or intentions, piecing together every shred of evidence that might prove my current theory; that he's staying, that he's going, that he loves me, that he never wants to see me again. There's a certain amount of confirmation bias at play here, but being aware of that doesn't stop me.

Of course, he could just tell me how he's feeling, but that would require self-awareness and communication skills, neither of which Theo possesses. So I settle for speculation. Today he's an enigma; he's gone from ignoring me to crying on me to insulting me to complimenting me to ignoring me again, and I don't know what any of it means. My head hurts. I check the map. Another hour to go.

We're driving to Dunkerton, a small village just outside Bath where Theo's grandmother grew up and where she'll be laid to rest today. I imagine the gravediggers at this very moment, opening a hole in the earth for Augusta next to her late husband, Jim. This seems like a romantic notion—two people who were once in love, separated by death, resting together for eternity—but the truth is that Jim and Augusta were already separated in life. Not in any official capacity, of course—it wasn't the done thing back then to leave one's spouse, even if they made you miserable. They barely spoke save for perfunctory conversation, they slept in separate bedrooms at night, and during the day they occupied different areas of their home; she took the parlor and he the conservatory, or the garden, weather permitting.

I never met Jim—he died when Theo was just a boy—but the stories Theo tells about him all seem to revolve around bike rides in the local park, games of kick-about in the garden, and reading together at bedtime. Jim sounds like a good man: a soft-natured, altruistic old soul who deserved better than a stern, scathing wife. I'm wondering how two such different people got together in the first place, and why they stayed together for so long, when my thoughts are interrupted by an impossibly loud bang, a sort of guttural, shredding noise that feels like it's happening inside my own head.

"What the fuck was that!?" shouts Theo, grabbing at the dashboard as the car swerves abruptly to the right. We're in the outside lane of the M4 motorway and I'm pretty sure one of the back tires has just burst. My instinct is to steer left out of the swerve, but some blessed part of my brain remembers being told not to do that or it could send the car into a spin. I grip the wheel and hold it straight instead.

"Stop the car!" shouts Theo.

"No," I say, pushing my foot down on the accelerator.

"What are you doing?" he screams, eyes wide. I don't answer.

I'm not sure who gave me this information or where it was being stored, but I know that slamming on the brakes is maybe worse than turning the wheel. So once again I ignore my instincts and accelerate.

As soon as I can maintain a straight line and a safe speed, I indicate left and move slowly to the inside lane, by which point Theo's panic has reached a crescendo and he's clawing at my arm and begging me to pull over.

"We can't change the tire here," I say.

"WHAT TIRE!?" he bellows. He has no idea what's happening. I just keep quiet and keep going until eventually I can exit off the motorway. Somewhere near Chippenham, we pull into a service station, and the moment the car crawls to a stop, Theo unbuckles his seat belt and gets out. I'm still staring straight ahead as he paces back and forth through my field of vision, holding his head in his hands and grabbing tufts of hair in his fists.

Finally, as though suddenly remembering I exist, Theo comes back to the car and opens my door. The wind catches the door, flinging it open as he crouches down next to me.

"Are you all right?" he asks.

"I'm fine," I say, much too quickly. He reaches in and turns the key in the ignition. The engine stops. I notice the absence of the sound.

"You can let go of the steering wheel now." His voice is gentle and far away.

"Okay," I say, but when I look down my hands are still clenched around the wheel, my knuckles turning slowly white.

Theo peels my fingers off the wheel, then takes my hands in his.

"You did good," he says. "You did so good."

A teardrop lands in my lap. Then another. I turn to look at Theo but there are no tears on his face.

"Am I crying?" I ask. Theo looks at me like he's searching my face for the answer to a math problem.

"Yes, angel," he says.

"Oh," I say. Then: "I'd like to get out of the car now."

With one arm around me, Theo walks me inside to a little café down the back of the service station. He bundles me up in his coat and deposits me in one of the booths while he goes to get help. The wallpaper is a grubby shade of maroon, peeling at the seams. I stare at it for an indiscernible amount of time.

When Theo returns, with two cups of tea and a bar of chocolate, he tells me about the nice young man named Derek who's going to fix our car. There appears to be a slight delay between Theo's mouth moving and the words coming out, like he's speaking over live satellite link. He tells me it's just a burst tire and the car will be ready in an hour. I hear this about three seconds after he says it.

"Why are we here?" I blurt at him.

"What do you mean?"

"I'm not sure," I say, losing my train of thought.

I might have meant why are we in this service station in Chippenham, or I might have meant our relationship, or the universe, but I can't remember now and every time I try to get hold of the thought it feels like I'm pulling on an elastic band until it snaps back and hits me in the brain.

"Why won't you talk to me?" I ask.

"I am talking to you."

I go back to staring at the wallpaper.

"What do you want to talk about?" asks Theo with a sigh.

"You know what I want to talk about."

"This isn't the time or the place," he says. "Drink your tea, please."

I take a sip and almost spit it back out.

"I don't take sugar anymore!"

"I know. But the lady said sweet tea is good for shock."

"What shock?" I ask. Theo doesn't respond; he just opens the chocolate wrapper, breaks off two squares, and hands one to me.

"I think you love it," I say through a mouthful of chocolate. "I think you love that I fucked up."

"Yeah, I love that you cheated on me." I wasn't ready to hear that word.

"Is that what you think?" I ask, and suddenly I'm crying again.

"Let's not do this now," he says, not unkindly.

We spend the rest of the wait in silence. Outside, I can see Derek changing the tire. The wind whips his ponytail against his head and I find this very satisfying to watch. As soon as the car is fixed, Theo drives us the rest of the way to Dunkerton.

Jocelyn is flapping about on the steps of the church when we arrive. Her sister, Eugenie, and brothers, Magnus and Halbert (I'm told Augusta named all of their children), appear to be consoling her. The service is due to start in ten minutes.

"Don't tell her about the car," says Theo as he pulls on the handbrake.

"Obviously," I reply.

He gets out and goes straight to his mum.

"Theodore!" she wails, throwing her arms around him and crying in great, heaving sobs.

"Sorry we're so late," I hear Theo say as I approach behind him, his voice muffled in the collar of Jocelyn's enormous faux-fur coat.

"What kept you?" She casts a scornful look over his shoulder at me.

"Traffic," says Theo.

"I told you to drive down with us," she says, and I know that by "you" she means him, singular.

While I wait for Theo to be set free, I offer my condolences to his aunt and uncles, who, despite being a glum old bunch of Tories, seem positively charming next to Jocelyn. We shake hands and nod solemn nods and they ask how the drive down was. I tell them it was fine. Just a bit of traffic.

Jocelyn's still nattering on about us being late when a very fidgety Eugenie steps in.

"Everyone's here now, Jossy; that's all that matters," she says, wringing her hands.

Jocelyn looks around, nonplussed, then finally relinquishes her grip on Theo and hooks her arm around his instead. His cheek is smeared with her magenta lipstick.

"I'm very sorry for your loss, Jocelyn," I say, now that she's no longer wearing my boyfriend like a shield.

"She was a great woman," Jocelyn replies. I can smell the booze on her breath when she speaks to me.

We all nod. Then Jocelyn turns to Theo and abruptly changes the subject.

"No sign of your sister," she says.

"Yeah. Sorry," says Theo, even though it's not his fault his sister, Octavia, isn't here. She moved to New Zealand nearly ten years ago and never came back.

"It's a long way to travel, Jossy," says Eugenie, ever the appeaser.

"Humph!" says Jocelyn. "She could at least have called." Theo and Eugenie share a confused look.

"She did call, Mum," he says. "You spoke to her last night." Jocelyn looks completely dumbfounded.

"Remember?" asks Theo.

"Of course I remember!" she snaps.

She doesn't. And we all know it's because she was drunk when her daughter called. Everyone stares at the ground or the sky or anything else, and suddenly I'm very jealous of Octavia, thousands of miles away from all this.

"We'd better be getting inside now," says Eugenie, and as we turn to go into the church, Jocelyn looks me up and down and says, "You look nice," leveling the compliment at me like an accusation.

"Thank you, Jocelyn," I say. "I like your coat."

We're making our way slowly past the small congregation when I spot Maya and Darren in the back row, and the sight of them almost reduces me to tears. I'm not sure how they found out but I'm so glad they're here. I smile at them and Maya gives me a little wink, which is our code for *You've got this*.

Jocelyn is still clutching on to Theo when they reach the

front pew. She drags him in alongside her, followed by the rest of the family. Theo realizes and looks back at me apologetically, but I just smile to let him know I understand, and then find a spot in the second row next to one of his cousins.

The service itself is like any I've been to, only much shorter; I'm used to Catholic masses and Theo's family is Protestant. I once asked Theo what the difference was between Catholics and Protestants, but aside from the length of the service he couldn't tell me. We were eating pizza in bed after a night out and were both far too drunk to figure it out.

"It's all made up anyway," said Theo, "so who gives a shit?"

"Hear! Hear!" I said, and we toasted by smacking two slices of pizza together. The next day I found several bits of pepperoni mashed into the sheets.

I'm smiling at this memory when Jocelyn throws another contemptuous glance in my direction and I suddenly realize everyone around me is standing as the coffin is being carried into the church. I immediately stand up and join them, but it's too late. I've already pissed her off.

I'm not really a fan of dead bodies. That is to say, I actively dislike them. So I spend most of Augusta's mass acutely aware that her corpse is mere feet away from me. Afterward, when the coffin lid is lifted and people are invited to come pay their final respects, I decide not to join the queue to see her. This isn't a traditional part of the ceremony, I'm told, but Jocelyn insisted.

Jocelyn is first in line, with Theo by her side. She howls over her mother's body, and it takes ten minutes and both of her brothers to finally tear her away and return her to her seat. All eyes are still on Jocelyn when I look back and notice Theo alone by the coffin, a lost child once again. I go to him and place a hand on his back, turning him away from the commotion and toward his grandmother instead. I gently rub away the lipstick on his cheek as I talk to him.

"Don't worry about your mum. She's okay. Just take your moment to say good-bye now."

Theo nods and looks down at his gran and I realize I'm in this now, until he's ready to go. I can't help but look at Augusta's face—a vague approximation of humanity—and I realize my problem with dead bodies is that they all look the same, which is nothing like their former selves.

When I was ten years old, Connor from Up the Road died from lymphoma. We called him Connor from Up the Road because there were two Connors, one of whom was from round the corner. After Connor from Up the Road died, we started calling both of them just Connor again, the new distinction being the tense in which we referred to them.

Connor played football for his school team and was an avid Liverpool fan, so they buried him in his jersey; I remember how the red cloth hung loose around his little body, made frail from months of chemotherapy. He was laid out in his living room and I had to stand on tiptoes to see inside the coffin. Lying there, his face pallid and his cheeks more rosy than they'd ever been in life, surrounded by folds of white satin lining, he reminded me of the hollow plastic dolls I used to push around in my toy pram.

For a whole day the neighbors came and went, visiting Connor's body, bringing food for his family, and keeping the kettle constantly on the boil, despite it being a hot day outside. I have a vague memory of one of the adults saying the heat could cause problems for the viewing, but when I asked what that meant nobody answered. I wanted to leave as soon as I saw the body and to this day I'm not sure what bothered me more: that I knew it wasn't Connor or that I felt like the only one who knew.

I can't count how many funerals I've been to since, but my nana's was by far the hardest; she had always been a fat, sturdy mass of a woman—even her laugh was big—yet here she was, small enough to fit into a little box. I watched as my family touched her hands and kissed her forehead and whispered good-byes into her ear, and I marveled at the love they still seemed to feel for her dead body. Not only could I not find love for it; I resented it, this thing that looked like her but wasn't her. I could see it, touch it, even talk to it, but I wouldn't be talking to her. It felt like a cruel joke.

My nana had been ill for a long time and I, of course, found solace in the fact that she was no longer suffering, but on a purely selfish level I wished there was some relief from the pain I felt in losing her. My usual information-gathering instinct was useless in this case—no matter how much I learned about death, she'd still be gone and I'd still be grieving—and so, having rejected religion at a young age, I found myself wishing for the comfort blanket that is faith.

I wanted to be able to blindly believe in something that might make me feel better, but I couldn't bring myself to do it because I feel much the same about the Church as I do about dead bodies—that they can both provide consolation, but only if you're willing to ignore some harsh truths. I find no more comfort in whispering in a dead person's ear than I do in whispering to a made-up God in the dark. Though sometimes I envy the fools who can.

Theo nods to let me know he's done and I take him back to his seat while the remaining mourners say their farewells.

It rains throughout the burial; thick, bulbous drops splash down on umbrellas and make mud of the soil. Afterward, the soggy procession shuffles quickly to a small pub down the road, and I stop at the B&B next door to drop off our bags. A silver-haired woman shows me to a poky room at the top of the stairs, where the carpet, curtains, wallpaper, and bedspread are all different shades of dusty pink. I make a vain attempt to dry my shoes with a whiny plastic hair dryer, and I spend the entire time wondering how many of these hair dryers were stolen over the years to warrant this one being attached to the wall by a too-short anti-theft cord. Eventually, I give up and crawl onto the bed, where I spend five glorious minutes lying on my back in complete silence, before squeezing back into my warm, damp shoes and heading to the pub.

Inside, Theo's family are crowded around wooden tables, somberly sipping their drinks and speaking in hushed tones. Hardly any light makes it through the bottle-brown windows and it takes a moment for my eyes to adjust to the gloom inside. *This is nothing like an Irish wake*, I think, where at least there'd be some respite from the sorrow; my uncle's funeral was a veritable hoot compared to this.

Jocelyn is at the bar, ordering what is probably her third or fourth drink of the day, and Theo is engrossed in conversation with Darren. I spot Maya at a table by herself and make a beeline for her. She's ordered me a bowl of vegetable soup and even though it's tepid by now, I am incredibly moved by the gesture.

"Hungry?" she asks as I guzzle it down.

"Starving. Haven't eaten today. Well, I had some chocolate . . ."

"Chocolate isn't food."

"It's not *not* food," I say, and she rolls her eyes. Then she drops her chin into her palm and glares with a sour expression at the pub full of wrinkly white Conservatives.

"I feel like I'm in *Get Out*," she says, and I look around and laugh.

"I'm surprised they don't have a 'No Blacks, no dogs, no Irish' sign," I say.

"Oh, they did," replies Maya, deadpan. "I asked them to take it down before you got here."

"You're a good friend."

I catch the attention of a waitress to order some drinks.

Maya says she's driving so I just get a glass of wine for myself.

"Soup and wine?" asks Maya.

"Good point," I say, turning back to the waitress. "Can I also get some chips, please? And a separate plate?"

"What's the extra plate for?" asks Maya.

"So I can douse my half in vinegar."

"I didn't say I wanted any," she says indignantly, but I only have to look at her before she acquiesces and her face melts into a cheeky grin.

Soon enough I've got chips and wine and time alone with Maya—I've even slipped my damp shoes off under the table—and I genuinely can't remember the last time I felt so content.

"Dare I ask how you are?"

"In this moment," I say, "I'm happier than I've ever been."

"And outside of this moment?" asks Maya as she blows on a piping-hot chip.

"Not great."

Maya was the first person I called when I got back from Paris. I told her everything that had happened, and while some details were sketchy because I was blackout drunk for the main event, the headlines were all there and I gave them to her as objectively as I could. She spent the first few days after I got home convincing me I'm not a monster and, once I believed this, she had to convince me that Theo wasn't a monster either, since he still wasn't talking to me. This is a prime example of my ability to think only in black and white, and it's often Maya's job to remind me that most things are actually interminable shades of gray. I haven't spoken to her much this past week; I tell her I've been busy, and even though she knows I've actually been wallowing, she doesn't call me out on it.

"How are you two now?" she asks, and I can't bring myself to tell her that Theo didn't call me until last night; she might get angry with him or she might side with him, but either way I don't want to hear it.

"I don't know," I say. "I'm not sure what he wants."

"Fuck what he wants. What do you want?"

"I want to talk. I want to fight, and cry, and spend days screaming at one another if we have to. Whatever it takes to sort this out and get back to being us."

"You want answers," she says.

"Yes."

"You want certainty and stability and a return to the status quo."

"Exactly!"

"Well," says Maya, "tough shit."

My mouth opens and snaps shut again.

"A big thing happened," she goes on, "and it doesn't matter who's right or who's wrong; this has changed things. They may never be the same again."

I can feel hot tears behind my eyes and I try to blink them away. Maya hands me a napkin before continuing.

"That doesn't mean things will be better," she says, "or worse. They'll just be different. But you need to accept it will take time."

"And what am I supposed to do till then?" I ask, like a petulant child. I hate the sound of my own voice right now.

"Just be there," she says. "Unless you don't want to be, of course. You can leave him tomorrow if you like, push the fuck-it button on the whole sodding relationship, and I'll be there to pick up the pieces. But if you want to make things right, you've got to resist the urge to force a resolution. Stop poking and prodding him and just bloody be there."

"Fine," I say, crossing my arms. Maya smiles at me.

"His grandmother died," she says pleadingly.

"His grandmother was a cunt," I reply, not noticing the waitress leaning over me to refill our water. Maya just about suppresses a smile but erupts as soon as the waitress turns her back.

"Do you think she heard me?" I ask earnestly, and Maya doubles over in another fit of giggles. Maya's laughter is infectious and

I can't help but join in. One by one, heads turn in our direction, a sea of bushy gray eyebrows all furrowing at the pair of us laughing in the corner, and all I can think to do is hand back the napkin Maya gave me, pat her on the shoulder, and loudly announce that she's very upset. Finally, Maya rights herself, wipes tears from her eyes, and whispers, "She called me a Negro once."

"She did NOT!" I say, incredulous, and Maya just nods. "Christ almighty. She was even more horrid than I thought."

With that, Darren joins us, sitting beside Maya and slipping an arm around her waist.

"What are we talking about?" he asks.

"That time Augusta called me a—"

"Ah yes," says Darren, cutting her off. Then, after a reflective pause: "May she rest in peace."

The three of us talk until it's dark outside and the room is bathed in tungsten light, meandering our way through various topics of little to no real importance. Chatting to Maya and Darren is familiar and comfortable, like slipping on a set of old pajamas at the end of a long day.

I notice that they seem especially loved up. Darren keeps nuzzling at Maya's ear while she speaks and asking if she's okay or if she needs anything. But despite Theo and I being distant at present (in every sense of the word), I'm not in the slightest bit jealous; if anything I'm glad of the reminder that relationships can be nice sometimes. I find myself scanning the room to check on Theo. He's forever talking with some cousin or other, but I give him the odd smile and he responds in kind. At some point there's a minor commotion at Jocelyn's table—an altercation with the waitress, I think—but when I look over I see Eugenie's got it under control.

The waitress, who now seems a bit disgruntled, stops by to ask if we'd like more drinks. I order another glass of wine and ask Darren what he's having. He says he can't drink because he's driving.

"I thought you were driving," I say to Maya.

"I am," she says, a bit flustered. "I mean, we both are."

"You're both driving?"

They nod in unison.

"We're taking it in shifts," says Maya.

"To drive back to London?"

They nod again.

I pretend that this is perfectly normal, order my wine, and turn back to Maya.

"So," I say, "how far along are you?" and the sweetest little smile creeps across her face. She looks at Darren and he just nods, exasperated.

"Five months!" she exclaims, and I squeal. I actually squeal. I never thought I would react this way, but here I am, squealing. Maya squeals back. Darren just sits there with a big, goofy grin, trying to shush us.

"We wanted to be certain before we told anyone."

I leap out of my chair and hug them both at the same time, practically sitting in their laps and planting kisses all over their faces while Maya giggles like an idiot. This hasn't been an easy journey for them, I know that, which makes it all the more joyful an occasion. I'm gushing about what wonderful parents they both will be when I notice the bushy-eyebrow brigade are staring at us again. This time I don't care. I want to stand up on my chair and announce to the room that my friends have created life!

"This is insane," I say, unable to properly articulate my thoughts on the matter. In trying to grasp the magnitude of it, I feel that rubber band around my mind again, expanding and snapping back each time I come close to comprehension. It's the same feeling I get when I think about the Big Bang, which I suppose makes sense since this is sort of the same thing; the sudden presence of life, the existence of something, where before there was nothing.

"It is a bit," says Maya.

"We're making a human," adds Darren.

"You're making a human!" I echo, beaming at Maya. "At this very moment you are growing a tiny body inside of you and one day it will come out and be a person who walks around and says things and eats cereal and watches TV and falls in love and makes more humans and—"

I stop myself before I say "dies," but that's what I'm thinking about. Suddenly that's all I can think about: how the only thing that's certain in life is death. *This baby might never watch TV or fall in love, I think, but it will definitely die. It might not even make it out of the womb alive.* And instantly I hate myself for having such a horrible thought. A quiet fatalism takes hold and I wonder how any parent can bear it—the inevitability, the futility—and now I feel the same resentment I felt for my grandmother's waxy, smiling corpse, only this time it's not for any one person or thing, but the universe, the grand scheme, the whole flawed fucking setup. Existence, I decide, is the cruelest joke of all.

"That's generally how it works," says Darren, bringing me back, but I can't remember what I was saying.

"How what works?" I ask.

"You know, the circle of life and all that," he says with an easy smile, which morphs into something sinister the longer I stare at it. The quiet chatter in the room seems to increase in volume, each voice flattened and hollow and indistinguishable from the next. There's something unreal about the texture of things; the table, the chairs, the walls—they could all be cardboard.

Maya leans over, places a hand on my knee, and asks if I'm all right.

"I'm great," I lie, looking around for Theo. "Does either of you know where Theo went?"

They both just shrug.

"I want to tell him the good news," I say, desperate to get away from this situation before I spoil the moment for them.

"How was he when you spoke earlier?" Maya asks Darren.

"Good," he says. "Definitely better than the other day."

I'm just about to walk away when this stops me in my tracks.

"Oh? When did you see him?" I ask as casually as possible.

"We went to a club in Hackney on Friday," says Darren, grinning. "Got absolutely smashed."

"Cool," I say. "I'm just going to see where he's got to."

I feel like a spring slowly coiling as I slip, seething, through the crowd. I ask Eugenie if she's seen Theo and she points toward a door at the back of the pub. Jocelyn is nearby, loudly prattling on about "the state of *her* country." I march toward the door, my panic slowly replaced by anger as my imagination flies into action, painting a picture of the past few days. He said he needed to be with family. He said that's why he hadn't called. But he wasn't at home, quietly mourning the death of his grandmother; he was out getting drunk with Darren while I googled last-minute flights to Paris.

What else had he lied about? Did he actually need more time? Or was he just dragging things out, trying to prolong my suffering?

By the time I reach the door, I have concocted an entirely new narrative of the past two weeks, wherein Theo went from one all-night bender to the next with a callous disregard for my feelings and no intention of ever speaking to me again. He only brought me here today to keep up the pretense, I decide, because he's too afraid to tell his mother she was right about me all along. Tomorrow, he'll go back to his swish Parisian bachelor pad and I'll go back to our shitty apartment with only the mice for company. *Bollocks*, I think. *I was supposed to ring the pest-control guy.*

I burst through the door ready for a fight and I find Theo sitting alone on a step outside. He looks up when he hears me, making no attempt to hide the fact that he's been crying; then he turns away again and continues staring out into the night. It's dark out here; muddy pools of light spill from the pub's beer-brown windows, providing no real illumination. The only sound is the breeze.

I stand for a moment, unsure what to do with all this unused energy; then I sit next to Theo on the step. He rests his head on my shoulder and weeps. A few minutes pass and I begin to feel the anger drain from me, like water through soil. After ten minutes or so, Theo stands, holding his hand out to me. I take it and we go back inside together.

• • •

The second we walk through the door I notice a change in the room, that sense of a party winding down. The already thin crowd has grown even thinner and the staff have started to clear away glasses and reset the tables for the night ahead.

"There you are, Theodore!" yells Jocelyn, and everybody turns to look at us. She's propped up at the bar by herself with a glass of whisky in front of her.

"Where'd you go?" she slurs at Theo as we approach, and I feel his fingers tighten around my hand.

"Just needed some fresh air," he answers.

She looks at him with a face that says, *Suit yourself*, like the very notion of fresh air is preposterous to her.

"What are you drinking?" Jocelyn asks us, and when Theo shakes his head, she looks at me expectantly.

"None for me, thanks," I say.

"But you're Irish!"

"Mum!" says Theo, then looks at me apologetically.

"What?" says Jocelyn, aggrievedly. "She is!" A moment passes.

"So, how's the *writing* going?" asks Jocelyn, with such derision that she might as well be inquiring after the well-being of my pet unicorn.

"It's going well," I say.

"She's a really good writer," Theo chimes in. "You should read one of her stories sometime."

"No, thanks, Theodore. I'm not interested in all that."

"What? Reading?" I ask.

"No," she says, "*stories*." And again this comes out like she's referring to some kind of mythical creature.

"Well, they're not for everyone," I say. "Now, who'd like a cup of tea?"

"I'd love one," says Theo, turning to Jocelyn. "Cup of tea, Mum?"

She drains her whisky and shakes the empty glass at the barman, who seems disinclined to pour her another. He looks at Theo, unsure what to do. Just then I spot Maya and Darren in my periphery, heading toward the door. I tell Theo I'll be back in a second and rush over to say good-bye.

"Sorry," says Maya. "We've got to get back."

"No problem at all," I say, hugging her and Darren and telling them how grateful I am that they came.

"I hope I didn't put my foot in it earlier," says Darren.

"It's fine," I say, waving it off.

"Did you not know they went out the other night?" Maya asks.

"I didn't know he was back in the country, Maya."

Her eyes widen at this, and Darren shuffles about like an awkward schoolboy. Suddenly we hear Jocelyn raising her voice at the barman and we all look at one another in silent understanding that I'd better go rescue Theo.

"Call me tomorrow," says Maya, pulling me in for another hug and squeezing extra tight this time. I tell her I will and congratulate them again as Darren ushers her out the door. I feel awful for the thoughts I had earlier. I hope that I at least gave the appropriate outward reaction to their good news, but I don't have time to dwell on that now.

• • •

It takes more than an hour to prize Jocelyn away from the bar, by which point the pub has all but emptied out; Eugenie is still there, along with her two brothers, and a couple of regulars who are settling into their usual seats in the corner. The barman caved when Jocelyn shouted at him and reluctantly poured her another drink. I ask him how many she's had today and he just shrugs and says, "A lot." Eugenie makes one final attempt to convince Jocelyn to go to bed, but Jocelyn sluggishly insists, "We're all having a nice time," and so, with the benefit of experience on her side, Eugenie hands me the key to Jocelyn's room and leaves. Magnus and Halbert, seemingly exasperated by Jocelyn's antics, quickly follow suit.

Theo never grows impatient with his mother—who by now is propping her own head up with one arm while continuing to spew gibberish at us—he just sits and waits and occasionally asks if she's ready to go yet. He keeps conversation to a minimum and responds to her questions in monosyllabic sentences. No matter what she says, or how hard she tries to get a rise out of him, he gives nothing in return, no hint of how it makes him feel. I recognize this behavior—the conversational equivalent of playing dead—I've used these tactics myself in the past and it saddens me now to see how proficient Theo is in them; it takes a lot of practice to learn how not to poke the bear. Watching Theo with his mother, I wonder if on some level I was drawn to him because his wounds look so similar to mine.

Finally Theo's efforts pay off, and, with no booze or banter to be got from us, Jocelyn gives up and lurches off her stool toward the door. We follow her as she staggers, one hand on the wall, all the way to the B&B. I run ahead and open the door to Jocelyn's room; then I wait for Theo to get her up the stairs.

He's practically carrying her by the time she gets to the top, and he has to drag her the remaining few feet into the room as she slips in and out of consciousness. He deposits her on the floor, then takes off his jacket and paces about the room for a while. Lying there, insensate in her fur coat with her chest rapidly rising and falling, Jocelyn looks like a dog on a hot day.

Theo finally stops pacing. He has refused my help until now, but with no other way to get his mother's body from the floor to the bed, he gives me a nod and together we lift her up. I remove what I can of her makeup with a damp facecloth and help get her under the duvet; then Theo says he's going to check her suitcase for pajamas, which I know means alcohol, so I pick up his coat and my bag and I go back to our room to wait.

I'm brushing my teeth when Theo's phone starts vibrating in his coat pocket. I take it out and see that it's Octavia calling. We've never spoken before.

"Hello?"

"Hi," she says. "Who's this?" She's picked up a bit of a Kiwi accent.

"Sorry. This is Theo's girlfriend. He's just with Jocelyn—I mean your mum—at the moment."

"Oh," says Octavia, "is she okay? I've been trying to call her."

"Yeah, she's fine," I say. "She's just—she can't come to the phone right now."

When Octavia sighs, she sounds exactly like Theo.

"Right," she says.

"The day went so well," I offer suddenly. "It rained. A lot. Absolutely chucked it down. But the service was lovely. The priest—or the vicar, sorry—he knew your gran from when she used to live here. So that was nice. Made it quite personal. And your aunt and uncles came. And all your cousins. And Theo was so great with your mum all day. He's just saying good night to her now, actually. I think she's just exhausted, to be honest. But I'll tell her you called."

There's a long pause, during which I can hear Octavia sniffling.

"Thank you," she says.

"That's okay."

"I'm sorry I wasn't there, I really am. I should have been there. But it's hard, you know?"

"I know," I say, not sure if she's talking about the funeral or the past ten years. Either way, I get it.

"Would you ask Theo to reply to my texts, please? I know he's upset. But I'd like to talk."

"I will," I say. "I promise."

"Okay. Thanks again. I'm glad you're there with him. You sound nice."

I smile and we say our good-byes.

A few minutes later Theo knocks at the door. When I open it he walks straight to the bin and drops a half-empty bottle of gin into it.

"You've done this before," I say, and he nods. He tries to pace up and down but this proves difficult in the tiny room, so he gives up and sits on the edge of the bed.

"Wanna talk about it?" I ask. He shakes his head. I sit down next to him, leaving a big gap between us, and I wait.

"I've been doing this my whole fucking life," says Theo finally, "as far back as I can remember. Whenever something bad happens . . ."

He gestures in the direction of Jocelyn's room.

"It used to last a few weeks at most," he continues, "but now it's all the time. She'd call them 'bad spells' and send me to go stay with Gran and Grandad for a while. Then it was just Gran after he died. That was shit. She wouldn't even let me kick a ball in the garden. But it was better than . . . that."

Theo gestures toward Jocelyn again, then drops his head into his hands. I stay quiet and wait for him to speak. This is called creative silence. My therapist used to do it to me. I hated it, but it works.

"I spoke to her doctor," says Theo, his voice muffled in his palms. "They're not supposed to talk about other patients but I already knew everything. I just wanted him to tell me how to help."

I nod and rub his back as he talks.

"He says she has a drinking problem, which, yeah, obviously, but apparently it's affecting her liver now. So he gave me a bunch of leaflets, about alcoholism and meetings and rehab and stuff, and he said I should try and talk to her, but she won't listen. She just tore them up and threw them in the fucking bin."

Theo sits upright and looks at me pointedly.

"What am I supposed to do?" he demands. "How the fuck am I supposed to fix this?"

"I know this is hard to accept," I say, "but it's not your job to fix her."

"That's what her bloody doctor said!" Theo blurts, sounding more and more like a child on the verge of a tantrum. "Of course I have to take care of her—she's my mother."

"You're her son. And she didn't take very good care of you today."

"Her mother just died," he snaps.

I take his hands in mine and look into his eyes.

"Your grandmother just died."

Theo stares back at me, his lower lip quivering. He takes a deep, shaky breath, then sighs it out.

"Why didn't you tell me all this?" I ask.

"You wouldn't understand."

This makes me laugh. Really, properly laugh. "Sorry," adds Theo, "I know your dad drank."

I roll my eyes.

"That's one way of putting it," I say.

"But at least you got *one* good parent! Your mother is practically perfect."

I laugh again.

"Theo, I love my mother, and I genuinely don't know what I'd do without her, but she is far from perfect. She's had some pretty 'bad spells' herself over the years. And whenever she did I always wound up feeling more like the parent than the child." Theo nods.

"How did you get over it?" he asks.

"Therapy," I reply quickly. "Lots and lots of therapy."

He smiles.

"But also," I go on, "I'm not really 'over it.' I don't think you ever get over it. You just learn to accept that people have their own fucked-up ways of coping with shit. And you decide whether you're willing to put up with it or not.

"Plus she's a lot better now. At least, she really tries to be better, which makes a big difference. And I just try to hold healthy boundaries, you know? Be there, but also observe it all from a safe distance.

"Like a nuclear explosion," I add with a smirk. Theo chuckles and I can feel the tension lift.

"Your sister called," I say. It takes Theo a second to realize I had his phone.

"What did she say?"

"That she's sorry for not being here." Theo nods but says nothing.

"Maybe you could talk to her about all this," I suggest. "She said she sent you some messages . . . ?"

"Yeah," he mumbles, "I'll get back to her soon."

I'm not sure if he will but I know that pushing the issue won't help.

"Do you think people can change?" he asks suddenly, looking up at me with wide, shiny eyes. The question is so pure, so earnest, that I'm almost afraid to give him an honest answer.

"Yes, I do," I begin, cautiously, "but I think you need to be both willing and able to change, and most people are only one or the other, or neither. A lot of the time people can't even see they have a problem. They get confused between what's right and what's familiar."

Theo says nothing for a minute or two. He just stares down at his hands.

"Why did you do it?" he asks finally, and I know we're not talking about our mothers anymore. We're talking about Paris.

"I was lonely," I say.

"I was only gone a month."

A sad, quick laugh escapes me.

"Not when you were gone, Theo. When you were gone and I was alone, it made sense. You're supposed to feel lonely when you're alone. But I felt lonely when we were together."

He stares at me for a moment, then announces that he's tired and wants to go to sleep. I resist the urge to poke or prod him further, and instead I pull the curtains. We undress and climb into bed in silence. As I lie next to him in the dark, Theo's unspoken words seem to dangle above me like knives.

"Were you lonely today?" he asks.

"No."

"Why?"

"Because," I say, turning over to face him even though I can't see him, "today we were a team. You let me help. You let me in."

"How is it usually?" he asks.

"I don't know," I say, trying to choose my words carefully. I want to be clear without upsetting him further.

"It's usually like you're right in front of me but I can't quite reach you. Like there's an invisible wall in the way."

"I like it when you explain things in easy-to-understand metaphors," he says, and I can hear the smile on his lips.

"I know," I say, smiling back in the dark. I hear Theo shuffling to face me. The sheets are scratchy and unfamiliar and I wish we were at home in our own bed.

"I went out with Darren the other night," he says. "My mum was doing my head in and I needed to get out of there. But then we got trashed and I felt like shit the next morning. It wasn't what I needed."

"What did you need?"

"You," he says. He sounds frustrated that I didn't know the answer already.

"You could've called me," I say.

"No, I couldn't. Not after sending you home from Paris alone. And ignoring you like that. How could I just call and dump all my problems on you?"

"I would have understood," I say. "I'm here, aren't I?"

"Yeah, I suppose."

I can feel his breath right in front of my face.

"I'm sorry," I blurt out, as hot tears trickle down my cheek onto the pillow, "I am so sorry for hurting you, Theo."

He pulls me into him and our limbs instantly weave around one another's like vines growing toward light.

"I just wanted you to see me," I cry into his chest. I can feel him processing this for a little while.

"I'm sorry you felt like you had to do that," he says, brushing the hair back from my face and resting his forehead against mine, "and maybe, if I'm being totally honest, I wasn't really looking for a while there . . . But I see you now." There's a pause before he adds, "Well, not now, obviously. It's quite dark in here."

I'm beginning to laugh through the tears when Theo's hand

finds my chin and lifts my face toward his to kiss me. His lips tenuously brush against the outer edges of my own, like he's making a mental map of my mouth, reacquainting himself with the terrain. He eases me onto my back and climbs gently between my legs and I feel as though he's discovering me all over again. We make love wordlessly, almost soundlessly, our other senses heightened in the dark, amplifying every movement and sensation. It feels like the first time, but better.

Afterward Theo lies with his head on my chest and one hand resting on my belly, which rises and falls with my breath.

"The doctor said I should maybe talk to someone about all this stuff," says Theo. "As in, like, a therapist."

"It couldn't hurt," I say. I've felt for some time that Theo should try therapy—truth be told, I think everyone should try therapy—but I knew he'd have to reach that conclusion on his own.

"I have to go back to Paris for another month or so, but I'll look into it when I get home."

He's coming home, I think, and something in me releases, like a fist unclenching.

"I'd like to see someone again too," I say. "I feel like the depression might be creeping back in." This is a massive understatement, but I don't want to mention my deep bouts of existential dread right now.

"All right, angel," says Theo, as his fingers idly draw circles around my belly button.

"I want to be better," he adds. "I will be better. Because I want you. And I want to make you happy."

"How about we make one another happy?"

"Deal," he murmurs into my chest.

"Also, I'm thinking about quitting my job. To write full-time."

"Wow. Okay," says Theo. "Well, you know how much I love your writing. So if this is what you want to do, I'm here for you, all the way."

A few minutes of silence pass. The next time Theo speaks, his voice startles me.

"Thank you for saving my life today," he says, and for a moment I've no idea what he's talking about. Then, like a long-forgotten dream, it comes back to me in fragments; the rain on the windscreen, the loud popping sound, my knuckles on the steering wheel, that man's ponytail flapping about in the wind. It doesn't feel like it happened at all, let alone a few hours ago.

"I'm glad we didn't die," says Theo through a yawn.

"Me too," I say, and I'm smiling as I drift off.

We stay this way all night, two bodies intertwined in the dark.

la petite mort

I SAW THE *Mona Lisa* yesterday. I stood in front of her and wept.

For most of the day before that, I'd felt detached, as though I were floating just behind and to the left of myself, observing life rather than living it. And so, in an attempt to either outrun or catch up with my own mind, I had traipsed for hours through the Louvre, aimlessly traversing its labyrinthine interior until I stumbled accidentally across this painting and was suddenly and inexplicably reduced to tears.

I've seen the *Mona Lisa* before, of course, but only facsimiles of her, and none of them had made me feel like this; here, even behind a wooden barrier and inches of bulletproof glass, she felt more like a person than a painting. It was like running into an old friend in a strange city.

Occupying the entire wall opposite her, *The Wedding Feast at Cana*, a monumental work by any standard, seemed somehow small in her presence; a busy, colorful scene depicting Jesus's first miracle unable to compete with the unassuming young woman across the way. People lingered there with Christ just long enough to be polite before shuffling away from him toward her. They spoke with the kind of hushed reverence reserved only for libraries and church, and all around me couples took turns taking photos with her. A scrawny man in a blue parka offered to take one of me but I declined.

My thoughts are interrupted by the sound of seat belts clanging open and a chorus of passengers all clamoring to retrieve their luggage from the overhead compartments. An air hostess loudly announces our arrival at Heathrow, and as I step off the plane she smiles broadly, wishing me a safe and pleasant onward journey.

On the flight back from Paris I was happily trapped in a state of limbo, unaccountable, uncontactable. For ninety blissful minutes I ceased to exist, but now, trudging through Heathrow airport, with a full signal and no missed calls from Theo, reality sets in like milk slowly souring in my stomach. I consider texting him, just to let him know that I've landed, but when I see my last drunken messages to him, I cringe and put the phone away.

I drag my suitcase onto a train with all the enthusiasm of a naughty child being marched to the principal's office, and once again I am without a signal for a while. As soon as the train surfaces overground, I check my phone. Still nothing from Theo. I've been doing this since I left the hotel and it's beginning to feel a bit masochistic.

A few stops later the urge to call him overwhelms me and I

just about manage to call Maya instead. This is our version of the AA sponsor system, except we don't call one another when we're tempted to drink; we call one another when we're tempted to make a desperate phone call or send an angry text to someone.

"Hey!" shouts Maya into the phone. I can tell she's got it wedged between her shoulder and her face.

"Hey. Is this a bad time?"

"No, no. Just putting out a small kitchen fire," says Maya.

"Oh. Are you okay?"

"I'm great!" she yelps.

"What's wrong?"

"Just fucking Darren." Her voice is strained, like she's lifting something heavy. I hear the rush of water, followed by an explosive sizzle. Then silence.

"Where are you?" asks Maya.

"On the Piccadilly line."

"I thought you were coming home next week," she says.

"So did I."

I can tell I have her full attention now.

"What's happened?"

"I fucked up," I say, fighting the urge to cry. "I really fucking properly fucked up."

"Okay, well"—and I hear her inhale deeply before plowing through this next part—"I've just made a cottage pie, from scratch, for Darren, because his mum used to make him cottage pie, but she's dead now, so she can't do that anymore, and apparently the mantle falls to me because I was bequeathed the bloody recipe, but he forgot we had plans and pissed off down the pub instead, so would you like to come over and tell me exactly how you fucked up and also eat some of Darren's dead mother's cottage pie?"

"Yes," I say, as tears break free and stream down my cheeks, "I really would."

A man sitting across from me averts his eyes, like me crying is somehow offensive to him. I throw a pointless scowl in his direction.

"All right, pull yourself together," says Maya. "I'll see you soon."

By the time I get to Maya's apartment, order has been restored to her kitchen. The whole place is immaculate, in fact. I try to neatly stack my handbag, suitcase, and coat in a little pile by the door, but Maya scoops them up and whisks them off to another room without saying a word.

"It smells great," I call after her.

"I know!" says Maya, reentering the room. She stands with her hands on her hips and a look of utter exasperation on her face. We stare at one another for a while, both nodding sympathetically; then we both take a deep breath and sigh it out in unison.

"Wine?" she asks.

"Obviously."

Maya and I talk the whole way through dinner, but she knows better than to mention Theo until I'm properly fed and watered. Instead she tells me about the new bakery on the corner, a subpar salad she had for lunch yesterday, her mother's upcoming knee surgery, and the dilemma over whether to paint the living room coffee, oatmeal, or biscuit. I also get the full story about Darren, which she tells me in one long, frazzled sentence. I struggle to keep up at times, but the short version is that Darren accidentally double-booked himself tonight and he didn't want to let his friend down, so he called Maya to cancel on her, thinking she'd understand.

"I was mid-pie at this point," she says, "and I got pretty upset, and he said he'd have some when he got home later, and I told him that wasn't the point, and he asked me not to make him choose between me and his friends, and I told him not to be so fucking dramatic, and he said I was the one crying over a pie, and I hung up on him."

"Wow," I say.

"I called him back, of course. To apologize for hanging up on him."

Without realizing, I've started crying again.

"Oh my God, what's wrong?" asks Maya.

"It's just. You had plans. He forgot. You made a pie. He didn't appreciate it. So neat. So simple."

I'm speaking through sobs, like an upset child.

"He'll come home," I continue, "and you'll make up. And it'll be lovely. Everything will be lovely again. Because you two are lovely together. You're just. Fundamentally. Fucking. Lovely."

"Say 'lovely' again," says Maya, and I laugh through my tears.

"Are you all right?" she asks, frowning at me.

"No."

"Okay," she says, "what the hell happened in Paris?"

I arrived at Theo's hotel on Wednesday afternoon. I was a little earlier than expected, but rather than call him and ruin the surprise, I decided to wait in the lobby until he got back from work. I didn't mind—there were comfy armchairs and I'd brought a good book with me, so I settled in. I got chatting to the waiter—a lanky Spanish teenager named Donato, who fidgeted constantly and insisted I call him Donny. He told me he was working here part-time while he studied hospitality management. I told him I'd just flown in from London to surprise my boyfriend, whom I hadn't seen in more than a month, and upon hearing this, Donny clasped his hands together and practically cooed at me. Then he took it upon himself to refill my tea all afternoon. He even stopped by from time to time with a tray of tiny complimentary cakes.

Two pots of tea and maybe six tiny cakes later, I was beginning to worry that Theo was out for the evening; then I finally saw him walk through the hotel's huge revolving doors. I giddily gathered up my things, and as I made my way to where he stood by the lifts, I noticed there was a woman with him. She was wearing a crisp white blouse and gray pencil skirt with a pair of black stiletto heels. They looked positively torturous.

It was too late to turn back, so I tapped Theo on the shoulder and in my most obnoxious French accent said, "*Excusez-moi, où est la bibliothèque?*"

The lady regarded me with a half smile and a cocked eyebrow. Theo turned toward me and I smiled cheekily, but instead of smiling back he just stood there, gawping at me like a dead trout.

"So . . . you don't know where the library is," I said, and the lady laughed. Theo appeared to be rebooting.

"Oh, for heaven's sake, Theodore," she said, only she

pronounced his name with a soft, French *r*, which made it sound far more sexy than I ever could.

"Sorry, Sophie," he said, snapping out of it as he turned to me. "What are you doing here?"

"Surprising you," I said.

"More like shocking the hell out of him," said Sophie with a smirk. At this moment I remembered Theo telling me about the brilliant Frenchwoman in charge of the new Paris office and I realized this must be her. I extended a hand and introduced myself, saying I'd heard a lot about her.

"All good things, I hope," said Sophie, shaking my hand firmly.

"No," I said, "really horrific things, actually. Couldn't possibly repeat them."

Sophie cackled. Theo looked like he might actually pass out. "I like this one," she said to Theo. "You should keep her."

"Yeah," he said, laughing awkwardly.

Just then, the lift doors opened with a ping.

"So lovely to meet you," said Sophie, sashaying into the lift. "Now, if you'll excuse me, I have a hot date with a bubble bath."

We said good-bye and as the doors slid closed she called out to Theo, "Get that poor girl a drink!"

I notice Maya is staring at me, her face fixed in a grimace.

"What?" I ask.

"Is he having an affair with Sophie?"

"She's his boss," I say.

"So?"

"She's, like, fifty."

Maya takes a sip of wine and throws her eyes sideways.

"They're not having an affair, Maya."

"Fine," she says. "Then what the fuck was his problem?"

I shake my head. "I don't know. Whenever I called he kept saying he missed me and he couldn't wait to see me," I say, like I'm retracing my steps after losing something. "He was the one who suggested I come visit sometime, so I don't get it."

Maya mulls this over for a moment.

"One Christmas," she says finally, "my brother got a brand-new BMX bike. He'd been banging on about that bike all year. All. Bloody. Year. And then when he got it he was so overwhelmed by emotion that he just short-circuited. He was catatonic for about fifteen minutes, actually; it was really weird. Anyway, this reminds me of that."

"Am I the bike in this analogy?" I ask.

"Yes," she says.

"Right."

"So what happened next?"

Theo and I went to the bar for a drink, and although it seemed less like he wanted to have a drink with me and more like he was obeying Sophie's command, I was glad to finally be alone with him. When Donny came by to take our drinks order, I introduced him to Theo and we shared a joke about all the cake I'd had that afternoon. As he walked away, Theo turned to me and said, "How do you do that?"

"Do what?" I asked.

"Make friends with complete strangers," he said, with a sort of incredulity.

"Is that a bad thing?"

"Just an observation," said Theo, shrugging it off and changing the subject to work.

He came alive when he talked about work, telling me all about the plush new Paris office with a view of the Eiffel Tower, and the keen young team of recruits he'd been brought here to train. It was refreshing to see Theo this passionate about something, especially when he'd been so apathetic lately. It reminded me of times, early on in our relationship, when he would gush about the plans he had for us—the places we'd go, the house we'd settle down in, the names we'd give our children. The memory brought with it a remnant of hope, like a bittersweet aftertaste in the back of my mouth.

"I've learned so much teaching them," Theo went on, "and I've got ideas for a whole new training program. Sophie wants me to meet with the other execs here next week."

I was immensely proud of him, and I wanted to see him succeed here, but the subtext was clear; he wasn't coming home anytime soon.

"That's wonderful news," I said, clinking my glass with his. "Congratulations!"

"Thank you!" He beamed.

"How much longer do you think you'll be here, then?"

"Another month or two. Maybe more. That's okay, right?" I didn't know if that was okay. It certainly didn't feel okay. Was it because he was staying here? Or because it felt like he'd made that decision without me? Suddenly my rib cage seemed to squeeze inward and my heart began pounding back in protest.

"Work is work," I said, ignoring my inability to breathe, "and you seem happy here."

"I am," said Theo, as Donny arrived with our drinks.

I was fishing for reassurance and I wasn't getting any. I had wanted Theo to tell me that he missed me too, or that he was just as happy at home as he was in Paris. I couldn't tell if he wasn't saying those things out of forgetfulness or because he didn't want to be dishonest.

Why was I finding this so hard? I wondered. We had lived long-distance before—he in London and I in Dublin—and we'd made it work. But back then we talked for hours every night and Theo would text me all the time just to tell me he was thinking about me. Lately I was lucky to get a reply or have more than a five-minute conversation with him. Even when we did talk, it wasn't us talking; it was me nattering on while he grunted the odd response. I could handle the physical distance as long as we were emotionally close and vice versa, but not both at the same time.

The result was that I craved him—his time, his attention, his touch—I was physically craving connection with him, and I thought coming here would fix that. But sitting in front of him in that bar, I felt farther from him than ever before. I wanted to tell him all this, but I know from experience that Theo is like a dog on a lead: the tighter I pull on it, the harder he pulls in the opposite direction. So I stayed quiet and sipped my drink.

"How long are you here for?" he asked.

"Five nights," I said. "I fly back Monday."

"Oh."

"Oh?"

"It's just—I'm really busy this week," he said.

"Well, I don't need a chaperone," I said. "I'm happy to explore Paris by myself. And in the evenings we can go out or stay in or whatever you fancy, really."

I was trying to sound casual, but in doing so I came off even needier.

"That's the thing," he said. "I'm kind of busy in the evenings too."

"Right," I said, trying not to visibly deflate. It was getting harder to act normal. I felt like my head was on fire and everyone was pretending not to notice, me included. Theo took out his phone to check his schedule.

"I'm free Saturday," he offered. "We can do whatever you want."

"Zoo?"

I hadn't planned to say that; it just came out. Theo's eyes widened and he let out a little laugh.

"Really?"

We had visited a zoo in almost every country we'd been to together, and bought the most hideous toy animal we could find in every gift shop. It had become a sort of unspoken tradition, and the "Gang of Freaks," as we lovingly called them, currently resided on a shelf in our living room. I could tell I was just trying to re-create nice memories, but I didn't see any harm in that.

"Yeah," I said, "that's what I want to do."

"Zoo it is," said Theo, smiling.

His hotel room was not at all what I expected; every time we'd spoken on the phone, I'd imagined him cooped up in a dark, cramped room with little more than a bed and a bathroom, but looking at it now, I couldn't believe I'd conjured up such an inaccurate mental image. The room was pristine—presumably someone had cleaned it while he was at work—and everything about the place, from the bedding to the curtains to the bowl of perfectly ripened fruit (which I had to touch to confirm it wasn't plastic), exuded a sort of business-class opulence. There was even a little chocolate, wrapped in gold foil and placed exactly in the center of one pillow.

"I'll have them bring up two tomorrow," said Theo, breaking it in half so that we could share it.

Theo's clothes were all hung neatly in the wardrobe, his toiletries lined up by the sink—I noticed he'd bought a new brand of moisturizer—and the large oak desk was covered in paperwork and Post-its, all arranged at perfect right angles, just like they were on his desk at home. While he took a shower I unpacked my things, careful not to take up too much space, and afterward, we lay on the bed and watched a movie. Theo fell asleep ten minutes in, so I turned it off and read my book instead.

When my eyes grew heavy, I got undressed and slipped under the covers. I had worn Theo's favorite lingerie that day—I remember smiling to myself on the plane at the thought of him discovering the lace bodice underneath my dress—and I felt a little pang of foolishness as I slid the black lace down my legs, folded it, and put it back in my suitcase.

"Ouch," says Maya, wincing as she tops up my wine.

"Yeah."

"We've all been there, though," she offers.

"I know. And he wasn't exactly expecting a wild night of sex. I just thought after a month apart . . ." I trail off, sulking into my chardonnay. "I don't know what I thought."

"You thought you'd get fucked," Maya offered.

"I did."

"Well, I'd have fucked you," she says, and I laugh.

"Thanks, babe."

"Did you do it the next night?" she asks.

"Yeah, but it was weird."

"Weird how?"

"He kept leaning to the left," I say.

Maya squints at me in confusion and tries to stifle a smile.

"What?" she asks.

"I wish I hadn't brought this up now."

"No, no." She giggles. "Explain, please."

"Well, when he was on top," I say, "he kept . . . leaning, so that all his weight was on my right leg. And I had to keep, sort of, hooshing him back to center."

"So what did you do?"

"I got on top, obviously."

"Obviously," says Maya, as she goes to the fridge to get another bottle of wine. "I mean, if you can't muster the energy to at least stay upright during sex, don't bloody bother, mate."

"Exactly," I say, holding out my glass for a refill. "I was tired too. I'd walked the length and breadth of bloody Paris all day!"

Theo had woken me up around seven a.m. to say good-bye, and after he left for work I decided I might as well get up and make the most of the day. I grabbed a fold-up map from reception and took it to breakfast with me—I could have used the map on my phone, but I liked the massive, cartoonish depictions of each landmark.

I scoffed down a plate of scrambled eggs and some orange juice while I studied the map, running my finger along the route I planned to take, and then I stuffed my pockets full of fruit and headed out.

It was a cool, clear day—perfect walking weather—and I managed to get to every spot on my list, including the Eiffel Tower, where I was approached every twenty seconds by loud men, all hawking touristy trinkets and tat.

I was here on a school trip more than a decade ago, but I could barely remember it. I'd been too preoccupied with Christopher, a boy from another school, whom I would later go on to have a brief fling with, despite the fact that he had a girlfriend and—as it turned out—was gay. Last I heard he was married to a hairy Welshman and they'd adopted two cats.

I do remember enjoying the trip to the top of the tower, but in hindsight that was probably because we were crammed together like clowns in a car and Christopher was pressed rather firmly up against me the entire time. Imagine being so exhilarated by someone that a view of Paris seems pale in comparison.

Suddenly I felt light-headed. Not in an unpleasant way; it was like I had downed a glass or two of champagne and my senses were just slightly dulled. I leaned against the base of the tower and stayed a while, mesmerized by the sheer size of the four metal feet planted firmly around me. They reminded me of the kind of hefty roots you'd find on an old, gnarled tree.

Lately I had felt untethered, like the slightest breeze might knock me over, and sometimes I would ground myself by imagining a huge tree, reaching fearlessly skyward while it's stalwart roots rose in mounds, then plunged back into the earth again. I thought of that tree now and my breathing slowed.

Soon enough, I grew tired of declining to buy shoddy metal replicas of the tower I was standing under, so even though my head still hadn't quite cleared, I set off through the Champ de Mars gardens toward the École Militaire. The buildings weren't open to the public, but I rambled around the outside, marveling at the fact that inside this exquisite facade was a military training facility; it looked like the kind of place where people should learn to paint or do ballet. Then I moved on to Les Invalides, where rows of enormous cannons stood guard like bright-green beasts. The plaque on one of the cannons reads "The Scourge," and my stomach turned slightly at the grisly sounding name. It was the first uncomplicated emotion I had felt all day, and driven by some morbid desire to feel more, I continued on into the Musée de l'Ordre de la Libération. At least, I thought, I knew how I was supposed to feel in a World War II museum, and I didn't have to analyze those feelings or feel guilty for feeling them.

I had been inside for more than two hours when I came across a series of drawings made in concentration camps. I pressed my hand against the cool glass and stared into the brightly lit display, transfixed by the sheer scale of tragedy. Sympathy and sadness swelled inside me until my vision folded inward and the edges of my sight grew dark. The room began to lurch around me, so I peeled my clammy hand from the glass case and rushed toward the exit, suddenly disgusted with myself and my motives for being there.

As I lay on the grass outside, numbness enveloped me like a shroud, and I listened to the muted sounds of traffic and chatter while I gulped down fresh afternoon air and stared vacantly up at the sky.

Sometime later, though I'm not sure how long, my phone rang and for a few seconds I couldn't comprehend the sound. Eventually, I picked it up and saw an unfamiliar Irish number on the screen.

"Hello?"

"My darling girl," boomed a woman's voice from the other end, and I recognized it immediately as that of my ex-boss, Ciara.

"How in God's name are you?" she demanded, not letting me answer. "It's been too long. Don't tell me how long! How are you? What are you up to?"

"I'm okay, thanks," I said. "Just having an existential meltdown. You know yourself."

"Oh dear. What are you doing that for?"

"Well, I'm in Paris," I said, "and I've just been walking around a World War II museum."

"Christ no, absolutely not," said Ciara. "Writers are far too sensitive altogether for that sort of thing. You're to leave that place immediately and go get a big, buttery pastry and some hot chocolate."

"It's actually quite warm here . . ."

"Just do as you're told, will you?"

"All right," I said, genuinely glad to have my problems boiled down so casually by an oblivious third party. They seemed instantly silly and unimportant.

"Now, I've got another call at half past so I'll cut to the chase," said Ciara, as though this wasn't the first time we had spoken in years.

"I want you to write for me again," she said. "I'm moving to London to set up a new fashion and lifestyle magazine and I think you'd be a great fit."

"But I'm not fashionable," I said.

"No, I know that, darling. But you've got all that mental . . . stuff . . . going on."

"My anxiety?"

"Yes," she said, "and the depression. And that's all very in right now."

"I see."

"So I need a high-functioning head case like yourself to write a column on mental health."

"And you want me?"

I was too confused to be insulted.

"Well, I won't lie, you weren't my first choice, darling, but my first choice is too busy writing a bloody book."

"So I was your second choice," I said.

"No. She has apparently fucked off to a monastery in Southeast Asia to 'find herself.' Which probably means she's in rehab."

"Right."

"Look, I'm offering you a job here; just be grateful for the opportunity."

I'd forgotten that every conversation with Ciara plays out in quick-fire mode. She's got the energy of a guinea pig on speed.

"I am grateful!" I insisted. "I'm just trying to figure out how I got on the list at all."

"Because most people are inept. Or cunts. Or both," said Ciara. "And you're neither."

"That might be the nicest thing anyone's ever said to me."

"Also," she continued, "I ran into Omar in the Shelbourne last month and he was singing your praises."

Omar is my writing teacher. He has never given me any indication that he likes either me or my work.

"How do you even know one another?" I asked.

"The literary world is deeply incestuous, darling; you really must be vigilant. Anyway, he sent me some of your latest stories. Hope you don't mind. But I liked them a lot. You've really found your voice."

Coming from anyone else I would find this pretentious and patronizing, but in that moment I was deeply flattered; Ciara's opinion always meant a lot to me, even when she had me writing fictitious travel reviews.

"So what do you need me to do?" I asked.

As it happened, she needed me to do quite a lot, and fast, and it wouldn't pay particularly well at first. As much as I wanted to say yes, I was worried about juggling this and my existing full-time job.

"You'll manage," said Ciara, "and if you can't manage, you can quit your job. Be a struggling writer! Create a bit of fucking impetus, darling! What are you doing these days anyway?"

"Writing press releases."

"Ugh. Horrid."

"I know." I sighed. "I swear to God if I have to write about the launch of one more miracle cellulite cream or antiaging, snail-slime face mask, my brain will liquefy and dribble out my fucking ears."

"Well, I'd suggest you get out of there. Fast. I've lost too many good people to shit jobs."

She always had a way of talking about her employees as though they were troops.

"You're right," I said.

"I always am. Now, go get that hot chocolate and look at some beautiful things."

"I will, thanks. Bye for now, Ciara."

But conversations with Irish people never end the first time you say good-bye.

"Speaking of beautiful things," she said, "Tim's living in Paris now."

"Tim who?"

"Tim!" she wailed. "Lovely Tim! Used to work at *Taisteal*. Nice lad. Built like a fucking tank. I'm sending you his number now. Give him a shout."

Bloody hell. I hadn't thought about Tim in years. He was a graphic designer at the magazine and the entire editorial staff used to call him Lovely Tim, simply because he was so lovely.

"I have a boyfriend, Ciara."

"What's that got to do with the price of cabbage?"

"Fine," I said, "I'll call him."

I had no intention of calling him.

"Great! Gotta go."

And with that Ciara was gone and I was left sitting on a lawn outside a war museum in Paris, with the phone number of a very attractive ex-colleague and a new job I definitely didn't have time to do.

"Oh my God," says Maya, aghast. "Did you sleep with Lovely Tim?"

I stare back at her nonplussed.

"That's a yes," she says.

"That is not a yes," I say. "I am trying to tell you the story."

"Well, you're not telling it fast enough!" she shouts in mock anger, and then her face lights up like she's suddenly remembered something wonderful.

"Cake?" she asks.

"Sure."

Maya pulls an entire homemade Victoria sponge out of the fridge and plonks it down in the center of the table. Then she grabs two forks and hands one to me.

"Did you tell Theo about your episode at the museum?" she asks.

"I tried. But he seemed a bit preoccupied that night. And explaining it only made me feel more crazy." Maya nods as we dig into the cake.

"What about the job offer? Did you tell him about that?"

I shake my head.

"I wanted some time to think about it."

"So you went to bed and had shit sex and called Tim the next day," says Maya casually.

"You should really consider a career in literature."

"I may not be a good storyteller," she says, "but I'm not wrong, am I?"

"No," I say, "unfortunately, you're not."

I woke up to a mammoth email from Ciara and spent the morning hunched over my laptop in a smoke-filled café trying to put together proposals for several different articles; she was meeting with her investors the next day and needed pitches from every department. I was now, I discovered, a department.

By two o'clock I had had enough, and I emerged from the café, blinking into the bright afternoon. Theo and I had plans to meet for dinner, but that was hours away and I wasn't really sure what to do with myself until then. I took out my giant map, but the prospect of exploring Paris alone had somewhat lost its charm and, faced with so many options, none of which particularly appealed to me, I began to shut down completely.

Once again I felt a dull numbness settle in, like I was cocooned inside a thin rubber membrane that kept me separate from the world around me. People appeared flimsy and incomplete, as though an important feature were missing from their faces, but I couldn't figure out which one. Buildings, too, seemed unfinished. As did the trees and the cars. They all looked like crude pencil sketches of what they should be.

I'd had panic attacks before—usually they were sharp and severe, and everything felt too bright, too loud, too harsh—but this was different: things weren't "too" anything; they were shapeless and distant and dark. I started walking, trying to put some distance between me and this sensation, and without meaning to, I gravitated toward the Seine. I wandered awhile along one bank, soothed by the sound of water gently lapping near my feet. It reminded me of Dollymount Strand—sitting by the sea on cloudy days eating sandy ham sandwiches—and the thought made me smile. Finally I reached a ticket booth for one of those open-top river cruises, and on a whim I bought one and got on.

It was good to be moving, to be speeding forward with what felt like purpose. My mood instantly lightened—I even laughed to myself at the irony of being asked to write about mental illness just as I was beginning to grapple with a whole new set of symptoms. I was returning to my body. To the present moment.

The boat whizzed past huge metal monuments and under ornate bridges, and all the while I stood at the front, savoring the breeze and the subtle spray of water on my face. I noticed the feel of the cold metal handrail in my hands, the way the wind plastered my blouse against my body, and the shift of weight from one foot to the other as the boat lurched in and out of every stop. When an automated voice announced, in both French and English, that we would soon be stopping at the Louvre, I remembered what Ciara had said about looking at beautiful things and decided to do just that.

Hours later, having spent an interminable amount of time transfixed by the *Mona Lisa*, I stepped back outside to see dusk was descending. I checked the time, and realizing I was late for dinner, I rushed back to the hotel to get ready as fast as I could. I had just squeezed into a short red dress and was stepping into a pair of heels when Theo called.

"Hey, honey," I said excitedly before he had a chance to speak, "I think I might be ten minutes late. I spent way too long in the Louvre. But I can't wait to see you and tell you all about it and eat *très* tasty French food! What's the name of the place again?"

"I'm so sorry, but I don't think I can make it to dinner."

I sat down on the bed with one shoe on.

"Oh."

"I have to work late. I wish I didn't."

"It's okay," I said, trying and failing to mask my disappointment. I reminded myself that this was what I had signed up for when I flew to Paris unannounced.

"Do you want to go without me or shall I cancel the reservation?" he asked. The thought of eating alone in a romantic restaurant was almost too much to bear.

"Cancel it, please."

"I really am so sorry, angel," he said, and I could tell he was.

"We'll have a nice day out tomorrow, I promise."

"Okay," I said. "See you later?"

"Yeah, I won't be too late."

I felt like I was struggling to swim, flailing about and surfacing just long enough to catch my breath before being pulled back under by my ankles.

After we hung up I lay staring at the ceiling for a while. I thought about cleaning my makeup off and climbing into bed, but the prospect was pretty depressing. Ten minutes later I found Tim's number and dialed it.

I doubted he'd remember me, or that he'd be free at such short notice, or that he'd want to see me if he was. In fact, I thought, I should just hang up now. But it was too late. The phone was ringing. He answered.

"Now, there's a blast from the past!" Tim bellowed when I told him who it was.

"I know," I said. "It's been a while, all right."

"How'd you get my new number?"

"Ciara gave it to me when she heard I was in Paris," I said sheepishly. "Hope that's okay?"

"Absolutely!" Tim laughed. "It's nice to hear an Irish accent, to be honest."

"I know the feeling."

"Of course, yeah, you're living in London now, aren't ya?" he asked.

"I am indeed. Few years now."

"So what brings you to Paris?"

"Just visiting my boyfriend," I said, glad to have got my relationship status out of the way. "He's working over here for a bit."

"Ah, right," said Tim. "Well, do you fancy a pint some night?"

Lovely as ever, I thought.

"Actually, I was sort of wondering if you're free tonight. He has to work late and I've found myself literally all dolled up with nowhere to go."

I winced as soon as the words left my mouth. I felt like I had just thrown a ball in the air and was hoping it didn't hit me in the face on the way back down. The silence on the other end of the line didn't help.

"Sorry, the signal's rubbish," came Tim's voice after an excruciatingly long pause. "Did you say you were free tonight?"

"I did, yeah."

"Perfect!" he said. "I'm just about to head out with a few mates if you want to join us?"

I exhaled for the first time since he'd answered the phone.

"That sounds great!"

"Great!"

Great.

I followed Tim's directions and found myself outside a dingy-looking bar down a back alley in the Latin Quarter. I can't remember the name of the place now—I think it had something to do with cows. Inside, Tim and his friends were huddled around a small table in one corner, and a string trio were setting up across the room. The place was all dark woods and purple walls and strings of multicolored lights.

Tim stood up when he saw me and hugged me tightly.

"It's so good to see you," he gushed. I felt a bit guilty that I'd forgotten about him until that call with Ciara.

He introduced me to his friends, Rob, Manon, and Claudine, who, together with Tim, were maybe the most gorgeous collection of humans I had ever seen. Rob had bushy black hair and a beard to match; Manon was short but striking, with beautiful brown eyes and bright-red lips; and Claudine was a tall, full-figured blonde who glided, swanlike, around the table to greet me. They each gave me a double kiss, then resumed their fast-paced

French chatter. I stared on helplessly until Tim realized I had no idea what they were saying.

Rob and Manon were fluent in English and could easily switch between the two languages, but Claudine didn't speak a word of it and so things needed to be translated back and forth. Sometimes Tim acted as a go-between, leaning in to explain things in my ear, or leaning the other way to tell Claudine something in French—albeit with a thick Dublin accent, which I found rather sweet.

There were two half-full bottles of wine on the table and Tim was quick to pour me a glass.

"Are you enjoying Paris so far?" he asked.

"I think so," I said, and he looked at me quizzically.

I found myself telling Tim that I'd come to Paris to surprise Theo but it hadn't quite gone to plan. He nodded sympathetically as I spoke, then told me he was moving to Berlin next year to be with his girlfriend; they only saw one another every few weeks, he said, and it wasn't enough. I couldn't believe how effortlessly we had slipped into such honest, open conversation about our relationships. It was nice to talk to someone else who knew how difficult long distance could be.

After that, we somehow got talking about the World War II museum, and I struggled to describe the enormity of emotions I'd felt there, or the cloud that lingered over me afterward on the lawn. My hands opened and clenched in front of me as I searched for the right words to make him understand, but just as I was about to give up, I noticed Tim gazing thoughtfully at me, his eyebrows collected in a scowl.

"I've been there three times," he said, "and I still can't figure out what keeps bringing me back."

How had I worked with this man for more than a year and never really noticed him before?

"I saw the *Mona Lisa* today," I announced, excited to tell Tim about the unexpectedly emotional experience I'd had. He was about to respond when Claudine muttered something under her breath. I asked Tim what she'd said.

"She says you didn't," said Tim.

"Didn't what?"

"You didn't see the *Mona Lisa*," he said.

"What?"

I looked at Claudine in complete confusion and she casually began to rattle off information in French, which Tim translated for me.

"Apparently," said Tim, half listening to her and half talking to me, "the real *Mona Lisa* is too precious to be put on show. So the one they display is a fake."

"But all that security . . ." I said.

"*Une illusion*," said Claudine, with a nonchalant wave of her hand. I was still processing all this when Rob chimed in.

"A Russian woman threw a mug at her once," he said.

"At who?" I asked, thinking for a moment he meant Claudine.

"The *Mona Lisa*."

"A Russian woman threw a mug at the *Mona Lisa*?"

Rob just nodded at me.

"What happened?" asked Manon.

"It smashed on the glass," said Rob matter-of-factly, and Manon rolled her eyes.

"*Oui, bien sûr, mais pourquoi?*" asked Manon. "Why would she do this?"

Rob shrugged and sipped his drink. This was apparently all he had to offer.

"It's called Stendhal syndrome," said Tim, and everyone turned to look at him.

"Bullshit," said Manon. "You have just made this up."

"It's true," he said. "Some people can't handle the experience— it's like overdosing on positive emotions or something—they get dizzy or hallucinate or go totally bonkers and attack the art."

Manon wrinkled her forehead in disbelief, then went to the bar for more wine, while Tim repeated what he'd just said in French for Claudine. She laughed dryly—presumably at the thought of all those nutters chucking mugs at fine art.

Drink and conversation flowed all night, and I just about managed to keep up with both. After my fourth or fifth glass of wine I realized I hadn't eaten since lunch; there was talk of going somewhere for food, but then the band struck up and we remained, entranced by the magnificent sounds they produced as their fingers and bows slid deftly across their instruments. I had never heard jazz played live before, but here it was, at once melodic and discordant and chaotic and harmonious. The music seemed to seep through me, oozing into every pore, filling me to the brim until I felt like I might overflow. Claudine caught sight of me, my face transfixed in a silly smile, and she leaned across Tim toward me.

"*C'est sublime, non?*" she said. I didn't need a translator for that. I just nodded, still smiling, my eyes never straying from the band. Tim placed a hand on my shoulder and squeezed it gently as though to say, "It's okay, we've all been there." I felt completely at ease, and without thinking I rested my head on his hand.

By the intermission the place was heaving with people and I had to elbow my way through the crowd to get to the bar. When I stood up, the wine hit me and I heard Theo's voice in my head reminding me to rehydrate. I downed a pint of water and brought more back to the table in a jug, but the damage was already done; I was drunk. The rest of the evening is patchy, but I remember the band refusing to play an encore, and an unassuming woman in a floral dress taking to the mic for a roof-raising a cappella rendition of "La Mer."

At some point there was a lengthy conversation at our table about death, the only part of which I can recall is Rob's assertion that we are all reincarnated as the animal we most detest.

"That's why there are so many wasps," he said, deadpan, and we all laughed. I'll never know if he was joking or not.

Eventually we all got up to dance, throwing ourselves about to a barrage of nineties pop classics being piped through the bar's shitty speakers. I wore myself out and then breathlessly stumbled back to the table to find Claudine sitting on Tim's lap, totally engrossed in whatever he was saying. I felt as though I was intruding on some intimate moment and was about to leave when Claudine caught my hand and pulled me into Tim's lap with her.

We each sat on a leg, facing one another, and I was incredibly aware of my ass on Tim's thigh.

"You're very beautiful," said Claudine.

"Oh. Thank you," I said.

Tim said something to Claudine in French and she pouted.

"I just told her you have a boyfriend," explained Tim, and I nodded even though I didn't fully understand; was she trying to set me up with him?

"She says she'd like to meet him," said Tim.

"My boyfriend?"

Claudine nodded.

"Okay," I said, and I took out my phone to text Theo. I think my plan was to ask him to meet us at the bar, but I never got that far because Claudine grabbed the phone out of my hand, opened the camera, and held it up to take a photo. Tim leaned back, not wanting to be part of it, but I don't think she meant to include him anyway; Claudine pressed her cheek against mine and took a selfie of us, me smiling broadly and her smoldering down the lens. Then she hit send and I watched the photo pop up in a message to Theo.

Within seconds, Theo replied: "You made a friend!"

I looked at Claudine then, unsure what to say back to him, and she kissed me. Quickly and softly and completely unexpectedly, she kissed me on the lips, then pulled back and looked at me mischievously. For the second time that night I didn't need a translator to know what she was trying to tell me.

Tim stared at us, mouth agape; then, like a man who just accidentally wandered into the lingerie department, he politely made his excuses and left.

Claudine and I were standing now, facing one another. She gestured for me to send another message and I felt like a bundle of raw nerve endings as I lifted the phone again and watched my fingers type.

"I made a friend! Can I keep her?"

"Where would she sleep?" Theo replied.

"I was hoping she could sleep with us," I said, with two winky-face emojis. I still can't quite believe I did that.

"Haha," was all he said, and I wasn't sure whether we were being serious, but a minute later he replied again, saying, "All right! I'm on my way back to the hotel now."

"Okay, see you soon," I said, and put my phone away.

I couldn't say for sure what my thought process was at this point, or whether I was thinking at all, but I remember feeling very bright, as though a light had just switched on inside me. The veil between me and the world had lifted and suddenly I felt naked, exposed, and dazzlingly visible.

We gathered up our bags and coats and Claudine marched off toward the toilets ahead of me, glancing back at me over her shoulder. The way she did it reminded me of someone, but by the time I caught up to her I'd already forgotten who. She pulled me into a cubicle with her and I remember wondering whether she planned to pee in front of me. *That would be weird,* I thought, since I didn't even pee in front of my own boyfriend. But instead she locked the door and kissed me again, more forcefully this time, pushing her body hard against mine so that my shoulders smacked against the locked door behind me.

When Claudine pulled away, I took in the sight of her perfect porcelain face, and I was overcome by the urge to destroy it. I didn't want to hurt her; I just wanted to smash her pretty face in. That was a weird thought. I didn't like that thought at all. So I pushed it away, and with that, I became aware of Claudine's hands squeezing down the front of my dress and grabbing at my breasts. Suddenly, the room was spinning, or I was being spun around, I couldn't tell which. Claudine kicked the toilet seat down behind me and, with both of her hands on my hips, she lowered me onto it. Then she knelt down in front of me and gently separated my legs.

The bassline of some distant song came thudding through the ceiling. I looked down at Claudine, her exquisite body kneeling before me on the grubby tiled floor, and wondered what the hell was happening. Did I want this? I wasn't sure I did. My body was betraying me, reflexively responding to the situation while some other part of me floated up and out of myself, regarding the whole scene from above. Something about it looked wrong, like a beautiful knockoff, flawless but nonetheless fake. No, I wasn't sure I wanted this at all, but still, when Claudine placed her fingertips on my chest and eased me gently backward, I let her.

Her mouth found me and my whole body shuddered, my palms flying out and planting themselves firmly into the walls either side of me for stability. I thought of the four metal feet at the bottom of the Eiffel Tower, hoping this thought would ground me as my back arched and my head rolled sideways, my brain lolling about inside it like a broken compass. A bright light blazed within me. Everything was spinning around me.

And for a moment it all began to spin so fast that I was convinced the toilet I was sitting on might actually be the center of the universe.

I wanted it to stop. I wanted everything to stop.

I sat up and Claudine pulled back, looking up at me with concern in her eyes.

"We should go," I said, touching her cheek softly, not wanting to be unkind. "We should go to the hotel now."

I turned up to Theo's hotel room with Claudine in tow, like a pet cat with a dead mouse between its teeth. Theo opened the door and stood there, immobile at the sight of us.

"Hello," said Claudine, and before Theo could say anything she stepped forward and kissed him, placing her hands on either side of his face and holding him there as he kissed her back, reluctantly at first, then with more vigor. My stomach turned a little to see this, but then Claudine let go and pushed past Theo into the room. I stopped in front of him and he kissed me, almost aggressively, biting at my lip and planting a hand on my lower back to pull me closer into him. When he looked at me again, it was like he could see the light I felt inside of me. I could last a lifetime on nothing but that look.

Inside the hotel room something changed, as though we'd all been listening to the same ear-splitting music, which had suddenly been cut off, leaving only silence. Theo poured us all a drink; then he stood a few meters away from us sipping on his.

We had inadvertently formed an awkward triangle.

"How long have you lived in Paris?" Theo asked Claudine, but she just looked at me helplessly.

"She doesn't speak much English," I said.

"Oh, right," said Theo.

His tension and uncertainty were contagious, and we all waited quietly for someone else to do something. I felt nauseous. I had to fight the urge to be sick.

In the end it was Claudine who made the first move, but as she stepped toward Theo, he downed his drink and made a dash for the minibar.

"Would either of you like another?" he asked. We both shook our heads.

A few more excruciating minutes passed before, finally, Claudine picked up her bag and coat. She looked at us both expectantly, maybe hoping we'd tell her not to go. I looked at Theo.

"Yeah," he said. "It's getting pretty late, so maybe we should just . . ." Then he stopped talking and opened the door for her instead. When Claudine hugged me good-bye, I whispered in her ear that I was sorry. She kissed me on both cheeks as she had when we met earlier that night. Theo shook her hand on the way out.

"Wow," says Maya. "I wasn't expecting that."

"Nobody was expecting that," I say.

We both sit back in our chairs, a half-demolished cake in front of us.

"We had a threesome once," says Maya. "Darren and I."

"How was that?"

"Fine."

I nod.

"Did you and Theo talk about it?" she asks, and I laugh.

"Kind of."

Maya looks at me in confusion and I have to gather myself before saying this next bit out loud.

"We had sex after she left," I say. "Theo asked me to tell him all about what happened with Claudine. And I did. I left some bits out so as to maintain the allure, of course, like me wanting to smash her face in and thinking a toilet was the center of the universe."

"And?"

"And he came. And then he fell asleep. And I went to the loo and threw up a lot."

Maya's head drops into her hands and she lets out a long sigh.

"Yeah," I say.

"Did you come?"

"No," I say.

"I meant with Claudine," says Maya.

"Oh. Maybe. I honestly don't know."

"That's upsetting."

"Yes, it is," I say. "On so many levels."

I woke up before Theo the next morning. My skin felt two sizes too small, like it had somehow shrunk in the night, and my skull seemed to be crushing my brain like a vise. I took some painkillers and got in the shower, turning the temperature up until the water practically scalded me.

Afterward, I wiped steam off the mirror with one hand and

stood staring at my naked body. I had erupted in bright-red patches, which turned white when I pressed down on them. Strings of wet hair clung around my throat like skinny orange fingers, and my shoulders dipped forward in defeat. I hated every inch of flesh in front of me. I repulsed myself.

My fists clenched, and I considered putting one of them straight through my reflection. I imagined thin slivers of glass slicing through my skin, lodging in my knuckles, and the thought brought with it a brief respite.

I didn't notice Theo knocking on the bathroom door at first.

"Are you nearly done in there?" came his voice, as though through water.

"Yeah," I said, wrapping myself in a towel and remembering to turn the shower temperature back down before I opened the door. When I did, Theo took one look at me and walked straight past me without saying a word. He showered, then came out to find me still sitting on the bed in a towel.

"Why aren't you getting ready?" he asked.

"For what?"

"The zoo."

"Oh," I said, "I didn't know if you'd still want to go."

He shook his head dismissively. "Why wouldn't I?"

"I just thought you might want to talk about last night."

"There's nothing to talk about," said Theo.

We hardly spoke at breakfast; I tried to make conversation but Theo just gave me the bare minimum response before going quiet again. This continued the whole way to the zoo.

At the ticket desk we were served by a very pleasant lady wearing a gray hippopotamus hat. She handed us each a brightly colored flyer with directions to the different enclosures and fun facts about each animal. Then she printed out our tickets and offered them to Theo.

"Isn't it cruel?" he blurted.

We both looked at him in confusion.

"I'm sorry?" asked the lady in a heavy French accent.

"Keeping the animals locked up like this," said Theo. "It just seems a bit cruel."

"Oh, I think the animals are very happy here," she replied, her smile unwavering.

"Well, what would you know?"

Was he trying to pick a fight with the hippo lady?

"We don't have to go to the zoo if it upsets you," I interjected.

A look of utter exasperation spread across Theo's face.

"It doesn't upset me."

"All right," I said, "but we can go somewhere else. I don't mind."

"No. You wanted to go to the zoo. So we're going to the zoo."

The lady was still holding out our tickets, her grin firmly glued in place.

"Our animals do receive very excellent care here, monsieur," she chirped.

Theo rolled his eyes, grabbed the tickets from her, and stomped off toward the entrance. I apologized on his behalf, then followed him into the zoo.

We walked side by side in silence for what felt like hours, and

I could sense the tension building while we pretended to be interested in lions and elephants and something called an okapi. It was like spending an afternoon with a pressure cooker.

Theo finally lost it at the penguin tank.

"What the fuck were you thinking?" he snapped, the severity of his outburst somewhat muted by a group of baby penguins swimming playfully behind his head. Several people turned to look at us.

"Let's go back to the hotel and talk," I said, trying to take his hand, but he just pulled away from me and walked off to a quieter spot.

"I don't understand," I said, when I caught up with him. "You seemed okay about it last night."

"Well, I'm not!" he barked. He was pacing back and forth, running his hands through his hair and making that awful, stressy face he makes. I waited for him to speak, terrified to say the wrong thing.

"Why would you just bring her back like that?" he asked.

"I thought you wanted a threesome."

"I do. I did," he said, getting more and more flustered as he spoke, "but I'd have liked to agree to it first."

"Wait. Didn't you?" I asked, struggling to remember. "Didn't we text about it?"

Theo stopped pacing and looked at me, incredulous.

"That was your way of asking?"

"I'm sorry," I said, "I was drunk and—"

"And that excuses it all, does it?"

"No, of course not," I said. "I really am sorry."

A family strolled past, chatting and laughing. They smiled at us and we smiled back, waiting until they were out of earshot to resume arguing.

"Why did you do it?"

"For you."

"For me!?" Theo forced out a fake laugh. "Seemed like you were having plenty of fun without me."

"Please don't be mean," I said calmly, but my composure only seemed to fluster him more.

"Mean!?" said Theo. "You let some stranger go down on you in a toilet and *I'm* mean?" I winced at this.

"That's not how I wanted it to be," I said.

"How you wanted *what* to be?"

"My first time with a woman."

"Your *first* time?" he scoffed. "So you're planning on doing this again, are you?"

Theo's words were coming out like bullets, each one aimed with the intention of doing maximum damage. When he looked at me, all I could see was pure, unfiltered hatred. This wasn't the same man who had kissed me in the hotel last night. I'm not sure I'd ever seen this man before, in fact.

"No," I said. "Please calm down. You're mixing my words."

"I'm not doing anything." Suddenly he was roaring at me, "THIS IS ALL YOUR FAULT."

Theo stepped toward me and instinctively I recoiled, lifting a hand to protect myself. He pulled away from me then, looking down at me in disgust.

"Oh, don't pull that card," he snapped, but I could tell he instantly regretted it; I watched as all the anger drained from him and was immediately replaced with guilt.

I looked away, embarrassed that my body had responded so dramatically, and furious that Theo seemed to think it was performative. I felt weak and silly and exposed and when I spoke my voice scraped out through gritted teeth.

"The way that men have treated me all my life is not a card, Theo."

"I know," he said. "I'm sorry I said that. It's just, I would never . . . I'm not them, I'm not your dad, and I'm not your shithead ex."

"Could've fooled me," I muttered.

A heavy silence hung between us until he spoke again.

"I don't like who I am around you sometimes," he said finally.

"Well, I despise the sad, sniveling little appeaser I've become around you."

I didn't even know if I meant it. But I sure sounded like I did.

Theo looked at me with tears in his eyes, then walked away with his head down and shoulders slumped. I went back to the penguin tank and sat watching them for hours. I felt absolutely nothing. The veil between me and the world had returned.

When I got back to the hotel I found Theo perched on the sofa and my bag by the door, packed and ready to go.

"I'd like you to leave," said Theo.

"Evidently."

"Stop it!" he shouted. "Stop this cool, calm, collected shit."

"Look, I know your flight isn't until Monday," he said, gathering himself. "But I'll give you the money to change it."

I couldn't help but laugh. "You're all right, thanks."

Theo glared at me from across the room.

"I was just trying to fix things," I said.

"What *things*?" He sighed.

"Well," I said, "the fact that you don't love me, for a start."

Theo flinched at this. It was subtle but I saw it.

"I'm just angry with you," he said dismissively.

"No, you've got it backward," I said. "I'm not saying you stopped loving me because of what I did. I'm saying I did it because you stopped loving me."

He leveled an indignant look at me.

"When?"

"I don't know exactly when it happened, Theo. All I know is that it's true." My voice sounded weary and resigned. "And for the record, I'm neither calm nor collected. This is just my default mode in a confrontation. But then you'd know that if you ever bothered to fight with me."

"What the fuck is that supposed to mean?" he asked. "You want to fight? Is that it?"

"Of course I don't *want* to fight," I said, "But sometimes things need to be talked about. Even if it's uncomfortable. Even if we disagree. Like, I know you're not happy with our sex life. How could you be? It's shit. I'm not exactly thrilled about it either. But you never want to discuss it."

"So, what?"

"So, maybe if we just—fucking—talked about things, it wouldn't have come to this."

"Are you honestly blaming me for what you did?"

"No! Jesus. I'm just trying to tell you that this, right here?" I gestured at the general vicinity of the argument. "This is the most invested you've been in our relationship in years."

"That's ridiculous," he said.

"Is it?" I asked.

"I think you should go."

"Of course you do. Just when we might actually be getting somewhere."

He stood there, staring at me regretfully, and I couldn't tell if he regretted the fight, the surprise visit, or ever having met me.

"Well," I said, grabbing my suitcase, "we'll always have Paris."

"You didn't actually say that," says Maya.

"I did. And then I made it all the way to the lift before I had a complete meltdown."

"Oh, you poor thing," Maya says. She's rubbing my back while I cry into my hands.

"I almost went back, Maya. I wanted to so badly. I just wanted to run back to him. But I couldn't take that look on his face again. I just couldn't bear it."

With that, we both notice Darren creeping through the front door. He's trying and failing to hide a big bunch of flowers behind his back.

"Is this a bad time?" he asks sheepishly. Maya smiles up at him while I dry my face with the back of my hand.

"No, no," I say, "just having a drink and a cry—the usual."

"Oh, okay," says Darren, still frozen.

"Come in, for Christ's sake!" says Maya, getting up to give him a hug.

While they're busy making up, I go into Maya and Darren's bedroom to get my things, and I find myself looking at a framed photo of their wedding day. It's a picture of the whole bridal party, and I'm on the end next to Theo. All the other couples are holding hands or draping arms around one another's shoulders, but Theo is just standing there with his hands in his pockets, like he doesn't even know me.

I've never seen anyone as happy as Maya was that day, but then, she's always happy. I mean, she's gone through breakups and been fired from jobs and for a few years in her early twenties she lived with a housemate from hell, but from what I can tell she had a fairly uneventful upbringing—her parents are about as loving and supportive as two people can be—and she's never experienced any real tragedy until recently; she had a miscarriage shortly before the wedding, and it was the lowest I'd ever seen her. Darren was grieving too, of course—he even called me a few times to talk through how he was feeling—but he never let those feelings affect Maya. As far as I know they're trying for a baby again, which to my mind is one of the bravest things a couple can do together after suffering a loss like that.

I sometimes wonder how I would have turned out if I'd had nice, stable parents and settled down with a nice, stable man; someone calm and kind who doesn't flap in the face of adversity. *I keep ending up with flappers*, I think, *but then I keep choosing them.*

Maya and Darren are tucking into the remains of the cake when I come back with my coat on and my suitcase in hand.

"Where are you going!?" asks Maya when she sees me.

"Home. I should leave you two alone. Thank you so much for looking after me tonight."

They both protest in unison, but I insist. I feel like my sadness is contagious and I want to take it as far away from these perfect people as I can.

"Besides," I say, "someone's got to feed the mice!"

Darren laughs at this. Maya gets up and hugs me.

"If you're sure," she says into my ear. Then Darren wraps his arms around the both of us. He smells of beer and day-old cologne and it makes me pine for Theo.

When I pull away, Darren holds me by the shoulders and stares at me with glazed eyes.

"Whatever's wrong, don't worry," he slurs. "Things could get much, much worse."

Maya squints up at him in confusion.

"Great," I say, patting him on the arm. "Nailed it, Darren."

On the way home I text Theo to ask if we can talk. He replies immediately to say he's not ready yet, but he's glad I landed safely. All very polite. All very cold.

I spend the next couple of weeks acutely aware of his absence, wondering if he's ever coming home, or if I even want him to.

knowing: part ii

MAYA AND DARREN'S WEDDING is a homemade affair, all tea lights and bunting and fresh lemonade in mason jars. In the cool quiet of a small stone church, Maya hands me her bouquet, and I go stand next to her sister and cousin—the three of us wearing the same blue satin dress. Maya's dress is made of delicate ivory lace, and her hair is adorned with a dainty flower crown. She's never looked more beautiful.

She's been beaming all day, since the moment I helped her into her dress in the morning—the pair of us giggling hysterically as she stood there in nothing but a white thong and heels, with me kneeling in front of her, trying desperately to shimmy the fabric over her not-insignificant hips.

At the altar, her face is set in a soft, serene smile, the picture of certainty and calm. Sunlight streams through a stained-glass window and the low hum of a tractor can be heard gently rumbling through a nearby field. The vows are flawless. Maya stumbles once but then I give her a wink and she lets out a nervous little laugh, which only adds to the charm of it all. Darren doesn't take his eyes off her once.

Chalkboard signs lead the small congregation from the ceremony to the reception, and we follow the happy couple down a cobbled country street to a converted barn, where we're seated at long trestle tables, each one lovingly strewn with flowers and candles, and a handwritten place card for every guest.

The speeches are just the right length, the meal is a giant cottage pie—made from scratch by Darren's aunt—and the band is surprisingly good. We drink and dance into the wee hours, belting our way through every chorus of every song, until the band have long gone and we're playing music off somebody's phone. Finally we collapse into deck chairs around a fire pit in the courtyard outside.

By now there are only eight of us left, all couples, and we're down to our last bottle of wine. We pass it around the circle along with a spliff that Miles, Darren's best man, has just produced from his jacket pocket. It's a warm night. Still and quiet. Maya lets out a satisfied sigh, and Darren looks at her and smiles.

"This woman," he announces, apropos of nothing, "this woman means everything to me. Without her, life wouldn't be worth living."

Maya smiles shyly but Darren continues to stare at her with sincerity and intensity.

"I mean it," he goes on. "You are the kindest, sweetest, smartest, sexiest woman in the whole world and I can't believe I get to call you my wife."

Maya leans out of her chair, grabs Darren by the shirt collar, and kisses him. Everybody whoops and cheers and laughs, and then, out of nowhere, Miles begins to speak.

"This woman," he bellows. His girlfriend, Alyssa, sinks into her seat, hiding her face in her hands. Miles carries on regardless.

"This woman is my rock," he says in a delightful Welsh accent, "and I know I myself may seem quite . . . sturdy." He pats his beer belly with both hands and chuckles. "But I'm just a softie, really. This woman right here . . ."

Miles looks at Alyssa with tears shining in his eyes. She peeks at him through her fingers.

"She's the strong one. She's my rock. She's got us through thick and thin, so she has."

Alyssa drops her hands and stares at Miles, mouthing the words, "Thank you."

I don't know what their story is, but I know they are both silently reliving it right now. I notice Maya wipe away a tear. Finally Joe pipes up to break the tension.

"This man!" he blurts drunkenly. He's referring to Kabir, the poor fellow whose lap he's currently sitting in.

"This man puts up with all my bullshit! He's a goddamn saint. And he's gorgeous! Look at him. Go on, I don't mind, look at him!"

Joe stands up and makes Kabir stand up too, then gestures for him to do a little spin. We all cheer and whistle our approval while Kabir takes a theatrical bow.

"I love you with all my heart, honey," says Kabir to Joe. They kiss—a little too passionately for the circumstances—and we all cheer again.

"Here's to love!" proclaims Joe, raising the bottle of wine in the air.

"To love!" we echo.

By this point a precedent has been set; the group instinctively turn to me and Theo, and I can't help but smile in anticipation. He shifts in his seat, and everyone thinks he's acting coy. They stare on with big, stupid smiles. But suddenly, my stomach drops. It's the same feeling you get when the phone rings unexpectedly at four a.m. Only some part of me was expecting this call. Some part of me saw it coming.

Now, I'm not the kind of girl to gush over weddings, but the marriage part—the idea of two flawed people being somehow perfect for one another, the odds of finding another human who can tolerate your specific brand of shit, and whose shit you can tolerate too—I think that's pretty special. All around me today, couples old and new grew visibly closer and more affectionate as they gazed dotingly at Maya and Darren and were reminded what real love looks like. And I think that's how a wedding should make you feel—closer and more affectionate. But I haven't felt particularly close to Theo today, and I certainly haven't felt any affection.

It's not that Theo has *done* anything wrong, exactly, but for a few months now I've had the oddest feeling that something is missing, and I can't quite put my finger on what. Today it's been especially palpable—he was one of Darren's groomsmen, he stood opposite me at the altar, and whenever I tried to catch his eye, I felt like he could sense me looking at him but chose not to look back.

After the ceremony he made every possible excuse to not be near me, as though standing next to me on a day like today—he in a nice suit and I in a pretty dress with a bouquet of flowers— was all a bit too symbolic for his liking. For a long time his energy around me has been that of a man who's bracing himself for impact, and for some reason this is only hitting me now.

Everyone's still waiting for Theo to speak, but he doesn't. He just stares down at his feet, pretending to be unaware of the seven sets of eyes on him. Nobody else speaks either. The moment balloons with expectation, expanding unbearably outward, until finally I can't take it anymore.

"Well," I say to Maya and Darren, "today was absolutely perfect, guys. Congratulations again, to both of you." Maya smiles back at me with pity in her eyes.

"To the bride and groom!" shouts Joe, raising the bottle once again.

"The bride and groom!" we all say together, and slowly but surely, the conversation sputters back to life.

This is the moment I know that Theo has fallen out of love with me.

the things we carry

I'M IN DOWNWARD DOG when my phone starts ringing, loudly, much to the dismay of all the other upside-down women in the yoga studio. I don't usually take my phone into class. I don't know why I did today.

I cut the call off quickly and put it in silent mode. It was Maya. I'll call her back later.

But straightaway the screen lights up again. And after it stops ringing, it lights up again.

Something's wrong.

I grab the phone and walk quickly to the door, dodging mats and disapproving glances as I go. As soon as I'm outside I pick up.

"Hey. I'm here. What's up?"

On the other end of the line, Maya is trying and failing to talk. I can hardly make out what she's saying. Something about a bathroom. And Darren. And . . . golf?

That can't be right.

"I need you to take a breath," I say. "I can't understand. Is Darren okay?"

They're due to be married in two months and my first instinct is that he's called off the wedding.

"He's playing golf," she stutters.

"Okay . . . ?"

Has Darren injured himself playing golf?

"I need—"

But her voice is cut off by a sudden, wracking breath. I'm already at the changing room, shoving my clothes in a bag. It's like my body is two steps ahead of my brain.

"It's okay," I say. "Take a breath. Tell me what you need."

"You."

"You need me?"

"Yes," she manages.

"All right. Where are you?"

"Bathroom," she says. "Restaurant. Can't . . . remember."

She's in shock.

"Are you hurt?" I ask. "Has something happened?"

She just starts sobbing.

"Please, Maya, I need to know if you're hurt. Should I call an ambulance?"

"NO!"

That was clear enough.

"All right," I say, leaving the gym and heading for the nearest Tube station. I somehow manage to talk her through sending me her location over text, guiding her step by step until, miraculously, a little pin pops up on my map. Thankfully, she's not too far.

"You're in a café in Soho, Maya. And I'm at King's Cross station."

"Okay," she mumbles. But I can tell this means nothing to her.

"I'll be there in twenty minutes, darling. Okay? Can you wait that long?"

"Okay."

The Tube journey feels impossibly long. Every few minutes the train stops, the doors hiss open, people jostle their way laboriously on and off, and I wait, not even realizing that I'm holding my breath until the blessed *beep* before the doors slide shut and we are moving once again. The worst part is I have no signal underground, so I can't even check on Maya.

I charge up the escalator at Leicester Square and practically run from the station to the restaurant, pushing past the crowds in Chinatown and all the way up Dean Street. I'm completely breathless by the time I reach the café, where I burst through the door and make a beeline for the toilets. I'm almost there when a haughty little waiter steps in front of me, blocking my path.

"Can I help you, miss?" he asks.

"Hi," I say, suddenly aware that I'm still wearing leggings and a sports bra. "I'm fine, thank you. I just need to use your bathroom."

He eyes me up and down.

"The bathrooms are for customer use only."

"My friend is in there."

"You can wait for her here then."

"This is an emergency," I say, moving to go around him, but he steps in front of me again.

"No exceptions, I'm afraid."

I look around for someone to sympathize with me but the place is completely empty; I've just missed the lunchtime rush.

"It really is an emergency, though."

I don't know what else to say. I still don't even know exactly what the problem is.

"No exceptions," he repeats through a phony smile.

I have never, until this moment, had such a strong desire to punch someone in the teeth.

"Sir," I say, "I am going to that bathroom."

And then I do something that shocks the both of us. I square up to him. I actually square up to the guy.

"Look. You can call the fucking police if you like." I notice my Dublin accent has grown suddenly thicker. "But I'm going to that bathroom whether you like it or not. All right?"

He stares up at me, holds my gaze for about four seconds; then his face twitches ever so slightly and he moves aside.

Prick.

There are no windows in the bathroom, just a sickly green light overhead. The piped music is crackly and low. Some old Frank Sinatra song. "That's Life"? Maybe? There are three cubicles with chipped wooden doors. Only one door is closed.

"Maya?"

No answer.

"Maya!"

And then, almost a whimper: "I'm in here."

I rush to the door and push it but it's still locked.

"Can you unlock the door, please?"

Again, no answer.

"Maya, please."

"I can't . . . move."

I consider slamming myself against the door, but that would probably break both my shoulder and her face. There's a two-foot gap at the bottom, though.

"I'm going to climb under, okay?"

"Okay," comes her little voice.

I crawl under the door and I find Maya sitting on the toilet, ankles splayed and knees pressed together, just sitting there, frozen. In any other circumstances she'd laugh at me squeezing under a toilet door to get to her, but her face remains fixed and vacant. Her fringe is wet with sweat and her makeup has all but washed off. There's mascara everywhere. And there's blood.

I didn't notice it at first, but then I see it on her legs and on the trousers bunched around her ankles. It's not like the blood that comes spilling from a wound, though. It's more like period blood, clotted and dark. And then, suddenly, I understand. I get to my knees in front of her and look into her eyes. When she looks back at me, I can see it; the grief, it's all over her.

"She's gone," says Maya.

She.

"Oh, Maya," is all I can say.

I fight back tears as I gently wipe the hair off her forehead, taking her temperature as I do. She doesn't feel hot.

"How long have you been here, my love?" I ask.

"I don't know. Hours. Maybe. I was having lunch . . ." But she just shrugs and trails off.

"It's okay. I'm here now. I've got you."

"I carried her," says Maya, holding her hands out, palms

upturned, as though measuring the weight of her loss. "I carried her for four months. And I'll never get to hold her."

Maya's eyes dart about, searching the middle distance for something that doesn't exist. Then her gaze drops and she starts crying again, but not the hysterical sobs I heard on the phone. This is worse; quiet and defeated, she lets the tears flow down her face in a state of near catatonia.

"I'm so sorry," I say. "I'm so, so sorry."

I take her hands in mine as I try to assess the situation. I wish I could just let her sit and cry, but I need to get her out of here. I need to get her home. Or does this require medical attention? I'm trying to bring my logical brain online and gather all I know about this, which it turns out is not a lot. I'm clutching at bits of films and TV shows I've seen, remembering my siblings all waiting until after their first trimester to announce their pregnancies. I think that's because this is quite common in the first three months. Right? But Maya said she was four months in. Does that mean she's in danger?

I hate this.

I'm usually good in a crisis; thanks to my anxiety I'm used to being on high alert, subconsciously scanning rooms for fire extinguishers, secretly planning escape routes, sensing danger a second before everyone else does. If Maya were drowning, or choking, I could handle it. If she'd broken a limb or accidentally chopped a finger off, I'd be all over it, elevating things or putting them on ice. But in this moment, staring at my friend, sitting on a toilet covered in her own blood, I realize how utterly useless I am. Nothing is, technically, happening. And yet it is. And I haven't got a fucking clue what I'm doing.

"Maya, darling, you've lost a lot of blood," I say finally. "Is that normal?"

Maya just shrugs. She doesn't know. Of course she doesn't know.

"I think we should go to the hospital, just to be safe."

But she snaps out of her stasis at the mere mention of a hospital, her eyes widen, and her head shakes violently from side to side.

"No," she insists, "I want to go home."

"Maya, the blood, I'm worried you might—"

She pulls her hands away from mine, clutching on to her own arms now, folding in on herself.

"It stopped," she cries. "The bleeding stopped. Take me home. Please. Just take me home."

"Okay," I say quickly. "Okay, no hospital. I promise."

This calms her somewhat but she's still shaking.

"Is Darren at home?" I ask.

"He's playing golf. I can't reach him."

"Oh!" I say, as our earlier conversation starts to make sense. But then I realize, he doesn't know; Darren's still existing in a universe where his wife-to-be is out to lunch, healthy and happy and pregnant with his baby girl. I think about him finding out and then I shove that thought down. It's not helpful now.

"All right, let's get you out of here."

"How?" she asks, looking down at herself.

Good question.

"My gym bag!" I say, suddenly remembering. "I've got clothes in there. I've even got clean underwear."

"Okay," she says, nodding feebly.

"We can do this. Trust me."

• • •

I go back to the main door of the bathroom and lock it. Then I help Maya out of the toilet cubicle. She's completely paralyzed at first; she can't even stand up. But slowly, cautiously, she gets to her feet and steps out of her bloody clothes. I fill a sink with warm water and soap, and we use the T-shirt she was wearing as a cloth to wipe off as much blood as we can. Then, once she's clean and dry, I give her my clothes to change into. She leans against me the whole time, one hand on my shoulder, like her legs might suddenly give way.

Later, when I look back on this, what I'll find most moving is how quickly we slip into these roles, how naturally the art of caring comes to us. We hardly say a word, we just do what needs to be done, and Maya lets me wash and dress her without a hint of shyness or embarrassment. It's as though her body is a separate entity, and we tend to it together as we would a wounded child, gently and with great affection.

I flush and clean the toilet quickly while she waits; then just as we're about to leave she says, "What if I start bleeding again?"

I hadn't thought of that.

There's a machine on the wall that dispenses tampons and sanitary towels. But it requires a two-pound coin. Of course it does. I look at Maya. She looks back at me and shrugs as if to say, I don't have it either. A look of desperation creeps across her face. She's beginning to panic again. I can't let that happen.

"Okay," I say. "Okay, let me think."

My eyes flit about the room, from the sinks to the toilets to the gym bag. All I have are her soiled clothes and the clothes I'm wearing.

"That's it!"

Maya just stares at me as I pull the pads out of my sports bra, place them on top of one another, and wrap them neatly in a wad of toilet paper.

"I'm sorry," I say, offering it to her, "best I can do."

But even though this must be humiliating on so many levels, Maya takes the makeshift pad from me, unzips her jeans, and shoves it into her pants. Then she looks at me with tears in her eyes and thanks me. *This is isn't fair,* I think. *None of this is fair.*

Outside, I hail a cab and climb in the back with Maya. About five minutes into the journey she doubles over, holding her stomach and groaning in pain. The driver catches my eye in the rearview mirror.

"She better not get sick in my car," he says, and once again I'm overcome with an urge to lash out violently. As though sensing this, Maya squeezes my thigh with her free hand.

"She won't," I say through gritted teeth.

Finally, we make it to Maya's apartment, but as we climb the stairs to her door, I notice a dark patch on the back of her jeans. I take her straight to the bathroom and she sits on the toilet while I run a bath and go fetch her some painkillers. Then, having taken twice the recommended dose—I'm certainly not arguing—she strips off and I help her to very delicately lower herself into the hot water. As she settles in the tub, Maya lets out a little sigh, and I feel myself exhaling with her.

I sit with her awhile, just holding her hand in silence; then I leave her to soak while I gather up all the bloody clothes and go put them in the washing machine. I hit the switch. The drum starts spinning. And I watch the clothes tumbling around inside.

The moment the water turns red is the moment I allow myself to cry. Sinking to the floor in front of the machine, I let the noise drown out my sobs as the day solidifies, making itself real inside my mind. At least Maya didn't have to see this, I think. At least I could spare her that.

I've just gathered myself and returned to the bathroom when Maya's phone starts ringing on the floor next to her. We can both see that it's Darren. Maya freezes, reverting to the same state I found her in earlier. All she can do is shake her head. But he'll have seen all the missed calls, I think. He must be absolutely terrified. I pick up the phone.

"Darren, hi, it's okay, Maya's okay," are the first words out of my mouth.

"All right," he says. "What happened? Where is she?"

"She's here beside me. She's just in the bath right now."

"Okay," he says, but I can tell he's still waiting for the hammer to fall.

"Listen, Darren. Maya is all right. I promise. I'm here with her and she's doing all right. But . . ."

I shouldn't be the one to tell him this. I look at Maya and she holds out her hand. I give her the phone.

"Hi, honey," she says, her voice incredibly calm. Somehow, she's found a pocket of strength inside herself.

"Yes, I'm okay. I have some bad news, though." She takes a deep breath and says, "I've had a miscarriage."

It's the first time someone's said it out loud. The word seems to linger in the room with us like some grim specter; a presence unseen but very much felt.

Darren tells Maya that he's on his way; then he stays on the phone for the whole journey home. Even after she's explained, and been reassured, even though there's not much more to say, he stays with her until eventually, the bath gets cold and I wrap her in a towel and help her to the sofa. They hang up just as Darren comes through the front door.

I will never forget the look on his face when he sees her; I'm expecting panic and despair, but all I see is love. Darren looks at Maya like a groom looking at his bride, like he's seeing her for the first time, maybe the only time. There are tears in his eyes but he smiles at her, the sweetest, saddest smile I've ever seen, then without a word he goes to her and scoops her up like an injured bird. They don't speak. He just holds her there for as long as she needs and lets her cry and cry.

Later, after we've put her to bed, Darren and I have a drink together and he tells me all about it; how they weren't expecting to get pregnant before they were married; how scared they were, and then excited; how Maya was having her dress altered to accommodate the bump. He even shows me the ultrasound from just a week ago. I hold the black-and-white photo in my hands and stare down at the blurry outline of their daughter's tiny face. It's like looking at a ghost.

"We were going to show this to you and Theo this weekend," he says, and this brings on a fresh wave of tears.

An hour or so later Darren follows Maya to bed and I let myself out. I get home around nine o'clock, expecting to find Theo on the sofa watching TV, but the flat is dark and empty.

He must still be at the office. I call him to tell him what happened and to ask if he'll be much longer.

"Just got a few more things to do here," he says. "I'm really sorry today was so tough. I hope Maya's okay."

He doesn't get it. How could he? I want to ask him to come home—I don't want to be alone—but instead I tell him I'm going to bed and ask him to be quiet when he gets in.

A few days later, Maya comes back to work. I call her the night before to say I'm worried she's not ready, but she insists she needs to get out of the apartment and at least try to feel normal for a few hours.

"I've been sleeping with the ultrasound photo under my pillow," she says, as though confessing to some awful crime.

"That makes sense," I say, "keeping her close."

"Yeah," says Maya, and I can hear the relief in her voice. "I might take it with me tomorrow, just to have in my bag. That's not weird, is it?"

"Maya, my love, that's not weird at all."

At work, she tells everyone she had the flu, but here's the thing: throughout the day I notice all the women in the office stopping by her desk. Our boss, Chetna, sits with Maya for a few minutes in the morning, just to chat. Elena brings her a plate of sliced apple, insisting that she "keep her strength up." And when Maya asks if anyone has painkillers, Sheena's over like a shot with a whole box of ibuprofen. After lunch, Joanne returns with a cup of raspberry leaf tea, which she hands over with a knowing look.

"This helped me," she says, "when I had the flu."

I watch Maya sipping her tea and I wonder how many women carry the memory of a child nobody knew but them. How many women grieve alone and in silence, without sympathy or ceremony, too afraid or ashamed to speak of their loss? And why should they feel ashamed, or afraid, or alone? When there are so many others, when this is so common, why isn't it something we talk about? And when it happened to my friend, why didn't I know what to do?

summer skin

IT'S MAY, AND ALREADY the nights are sticky. I can't sleep.

Our flat is stifling. Even the furniture seems to sweat. I lean against a kitchen cabinet and my shoulder leaves a moist patch on the wood. I sit on the leather sofa and I have to peel my thighs off it as I stand up. I didn't want a leather sofa—they're hot in summer and cold in winter and they make awkward, squeaky noises every time you sit on them—but Theo wanted one and I wanted to be amenable.

We've moved into a new place on the second floor of a shabby Georgian house in Marylebone. We were so desperate to find somewhere fast that I overlooked the flat's less-than-perfect features—like the light with no switch, the switch with no light, and the boiler that turns itself on and off at seemingly random intervals. I focused instead on its proximity to the Tube station, the marble fireplace, and the bright, airy living room with enormous sash windows. But the things I once found quirky and charming have quickly become irritating.

Also, I think we have mice.

Every day now the sun blasts through our sash windows from early morning until around five o'clock, then concentrates its efforts on our bedroom until an inevitable evening mist takes the heavy heat away. Each time I come home, I feel a wave of hot, lavender air hit me in the face. Instead of hanging above things, the way air should, it seems to sit on them, on me.

The lavender was supposed to help me sleep; Maya said a few drops of essential oil on my pillow would cure my insomnia. Instead I've spent the past four nights flipping my pillow over, throwing my head from one side to the other, trying to find a spot that hasn't been contaminated. I send Maya a text message: "Take one pillow. Marinate in lavender. Cook in a preheated bedroom at gas mark 6 for two weeks. Come home. Enter bedroom. Faint."

She responds with an extremely close-up photo of her derpy face, taken from just beneath her chin. This is her version of an apology.

I tell her to piss off.

She sends me another photo of herself and Darren on a sun-drenched beach, both sipping impossibly yellow cocktails.

I call her a cunt and tell her to come home soon. She says she misses me too.

Theo is in Las Vegas at a conference. Every year the company we work for makes some extravagant, insanely expensive effort to distract its employees from the crappy reality of their cubicled existence, and this year is no different; more than two thousand people from six different offices were flown to Vegas on Monday morning for a weeklong booze cruise disguised as "team build-ing." Theo thought I was joking when I said I didn't want to go.

"I'd rather eat my own shit," I told him. He laughed and said that wasn't true.

"Well, either way," I went on, "I could happily live my entire life without sitting around a continental breakfast buffet listen-ing to laddish banter from male colleagues who just rolled in from an all-night strip club."

We were watching commercials silently flash by on the telly while we waited for *Game of Thrones* to start.

"And what if I go to a strip club?" he asked. Defiance does not come naturally to Theo, so his question came across bolshie and a little pathetic.

"You can do as you like, honey. Just know that no little girl dreams of one day dancing naked for you and your dickhead mates. Most of them have no other choice."

"Jesus Christ," he said, and he skulked off to finish the tea he'd left brewing. I turned around to look over the back of the sofa at him.

"What?" I said.

"Oh, are you still here?" he asked, feigning surprise. "I thought you might have another parade to go piss on."

I pulled a pouty face and placed my chin on my arms coyly, speaking in a baby voice that I know he detests. "Oh, I'm sowwy, sweetie. I'm sure the nice ladies are all rich CEOs who let drunken men maul them cuz they love it so vewy much!"

I could see him trying not to smile as he stirred the tea.

"Fucking feminist," he grumbled, and I laughed.

"That's not actually an insult, you know."

"Yeah, well, it used to be!" he cried, in faux rebellion. "Back when men were men and strippers were just . . . objects. Then you lot came along, fucking personifying them!"

"Come watch *Game of Thrones* with me," I said. "There might be tits!"

"Yeah, okay," said Theo as he rejoined me on the sofa and handed me my tea.

"I put too much milk in yours on purpose," he muttered. I just rolled my eyes.

A few minutes later, while some poor fellow was being beheaded on-screen, Theo randomly announced that he went to a strip club once and it was shit.

I appreciated the olive branch, but what Theo doesn't understand is that my problem with Las Vegas is far less literal than strip clubs. Something about the synthetic nature of the place unnerves me, as though at any moment the veneer might crack and I'll be face-to-face with whatever it was hiding. It's the same problem I have with Disneyland, which I've been to several times and hated even more with each visit. I'm simply averse to any place or event where I'm supposed to feel a certain way—that includes Christmas, New Year's, and Valentine's Day. As far as I'm concerned, failed actors in gaudy costumes, ten-dollar bottles of water, and a polystyrene castle do not a magic moment make. I'll feel magical when a goddamn miracle happens, and not a moment before.

My boss gave me the option of "working from home" for the week, knowing full well there was nothing for me to do while the rest of the company took part in a glorified piss-up. So I've decided to use the time to work on a new story. I recently graduated from an intermediate to an advanced creative writing class, and the caliber of my new classmates is nothing short of debilitating; their work at once inspires me to be better and to just give up because I will always be trash by comparison.

There's another Irish girl in the class. Maureen. She's lived in London for six years and her work has been published in several journals. On weeks when we hand in assignments I always read hers first, usually on the bus ride home. Her last piece was a personal essay about motherhood. It was devastating.

We have a reading coming up, which means our friends and families will drink cheap wine and eat cubes of plastic cheese from paper plates while our teacher, Omar, a stern-looking bald man with a formidable goatee, introduces us in far too formal a fashion. Then I, along with my twelve classmates, will read a story in a very-serious-writer voice reserved solely for very-serious-writer occasions. I know my story won't be the best—Maureen's will be the best—but I want so desperately not to be the worst.

I asked Omar if he'd like us to focus on a particular theme for the reading, but he just told me to write "whatever story keeps me awake at night." I thought that was incredibly profound, but then everything Omar says seems incredibly profound. I think it's his goatee.

Omar finds me infuriating. I know this because he told me so last Tuesday night in front of the entire class.

"I find you infuriating," he said, cutting off a small, pointy woman named Pamela, who was giving me feedback on my latest story. Omar was sat at the head of a large wooden table, which we were all gathered around. We watched as he shook his head slowly from side to side, then drew his lips into a tight, straight line.

A long silence followed.

Pamela glanced at Omar, the way you might check for oncoming traffic. Then, presuming it was safe to proceed, she continued her critique.

"So, um, I was quite drawn in by the—"

"Everything you write begins with such promise," blurted Omar, "but the endings . . ."

He dragged the palm of one hand down the length of his face, as though the mere thought of my endings caused him great physical distress.

The class nodded along solemnly.

"They're so . . . fucking . . ." said Omar, presumably struggling for a suitably cutting adjective.

"Nice," Maureen offered, her face a sympathetic grimace.

"Yes!" Omar erupted, pointing a pencil at her with gusto. "Nice!" he repeated.

Several "mmm-hmms" echoed around the room while Omar stared at me, unblinking. I waited for an uncomfortable amount of time to pass before finally speaking.

"I struggle with endings," I said.

"You do," said Omar. "I'm glad you understand."

Then we moved on to Edgar's story about a mushroom he found outside Sainsbury's last week, and I resumed breathing.

This isn't the first time my endings have been called into question, but they've never been described as "nice" before. I hate that word. I hate the idea that anyone would ever describe me, or my work, as "nice." I'd rather be loved and loathed in equal measure than for everyone to just tolerate me.

What did you think of her? Yeah, she's nice.

Fuck that.

And fuck Maureen. That talented cow.

I know full well what my problem with endings is; I hate closing doors on my characters. In my mind, each one is like a train, and their story is a track that branches off into infinite possible outcomes with every decision they face. I sketch out diagrams of these timelines to try to make sense of them, turning my pencil over every now and then to use the eraser, and brushing away the tiny pink fragments until my page is covered in the faint indentations of tracks that never were.

Each time a character chooses a track, all other possibilities are erased by default. And I can't bear it. I imagine little pieces of them being left behind; a faded copy traveling along one of the ghost-tracks. This is why my endings are lacking; I can never fully commit to one.

I find myself drawn to science fiction—in particular time travel and alternate universes—because this way I can explore numerous eventualities within the same narrative. Maybe that's cheating, I don't know.

The story I'm working on for the upcoming reading involves a woman who can visit her past and future selves. That's not what my story is about, of course—it's about regret—but this is why I love sci-fi—it's never about the aliens or the robots or the wormhole to another dimension; it's about human nature, and how we might react to such phenomena. I can give a character the ability to time travel, then see what she does with it. Like giving a lab rat a laser gun, I suppose.

I've been working on this new story for a while, on evenings and weekends, and I thought this week off would be enough to finish it. But instead of helping, the alone time seems to have hindered progress. I am desperate to write. I know the words are in there—I can feel them piling up inside my head like water behind a dam—but right now I've got creative constipation. Eventually the dam will break and the words will gush forth, like so much proverbial shit, but until then I can only sit and wait with a pencil at the ready.

Theo has been gone for five days now. Every day I open all the windows and doors to let a draft through; then I sit in the middle of the sofa and build a nest out of books, notepads, and loose pages. There I stay, sometimes scribbling notes, sometimes staring intently at nothing for hours on end. Occasionally the curtain billows inward, impregnated by a thick, warm breeze. Scraps of paper, weighed down by random objects—a spoon, a remote control, some sun cream—flutter wildly for a moment, as though excited by the prospect of escape. Then, wearied by the attempt, they settle once again.

I have discovered that one o'clock is the optimal time to observe dust motes. I imagine that they're alive and my living room is their universe; an entire race of tiny life forms going about their business—things to do, places to be—never stopping, never waiting, never lying in a lavender-soaked room unable to sleep. Sometimes I choose one and follow its trajectory around the breezy room. I had one for more than two minutes once; then a bird flew by my window and I lost it. I was angry—with the bird for distracting me and with the dust particle for escaping me.

I go for long walks to inspire myself. But the city feels somehow more oppressive than the apartment; people everywhere, all cleavage and bare legs, breathing and walking and sweating together. The weather forecast says it will get hotter.

I bought a new pillow today and threw the old one out. This evening I lit jasmine- and eucalyptus-scented candles—anything is better than lavender—then I rolled up my duvet and shoved it on top of the wardrobe, opting to sleep naked under a cotton sheet instead.

Lying in bed, I wonder if I miss Theo. We've barely spoken this week save for a few perfunctory texts—on the first day he let me know he'd landed safely and sent me a photo of the view from his Las Vegas hotel room: a fake Eiffel Tower amid buildings and branding. I replied to say the weather looked nice. Since then it's been brief reports on each other's activities; he seems to be having fun and I've lied several times about how much writing I'm doing.

I check the clock—midnight—then count backward eight hours on my fingers. Four o'clock in the afternoon. I call Theo but there's no answer, so I decide to reread *Story of Your Life* (for the hundredth time). I drift off after a couple of pages.

Sleep comes in short bursts, one or two hours at the most. At some point I wake and I can't move my arms or legs; they're bound in awkward directions by what feel like ropes. I was dreaming of drowning again and I can't shake the sensation of sinking slowly through salty water. The more I struggle the tighter the ropes squeeze around me, like a Chinese finger puzzle. My panic reduces me to paralysis. I give up and allow myself to sink. But as soon as I stop fighting, one of my hands comes free, so I reach to free my other arm and find that I'm tangled up in my sheet. I sit up, fully awake now, and unwrap the sheet from around my ankles; then I toss it at a chair in the corner, where it lands soundlessly and seems to hover in the dark, like a cloud in the night sky.

The back of my neck is wet and there are trickles of sweat under my breasts. I move toward the open window, desperate for even a gust of cool air, and I see another girl in the window opposite. She's smoking a cigarette. I watch its orange tip glow brighter every time she takes a drag, and then I notice a low, monotonous chugging coming from outside.

Craning my neck to the left, I spot a bus waiting on the corner with its engine idling. Just then, a gaggle of chirping women emerge from a nightclub. They stagger to the bus, shrieking laughter, and as each woman steps inside, the volume gradually lowers until they are muted completely. I watch them move soundlessly down the aisle and clamber into the seats on either side. Silence returns to the street, save for that deep hum from the bus. When it pulls off, I look for the girl in the window, but she's gone. I lie back down and wait for sleep.

I wake around midday to the muffled din of daily life outside: a car horn, a child wailing, the *beep, beep, beep* of a reversing truck.

Noise rises like heat from the street below and seeps into my room. I feel separate from it. Apart.

I have a missed call from Theo so I call him back, but there's no answer. It's four a.m. there now. He's lived a whole day.

After twenty minutes of staring at a small patch of sky, I pull on a sloppy T-shirt, pad down the corridor to the living room, and open the windows and doors as usual. Then I stand in the kitchen, drumming my nails against the countertop while I stare into a cupboard, trying to decide between cornflakes and Coco Pops.

I have no appetite lately, for food or for sex. Theo and I are still having sex; we did it on Sunday night before he left, and I enjoyed it in the moment—just like I enjoy food when I do eat—but lately, eating and fucking both feel more like necessities than luxuries. This would usually worry me, since my appetite and anxiety are intrinsically linked, but I put it down to the heat and go back to choosing cereal.

A few minutes later, I'm draining the dregs of chocolate milk from a bowl when a bumblebee drifts through the front door. I watch the bee navigate the room, dipping and diving, inspecting objects, then quickly losing interest in them. He reaches the window and bumps clumsily against the wooden frame over and over. I grab a notebook from a stack on the sofa and try to usher him outside with it, but as I lean across the ledge, my knee knocks against something. I turn just in time to see a potted plant teetering toward the edge and I dive to catch it, but I'm too late; the clay pot plummets downward, crashing onto the bonnet of a parked car below. The sound blasts through the empty street and a man walking his dog stops to glance in my direction, before carrying on, uninterested.

The bee glides casually past my face and out into the day.

I hear a woman's voice say, "Oops," and I look up to see the girl in the window again. She's sitting with her back against the frame and one leg on the ledge, and she's wearing what looks like a man's pajama shirt. Her hair, which I can now tell is blond, is piled in a loose bun on top of her head. She has a book in her hands but she's not looking at it, she's looking straight at me, and I am suddenly aware that I have no underwear on.

"Please tell me that's not your car," I shout across to her, as my hands instinctively tug the hem of my T-shirt downward.

"That's not my car," she replies, and I'm about to exhale in relief when she adds, "It belongs to my neighbor."

I must visibly deflate because she smiles at me then. It's more of a smirk than a smile, really; there's something quite knowing about it, as if some brilliant joke hangs in the air between us and only she can see it.

"Don't worry," she says, "he's not home. And also he's an asshole."

I notice her accent now but I can't quite place it. Scandinavian, maybe. Something about the way she bounces off certain words is very satisfying.

"Good to know," I say.

"I can help you to clean it," she offers.

"Oh, thanks. You really don't have to do that."

"It isn't a problem," she replies, "I'll be down in a moment," and she disappears from the window before I can protest further.

A few minutes later I'm standing by the car surveying the damage when the girl emerges from a door across the road. She's still wearing the pajama top, now tied at the waist over a pair of denim cutoffs. I've thrown on a pair of shorts too, but while mine hang loose around the ends, as though my pale legs have shrunk inside them, hers seem to hug her thighs as she walks. I can't help but watch. I am instantly jealous of her figure.

"Thanks again," I say as she approaches.

She shrugs. "I was bored."

I don't know how to respond to that. She raises an eyebrow at the car.

"It's pretty bad, no?" she asks.

"No," I say, nodding, then: "I mean yes, it is. Bad." Jesus.

People often tell me they were intimidated by me when we first met. And I've always found that silly. But right now I'm beginning to understand what it feels like.

A moment passes; then the girl holds out her hand, palm up, and nods to the plastic bag under my arm.

"Shall we start?"

"Oh," I say, handing her the bag. "Sure. Thanks."

She holds the bag open for me as I carefully collect the shards of broken clay and drop them in. The windscreen is covered in soil—I'm amazed by how much there is—and the plant is lying on the ground next to the car with its limp, white tangle of roots exposed. It looks like a dying alien. I pick it up and throw it in the bag.

The girl and I work quickly and quietly. At one point she asks if my hair is naturally red. I tell her it is. She says she likes it. I say thanks. A while later I ask where she's from. She says Sweden. I say I've never been. She tells me it's fine.

She sits smoking on my front step while I go upstairs for a

bucket of water, which I throw over the car, and then run back for another. The soil washes off in muddy little rivulets. Luckily there are no dents, but there is one big scrape in the middle of the bonnet where the pot landed and shattered. I lean in, frowning as I run my finger over its silvery edges. I can feel the girl watching me and I turn to look at her.

"I won't tell him," she says, as though reading my thoughts. She squints up at me and sucks on her cigarette while I think this over.

"In what way is he an asshole?" I ask finally. This makes her smile, that same smirk of a smile, and I imagine the invisible joke floating between us again.

"Like, is he just a typical twatty man or is he a real monster?" I continue. "Does he beat his wife? Does he starve his dog?"

"He doesn't have a wife," she says. Then, "His dog seems fine."

"Right," I say.

"I just don't like how he regards me," she admits finally.

"How he regards you?"

"He is . . . a bit . . ." She pauses, searching for the right word. "Pervy?"

"Oh!" I say. Then I mull it over in silence for a few moments more and sigh.

"I think I should tell him."

Without another word, or seemingly any emotional investment in my decision, she stubs out her cigarette on the ground, stands up, and brushes the dirt off her legs.

"We'll leave him a note," she says, and once again she's off before I can say or do anything in response. As she crosses the street she calls back at me over her shoulder. "Follow me." And I do.

Her apartment is deliciously cool and shady. It's a studio with a kitchen, living room, bedroom, and office all in one room, but somehow the efficient, immaculate decor makes them feel like separate spaces. The walls are stark white, adorned by sparsely placed artwork—including a papier-mâché moose head—and the furniture looks stylish but comfortable. For the second time today I find myself envying this girl I've just met.

"Your apartment looks like an IKEA showroom."

She's rummaging through a drawer in the kitchen.

"Sorry," I add, "is that racist?" and she laughs. This is the first time I've heard her laugh. It's a raw, raspy sound.

"It isn't my apartment," she says. "It's his," and she nods to a wall of photos on my left.

The pictures are all black-and-white, and perfectly arranged in thick, monochrome frames. They mostly feature a beautiful blond man with a full eight-pack and a jawline that could cut through glass. He looks like a Renaissance sculpture come to life. *Of course this is her boyfriend*, I think.

Here he is in graduation robes. Here he is rock climbing with friends. Here he is riding a fucking elephant! It would be funny if I weren't so sickeningly jealous—of what, I'm not sure, but I feel it bubble in the pit of my stomach and rise toward my throat.

There's only one photo of her; she's posing with him on a bridge in front of a gigantic waterfall. One of his stupidly chiseled arms is draped around her shoulders, pulling her close. She looks happy.

"Aha!" she says, holding up the notebook she's found. "Here you go." She rips out a page and places it on the countertop next to a pen.

"Great," I say, walking over to join her. As I begin to write, I'm aware of her sidling up beside me to watch.

"You are left-handed," she says when I'm almost done, and I become instantly and irrationally conscious of how ugly my hand is, clutching the pen, clawlike, at an impossible angle.

"No, I'm not," I say, without looking up. "I just do this for fun." It comes out more curtly than I'd intended.

She smiles and the moment passes, but even so, I find myself trying to adjust my hand into a more natural position.

"Hey," she says, noticing, "I'm sorry if I was rude."

She wasn't rude. She was just making conversation. But something in me is resisting her kindness now. As though she couldn't actually be this perfect. As though her perfection is, in fact, a personal affront to me.

"It's fine," I say, and again it comes out clipped.

"No, really," she says, playfully bumping her hip against mine, "I like it."

Then, without a moment's hesitation, she lifts my left hand to her lips and kisses it, just below the knuckles.

My body responds before my brain does, giggling at the absurdity of the situation. She seems amused by my confusion and she laughs as she lowers my hand back to the page, then resumes watching as I write my name and number at the bottom. She tells me I have a pretty name and I ask what hers is.

"It's Lena," she says as we shake hands, which seems an oddly formal gesture now. "Pleasure to meet you." Then she whips up the page, turns on her heel, and leaves.

I follow her to her neighbor's front door, where she pulls some tape from her back pocket, breaks it with her teeth, and unceremoniously sticks the note to the door with a smack. Behind the door, a dog barks back in protest. Lena tells it to shush.

"Would you like to come get ice cream with me?" she asks suddenly. The question is both forceful and vulnerable, and I feel like a broken magnet being drawn to her and repelled by her all at once.

"I'm sorry," I hear myself say, "I have loads of work to do."

Then I go back to my apartment and loaf about until it gets dark.

Around eleven o'clock I realize I haven't eaten since breakfast. There's no food in the house—Theo usually cooks and I do the cleaning—so I make a bowl of overly salty spaghetti and slather it in butter, promising myself I'll eat something green tomorrow.

Theo calls just as I'm about to dig in and I answer straightaway.

"There she is!" he roars down the phone.

"Here I am!" I say. "Right where you left me."

He laughs, and the sound makes me smile. "So you haven't burned the place down yet?"

"Not quite . . ." I say.

"Oh God, what's happened?"

"I just knocked a plant out the window; it's fine," I say, shoveling spaghetti into my face.

"How'd you manage that? What are you munching on there?"

"Pasta," I say. "There was a bee."

"A what? Have you been eating properly?"

"Yes," I say, swallowing a mouthful. "There was a bee."

"Oh!"

There are splashing sounds in the background, and lots of voices shouting and laughing.

"Where are you?" I ask.

"The pool," he says. "Hold on."

I hear the noise fade as he walks away from it.

"Anyway," I say, "the pot hit a car but it's sorted now."

"Fair enough."

"A woman across the street helped me out."

"Aw, that was nice of her."

"Yeah," I say. "She's a bit weird, though."

"Is she fit?"

"No," I lie. "Why?"

"Fit women are always weird," he says nonchalantly, like this is a fact of nature. "There is no such thing as a sane, fit woman."

"Oh?" I ask. "Then what am I?"

"You, my angel, are gorgeous. And absolutely mental," says Theo.

I laugh and ask how his trip has been. There's another loud splash and a cheer in the background. A man's voice shouts something to Theo.

"Yeah, just a sec!" Theo calls back. Then to me he says, "Oh, you know how it is, wall-to-wall strippers and meth. Also, I've lost fifty grand on roulette. Sorry about that."

This is the kind of humor that makes me roll my eyes and giggle in spite of myself.

"I miss you," he says, suddenly earnest. "I can't wait to see you."

"When do you get back?"

"Around five a.m. on Sunday. Don't wait up!"

"Shan't," I say with a smile. "Good night."

"Good afternoon!" he says.

After we hang up I write frantically for a few hours. I'm tired but the words are ready to come out now and I know if I don't let them they'll keep me awake all night. I finish a first draft of the story for my reading; then I wash the dishes and go to bed.

Before I lie down, I look for Lena in the window. I tell myself I'm not looking for her, but I'm disappointed when she's not there. Her apartment is dark, save for the faint flicker of blue TV light. I imagine Lena and her Adonis curled up on the sofa together and I wonder what they're watching, whether they have popcorn, whether they've made love tonight, if she's fallen asleep with her head on his giant, too-smooth chest. Then I lie down and try to push that thought aside.

I nod off thinking about Theo. I do miss him. I miss how easy "us" is. I miss his cooking. And I miss his body in the bed next to me, the reassuring mass of him. I don't know why I lied to him about Lena; she's objectively very attractive. Maybe I didn't want him to know about the Hot Girl Across the Road. Maybe I don't want to add that particular character to our narrative. I'm probably just feeling insecure, I tell myself. I'll get up early and do some exercise.

I wake up at midday again. It's a Saturday and the world outside is much quieter. The first thing I do is look out my window.

Across the way, I can just about make out the shape of Lena's boyfriend in their kitchen. He's even taller than I'd thought, and he's standing in the same spot where we wrote the note yesterday. I flash on the memory of her kissing my hand; it wasn't sexual, just oddly intimate. The memory makes me a little queasy. *She's definitely weird*, I think, *very fit and very weird*. Eventually he leaves the kitchen and I get bored waiting for something to happen. I drag myself into a pair of leggings and a graying sports bra, then pull my yoga mat out from behind the vacuum in the hall cupboard and work out for an hour.

Afterward, I'm lying on the floor recuperating when my phone beeps on the table next to me. I wince as I do one last sit-up to get it; then I ease myself back down and hold it above my face. I have a text from an unknown number; the message is just an ice cream emoji and a question mark.

I reply: "Hey Lena!"

A few minutes later she sends back a smiley face, followed by: "Well?"

I write back: "Sure! Gimme 20?"

She replies: "Meet you then xx"

Stepping out of the shower, I catch my reflection in the bathroom mirror and frown; I haven't so much as moisturized all week. I decide to put on some minimal makeup—concealer, mascara, and lipstick. And a bit of blusher. And actually my eyebrows need filling in too. But that's it. I catch my damp hair up in a bun, then glance out the window at a cloudless sky as I grab an old reliable sundress from my wardrobe and shimmy into it. I always feel good in this dress; the shoestring straps sit neatly on my shoulders, and the thin yellow material falls flatteringly in an empire line, making me look more shapely than I am, with a bigger bust and a smaller waist.

"Good job," I say out loud to my own reflection; then I slip on a pair of sandals, shove my phone, lipstick, and credit card into a small handbag, and head downstairs to meet Lena.

She's waiting for me just outside my building, smoking a cigarette as usual; I've only known Lena for a day but already this habit feels familiar. She gives me a cursory nod, then gestures toward her neighbor's car, which hasn't moved since yesterday.

"Has he called you?" she asks.

If she's happy to see me I can't tell.

"Not yet," I say.

She makes a short *hmph* sound.

"The note wasn't on his door today," she says.

I shrug my shoulders.

"So, where do you want to go?" she asks, flicking away the cigarette stub.

"Oh," I say, "I assumed you had somewhere in mind."

I'm a little thrown already, partly because the pressure is now on me to suggest a good place to go, and partly because my ego cannot withstand this proximity to her. Lena looks even better than she did yesterday. She's wearing the same shorts, paired with a white cropped T-shirt, and while her figure is much fuller than mine, she's curvy in all the right places. She looks like a woman, and I look like a lanky little girl.

"I don't mind," she says with an easy grin. "Let's walk and see what we see."

I agree to this plan, and we set off toward the main street.

My anxiety about finding somewhere to get ice cream was, as with most anxiety, stupid and unfounded; almost every café, shop, and restaurant we pass seems to be selling it in some form or another. After ten minutes or so of ambling along, making small talk, we come across what looks like an authentic Italian gelateria. The green, sun-faded awning reads "Mimi's" in white cursive letters, and beneath it, a couple are trying to share a chocolate sundae across a wobbly metal table. There are no other customers inside, just a papery old woman waiting behind a freezer full of ice cream.

"*Buongiorno*," says the woman, first to me and then to Lena. Her expression is stern.

"Hello," says Lena.

"*Buongiorno*," I say, then: "*Posso, per favore, avere due gelati?*" I hope I've just asked for two ice creams.

"*Sì, naturalmente*," the woman replies. Then, moving at a glacial pace, she plucks the scoop from its bucket of water and lifts two cones off the top of the stack. Lena peruses the flavors of ice cream and smiles to herself.

"*Allora*," I say.

Allora doesn't really mean anything; it's more like punctuation than a word in itself. Italians use it in the same way the Irish say "now" before going on to say or do something else. I use it to sound like I know how to speak Italian, and right now I'm using it to buy time while I try to remember the word for strawberry.

"*Vorrei un gelato alla fragola e . . .*" I continue, then turn to Lena and casually ask which flavor she would like.

"Mint, please," she answers, still smirking.

"*Sì, e un gelato alla menta, per il mio amico, per favore,*" I say.

My words are stilted and my accent is appalling, but the woman nods and begins to slowly scrape ice cream into a cone.

"Do you think she is Mimì?" Lena asks into my ear. I smile and shrug, then turn to the woman.

"*Scusemi,*" I say, "*il tuo nome è Mimì?*"

"*No, no,*" says the lady. She softens a little and gestures toward an old, yellowing photo Scotch-taped to the cash register. It's of a woman in her fifties or sixties, standing outside this café with two little girls at her side.

"*Mimì era mia nonna,*" says the woman.

"Ah," I say. Then I turn to Lena and say, "Mimì was her grandmother."

Lena nods and smiles sweetly.

"Is this you?" I ask the woman, leaning in for a closer look at the photo.

"*Sì,*" replies the woman, "*con mia sorella . . .* with my sister."

Back outside the afternoon swelters on. Lena and I have notions of eating our ice creams in Regent's Park but instead we have to gobble them down before they melt, making complete messes of ourselves. We stop at a shop on the way and pick up some wet wipes and a bottle of rosé. The store clerk looks bemused as he scans them through.

As we approach the iron gates on the south side of the park, Lena opens the wine and swigs it.

"So, you speak Italian," she says.

"Not really."

She hands the bottle to me and I take a sip.

"How many languages do you speak?" I ask.

"Five."

"Five!?"

Lena laughs.

"Which five?"

"Let's see," she says, "English, Swedish, of course, Norwegian—quite similar to Swedish—also French . . . aaaand . . . oh yes . . . Italian."

I stop dead in my tracks. Lena keeps walking. From the back of her head I can tell that she's smirking.

"No," I say.

"Yes," she says, without looking back.

I feel my face flush bright pink.

"Come on," she says, over her shoulder.

"You didn't say!"

"You didn't ask," she says, turning around to face me. We stand this way for a while, her grinning, me glaring; then I give up and cover my face with one hand. I am absolutely mortified. *Serves me right for trying to show off*, I think.

Lena walks coyly toward me, peels my hand from my face, and looks into my eyes, smiling sympathetically. As soon as I smile back she grabs the bottle of wine from my other hand and sets off again, giggling.

"You're a fucking troll," I shout, hurrying after her. She guffaws.

"Now, that's racist!"

She takes another swig of wine before I grab the bottle back off her and gulp some down; then we fight about it awhile, doubled over laughing and spilling it everywhere.

Lena and I languish in the park all afternoon. We find a spot right by the pond, beneath a cluster of trees, so that she can lie in the sunshine while I sit just left of her in the shade. She says she can't believe that I burn so easily and I tell her I'm not willing to prove it today.

Couples paddle up and down in little blue boats, and geese waddle this way and that, accepting scraps of bread from picnickers all along the length of the pond. Several dogs jump in the water and emerge dripping and delighted with themselves. At one point a toddler breaks free of her mother's grip and runs headlong toward the water, arms outstretched, her face the picture of unbridled glee. People gasp and the mother gives chase, catching her at the last possible second. Peace returns to the pond.

We watch this tiny drama unfold; then we lie down on our backs. Lena closes her eyes and tilts her chin up to the sky. I turn my head to look at her and find myself staring at her throat.

"Shall we have dinner tonight?" asks Lena without opening her eyes.

"All right," I say, not letting myself think about it too much.

Thus far I've found our interactions exhilarating but tense, and I'm not sure I can take much more, but I want it all the same.

"I'll cook," she says.

"You'll have to. Unless you want beans on toast or over-cooked pasta."

I watch as a little smile forms on her lips. I like conducting the conversation this way, with her eyes closed and me able to observe her at will.

"We can cook at my place," I say. "My boyfriend's away."

"Oh," says Lena, and her smile drops momentarily. "Yeah, sounds good."

I wonder then if she was suggesting a double date. *She probably doesn't want to spend an entire evening alone with me*, I think.

"Would your boyfriend like to join us?" I ask, and her eyebrows creep toward one another like two furry little caterpillars.

"My boyfriend?"

"Yeah."

Now I'm afraid she thinks *I* don't want to spend a whole evening with her. I find this all incredibly stressful.

"The guy in the pictures," I add.

She doesn't say anything for a long time. If she's confused, she doesn't let on. Finally something clicks, and that knowing smirk returns to her face.

"That's my brother," she says. "I'm visiting him this week."

I instantly replay the events of the past twenty-four hours in my head and am almost impressed by how magnificently wrong I was. I flash on my reverie about them fucking on the sofa last night and wince.

"You're more my type anyway," says Lena.

Wait. What?

I'm still trying to figure out exactly what that means when she changes the subject completely.

"What would you like to eat tonight?" she asks.

We decide on risotto and talk about food for a while—mostly the dishes our mothers would cook when we were little—then I close my eyes for what feels like a moment and when I open them again the sun has dropped notably in the sky. The park is quieter and several sunbathers have vanished. Lena is snoring softly beside me.

I check the time: half past six. We've been asleep for more than an hour.

I lean up on one elbow toward Lena, and as I do I notice my right shoulder is a vivid shade of pink. The sunburn spreads down my arm and halfway across my chest; my left side is still in shade.

"Fuck!" I say, waking Lena up.

"What?" she mumbles, half opening her eyes; then she notices my arm and her eyes fly open.

"Oh fuck!" she says. "Shit. Sorry."

"Why are you sorry? It's not *your* fault."

"I made us lie here," she says, and I find her concern quite sweet. She's just woken up and her guard is down.

"It's my own dumb fault for not wearing any sun cream," I say, pulling the strap of my dress gently to one side. There's a perfectly thin white line on my shoulder that looks like a string of spaghetti.

On the way home, Lena offers me her T-shirt to cover my shoulders, which I think is incredibly kind, since that would mean her walking the whole way back in her bra. But then, I'm not sure Lena cares about that sort of thing. I certainly wouldn't if I looked like her.

The first thing I do when we get back to my apartment is take a cold shower. Lena gets straight to work on dinner, since we're both starving. In my bedroom afterward, I carefully pat myself dry, then lather my arm and chest in aloe vera lotion. There's a knock on the door and I open it a crack to see Lena with a glass of wine. Her face is turned the other way.

"I thought this might help," she says to the wall opposite.

"Oh my God, yes, please!" I say, taking the glass from her. I watch her walk back toward the kitchen and the smell of lemon wafts past me. I can actually feel my mouth salivating.

I stand naked in my bedroom for a while, sipping my wine and relishing the cool breeze on my skin as the lotion soaks in. I put on a strapless dress—the only thing I own that won't hurt me to wear—and grimace at my reflection. I look like a drumstick lolly; bright pink on one half and cream on the other.

When I emerge from my room, the risotto is simmering away and Lena is standing by the window with her own glass of wine. She takes one look at me and covers her mouth with her hand, trying to suppress a laugh.

"It's okay," I say. "This is definitely funny."

Just then I notice the pages in her hand. It's the story I finished last night. Lena looks at me sheepishly.

"I hope you don't mind. I found this on the table and I read it."

"The whole thing!?"

"Yes," she says, "I liked it a lot."

"Thank you," I say, suddenly self-conscious. "It's not done. I still need to edit it."

"Pffft!" says Lena, waving her hand at me. "It's good already. I know because I forgot where I was while I read it."

I don't know what to say. I can't help but clam up when people give me compliments.

"Thank you," is all I can manage.

"So this is your job?" she asks, and I laugh.

"I wish! My job is to write press releases for a pharmaceutical company."

"Oh. Well, you should do this instead."

"Noted," I say with a smile, as though it's that easy.

"You write in pencil?"

"I do. But I'll type it up later."

"How did the pot fall?" asks Lena, leaning out the window now. I like how she constantly changes the subject without warning. As though she got what she needed from the last one and has no desire to linger.

"I was trying to get rid of a bee." Lena looks at me quizzically.

"Do you not like bees?"

"Not particularly," I say. She frowns like that's an odd stance to take on bees. I feel the need to explain.

"When I was a kid," I say, perching on the arm of the sofa, "there was a boy on my street called Thomas who collected bees."

"Aw," she says.

"No," I say, "not 'aw' at all, actually," and Lena frowns at me in anticipation.

"He would put the bees in his freezer, then attempt to resurrect them."

"Resurrect?" she says, trying to place the word.

"Bring them back to life," I say.

"Oh! Like Jesus!"

"Yes! Exactly, like Jesus. But with bees."

She sips her wine, cautiously invested in my story.

"Anyway, one summer he froze an entire jar full of bees. Then, months later, he took them out one by one and tried to heat them up in the sun with a magnifying glass. Every kid on the street turned up to watch."

Lena's face contorts in a scowl.

"Did it work?"

"Of course it didn't work!" I say, laughing. "He just scorched a load of dead bees!"

She laughs and shakes her head.

"The smell was awful . . . I remember the smoke rising up off their singed little bodies." Then I realize I haven't thought about Thomas and his bees in years.

"I don't think I've ever told anyone about that," I say.

"It's a good story," says Lena. "You should tell it before dinner always." Then she crosses back to the kitchen to check on the food, emphasizing her punch line. I'm definitely starting to get a read on her humor now.

"This is ready now," she says, bringing the pot to the table. I grab two bowls and some cutlery and follow her.

"Tell me about your boyfriend," she says while she dishes out the food.

"Oh, well, he's nice," I begin, pouring us both more wine. She gestures for me to say more.

"He's very caring, reliable, calm . . ."

"Fun?" she asks as we sit down, and I'm surprised by my sudden candor.

"He used to be. The past year or so has been kinda shit, to be honest."

"Where is he now?"

"Las Vegas."

"Ugh," she says, and I nod.

"This is sort of a welcome break for the both of us."

She pulls a face that says, *Tell me about it*, and I ask if she's seeing anyone. She says she was, but they broke up a few weeks ago. From the sounds of it, the girl she was seeing hadn't quite come to terms with her sexuality; she wanted Lena in private but wasn't ready to display affection in public or introduce Lena to her family, even after three years as a couple. Lena ended it, but I can tell it broke her heart to do so.

"Is there any chance you could work it out?" I ask.

"Maybe we could. But sometimes I don't know if we should."

"Yikes," I say, and the heavy mood lifts a little when she laughs.

We chat for hours, abandoning the empty dishes when we're done with dinner and relocating to the sofa. It's easy to talk to her, maybe because of the transience of our relationship—she's going back to Sweden tomorrow morning—or maybe because of the wine. I find myself talking to her about my childhood, things I've only ever discussed with Theo and my therapist. She tells me about her job, her first kiss, the kids who bullied her at school, and the time she almost drowned. This reminds me of the dream I had the other night, and I tell her about waking up all tangled in my sheets. I confess that I saw her in the window that night, that I've looked for her there since. She smiles at this but says nothing. Then she asks why I didn't go away with Theo. I try to explain my feelings about Las Vegas, and by extension Disneyland, but I'm quite tipsy at this point and I'm not sure I'm articulating myself very well.

"I just hate places and events where I'm *supposed* to feel something, you know?"

Lena nods.

"Like Christmas," I go on, "or New Year's."

"Fuck New Year's," she says. "Needing to be happy at an exact time. Worrying you're not happy enough. Or that next year you still won't be. Too much pressure."

"That's it!" I say. "It's the pressure. To feel stuff. That I can't always feel."

We both nod and sip our wine; then Lena says, "Nobody has ever died in Disneyland."

"Bollocks," I say. "Somebody must have." She shakes her head solemnly.

"If you die there, they take your corpse off their property before declaring you dead."

"Why?" I ask in horror.

"So it stays magical, I guess," says Lena. Then she sees the yoga mat on the floor and asks me about my exercise routine.

"That's the first time I've exercised in months. Because I was jealous of you!" I blurt out.

"Me? But you're so skinny!"

Neither of us can believe this. She wants smaller boobs and thighs, and I'd give anything for her curves. She grabs a handful of flesh on her tummy and says she needs to lose weight. I tell her not to change a thing. She's perfect. Actually perfect. If I could be any woman I would be her.

The conversation turns to sex, as it so often does late at night with a head full of wine. Lena has never been with a man and I find this fascinating.

"You've never had a penis in you!"

She throws her head back and laughs.

"Have you ever been with a woman?" she asks.

"Not really," I say.

"Not really?"

"I've kissed women," I say, suddenly very aware of myself, "and done . . . you know . . . stuff."

"It's called a va-gi-na," she says mockingly, and I put a finger to my lips and shush her, pretending someone will hear us. This makes her laugh again. I could get drunk on just her laugh.

"Anyway," I say, "I got with my ex when I was seventeen, and after that I met Theo, and I never really got to, you know, explore that side of me."

"Have you said this to Theo?" she asks, and I nod.

"He said it was hot. And he mentioned maybe having a threesome."

Lena winces and I feel immediately embarrassed, for telling her and for choosing to be with a guy who said that. It hadn't really bothered me before, but now, saying it out loud to someone else, I feel a sudden flash of anger toward him. I confided in him that I might be bisexual and his first instinct was to fetishize it.

"It doesn't make him a bad person," Lena says, as though reading my thoughts again. "A bit immature, I think." She has a way of instantly putting me at ease.

"Maybe you could help him understand," she continues. Then, perking up, she adds, "And hey! A threesome could be fun!" She grins at me and lifts her eyebrows comically and I burst out laughing.

We're still talking at one a.m., both of us getting sleepy, when I decide I should tidy up. I'm not sure why, but I don't want the remnants of this evening still here when Theo gets home. I haven't done anything I couldn't tell him about—in fact, I probably will tell him all about my day with Lena, so I know it isn't guilt that's driving me—but somewhere in me is a deep desire to erase all physical evidence of this night and keep a mental picture of it that only I can see.

I'm stood at the sink, elbow-deep in sudsy water. Lena is sprawled out on the sofa.

"Are you happy?" she calls out.

"I'm not unhappy."

"Wow."

She sits up to look at me. Her face is unapologetic and flushed from all the wine.

"Do you love him?"

"Yes," I say, without hesitation, "and I know he loves me too. It just feels . . . different from how it used to."

I can hear myself slurring. I'm drunk.

"Sometimes I feel more like his flatmate than his girlfriend," I admit.

"Then why do you stay?"

"You ask that like it's so simple," I say, a little frustrated with her now, "and maybe it is. But there's this paradox with relationships, isn't there? The more time you've spent trying to make it work, the more time you're willing to keep spending, trying to make it bloody work. I stay because I genuinely believe, if we both try hard enough, we can get back to the way it was before. But—I don't know, maybe I should just accept that what we had is gone. Maybe it's more like a building that's been burned to the ground than some lovely home I could return to and find everything intact and in its place. Maybe I'm not willing to admit to myself that it's just a pile of fucking ashes."

I hear a little sniff and turn to see Lena wipe away a tear.

"You have such a way of choosing words," is all she says.

I go back to the washing-up, scrubbing each bowl a little too aggressively, and a moment later Lena approaches with our empty wineglasses and adds them to the stack of dishes next to me.

"Can I help you, please?" she asks.

"All good, thanks!" I chirp back, maybe too chirpily.

I can feel her eyes on me.

"Hold still," she says, and before I have time to react she's stepped right up behind me. I can feel her breath on my neck.

"Lena?" I say, uncertain what's happening.

"Your shoulder is peeling," she says, and I look down to see that it's red-raw and flaking.

"Fuck's sake," I say.

"May I?"

"May you pull my skin off?" I laugh, looking back at her over my shoulder.

"Yes," she says, earnestly. She's staring into my eyes. I can smell the wine on her breath. "Please?"

I grab a towel to dry my hands; then I hold on to the edge of the sink. Lena steps closer and brushes my hair to one side, letting it fall across the front of my shoulder. She places one hand on my left arm to steady me, and I find myself looking down at her fingers pressing into my arm. Her right hand reaches toward me and I flinch.

"Hold still," she says. "Sorry."

Lena begins to slowly peel the skin from my right shoulder. It's a strange sensation. Like glue that's hardened there. Like I'm losing something that was never really mine. There's a slight twinge as it breaks off and my body tenses. She tightens her grip on me and pulls another strip, and then another.

"All done," she says.

But instead of letting go, her fingers drop from my arm to my hip. She moves closer, so that our bodies are practically touching, and in that moment I do something that surprises me; I step back, closing the gap between us. I can feel her breasts against my back now, and her hipbones pressing into me. Her right hand slips down my arm to my hand and I watch as her fingers mingle with mine. She runs the tip of her nose up my neck to the back of my ear, her lips brushing my hairline, hot breath escaping from them as they part in what is almost a kiss. I shut my eyes tight, because my kitchen looks too real and what I'm doing right now can't be.

We stay this way, our bodies moving against each other,

softly swaying like seedlings in a gentle breeze. Lena's hand leaves my hip and her fingertips graze my stomach, resting there a moment before sliding slowly downward.

Without thinking, I feel my free hand fly up to meet hers. I hold it there, squeezing it tight, and I almost let her hand go, to continue on its journey, but I can't. I step forward, pulling my body away from her.

Lena rests her forehead on the back of my head for a moment, a few inches between us now, and I can feel her whole demeanor change.

"If I had you," she whispers into my hair, "I wouldn't share you."

I turn to face her then, and I'm not prepared for what I see: shame for what she almost did, regret for what she didn't do, and somewhere in there an intense desire for me. It's been a long time since somebody has looked at me this way, and I know there's every chance that I may never see it again. I gaze back at her with what I hope is enough to convey how I feel; then she turns and, without a word, she leaves. I dry the dishes and go to bed.

I think about her that night. I allow myself that. Alone in bed my body shudders at the thought of all the things we didn't do. Afterward, I drift into a deep sleep. And somewhere in the night, Theo returns home, slipping into bed beside me without me even stirring.

In the morning I wake to the sound of the blender noisily whirring and I stumble from bed to find Theo in the kitchen, already back from a run. He jumps when he sees me and turns the blender off.

"Sorry!" He practically shouts it, pulling his headphones out of his ears. I can hear a tiny, tinny version of "This Charming Man" come floating out of them. I put my finger to my lips and smile.

"Sorry," he whispers. "Thought you'd be up already."

"That's fine, honey," I mumble back, looking toward the window at yet another blue sky.

He hugs me and I wince as he wraps his arms around my burned shoulder. His clothes are damp with sweat.

"Fancy some pancakes?" he asks into my ear. My gaze drops to the tiles next to the sink and I squint down for a long time at the silvery slither of skin before I realize what it is: a little piece of me on the floor.

"Sounds lovely," I say.

While Theo makes us breakfast, I sit in the window, drinking a cup of tea.

"Wanna go to the park today?" I ask.

"Can't," he says, deftly flipping a pancake in the air, "I'm seeing my mother."

"Oh, okay."

"Sorry I didn't ask," says Theo. "I assumed you'd be writing." That's half-true.

"I finished that story, actually," I say.

Just then, Lena emerges from the door across the way. She's wearing loose white trousers and a pale blue blouse. Even from here I know it's the same color as her eyes.

"Well done!" says Theo.

"For what?"

I don't take my eyes off Lena, who's putting her suitcase in the back of a taxi now.

"Finishing the story." Theo laughs.

"Oh. Yeah. Thanks. Would you like to read it?"

"Sure! Later," he says. "Lemon and sugar?"

Lena's opening the passenger door. She's about to get inside. I want to call out to her. I want her to look up. And with that, as though sensing me somehow, she does, and I smile.

Lena waves to me and I wave back, but instead of getting in the car, she hesitates. Still staring up at me, she waits, and I know exactly what she's waiting for.

I could go, I think. *I could go with her and leave all this, leave everything up till now right where it is.*

I see us, Lena and me, lazing in the cool, quiet dawn of languid summer nights. The soft, sweet taste of one another and the dregs of some cheap, pink wine. Me writing the story of my life so far and she by my side for the rest of it.

"Hey," says Theo, placing a hand on my shoulder.

I look up at him, a little startled and suddenly aware of the tears in my eyes.

"Are you all right?" he asks, but I can't speak so I just nod. Theo touches my face softly and looks at me like he's searching for something. Then he kisses me on the forehead and hands me a plate of pancakes.

"Thank you," I say, and when I look back out the window, she's gone.

splinter

✦

I DON'T REGRET MOVING to London.

When I got here, I moved into the flat Theo was sharing with his friend Isaac. They both studied accounting at uni and had been living together in what Isaac unironically referred to as the "Lad Pad" since Theo left Dublin eight months earlier. The estate agency described the flat as "rustic but cozy"; there was mold growing in the kitchen—which also functioned as the living and dining rooms—and Theo's bedroom was so small that the door wouldn't open fully without hitting the edge of his bed, the only item of furniture in the room.

We'd been seeing one another in Dublin for more than half a year when Theo was offered a job in London with a salary too good to turn down. The plan was always for me to follow him when I could, but I'm not sure Isaac ever really believed that that would happen; apparently, he tried to set Theo up with a number of women during our time apart, usually in the form of a surprise double date, and always with girls who claimed they "weren't looking for anything serious." Theo would call and tell me about whatever awkward situation Isaac had got him into that week, and we'd laugh it off together. Harmless mischief, what a cheeky chappy, et cetera. But it got old fast.

Isaac "chooses to remain single," he says, "because you get way more pussy playing the field." It's true, you certainly get a wider variety of pussy that way, but I suppose it depends on whether you want quality or quantity. Personally, I'd take quality any day, but Isaac clearly favors the latter.

I had built him up in my mind as some kind of heartthrob and was surprised to find that he was in fact an average-looking twenty-five-year-old with a trust fund, a signed copy of *The Game*, and what Theo and I lovingly called "the sex light"—a red bulb in a cheap plastic lampshade, which Isaac claims can "get any woman in the mood." In the two months I lived with Isaac he did sleep with a lot of women, but it's impossible to tell whether they did so because of his sex light or their low standards. I met one of them the next morning over a bowl of cereal but I didn't have the heart to ask. Nice girl, actually. Quite pretty. And she put the milk back in the fridge when she was done, which is more than I can say for Isaac.

The rest of Theo's uni friends are friendly enough; they're all extremely rich and a bit aimless—none of them quite knows what to do with their art history or social sciences degree—and the first question every one of them asked me was what university I went to, but they're a fun bunch and they've made me feel welcome. I know that's less to do with me and more to do with the fact that they idolize Theo—any friend of his is a friend of theirs and all that—but I think they're also the kind of friends who would tell him if they thought he was making a massive mistake, and to my knowledge none of them have done that, with the exception of Isaac, of course, who we've already established is a bit of a twat.

I first met them all the week after I moved here, at a charity event hosted by Theo's university; a gang of wealthy alumni had been invited back to have their pockets picked for a new library or science lab or some such, and most of Theo's class were there. I was being introduced to Kara, James, and Trinny when we were interrupted by Isaac. He had brought a date but seemed more interested in flaunting her in front of everyone than actually speaking to her. I noticed Trinny in particular grow increasingly uncomfortable with this embarrassing display, and after ten minutes of polite but strained small talk, she excused herself to go to the bathroom. I offered to go with her, not because I needed to go but because anything was better than staying there with Isaac. Or so I thought; we'd barely made it a few steps before we were accosted by Gemma.

"Incoming," muttered Trinny as Gemma approached, arms outstretched, head tilted precariously to one side. I was being assaulted by air kisses before I had time to register what Trinny had said.

"So good of you both to come," bellowed Gemma, as though she were hosting the event herself. "I'm thrilled you could make it."

"Hi, Gemma," said Trinny, throwing me a look that said, *Run, save yourself.*

But it was too late.

"You must be Theo's new beau," said Gemma. She spoke without ever really opening her mouth and dragged out every vowel sound to an excruciating degree.

"We were just on our way to the bathroom, actually," said Trinny, but Gemma ignored her and continued speaking directly to me.

"What a lovely dress. Very . . . *daring*."

I was wearing a long-sleeved, plunge-neck gown, which I'd bought especially for that night, knowing I'd be introduced to all of Theo's posh mates. I'd kept the tags on and was praying that nobody noticed.

"Thanks," I said. "I like yours too."

"What, this old thing?"

Gemma lightly brushed the gold sequins on what was clearly a new designer dress and tried to feign humility.

"You know, I used to live with Theo," said Gemma.

Trinny sighed and folded her arms, like a woman accepting her fate.

"Is that so?" I asked.

"Mmm, for three months. In Vienna."

"We all lived together on sabbatical there," Trinny explained. "Seven of us. In a big house."

"We had the best time," said Gemma, staring intently at me. "We'd all watch movies together and study late into the night, and on weekends we threw the most amazing parties. Didn't we, Trin?"

Trinny nodded but said nothing.

"Theo was a bit of a 'player' back then, as I recall." Gemma actually did the air quotes.

"He wasn't that bad," Trinny interjected.

"Oh, stop! He brought a new girl home every week!"

Gemma searched my face for a reaction. A moment passed.

"Lucky them," I said.

Trinny smirked and Gemma forced out a laugh that sounded uncannily like a machine gun firing.

"Lucky them indeed," she said, "although I'm sure he's changed now, of course. And I'm sure he's a better housemate too! God, he was such a mess back then, wasn't he, Trin?" Trinny nodded.

"He never washed the dishes. Not once!" said Gemma.

"Well, he always washes the dishes for me," I said, smiling sweetly.

Gemma smiled back. Nobody spoke. It was a Mexican smile-off.

"I'm absolutely bursting," said Trinny finally, grabbing me by the wrist and dragging me off toward the toilets.

"It was lovely to meet you, Gina," I called back over my shoulder.

"Gemma," she corrected. I knew.

Trinny and I chatted to one another's reflections in the bathroom mirror as we reapplied our makeup and recovered from whatever the hell that was.

"Is she one of Theo's exes?" I asked.

"Hardly. They just slept together a few times."

"Oh."

"Don't worry," she said, "his real exes won't speak to you; they'll just throw daggers from across the room."

Theo told me he'd had a few flings in college, but that none of them had ended well; they all turned out to be crazy bitches, apparently. He hadn't spoken to any of them since.

"I noticed a few filthy looks being thrown my way, all right," I said, trying to make light of it. Trinny clearly sensed my unease. She lowered her lipstick and leveled a no-nonsense look at me.

"Look. He was a bit of a slut back then," she said. "But every guy goes through a phase like that. Just be glad Theo's done with his."

"I suppose," I said.

"I don't know how you did it, but you've . . . tamed him. That boy is clearly besotted with you."

"Really?"

"Really!" said Trinny. "He hasn't shut up about you since that bloody Christmas party last year."

"He told you about that?"

"In agonizing detail."

Trinny gave me a withering look, then resumed applying her lipstick.

"And you look gorgeous, by the way," she added through taut-ened lips. "I wish I could pull off a dress like that."

"Thank you," I said. "Yours is beautiful, though."

Trinny is a willowy, flat-chested girl who looks like she might at any moment be cast in an adaptation of a Jane Austen novel.

Her dress that night was considerably more conservative than mine, but nonetheless stunning.

"Did you two ever . . . ?" I began, hoping I wouldn't need to go on.

Trinny seemed confused at first; then she cracked up laughing.

"Me and Theo? Ugh! No!" she said, screwing up her face. "No offense, it's just, he's like an annoying little brother."

"Got it," I said, smiling. I had made a friend. More than that, I had made an ally.

"Speaking of slutty men, what's up with Isaac?" I asked.

Trinny rolled her eyes.

"We used to be together."

Suddenly his disgustingly macho behavior tonight made sense.

"What happened?" I asked.

"One day he just ended it. Said he was wasting his twenties on me."

I sucked in air through clenched teeth.

"It's pretty obvious he's just trying to fill a hole," I said.

"From what I can tell, he's filling many, many holes," she said, before throwing her lipstick back in her purse and clicking it shut.

"Men are idiots."

"Agreed," said Trinny, "but not your man—you got a good one."

She was right, I thought, Theo was a good man, and I was nothing like those crazy bitches he'd dated in college. What we had was different. What we had was lasting.

Trinny and I headed back out to the party and Theo lit up when he saw us.

"There's my angel now!" he said, slipping an arm around my waist and planting a kiss on my cheek.

"For the love of God, Theo, she was only gone five minutes," said Trinny.

"Well, I missed her."

Trinny looked at me as though to say, *I told you so.*

I spent the rest of the night on Theo's arm, sipping champagne and being introduced to old friends and college professors, every one of whom spoke about him with great affection and inevitably told me some embarrassing anecdote or other before commenting on my appearance and/or heritage. The professors in particular liked to refer to me in the third person even though I was right in front of them.

"She's a beauty," said Theo's business professor, a boisterous, silver-haired man by the name of Hayworth.

"She speaks too!" I said with a broad smile.

"Oh, and feisty," said Hayworth. "That's Irishwomen for you."

We all laughed but I could feel Theo cringing internally, so I decided to add some fuel to the fire.

"I come from a long line of feisty Irishwomen, sir," I said. "In fact, I'm pretty sure I'm related to Queen Maeve herself!"

"Is that so?"

As a foreigner, you can tell English people pretty much anything about your culture or upbringing and they'll believe it. Even clever old professors.

"Well, you've certainly landed on your feet there," Hayworth said to Theo. "Mind you, you always did land on your feet."

He nudged me with one elbow and said, "This young fellow once snuck out of a fourth-floor window to go to a disco!"

As Theo ushered me away to our next encounter, he took my glass of champagne away.

"No more of that for you," he said jokingly. "And stop lying to my professors."

I was giggling uncontrollably. "But he lied to me!"

"About what?" demanded Theo.

"You climbing out a fourth-floor window!"

"Fine," said Theo, handing me back my drink. "It was a ground-floor window. But it gets higher every time he tells that bloody story."

I behaved myself for the rest of the night; I laughed at every joke—even the offensive ones—I didn't curse once, and I only lied a few more times.

We got home at two a.m. Understandably, Isaac's date had chosen to leave halfway through the evening, and as soon as we got in the door, he skulked off to his room, switched the sex light off, and went to sleep. Theo and I reheated some leftover curry and stayed up watching TV for hours, curled up together on the sofa in our formalwear. It reminded me of our early days in Dublin, cocooned indoors for days.

It was getting light out when we went to bed, shuffling around each other in Theo's tiny room, trying to get undressed.

Theo unzipped my dress and kissed me on the back of the neck.

"Tonight was perfect," he whispered. "You're perfect."

I smiled and turned to kiss him, then unbuttoned his shirt. As he pulled his arm out of one sleeve he banged his elbow on the wall, then almost shouted "Fuck!" but caught himself and mimed it instead so as not to wake Isaac. I covered my mouth to stifle a laugh.

"We need to move," he said, rubbing his elbow and frowning.

A few weeks later we had our own place—twice the rent and only slightly bigger in size. It wasn't perfect but it was ours, and the freedom was glorious; I no longer had to get dressed to go to the toilet in the middle of the night, or keep quiet during sex, or worry about finding milk curdling on the counter.

Every morning and evening Theo and I traveled to and from work together—I'd spent months searching for jobs at London-based magazines, newspapers, and publishing houses to no avail, and in the end Theo had wrangled me a job writing press releases for the company he worked for. The accounts department was based in a different building from my team, so we didn't see one another all day, but sometimes we'd eat lunch in Soho Square together if the weather was good.

I abhor press releases; they are the very antithesis of what I want to write—soulless, exploitative, forgettable nonsense—but it turns out I'm really very good at them. The job was supposed to be temporary, of course, but within months I was promoted and given my own client list. I began attending weekly strategy meetings, where phrases like "up and to the right," "move the needle," and "negative growth" were commonplace. I soon learned it was not possible to simply "talk" to one's clients: one must always "reach out," "touch base," "take it offline," or of course, "push back," if need be.

It was in one of these meetings that I met Maya, who had just joined the company that week. We locked eyes during a particularly painful presentation from our boss, Chetna, and in an instant we were both twelve-year-old schoolgirls again, desperately trying not to lose our shit at some dumb thing our teacher just said. I believe it was the phrase "next-generation mission-critical sweet spot" that finally broke Maya. She tried to disguise her laughter as a deep, hacking cough, but her efforts were in vain. When Chetna asked what was so amusing, Maya told her she'd just remembered a funny meme she'd seen earlier. I had to bite down on the inside of my cheeks to keep from laughing.

"What a pile of wank," said Maya on our way out the door. These were her first words to me.

As it transpired, Maya had been given the vacant desk next to mine, but after two weeks sitting beside one another, she was moved to the other end of the department—Chetna said our "constant banter was causing a disruption." Our colleagues couldn't believe we had actually been separated like a pair of kids in class, but Maya and I were secretly quite proud of it. From then on we spent most of our days messaging over the company's internal chat system. You could tell when we were doing this because our laughter alternated back and forth across the department like a tennis match.

My favorite-ever interaction, which I have since printed out and framed as a birthday gift to Maya, was the following:

11:53 A.M. **MAYA:** I just farted

11:53 A.M. **ME:** ok

11:53 A.M. **MAYA:** But I'm wearing headphones so I
can't tell if anyone heard

11:53 A.M. **ME:** oh

11:53 A.M. **MAYA:** I'm gonna take them off and do it
again to check

11:53 A.M. **ME:** good idea

11:54 A.M. **MAYA:** yeah they heard

My birthday present from her that year was a voucher for a ten-week writing course, which she and Theo pitched in on. They gave it to me over dinner one night.

"We don't want you to forget how good you are," said Theo as he handed the envelope across the table to me. He had already treated me to the best birthday on record, so I wasn't expecting a dinner or any more gifts.

"You're too fucking good for press releases, that's for sure," added Maya. The mixture of thoughtfulness and practicality was almost too much to bear. I looked at her with tears in my eyes and instantly she began to cry. Her new boyfriend, Darren, stared on as we held one another and half laughed, half cried into each other's hair.

"You'll be seeing a lot more of this if you decide to stick around," I said to him over her shoulder, "so you'd best get used to it."

Darren did stick around, and after that the four of us started spending more and more time together; we even held our first Fakemas that winter, before heading home for the holidays.

Maya and Theo cooked a turkey with all the trimmings, and I tried to bake a pudding from scratch but failed miserably and was relegated to keeping everyone's drink topped up. We all returned to London several days later, exhausted from having spent a short amount of time with our respective relatives and happy to be back with our chosen family instead.

On New Year's Eve we snuck up to the roof of our apartment building and downed innumerable bottles of Tesco Finest's champagne as fireworks exploded in the distance, illuminating the cluttered expanse of rooftops and chimneys that stretched out before us. For the first time since leaving Ireland I felt tethered to a time and place, like a ship moored to shore.

Sometime in late January, Theo and I were walking to Trinny's house for a games night when he got a call from his mother. It was a bitingly cold day, and I remember he had to take one glove off to answer the phone. The instant he did I could hear Jocelyn wailing on the other end. I couldn't make out what she was saying, but the pitch and cadence reminded me of the desperate, agonized sound my nieces made when they'd badly hurt themselves or had a precious toy stolen from them. I placed a hand on Theo's arm and searched his face for a clue as to what was wrong, but he just took my hand in his and kept walking.

By the time we arrived at Trinny's almost twenty minutes later, Theo was still clutching the phone to his ear, his bare hand shriveled and turning bright red from the cold. When Trinny answered the door he walked straight inside and sat down on the stairs.

"It's okay, Mum," he said into the phone. "It'll be okay."

Trinny silently asked me what was going on but I just

shrugged, so she hugged me and left us alone in the hallway, cutting off the sound of chatter from the living room as she closed the door softly behind her. I sat down next to Theo and rested my head on his shoulder for a while.

"Listen, Mum," he said, "I'm at my friend's house now, so I need to go." A pause.

"Trinny."

A pause.

"Probably not tonight, but I'll come home in the morning, okay? We can go and see her together." A final, long pause.

"Okay. See you tomorrow, Mum."

As soon as Theo put the phone down I took his frozen hand and sandwiched it between mine, rubbing it gently and breathing hot air onto his fingers to thaw them out. I waited for him to speak first.

"My gran's been moved to a nursing home," he said finally. Theo's grandmother Augusta had been living alone since her husband passed away more than a decade ago.

"What happened?" I asked, still bracing myself for bad news. "Is she okay?"

"Yeah, she's fine. Just getting old and forgetful, I think."

"Right."

I couldn't believe it. Based on what I'd just heard, I was convinced that Jocelyn had found Augusta dead at the bottom of the stairs, or at the very least that she herself was standing in a pool of blood somewhere with one of her own limbs hanging off.

"Well," I said, "I'm glad your gran's all right."

Theo dropped his head and began rubbing his temples with

his free hand, something I'd only ever seen him do after speaking to his mother.

"Jocelyn seemed pretty upset," I said, careful not to sound judgmental.

"Of course she's upset. Everything is different now. She can't just walk round the corner and see her mum anymore. She'll have to visit her in a nursing home, which is a forty-minute drive away, and full of strangers, and it's not cheap either. Where are they gonna get the money from?"

I'd never heard him speak like this before. He was parroting his mother. Even the tone of his voice sounded more like her than him.

"How do you feel?" I asked.

"What do you mean?"

"That would be funny if it weren't so sad," I said with a sympathetic smile, but he just looked at me quizzically.

"I mean how do *you* feel? Are you okay?"

"Oh. I'm fine. Just worried about Mum."

"Of course," I said. "But she'll be all right. She'll adjust. And so will your gran. Augusta's a tough old bird."

He lifted his head then and rested his forehead against mine. I could sense the tension drain from him a little.

"This is probably for the best," I continued. "She was living in that rickety old house all by herself. It's better that she move out now than wait for something bad to happen."

"You're right," said Theo. "Thank you."

I took his face in my hands and kissed him lightly on the forehead.

"Now let's go play silly games and forget about the real world for a bit," I said.

"Good plan," he said, standing up and helping me to my feet.

We were a great team that night. We always were. So much so that after we'd won five games of charades in a row, Trinny split us up and made us captains of opposing teams. She insisted we were using some kind of secret code.

"We can't help it if we're really good at charades," protested Theo.

"Nobody is *that* good at charades," Trinny replied.

"I am," I said. "I was the Irish charades champion three years in a row."

Trinny looked at Theo skeptically.

"No way," she said.

"It's true," said Theo. "She competed internationally."

Trinny's head whipped back toward me as a big, goofy grin spread across her face.

"Really?"

"Really," I said, dramatically staring off into the middle distance. "I'd be world champion now if those blasted Russians hadn't slipped a laxative in my drink . . ."

Theo nodded solemnly.

"I still can't believe you shat yourself onstage," he said wistfully.

At this everyone in the room started chuckling, except for Trinny, who threw her eyes to heaven and sighed.

"You're both banned from all future game nights," she said with a scowl, so I threw my arms around her and begged for forgiveness until she started laughing in spite of herself.

That night in bed, Theo drifted off with his head on my chest and me stroking his hair. I offered to go with him to visit his gran the next day, but he mumbled something about Jocelyn only wanting family there. Truth be told, I was relieved; as much as I wanted to support Theo, I also wanted to keep my distance from his mother, who remained the only difficult part of my life in London.

In the previous ten months or so everything had come together— Theo and I were happily cohabitating and still sickeningly in love, I'd made new friends and was getting along well with his, I was earning a decent wage doing a job that required minimum effort, I was writing again, and I'd even stopped taking sugar in my tea—my life felt like a jigsaw puzzle where all the pieces magically fall into place, and Jocelyn was the one piece that just wouldn't fit.

I'd finally met Jocelyn on a trip to London one weekend, when I was still living in Dublin. I was delighted, of course, taking it as a sign that our relationship had just leveled up, but I was also scared shitless; I stopped several times on the walk from the Tube station to her house just to gather myself. I kept asking Theo if he was sure this was a good idea. What if she didn't like me? What if she hated me? What if I blocked up her toilet? Or accidentally mentioned the IRA? Or said the word "cunt" a bunch of times?

These all seemed like very reasonable concerns at the time.

I didn't know much about Theo's family then. He'd been reticent about them—about his father in particular—and being someone who understands what it's like to not want to talk about your own father, I never forced the issue. What I did know I had pieced together from fragments of conversations: his mother came from a wealthy family but her brothers had lost a lot of money on bad investments. She married young and had two children—Theo and his older sister, Octavia, who moved abroad when she was twenty-one. Theo's father was an aggressive drug addict who left when Octavia was nine and Theo was only six years old, and aside from a few compulsory visits as a child, Theo hadn't seen him since. As it happened, Theo's father also cheated on Jocelyn with an Irishwoman, and Theo had often joked about how much his mother hates the Irish as a result. Suddenly this sprang to mind.

"You *were* joking about her hating Irish people, weren't you?" I asked, stopping for the fifth time on our short walk.

"Kind of," said Theo.

"Kind of?"

"She probably didn't mean it."

"Probably!?"

I have since found out that when Theo told his mother he was dating an Irish girl, she broke down in tears. Jocelyn told me this herself, as though it were a funny anecdote.

"Look," he said, taking my hand again, "I'm sure she will meet you and love you and everything will be fine."

He was right. Everything was fine that day. Jocelyn was warm and welcoming and I felt like a fool for ever worrying about her. Theo told me she loved gardening so I stopped one last time to buy her some pink peonies, which she planted in her flower bed while Theo and I drank tea on the patio. Afterward she gave me a tour of the garden, explaining which flowers and fruits and vegetables were planted where, and when each one would come into season. That day was perfectly pleasant, and we've never had another one like it.

The next time I saw Jocelyn was after I moved to London. On that visit she was so cold toward me that I wondered if I had only imagined our day in the garden. Since then, she has made a concerted effort to put me down—making snide remarks about my looks, my education, even the way I hold my knife and fork—delivering each blow with just enough force so that I feel it, but to everyone else it passes for a joke. She constantly references Theo's "other girlfriends," all of whom she seems to like more than me and all of whom, I'm sure, she treated with equal contempt while they dated her son. She even calls me by their names occasionally, always insisting afterward that she did so by mistake.

Assuming that Jocelyn no longer considered me good enough for Theo, I tried to counteract this by always looking my best around her and speaking pointedly about my ambitions and achievements. But that only made things worse: the term "glamorous" got thrown about like an insult, and as for my ambitions, Jocelyn views medicine, law, and whatever job her son is currently doing as the only worthwhile professions. Writing, she says, is for children in school.

I once asked about her favorite books and films and tried to make the point that they were all written by somebody, but she doesn't read books and "films are written by people in Hollywood," apparently, so that was the end of that talk.

* * *

Jocelyn states each one of her opinions as though it were a fact and seems not to understand the difference between the two, which makes it both impossible and pointless to try to reason with her.

All the while she dotes on Theo, calling him every day, insisting he bring his laundry home to be washed, and even cutting the crusts off his sandwiches—I wouldn't have believed this last one if I hadn't seen it with my own eyes. I personally find her particular brand of love a bit suffocating, but Theo seems to like it. We accept the love we're used to, I suppose.

Things came to a head one evening after a family dinner at Theo's aunt's house. We were all sitting around watching the news when a report came on about a lesbian couple who had been attacked on their way home from a nightclub. The woman being interviewed had a black eye and stitches in her bottom lip, and her girlfriend was still in the hospital in critical condition.

"Pair of lezzers," Jocelyn muttered under her breath.

Maybe the family didn't hear her. Maybe they were just pretending not to. Either way, I couldn't let it slide.

"What was that, Jocelyn?" I asked.

"Nothing," she mumbled, sipping from a can of cider.

A few moments passed and the report concluded with an appeal for any witnesses to come forward.

"I think it's really sad that those women were attacked," I prodded, "don't you?"

"Jesus," said Jocelyn, "it's not like I attacked them!" Then she drained the rest of the can and went to the kitchen to get an-other. Once she'd left the room Theo threw me a reproachful look, as though *I* was the one who had behaved inappropriately. When I tried to talk to him about it afterward he said there was nothing to talk about.

I realized two things that night. Firstly, that Jocelyn is the worst kind of working-class conservative—a common bully who fears what she can't understand, blames everyone else for her problems, and simultaneously believes that she is both oppressed by and better than everybody else—and secondly, that when asked to side with his mother or his girlfriend, a man will always choose his mother, no matter how awful or irrational she is. Joc-elyn's behavior was normal to Theo, like a dark spot in his vision that he was accustomed to looking past.

After that, I decided to stop calling Jocelyn out on her bullshit. I would be quiet and excruciatingly kind. I would give her noth-ing to grip on to. And she'd be left scrambling for purchase, like a rock climber on a perfectly smooth wall. Eventually, I thought, she would go too far and Theo would see what I saw, but until then, I would spend as little time with her as possible, in order to reduce the probability of an altercation.

So far, my plan had been working quite well.

When Theo returned from seeing his gran the next evening, he was surprisingly upbeat. He talked to me while I got dinner ready, telling me all about Augusta's nice private room in the nursing home, and the lovely staff there, and how well she was being looked after. I was relieved to hear it had all worked out for the best. And then he announced that he wanted us to move into her empty house.

"Oh?" I said, my hand freezing in midair as I lifted a spoonful of broccoli from pot to plate.

"Yeah," he said. "My mum says we can move in straightaway."

I had only been to his grandmother's house once, for her ninetieth birthday party. It was a massive detached house with four bedrooms and an enormous garden, and it was probably worth a small fortune, but it was also absolutely filthy and falling apart; the place hadn't seen so much as a lick of paint in decades. It would take a lot of time and money to clear it out and make it livable again, and even then, it would still be just around the corner from Jocelyn's house, which was really my main concern.

"I thought you were happy here," I said.

"I am," said Theo, "but we'd only be paying half the rent we pay here."

"To your mother?" I asked.

"Yes, of course."

Even with my back to Theo I could tell he was perturbed; he'd come home excited to tell me about this and he expected me to be excited too.

"So she'd be our landlord?"

"I suppose so, yeah," he said.

I handed him his dinner and sat to the table to eat mine, moving slowly to buy myself time while I decided how to navigate this conversation; everything to do with his mother was a fucking minefield, but this time there were finances and heightened emotions involved too.

"Are you sure that's a good idea?" I asked.

"Why wouldn't it be?"

"Well, your mother is . . ." I began; then, realizing I couldn't call her a lunatic to his face, I stopped and rephrased. "I'm just not sure she's fully thought through all the pressures of being a landlord."

"She's not an idiot," he shot back.

"Of course not. It's just, she'd be responsible for sorting the house out and fixing anything that breaks, and it might be difficult to ask for those things from your own mother. It could get complicated is all I'm saying."

"My gran lived there just fine."

"Well, actually, she complained about the cold a lot," I said, "and she didn't really need the things we need. There's no shower. There's no wi-fi. There's no cable. Plus it's still full of her things. And everyone else's."

When Jocelyn moved out almost thirty years ago, she left her room in Augusta's house exactly as it was; clothes still in the wardrobe, sheets still on the bed. Her siblings had done the same, and after Theo's grandfather died, nobody went through his things or threw any of them away. Now that his gran had moved out, I just didn't believe that Jocelyn would deal with it all—she couldn't even take care of her own house, in which there was an entire bedroom full of old clothes and toys and stacks of dusty, yellow newspapers. The room, like her behavior, was another very obvious problem that we all pretended not to see.

"You're so pessimistic," he said.

"No, I'm realistic."

"Well, realistically, we can't keep pissing money away on rent. We've got to start saving if we want to buy somewhere."

"You want to buy somewhere?" I asked. In hindsight, this was the moment I got derailed.

"Eventually, yeah."

"With me?"

"Yes, of course with you." He laughed.

"And then what?" I asked.

"What?"

"Then what happens?"

"Well," said Theo, "I kind of figured we'd spend our whole lives together. If it's all the same to you."

"Oh."

I suppose in every relationship an assumption is made at some point that you're in it for the long haul. I'm not sure at what point Theo and I made this assumption, but suddenly it was clear that it had been made.

"Okay," I said.

"Okay, then."

I agreed to go see the house. That was all I agreed to. But somehow one viewing turned into three viewings and the next thing I knew we were deciding where the desk would go. Theo's enthusiasm was infectious and he painted such a pretty picture of the life we'd have there that I couldn't help but be excited for it too— the spare room for guests to stay over, the dinner parties we'd throw for our friends, the summer afternoons we'd spend lounging in the garden. There was still the delicate matter of Jocelyn, of course, but Theo assured me he would handle it, and handle it he did; on our fourth and final viewing, Jocelyn joined us on a tour of the house while Theo asserted our list of demands. Jocelyn hemmed and hawed over one or two things but ultimately agreed to give us everything we'd asked for—including wi-fi and an electric shower—and while she couldn't clear out the whole house, she said she would have everything boxed up and stored in two of the bedrooms out of our way. She seemed uncharacteristically capable and cooperative—she even hugged me on the way out—and once again I found myself questioning my own sanity; had she really been that bad before, or had I been oversensitive?

On the train home, Theo told me he that he'd had a quick word with her about respecting our privacy.

"How did that go?" I asked.

"She got a little bit upset," he said. "But I explained that she was welcome to come and visit; she just can't pop round anytime she likes. And she can't let herself in without notice."

"And?"

"And she was totally fine with it. All of it. She says she's going to ring the plumber about the shower today. And she'll sort out the wi-fi tomorrow."

"Wow," I said. "Maybe I underestimated her."

"I think you two just got off on the wrong foot," said Theo, acknowledging for the first time that there had ever been a problem. "It's nice to see you getting along now."

It was nice, actually. It felt like the last piece of the puzzle had finally clicked into place. The train rattled along for a little while before Theo spoke again.

"Look, I know I'm asking a lot," he blurted. "You already

moved to another country for me and you just got settled and now I'm making you move again. And I know this isn't exactly your dream home. And, yeah, I know my mother can be difficult. But just give it eighteen months. Eighteen months of saving and we can afford a deposit on our own place, and maybe you can quit your job and write. I know that's what you want to do. And I want to help you do it."

He was talking so fast I could barely take it all in.

"Theo, it's okay," I said, placing a hand on his leg. He took my hand in his and looked me in the eye with such sincerity that I was sure he was about to crack a joke.

"But I want you to know how much I love and appreciate you," he said, squeezing my hand. "I love you so fucking much that . . . it's not very nice sometimes. It's horrible, actually. I think about losing you and it's like someone's standing on my chest. You could break me. If you wanted to. You could absolutely fucking break me."

It was as if he had only now, in this moment, come to this realization.

"Sometimes," I said softly, brushing his hair back away from his eyes, "I love you so much that I want to bash in your skull with a blunt instrument." He nodded.

"Same."

We both sat back in our seats and didn't speak for a minute while the train chugged noisily through a tunnel. When we emerged on the other side, daylight flooded the carriage and I turned to look at Theo.

"Eighteen months," I said, extending my hand.

"Eighteen months," he said, shaking it.

*   *   *

When moving day came, I stood in the doorway of our empty flat and sobbed; I had never wanted to stay in a place I was forced to move out of before and it felt strange and unfinished, like breaking up with someone you're still in love with.

Theo gave me as much time as he could, but there was a man named Gregor waiting outside with a van full of our stuff and he was charging us by the hour. Before we shut the door for the last time, Theo pulled me into him, letting my body lean against his. Then, with my head resting in the hollow of his chest, Theo promised me that everything would be fine. He held my hand the whole way to his gran's house too, the pair of us squished into the front seat next to Gregor, and he even made all the necessary small talk on my behalf, knowing that I wasn't in the mood.

Jocelyn was waiting for us when we arrived. She helped Gregor reverse into the drive, then immediately started helping him to unload boxes from the back of the van. From the sounds of it, she'd been working tirelessly to get the house ready for us and I couldn't wait to see it. She handed us the keys she'd had cut for us both and Theo let us into our new home.

When we stepped inside I looked around and felt my stomach turn; the house was almost exactly as we'd left it a month ago. It was tidier; the kitchen had been cleaned and the whole place had been hoovered, but none of the family's belongings had been moved. Everywhere I looked I saw the detritus of someone else's life, filling every cupboard and drawer and covering every single surface. The place was completely cluttered with old furniture, half of which was riddled with woodworm, and while the doorframes and skirting boards had been painted, whatever cowboys Jocelyn had hired to do the job hadn't sanded down the old, flaking paintwork—they'd just painted over it. They also hadn't bothered to paint behind any of the furniture, so if you moved anything you'd find a filthy patch of skirting board behind it.

Jocelyn was prattling on about the boiler but I couldn't listen to her. My brain was scrambling for an answer, as though maybe I had missed something, or misunderstood. What had she been doing this whole time?

Theo could clearly sense my distress. He placed a hand on my shoulder and was about to speak when I spoke first.

"I'm just going to the bathroom," I said. I needed to be alone. I needed to think.

Upstairs I walked straight to the back bedrooms where everything was supposed to be stored and found only a small stack of boxes in one; this was the extent of Jocelyn's clearout. In Augusta's room the bed had been removed to make way for our own bed, but otherwise her belongings were just as she'd left them, strewn about as though at any moment she might come back and have need of them. Every room was the same, filled with the possessions of people long gone. It was more like a tomb than a home.

My breath was starting to speed up. I could feel my hands grow clammy and a wave of heat begin to crawl across the back of my neck. I hadn't felt this way in so long that the mere possibility of a panic attack, after all this time without one, was enough to send me spiraling straight into one.

Theo came running up the stairs behind me. He seemed flustered.

"Have you been to the toilet yet?" he asked.

"No, why?"

"Don't freak out," he said.

"What?"

"She just told me," he said, but before he could finish I stormed off into the bathroom. There was a gaping hole in the wall above the bath and exposed pipes sticking out.

"Where's the shower?" I asked. I could barely breathe, but panic wasn't an option. I had to focus. I needed to think.

"It's not finished."

"No shit," I snapped.

"There's no need to get angry," Theo said calmly. How was he so calm?

"Isn't there?"

We were both speaking in a hushed but urgent manner.

"Look," he said, "I know this isn't ideal—"

"Ideal!?"

"I'm upset too."

"Good," I said, "you should be. This is pretty fucking upsetting."

"We'll sort it out. I promise. But right now we need to unload the van."

"No. No way," I said, sitting on the edge of the bath, half in protest and half because I thought I might pass out.

"Angel, please—"

"Don't you dare angel me right now."

"Okay," he said, hunkering down to be on my level. "Breathe. Please. Just breathe."

He breathed slowly, as though to remind me how it's done, and I looked into his eyes until I could breathe in unison with him.

"There," he said, very gently. "That's good. Really good."

I nodded.

"Now, I understand why you're upset. But the thing is, we have to bring the boxes in."

My eyes widened but he kept talking before I could interrupt.

"We don't have to unpack. But it's raining. And the movers need to go. So let's just bring everything in; then we can figure this out. Together."

He was right. As much as I hated to admit it. As much as I wanted to tell Jocelyn to shove this fucking crypt up her arse and leave here forever, Theo's plan was somewhat more logical.

Once we'd brought everything inside, Theo sat Jocelyn down in the living room and asked her why she'd lied to us about the place being ready.

"I already told you, Theodore, the shower will be sorted in a few weeks," she said. "The guy took my money and never came back."

Where was she finding these people?

"All right," said Theo, rubbing his temples with his fingertips, "but it's not just about the shower, is it?"

"What do you mean?" she asked, all innocent, like butter wouldn't fucking melt.

"I mean, there's nowhere for us to put our things, Mum. The place is full to the brim and we have all this to unpack."

He swept one hand across the room, highlighting the dozens of boxes we'd just brought in. There were more filling the kitchen and hallway.

"Well, how was I to know you had so much stuff?" she spat indignantly.

Theo looked at me. I said nothing. I was literally biting my tongue.

"Of course we have stuff," he said. "We had an apartment together. It was full of stuff. And, generally speaking, you take your stuff with you when you move."

"Don't patronize me," she said.

"I'm not patronizing you."

"Well, I don't like your tone!"

Theo took a deep breath before replying. I couldn't believe how calm he was; this was the second time today he'd had to keep his cool for the sake of an emotional woman, and while I knew on some level my distress had been warranted, seeing him having to handle his mother like this, I felt suddenly guilty for losing my shit earlier. None of this was his fault, after all.

"Mum," he continued, "it's quite simple. You said you would have the place ready for us. You said you would clear it out. And you haven't."

She started to tear up. I saw it. Theo saw it too.

"It's okay," he said. "Nobody's angry with you. We just need to figure out how we're going to sort this out. Otherwise we might have to find another place."

There it was. Our only bargaining tool. Jocelyn suddenly

snapped to attention, her eyes darting to Theo and fixing on his face. She looked like a child afraid of being punished.

"There's no need to be like that, Theodore," she said, tears spilling down her face now. "I tried. I just couldn't do it all myself. The gutter fell off last week and I didn't know what to do."

"Bloody hell," said Theo.

Part of me wanted to run to her, to soothe and comfort her, to tell her everything would be all right. Another, much bigger part of me wanted to grab her by the shoulders and shake her so hard that her head whipped violently back and forth.

Snot was streaming out of her nose now. I had to look away.

"Why didn't you ask for help?" he asked. "Why did you tell me it was done if it wasn't?"

"I don't know," she bawled, wiping her nose with her sleeve. "I'm sorry."

There was no talking to her after that. She was inconsolable. And even though we were the ones who ought to be upset, she was the one being comforted. It made my blood boil.

Eventually Theo took her home and got her settled, then came back to find me sitting on the floor, staring at boxes. He was stuck firmly between a rock and a hard place and I felt for him, which is the only reason I didn't say, "I told you so." That, and I was too tired for a fight. He leaned in the doorway and looked down at me.

"Are you hungry?" he asked.

"Not really."

"You should eat."

"Okay."

"Pizza?"

"Fine."

We ordered pizza and ate it in silence. After that we dragged our mattress into the living room and I found the box with our sheets in it and made up a bed for us. Theo fell asleep within minutes. I was awake for most of the night.

By the time he woke up at nine a.m., I'd already been clearing out Augusta's bedroom for three hours. The wardrobes and drawers were all empty now, and every surface was clear; all that remained was a thick layer of dust, and the odd clean patch of wood here and there in the shape of whatever object I had removed: a hairbrush, a jewelry box, a porcelain pot from a long-dead plant. I heard Theo shuffling about downstairs, ripping boxes open; then came the blessed sound of a kettle boiling and a teaspoon clanging against the edge of a mug. When he came upstairs with two cups of tea, I accepted mine gratefully and we sat on the window ledge together, sipping quietly.

"Every cup of tea here tastes faintly of the Thames," I said.

"Just tastes like tea to me." He shrugged then said, "I didn't think you'd want to stay."

"I don't," I said, "but I spent hours looking for apartments last night and couldn't find a single decent one in our price range."

As I lifted my mug to my mouth, Theo noticed the haphazard bandage on my index finger; I'd been wiping dust off a shelf when a broken piece of wood tore through the cloth and stabbed me in the finger—I pulled out all I could but I suspected there was still a shard of wood lodged under the skin.

"What happened?" he asked.

"Just a splinter."

He nodded, then scanned the room.

"You've done a great job," he said. "I'll move those boxes into the other room now and then I'll help you finish cleaning in here."

"No," I said.

"No?"

"No, you're going to your mother's house to get the name and number of every person she's hired to install a shower or fix a gutter or set up wi-fi or whatever else needs doing. And then you're going to deal with them all yourself."

"Okay, boss," said Theo, smiling. "And what are you gonna do?"

"I'm going to sort this place out."

"By yourself?"

"No," I said. "I called my mam this morning. She was on her way to the airport before we even hung up. So she'll be here soon. Maya and Darren are on their way too."

Theo looked at me with wide eyes and I couldn't tell if he was angry or appreciative. He was probably embarrassed about everyone seeing the state of the house, or hearing about his mother's behavior, but either way he'd have to suck it up; I needed reinforcements.

"What will I tell my mum?" he asked.

"I don't care what you tell her," I said. "Just keep her out of my way."

Maya turned up that Saturday morning with two bags full of cleaning products and cloths. My mam arrived shortly after with a small suitcase containing only comfy work clothes and a pair of heavy-duty rubber gloves. Maya said she'd brought gloves for everyone but my mother insisted on using her own. The pair of them hit it off immediately.

We worked all weekend and by Sunday night the house was unrecognizable: anything we didn't need had been boxed and stored in the spare bedrooms or the garage; Darren finished painting the skirting boards; I hung all our framed pictures; we turned Jocelyn's old room into a cozy spare bedroom; and Augusta's room was now very much our room. I made sure to keep all the photographs of Theo's family dotted about the place, as well as any special items he was fond of, like his gran's serving dishes or his grandad Jim's leather armchair. The armchair was still nestled in the corner of the conservatory, Jim's favorite spot in the house, and next to it was a mahogany bureau full of his notebooks and ancient gardening magazines. I remember sitting on the floor, flicking through a fifty-year-old article about daffodils, and deciding to plant some in the garden this winter so that they'd bloom in spring. I caught myself making plans and smiled to myself.

We capped off the weekend with a late Sunday roast—which Theo cooked by way of thanks—and as the five of us sat down to eat, I realized our efforts that weekend had not only restored the house physically; they had imbued it with an intangible sense of home, the kind that comes not from a place itself, but from the people in it.

Theo and I returned to work on Monday morning and left my mother to relax back at the house. She called me at around three p.m. and the first words out of her mouth were, "Everything is fine," which meant something was terribly wrong.

"Jocelyn's here," she said. "She's going a bit ballistic."

"About what?" I asked—I honestly thought Jocelyn would be delighted when she saw what we'd done with the place.

"I don't know, love, she's not making much sense. But she's really pissed off. And I think she's been drinking."

"Jesus Christ," I said. "Are you okay?"

"Grand, yeah. Just speechless, to be honest."

If my own mother—whom we frequently call "Meryl" because of her Oscar-worthy histrionics—was rendered speechless by Jocelyn's display, it must have been quite the meltdown.

"Where is she now?" I asked.

"Upstairs. Going through the boxes we packed. She kept saying her things had been stolen. I told her it's all there, safe and sound, but she wouldn't listen."

"Right," I said, "I'm on my way. I'm so sorry about this."

It was the first time our mothers had met and I was mortified. My plan was to call Theo straightaway, but before I could dial his number I saw him come marching toward my desk, his face turning slowly purple.

"My mother just rang," he said.

"Yeah, so did mine."

By the time we got back to the house, Jocelyn had made a list of all the things she maintained had been stolen, and the only way to alleviate her fears was to empty out every single box until she had marked each item as present and accounted for. She was only doing this to flex her control over us, of course, but we went along with it. After that, she stalked restlessly about the house, silently selecting her next target. She kept mumbling under her breath, "Everything is different."

"We'll put everything back where it was when we move out," I said. "This is just temporary."

Jocelyn eyed me up and down skeptically.

"You did this," she said. "Why couldn't you just leave things the way they were?"

"Mum," said Theo, "it's not her fault. I thought you'd be glad we sorted the place out for you."

"She's no good for you, Theodore."

"That's enough!" Theo said, but Jocelyn wasn't listening to him; she was staring at the pictures I'd hung on the wall. "I didn't say you could hang those. Take them down right now."

"No," said Theo.

"Take them down!" she screamed.

"I think you should go home, Mum. I can't talk to you when you're like this."

Without warning, Jocelyn leaped at the wall, trying to remove the pictures herself. When Theo stepped in to stop her she shoved him out of her way. He stumbled backward and smacked his leg on the table.

"I SAID GO HOME!" he shouted.

"I AM HOME!" she roared like a petulant child.

"If you don't go, right now," said Theo, gathering himself, "I will leave and I will never come back."

And there it was again; the threat of losing her son was the only thing that kept Jocelyn in check, and while that was undoubtedly a pretty fucked-up dynamic, it worked; she went straight home and the next day, when Theo went to see her, she apologized profusely for the way she'd behaved. Theo told her that we'd stay—we had worked too hard on the house to leave it now—but he reiterated that one more outburst like that would mark the end of this arrangement.

Jocelyn kept her distance after that and we had a few months of relative peace and quiet. The shower was eventually installed and the gaping hole in the bathroom got tiled over. One by one things got sorted, although new problems presented themselves all the time. Jocelyn told us to pay for them ourselves and invoice her later, which we agreed to, and slowly but surely we settled in.

I was right about the splinter; weeks after we moved in I could still feel something under the surface of my skin, and I tried just about everything to get it out—I went at it with a needle and tweezers, I wrapped my finger in duct tape and ripped it off after half an hour, I even soaked the finger in baking soda overnight to try to draw out the splinter—but nothing worked, the skin had grown over it. I kept meaning to register with a doctor in the area but just hadn't got around to it, and then one night, when my finger swelled up and started oozing pus, Theo insisted on taking me to the hospital.

We waited for hours to be seen—I obviously wasn't a high priority—but eventually a doctor took me to a small examination room where she cut open my finger and pulled out a centimeter-long splinter.

"Congratulations," she said dryly, "it's a piece of wood."

She held it up with her tweezers and we both leaned in to look at it.

"Fucking hell," I said; then I immediately apologized for my language.

The doctor just laughed.

"Don't worry, I've heard worse," she said.

She stitched my finger up and sent me home with a course of antibiotics for the infection and a small test tube with my splinter inside, still covered in blood and resting on a piece of gauze. Theo gagged when he saw it.

When summer came we cut back all the overgrown plants and bushes in the garden and made a little haven for ourselves outside. On weekends, I'd sit on the patio and write while Theo lazed in his grandfather's old armchair and read the newspaper from cover to cover. Sometimes we'd have friends around for evenings in the garden; we'd eat and drink and play games, and soak up the balmy evening air till it got dark. Things felt almost normal for a while.

But winter brought with it a whole new set of problems; the pipes froze and burst and the garden needed to be dug up to fix them. Only the garden was frozen too, and for weeks nothing could be done about it. We soon discovered that the window frames had warped over time, leaving massive gaps between the wood and the glass, so that even with the central heating running constantly, it was impossible to keep the house warm. It was so cold that I could sometimes see my breath as I lay in bed at night. I hung heavy curtains in every room and sealed up all the gaps I could with insulation tape, but it still wasn't enough; the windows needed replacing.

Theo approached Jocelyn about all these things, but she had fallen back on old habits and was refusing to make any further changes to the house. I tried to stay out of it, but inevitably I wound up pestering Theo to sort things out; then he'd pester Jocelyn, she'd break down in tears, he'd end up comforting her, and it wouldn't get done. A few days later I'd pester him again, and round and round we went until he resented the both of us equally.

More and more, Jocelyn came around uninvited, always smelling of booze and always with some weak excuse like needing to borrow the vacuum or return a casserole dish. One time we got home to find her in our kitchen and she claimed she'd seen a burglar trying to break in.

"Why didn't you call the police?" I asked.

"I didn't think they'd get here on time," she replied.

Theo knew she was lying but I could tell he felt guilty anyway; she had changed tack once she realized her tantrums weren't getting her anywhere, and started projecting a sort of saccharine submissiveness instead. I found this emotional manipulation transparent and grotesque, but Theo fell for it, and as December rolled in, I sensed his resentment of me growing. After all, if Jocelyn was the victim now, then someone else must be the villain. We were fraying at the edges; I could feel it.

I found myself thinking about Christmas the previous year, how perfect and peaceful it all had been. I suggested that we host Fakemas again, knowing full well we could never re-create the magic of last year, but hoping, I suppose, that it might remind Theo how good we had been, how good we could be. We invited Maya and Darren to begin with; then Theo invited Isaac without realizing I'd already invited Trinny and her new boyfriend, so to avoid any awkwardness, we asked a few more people to come. Before we knew it we were throwing a full-blown party.

We decorated the tree the night before and hung decorations everywhere, and on the day of the party we baked tray after tray of mince pies and gingerbread biscuits. I piled them high on silver plates and dusted them with icing sugar, then we got to work on a huge pot of mulled wine. The whole house looked and smelled divine. Theo and I got ready together in the bedroom, dancing around to Christmas music, and by the time our guests started to roll in, we had reverted to a former version of ourselves.

"The place looks amazing!" shrieked Trinny as she took off her coat. Her new boyfriend, Flaubert, stood beside her, nodding his agreement. Darren and Maya arrived soon after, followed by our friends from work, then a bunch of Theo's uni mates, including Gemma—I wondered who had invited her. Isaac showed up late, drunk and with a noticeable lack of hot young model on his arm. After him came some friends from my writing class. They all brought extra red wine for mulling, which I was very grateful for, since we were already running low.

Theo and I circled the room introducing people—it was heartening to see the different factions mingling with one another—and occasionally handing out more food and drink. I noticed Theo seemed a little tense, but every time I tried to talk to him, one or the other of us would get distracted. At one point I saw him in the back garden talking to Gemma, who was laughing wildly at something Theo had just said. She shoved him playfully in the chest and left her hand resting there. Isaac caught me watching them.

"They used to fuck, you know," said Isaac far too loudly into my ear.

"I'm aware, thank you."

"Best sex of his life apparently," he added.

"She's also a—"

"Crazy bitch?" said Isaac, cutting me off. "Yeah, they all are once you're done with them."

I opened my mouth to speak but couldn't find any words.

Isaac held his hands up and shrugged.

"Just sayin'," he said.

I turned to leave and bumped into Trinny. She could tell I was upset.

"What's wrong?" she asked; then she noticed Theo and Gemma outside, and Isaac standing behind me, and she joined the dots herself.

"What did you say to her?" she demanded. For such a waifish woman, Trinny's voice really carries. People turned to look at us.

"Just dropping some truth bombs," said Isaac with a stomach-churning smirk.

"You're pathetic," she said.

"Hey, I'm not the one dating a tiny magician," said Isaac.

To be fair, Flaubert was quite short and had chosen to wear a shiny burgundy suit. Also his name was Flaubert. But he seemed like a nice guy in spite of all that.

"You're not *dating* anyone," said Trinny, stepping forward and glaring straight into Isaac's eyes. "You're mounting anything in sight and claiming to be happy about it. You love no one. And no one loves you back. You're a joke, Isaac. Only it's not even funny; it's just sad."

The room grew silent and still as Isaac stepped toward Trinny, squaring up to her almost. Theo appeared beside me. "Everything all right?" he asked, and without looking at him or anyone else, Isaac stomped out of the house, slamming the front door behind him.

Theo took me and Trinny to the kitchen for a debrief. He was shocked by Isaac's behavior, but he was the only one; everyone else was pissed off but unsurprised. Afterward, Theo pulled me aside and assured me he had absolutely no interest in Gemma.

"She does my bloody head in," he said. "There's a reason we never properly dated."

"I suppose."

I was still a little unsure. Isaac had a way of getting under my skin.

"Her laugh alone is enough to drive anyone mad," he added, and I smiled.

"It's like a machine gun," he said.

Around twenty minutes later, I was taking a bag of empty bottles out to the front garden when I found Isaac standing alone outside the house.

"I thought you'd left," I said.

"Sorry to disappoint," he sneered, angrily wiping his face with the back of his hand. He'd been crying. I leaned against the wall next to him and he rolled his eyes.

"Why do you hate me so much?" I asked. "Is this some kind of *Love Actually* thing? Are you gonna turn up with cue cards some night and tell me I'm perfect?"

Isaac scoffed.

"Is every one of your home movies just creepy close-ups of me?" I continued.

"Please shut up," he said.

"What then? You're angry I took your friend away?"

Isaac said nothing.

"You're angry I took your wingman away?"

Still nothing. He just stared at me, unimpressed.

"You're secretly in love with Theo!" I said, and Isaac rolled his eyes again.

"It's all right if you are, you know."

"Fuck's sake!" he snapped. "I'm not gay."

"Look, I know you're upset about Trinny . . ." I said, and at the mention of her name, a look of guilt swept across Isaac's face. Suddenly it dawned on me.

"Oh my God, you still love her."

"So?"

He said it so quickly and defensively that it almost made me laugh.

"So why did you break up with her?"

He shrugged.

"Brilliant," I said. "What's the plan, then? Keep acting like a prick around her till she falls back in love with you?"

"She was never in love with me."

"I wonder why," I said, and he just stared down at the ground.

"Sorry," I said, "that was mean."

"Don't you have a party to get back to?" he asked without looking at me.

"Yeah," I said, and I took a step toward the door.

"That's why you didn't bring a date tonight, isn't it?" I asked over my shoulder. "You were hoping Trinny would be here alone." Isaac looked up at me and I saw more honesty and vulnerability in that look than I ever thought him capable of. There was fear too, real, raw fear, and it reminded me of the way Jocelyn had looked at Theo when he threatened to move out.

Theo once told me that when he was offered his first job in Dublin—a well-paid accountancy job for a reputable company— Jocelyn turned her nose up at it and told him he should hold out for something better. This happened in the midst of an economic crisis, however, and Theo had been out of college for more than nine months already without a single offer, so he took the job in spite of her advice.

She refused to see him off at the airport, she said she was busy that day, then after he moved she would call him a lot— usually late at night and after a few drinks—to cry down the phone at him about how lonely she was. For days after these calls, Theo seemed completely dejected, and I would help as best I could to convince him that his mother's loneliness was not his fault. It was as though Jocelyn had poured all her problems into him and I was left to scoop them back out again.

Suddenly it was clear that, to Jocelyn, that job represented the same kind of unknown factor that I represent now: she doesn't see an opportunity for her son to thrive and be happy; she sees something that threatens to take him away from her. Back then, I was just some girl he was dating, not worth worrying about, but as soon as I moved to London to be with him, I became a threat.

Isaac was no different, I thought. They both held people back out of fear of being left behind, and when that didn't work they lashed out, desperate for any kind of attention. I wasn't sure if either of them knew what they were doing or why, but I suddenly felt very sorry for them both.

"You could come back inside with me," I said to Isaac, "and sort things out with Trinny. You can still be her friend, you know, even if she's in a relationship. Same goes for Theo."

"Yeah, I'll follow you in," said Isaac, but I knew he wouldn't.

Theo and I were tidying up after the party when I told him about my conversation with Isaac and the revelation I'd had about both him and Jocelyn.

"You think my mother would rather I was miserable with her than happy without her?" he asked.

"I didn't say that exactly," I said. "I just understand it better now. She's scared. They both are."

Theo mulled this over for a moment and then plonked himself down on the sofa. I noticed myself rubbing the spot on my finger where the splinter had been, convinced there was still something in there, just under the skin. This had become a bit of a habit lately, whenever I was worried.

"I was afraid she might come over tonight," he said finally; then he looked up at me for a reaction. I sat beside him and took his hand.

"That's not normal, is it?" he asked.

"I'm hardly an authority on normal parent-child relationships, Theo."

He smiled and nodded; then we sat in silence while he

fidgeted with his sleeve like a little kid. I so rarely saw this side of him. It made me want to wrap him up and protect him from the world.

When Theo spoke again it was as though he was trying to resolve a particularly complex riddle.

"It isn't normal to be afraid that your own mother might come round," he said, "is it?"

"No, honey, it's not," I said.

Another few moments passed before he spoke again. "We need to move, don't we?"

I nodded.

It took us almost two months to find a new apartment. It's nice. But it doesn't quite compare to our first flat. I haven't explicitly said this to Theo, of course, but he probably knows I'm thinking it.

Financially, we're worse off than before; what we saved in rent this past year we've all but lost on heating bills over the winter, and Jocelyn is refusing to pay us back what we spent fixing up the house because we left before our imaginary lease was up. She also claims that a lot of work needs to be done putting it back the way it was. We offered to do it ourselves, but she refused. We can't be trusted, she says.

To add to this unfunny comedy of errors, our sofa was destroyed by a leak in the garage roof, so we've had to fork out for a new one. We got it in the January sales, but still, it wasn't cheap.

So with all that, plus the time we've taken off work to find a new place and move again, I reckon we're about two grand down. I try not to think about this last part too much. If I do I'll just start crying.

I'm managing okay, though. I've had Maya, my mother, and my sister, Una, checking in on me. I even went for coffee with Trinny last week and vented for nearly an hour.

Theo won't talk about it. Not to me anyway. And Darren says he's not mentioned it. He hasn't said a word, apparently, about the house or the money or his mother, whom he hardly ever visits anymore. When she does call, crying down the phone like she used to, it takes him even longer to recover now. I try to help him but it's getting harder and harder for me to scoop all the problems back out.

He's been working longer hours and finding more ways to distract himself; running, mostly, which I suppose is healthy, but it means we see one another less. Hopefully he'll get through this patch soon and he won't need to keep himself so busy all the time. And hopefully he'll start talking to me again. We were always able to talk about anything, and now every conversation with him is like pulling teeth.

Writing is about the only thing that feels stable lately—the only place I feel safe and in control. I look forward to my weekly classes, and in between them, stories are pouring out of me so fast I can't keep up. I find myself waking up at all hours to jot ideas down. Sometimes it gets light outside before I realize I'm still writing, and it's jarring for my mind to return to the real world, having spent so long in the one it just created. I think I'm happier in there, most of the time.

Maya and Darren just moved in together, so we've not been hanging out as a foursome much. I get it; Theo and I were the same when we got our first place here—nestled in like newlyweds. I think about that place a lot, how we were then, how we are now, and even though on the surface nothing has changed, I can feel something just beneath it, niggling away at us.

rivers and roads

"A LITTLE TO THE left," shouts Theo.

I shift my body to the left.

"No. Sorry. My left. Your right."

"Got it," I yell as I shuffle to the right, still maintaining my pose: arms outstretched, one at hip height, the other just above my head.

"Back the other way a bit."

I adjust accordingly.

"That's good. Yeah," says Theo, one eye squeezed shut as he looks at me through the lens of his camera. "Now, down a smidge."

I lower my arms.

"I said a smidge!"

I sigh begrudgingly as I lift my arms back up.

Theo laughs. "You're the one who wanted to do this!"

He's right, to be fair. Several weeks ago, we were snuggled up watching *Mary Poppins*, and as she floated over London, clutching her umbrella, I mentioned that I'd never seen Big Ben. Theo paused the film and sat up to look at me.

"What do you mean you've never seen Big Ben?"

"I mean, obviously I've seen Big Ben," I said, gesturing at the TV. "There it is right there. But I've never, you know, seen it in person."

Theo dropped his head in faux shame.

"I'm so sorry," he said. "I've really let the side down there."

I laughed. "What are you on about?"

"You've lived here nearly four months and I haven't even shown you the sights!"

"Yeah, it's a fairly shocking display. I mean, what kind of tour guide are you?"

"I am actually an excellent tour guide," he said, which made me laugh more.

"Are you indeed?"

"Yes. I'll prove it to you."

"Oh my God," I said, suddenly excited, "can we be tourists for a day? And wear those awful 'I heart London' T-shirts?"

"Yes," said Theo, but I wasn't finished . . .

"And have afternoon tea? And fish and chips? And take photos where it looks like we're holding famous landmarks?"

Theo just grabbed me and kissed me, and before I knew it we were making love on the sofa.

There's been a lot of that lately—impromptu lovemaking—and I must say I'm a fan. If I had to sum up sex with Theo in one word I would say that it's fun. It's really fun! We talk and we laugh and we're not afraid to be silly or ask for what we want or try new things together. In fact, he's far more adventurous than his shy demeanor and dry sense of humor would have you believe. We watch porn together and read books about sex together and sometimes we go shopping for "props" (as we call them). We've got an entire prop box now, in fact, having accumulated quite the collection of handcuffs and blindfolds and cock rings and vibrators. Anything that claims to increase either my pleasure or his, we're willing to give it a go, and if it's a complete disaster we laugh it off and move on. We've recently started to introduce food into the equation, which has been a real learning curve; suffice to say, if you're planning on using a banana, don't peel it first.

Theo emerged from the kitchen the other night with a jug full of custard, which he proceeded to pour on my tits and lick back off again. That was worth washing the sheets for. But don't get me wrong, it's not all custard and cock rings. There are of course those mornings when we roll into one another and make lazy love before even saying good morning or brushing our teeth. And those nights when we're too tired to have sex, so we settle for a cuddle instead. There are also the times we hardly speak, and stare lovingly into one another's eyes instead—the very antithesis of porn. The times when we come together and then afterward collapse onto the bed and fall asleep, intertwined and oblivious to the mess and the sweat and the wet patch we're lying in.

Sex with Theo is messy. As sex should be. And the most beautiful thing about it is I'm never ashamed of my messiness, never embarrassed by the sounds my body makes or the fluids it produces, or the lack thereof. If we need to use lube, we use lube. If I'm on my period, we put a towel down and crack on anyway.

And I'd like to think I make him feel the same, as though nothing is too gross or weird to at least talk about, and no part of his body or the experience of making love to him is ugly or unenjoyable.

I feel like we're in a sort of second honeymoon phase; having lived long-distance and then shared an apartment with Theo's friend, we finally have a place of our own, and I'm milking our newfound privacy for all it's worth. I've never been particularly loud during sex, but I'm really going for it lately. There's something terrifically liberating about vocalizing an experience of intense pleasure without worrying someone will hear. That said, we recently heard our neighbors "going for it" too and realized just how thin the walls are. I passed them on the narrow stairs the other day, polite smiles and nods all round, and all I could think was, *You know what my orgasms sound like.* I wonder if they were thinking the same thing.

Sex aside, I'm relishing the little things; chilling on the sofa together after a long day, nipping to the corner shop for bread and milk, ordering pizza when we can't be bothered to cook, late-night chats after all the lights are out, waking up every day and knowing, without fail, that Theo will be there next to me.

Which might all sound dreadfully mundane to some people, I'm sure, but I've been craving this kind of mundanity my whole life: a stable, calm existence that ticks along steadily without much effort. No chaos. No confusion. Just simplicity and ease. Things with Theo are, dare I say, good? I'm happy. And while that feeling brings with it a brand-new kind of anxiety—a sort of foreboding joy, where the very presence of happiness only serves as a reminder that happiness can so easily be taken away—I'd take joy with a splash of fear over fear with a splash of joy any day.

Today is my birthday. I was woken this morning by the smell of bacon frying and the sound of a kettle boiling—my favorite way to wake up—and soon afterward, I was presented with breakfast in bed. Theo beamed as he handed me the tray, on the side of which he'd placed a small gift wrapped in Union Jack paper.

"What's this?" I asked, tearing it open to reveal a white T-shirt inside. Theo could barely contain himself as I turned it around to reveal the words "I Heart London" in massive Comic Sans lettering. Just as I was beginning to get it, he ripped open his dressing gown to reveal he was wearing the same hideous T-shirt. At this point he had to take the tray away because I was laughing so hard that my tea was about to spill.

"I can't actually believe you've done this," I said, in a fit of giggles.

"Oh, this is just the beginning," Theo cooed, snuggling up next to me on the bed. "Get that breakfast into you. We've got a very busy day ahead!"

Our first stop was just outside Waterloo Station: a little shop selling all manner of British-themed paraphernalia.

"Right," said Theo, eyeing up a display of brightly colored caps, "if you're going to be a tourist, then you need to look the part."

"Understood," I said, playing along with the pretend importance of this exchange.

"We'll need a cap," he mused, "and a backpack. And maybe a bum bag, so that everyone knows what a serious sightseer you are."

"Of course."

He held up a hat that said "God Save the Queen."

"Too far?" he asked.

I just stared back, nonplussed.

"Too far," he said as he put back the cap and picked up another with a picture of Paddington Bear on it.

"Now, there's a Brit I can get behind!" I said, placing the cap in my basket.

By the time we reached the till I had also picked up a backpack with the slogan "Keep Calm and Drink Tea," as well as a bum bag in the shape of a red double-decker bus, and an enormous mug with a picture of Maggie Thatcher's face on a psychedelic background.

"That's not for me," I said to the clerk as he scanned through the items, terrified he might think I was actually a Thatcherite. Theo smirked and shook his head.

"Just a little private joke," I added.

And so, here I am, standing on Westminster Bridge in this ludicrous outfit, while Theo tries to take "one of those photos where it looks like I'm holding a famous landmark," as per my request. All around us, busy Londoners roll their eyes and grunt pointedly as they veer around what must look like a pair of idiot tourists, incredibly dedicated to getting this "iconic" shot with Big Ben.

"It's her first time in London," says Theo to one particularly disgruntled passerby.

"Tourists, eh?" he says to another, and I laugh through clenched teeth, determined not to break my pose.

I suppose in some senses I am still a tourist, because I haven't quite settled in London yet—like my body made the journey but my heart hasn't quite caught up. I notice it in my language, mostly. Whenever I talk about my mam's house in Dublin I call it "home," but here I'll say "the apartment" or "our place." Some mornings I wake up and need a minute to remember where I am, and on days when I'm tired or hungover and I can't wait to go to bed, it's my bed back in Ireland that I think of automatically, before readjusting the image in my mind's eye.

I get homesick some days, and then I feel silly for feeling that way. It's just a different patch of land, I tell myself, just another jumble of rivers and roads.

"That's it. Don't move," says Theo, and I freeze, smiling broadly as he snaps the shot.

The photograph rolls out of his Polaroid camera and I run back to him, giddy and giggling; then we lean against the edge of the bridge and watch the London Eye slowly spinning while Theo shakes the photo back and forth.

Finally, the picture materializes.

"Nailed it!" says Theo.

"We really did," I say. It's perfect; the angle, the outfit, my goofy tourist grin.

"You know," says Theo, "the clock itself isn't actually called Big Ben."

"Yeah, I know. It's the name of the bell inside."

"No," he says, "that's also a common misconception. Big Ben is actually the guy who built the clock."

"Is that right?" I say with a smile. "Was this Ben quite a tall fellow, then?"

"Hung like a fucking horse," says Theo, straight-faced.

I laugh and roll my eyes at Theo's awful joke.

"What's next?" I ask. Theo takes my hand and leads me across the bridge, first to Westminster Abbey and then to 10 Downing Street. He spews made-up history the whole time.

"Ah yes," he says, rubbing his chin earnestly. "Here we see 10 Downing Street, home, of course, to the Earl of Downing, built in 1066 as a wedding gift for his wife, Penelope Downing."

"Will you be doing this all day or just for the first few stops?" I ask.

"All day, I'm afraid."

"Cool."

We stroll through St. James's Park, past the lake, and on to Buckingham Palace, where we ask someone to take a picture of us in front of the famous wrought iron gates. I also get a photo on my phone, which I send to my mother, sister, and brother. I receive some very mixed responses in return.

From my mother: "Lovely. I hope you've brought a coat."

From Una: "What on earth are you wearing? Is that a bus-shaped bum bag?"

From Donal: "Give old queenie two fingers up for me, yeah? BRITS OUT! HOME RULE!"

"Jesus," says Theo, when I read him the message.

"He's quite the patriot is our Donal," I explain.

"Rebel scum," says Theo.

"Imperial trash!" I retort a little too loudly, and an elderly lady turns to look at me, eyes wide.

"She's Irish," Theo explains apologetically. We're still laughing as we make our way toward Green Park.

We find a spot under a tree just as a light drizzle begins to fall. Theo pops his backpack down on the grass and for the first time I notice how full it is.

"What have you got in there?"

"Well, it's funny you should ask that," says Theo, "because I'm getting a bit peckish, actually."

I stare on with a wary smile as he crouches to unzip the bag.

"No peeking," he says over his shoulder. I chuckle as I cover my eyes, and when I open them, there's a green-and-white gingham blanket laid out in front of me with a flask of tea and two china mugs and saucers, a jug of milk, paper plates full of finger sandwiches, sultana scones with little jars of cream and jam next to them, and, most impressive of all, a tiny three-tier cake stand full of mini Battenbergs, Victoria sponge, and carrot cake.

"Afternoon tea is served, madame," says Theo with a flourish.

I genuinely don't know what to say. This is one of those very rare moments when I can't seem to call a single word to mind, so I just kneel down next to him and cover his face with kisses.

"Thank you," I say finally. "I love this. I love you."

Theo smiles up at me with his arms around my waist.

"I love you too, angel."

I kiss him once more on the forehead; then I lean over and unscrew the lid on the flask.

"Cup of tea?" I ask.

"Sure, thanks!"

Half an hour later, despite being well and truly stuffed, I'm eyeing up the last piece of Victoria sponge.

"I wish someone would look at me the way you look at cake," says Theo.

"Tough shit," I say, ramming the whole slice unceremoniously into my mouth.

"Wow. That was actually kind of sexy."

I laugh through a face full of sponge.

"No, really," he adds, deadpan, "I'm a bit turned on by that. Can you do it again please? But slower this time."

I shove him lightly in the arm and he lies back, smirking. I lie down next to him while we wait for the rain to pass, snuggling up to him and chatting about the day thus far.

A family passes by with three young boys, one of whom is sitting on his father's shoulders, kicking his poor dad like he's riding a horse. The kid waves at us and Theo waves back.

"Do you want one?" I ask.

"I'm not sure they're giving one away, babe," says Theo. I groan audibly and roll over, turning my back to him, then he follows me, laughing at his own dumb joke as he wraps his arms around me and nuzzles his cold nose into my neck.

"Yes," he says. "Someday." Then: "Do you?"

"I think so," I say.

"You'd make a really great mum," he says, and for the second time today I'm totally lost for words.

As soon as the sun comes back out, we pack up the picnic and stroll all the way through Hyde Park and back around to

Harrods, where we skip the jewelry and clothing departments and head straight for Toy Kingdom. We spend well over an hour navigating several stories full of life-size Lego figures, train sets, teddy bears, jugglers, and magicians, and I catch myself daydreaming about Theo and me as parents, taking our kids on days out to parks and toy shops. I'm surprised how unafraid I am of this thought. If anything, I find it calming.

Back outside it's starting to get dark when Theo reaches inside his bag and produces two tickets to *Les Misérables*.

"You're joking!" I say, wide-eyed. "No way. You're joking."

He just smiles and takes me by the hand again as he leads me all the way through Mayfair, past the brightly lit, obscenely expensive shops there, and up through Piccadilly Circus. There's a busker on one corner playing "Hallelujah" and even though we're in a hurry, we stop to listen for a minute before rushing on up Shaftesbury Avenue to Sondheim Theatre, where we're just in time to take our seats. I'm starting to feel a little silly in my tourist T-shirt when, without saying a word, Theo pulls a jumper from his backpack and hands it to me.

I keep thinking the day is done—after the picnic, after the walk, after the toy shop, and now, after the show. I'm struggling to recall a birthday I've enjoyed more than this, one where I felt so thoroughly taken care of, so considered, so loved. I'm ready to call it a night when we step out of the theater and I instinctively head toward the nearest Tube station, but Theo takes me in a different direction, telling me there's one more place he wants us to go.

"As your tour guide," he says, "I can't let you end a day out in London without some proper fish and chips."

And so, despite the fact that we're both still a bit full from lunch, we walk to Poppies in Soho and we each order a battered cod and chips. The restaurant is quite busy, so we wander toward South Bank and eat our food on a bench overlooking the river.

"What did you think of *Les Mis*, then?" I ask once we're situated.

"Bit depressing, innit?"

"Yeah," I say. "The clue is sort of in the name, though."

"Fair."

"Maybe next time we should go see *Everything's Actually Fine and Everyone's Doing All Right Under the Circumstances*."

"Sounds great," he says with a grin.

When we've finished our food, Theo starts unzipping his backpack again.

"What now?" I joke, and he smiles but he seems suddenly bashful.

"There's one more thing I wanted to give you today," says Theo. "I actually found it a while ago but I was waiting for the right moment."

I have absolutely no idea what it could be. For all I know it's another silly joke.

With that, Theo reaches into his bag and pulls out a flat square, about ten inches wide, wrapped in the same paper as the T-shirt this morning. He hands it to me and it's heavier than I expected. Gently, I remove the paper to reveal a picture in an ornate gold frame. Only it's not a picture; it's a map. The paper is old and yellowing and the ink has faded somewhat, so it takes me a second to understand. But as soon as I do my eyes fill with tears, which tumble quickly down my cheeks.

It's an antique map of Dublin.

"Theo," is all I can say.

I trace one finger along the river Liffey, past all her little bridges, to where she ends at Dublin Bay, and I'm completely overcome with emotion.

"I thought we might hang it in the living room," he says, and I break again.

"Thank you," I blubber through tears. "Thank you so much."

"Happy birthday, angel," says Theo, and for the first time since I've known him, he starts to cry too. We kiss then, our lips still greasy from all the chips, and we hold one another for a long time.

"Come on," I say finally. "Let's go home."

canadian geese

I AM MY MOTHER'S daughter. For better or for worse. I gravitate toward water when I'm sad. I'm always cold (except when I'm too warm). I can't drink milk from a cup or eat soup with a dessert spoon. Driving feels like freedom. Pink suits me. Ice cream gives me indigestion. I bruise easily. I never take the first room I'm offered in a hotel. And I can't get into an unmade bed. Last time Theo came to visit, he found me making the bed at midnight and asked why I was bothering to make it only to mess it up again. I stood there with the duvet in my hands, and all I could say was, "I have to." I told my mother the next day and she said, "You get that from me."

I'm also riddled with anxiety and plagued by depression, and occasionally I find great comfort in the thought of not existing. Do I get that from her too?

She drove down to the beach once with a bottle of brandy, a box of pills, and no intention of coming home. I was seven years old at the time. She'd left me back at the house with my father, sister, and brother.

I think about that day a lot. I wonder where she parked, what her hair looked like, whether she was crying. I walk through the story in my head and see it playing out from different angles: sometimes from the water's edge, sometimes from the dunes behind the car, sometimes from the perspective of a bird flying overhead. Occasionally I'm sitting in the back seat, but I can only watch the scene unfold; I can never change it.

In the end, the thought of leaving her children at the mercy of her tyrannical husband—the very reason she wanted to kill herself in the first place—was enough to make her change her mind. And so my mother drank some brandy and drove herself home, and a year later she filed a restraining order against him.

I have driven down to the beach today—the same beach my mother drove to all those years ago—and parked my car on the sand. The gray-green sea spreads out in front of me, its soft waves undulating like creases in some endless linen skirt, and here I am, like a scared child clinging to its hem.

In the distance I can see the smokestacks, standing like sentinels over Dublin Bay. Just above them, a flock of Canada geese take flight, little brown M's against an overcast sky, all turning and diving in unison, unfaltering in their formation. I watch them for a while and marvel at how they know.

• • •

I grew up near the sea. A ten-minute drive to the beach, straight down the Kilbarrack Road to the coast. To my left Howth Head, and to my right Bull Island, and the causeway where I learned to drive in my little red Toyota. I've taken her out today for one last spin.

A young girl from Sutton is buying my car from me. Niamh is her name. She came by last week and stood in my driveway with her hands shoved deep in her pockets, regarding the car as though it were some huge, unpredictable beast.

"Do you know much about cars?" I asked.

"No," she said, "I'm starting lessons next week."

I nodded.

"My dad says Toyotas are safe, though, so . . ." She trailed off, tucking a loose string of ginger hair behind one ear.

"Would you like to sit in it?"

She nodded and climbed with forced confidence into the driver's seat, like a child trying on her mother's high heels. I sat beside her in the passenger seat and couldn't help but smile at the sight of this young girl shifting uneasily behind the wheel, her pale, bony hands folded in her lap, too afraid to touch anything.

"It's okay," I said, "she doesn't bite."

Niamh smiled and placed her hands delicately on top of the steering wheel.

"Have you had any problems?" she asked.

"Plenty," I said, "but they weren't the car's fault."

That got a laugh out of her. She relaxed a little and started fidgeting with the rearview mirror, looking at herself, dragging a finger across one freckled cheek.

"Why are you selling it? Sorry. Do you mind me asking that?"

"Of course not," I said. "I'm moving to London next week."

"Oh my God," she said, perking up. "So jealous. I want to move there after I finish school but my dad says I need to get my degree here first. I think he's buying me a car to bribe me into staying."

"Fair deal, though," I said, smiling. She smiled back.

"What are you going to study?" I asked.

"Nursing in DCU."

"I went to DCU," I said.

"No way!"

She absentmindedly flicked the indicator up and down. "That's mad. Did you like it there? All my friends are going to UCD. I'm gonna be such a loner."

"You'll be grand," I said. "I made great friends there."

"Yeah?"

"Yeah."

Niamh decided to buy the car without even test-driving it. I think she mostly liked the color. And the chat. I suggested she send her dad round to check it out just in case, and so the next day Colm, an unassuming man with thinning hair and a flat pink face, arrived on my doorstep. Colm stood with his hands in his pockets, just as Niamh had, and as he spoke he bent forward slightly, as though in a constant state of apology.

We drove around the block a few times and made idle conversation about Niamh, the only thing we had in common. There was no mention of Niamh's mother, so I assumed it was just the two of them. No wonder he was so keen for her to stay.

"Niamh tells me you're off to the Big Smoke," said Colm as he pulled my car up outside my house.

"I am indeed."

"Fair play to ya," he said. "You've got to go where the work is."

I'm not going for work—I have a great job here, in fact—but for some reason I couldn't bring myself to tell this man that I'm actually chasing a boy all the way to London.

"I lived there meself," he went on, "in the eighties. Before the boom."

"Did you like it there?" I asked.

"I did."

"But you came back, though."

"I missed the horizon," he said, without a hint of irony or embarrassment, and my breath caught in my throat.

I had never really thought about the horizon before. It was always just . . . there.

I stare out now through my rain-spattered windshield at that sharp, bluish line beyond which the whole world might simply fall away, and I imagine a life where buildings block my view in all directions, a life where the horizon isn't just down the road. Sitting here now, that life feels almost inconceivable.

I roll down my windows and a gust of delicious salt air rushes through. Instinctively I suck it deep into my lungs, wishing I could hold my breath and take it with me. Nearby the waves wash steadily in and out, and I close my eyes to savor the sound of their endless ebb and flow.

Suddenly I'm reminded of a dream I had last night; I was trying to collect the ocean in jars. I ran the length of the shoreline with a jar in one hand and a lid in the other, scooping and twisting, scooping and twisting. Piling them high on the sand. But there weren't enough jars.

I woke from this dream to the sound of my mother's voice floating through my window with the morning light. Without even looking, I could see her propped against the pillar at the end of our garden, chatting to the next-door neighbor. Her words were muffled, but the cadence of each sentence was familiar to the point of predictability, like some fond old melody. I rolled onto my side and dozed awhile, till she came and knocked on my bedroom door.

"Come on, now," she said, "you can't sleep all day."

"Is that a challenge?" I mumbled into my pillow.

She smiled and shook her head as she placed a cup of tea on my bedside table—sliding a coaster underneath it first—then, like clockwork, she threw back my curtains, announced what a beautiful day it was, and listed all the things she needed to get done. Then she exited the room, intentionally leaving my door wide open behind her.

Neither of us mentioned the significance of the day—my last full day in Ireland—nor did we acknowledge the two huge suitcases standing just outside my bedroom door, harbingers of my impending departure. As she shuffled past them on her way out, I thought of the night my father left; the half-packed cardboard boxes stacked outside my door and how my mother had squeezed past them after putting me to bed.

In the morning, my father was gone and so were the boxes, along with the TV, the toaster, and his extensive record collection, which had filled a massive cabinet in the living room. Pale rectangles appeared on every wall—replacing framed pictures that had hung there—and in the garden an oily stain marked the spot where his car had been. Half the house was missing. We spent weeks reaching for things only to find them gone: the iron, the alarm clock, the first-aid kit. Who takes a first-aid kit?

I'm not sure what I expected to happen when he left. Maybe years of reading fairy tales had convinced me that the nightmare would end once the monster was gone. But that's not how it was. In my father's absence, certain fear was replaced by uncertain calm, and a quiet, creeping dread descended on the house. We waded cautiously into our newfound freedom, hesitant to accept that we were in fact safe and he was in fact gone. It was as though we had collectively lost sight of a spider.

The tide is coming in now, licking at a patch of sand just in front of my car. I start the engine, reverse a few feet, and switch the engine off again, buying myself a little more time.

Nightfall has settled on the edge of the horizon, like ink sinking to the bottom of a glass, and a deep, violet line stretches endlessly in both directions. All the picnickers and dog walkers have dispersed, and a swarm of seagulls have gathered on the sand, noisily scavenging for scraps. Their raucousness is oddly relaxing, so I sit and listen for as long as I can. But the water inches inexorably closer and eventually I have no choice but to take a few more gulps of precious sea air, roll up my windows, and make my way slowly back toward the road.

My phone rings as I reach the causeway. It's my sister, Una. When I answer, her voice comes booming through the speakers in my car.

"Well," she says, "are you all set?"

"I think so," I say, taking a right turn onto the coast road toward home.

"Are you driving?" She must be able to hear the indicator ticking in the background.

"I was just down the beach."

"Ah, God." Una drags each word out sympathetically. "Are you all right?"

"Yeah," is all I can say. I feel tears gather in the edges of my eyes.

"You'll miss it," she says.

"I will."

A brief pause. We both inhale and exhale together.

"How's Mam holding up?" she asks, and I laugh pointedly.

"Sorry. Stupid question," she admits.

"We haven't actually *spoken* about it, obviously; she just keeps dropping these massive emotional bombshells and expecting me to know what to do with them."

"Mam? Really? That's not like her at all," says Una dryly.

"It's absolutely infuriating!" I blurt. "She keeps staring wistfully into the distance and announcing her feelings out loud, like she's delivering some sad soliloquy. Everything is 'the *last* this' or 'the *last* that.' You'd swear I was dying or something. I was leaving the house today and she just stood there, all hunched and sad, watching me put on my coat. 'One *last* drive down the beach,' she said, to the nonexistent fourth wall, 'before she leaves forever.' I swear to God, Una, she actually referred to me in the third person! It's like being followed around by some miserable fucking narrator whose job it is to remind me of all the shit I'm trying not to think about. You'd think *she* was the one uprooting her whole bloody life."

The sound of Una guffawing on the other end of the line makes my anger dissipate, leaving only disgruntled amusement in its wake. This is how we put up with it, Una and I—we turn it into comedy. We do little routines just for one another. Because if you can make yourself laugh, then maybe you won't cry.

Una is the eldest of us three kids, and thirteen years older than me. I'm "the baby," as they all still insist on calling me. Una was already grown up and living in an apartment of her own when our dad left, but when Mam broke down she decided to move back in for a while to help look after me and my brother, Donal.

I don't remember the details of the breakdown, only that my mother stayed in bed with the curtains drawn for what felt like a very long time. She stopped working, which to my child's mind was the biggest indicator that something was wrong. She ran an interior design company that she built herself from the ground up—her fourth baby, we called it—and over the years I'd watched her drag herself out of bed and go to work despite colds, the flu, heartbreak, and even a hysterectomy. But this time she just couldn't bring herself to care, and so her sister had to step in to keep the business afloat.

From what I could tell, my mother had stopped eating too. Trays of food were delivered to her room and then taken away hours later with plates still practically full. I saw her getting undressed one evening through a crack in her bedroom door and was horrified by the sight of her. I remember the sharp protrusion of hipbones and the roll of ribs under her skin. Una caught me looking, and she quickly closed the door. Later that night she told me Mam was sick but that she would be better soon.

This wasn't a lie; several months later, fueled by fear and a stolid sense of determination, my mother managed a resurrection of sorts. She teetered back into the world like a fawn on fresh legs, returning to work, making new friends, and resuming her motherly duties. She also took up tennis and changed her entire wardrobe. The word "thriving" was thrown about a lot.

To this day, I'm not quite sure how she did it. If I asked her now, she would tell me that "she had to."

Una stayed with us for two more years, occupying a role somewhere between a sister and a surrogate mother. She slept in my room, and every night we'd chat about our days while she took off her makeup and got ready for bed. Some nights we'd spoon until one or both of us fell asleep—she was the big spoon and I was the little spoon, which seems odd to me now that I'm taller than Una—then in the morning, she'd get up and leave for work before my alarm even went off.

I was first home from school in the afternoon, followed closely by my brother, Donal, who worked in the local library. He watched *Star Trek* with me every day at five p.m., and we took turns making tea during the ad breaks. After years of practice we could time each trip to the kitchen with exact accuracy.

In the evenings, Donal helped me with my homework. I was oddly meticulous about schoolwork—desperate to be right, to be special, to be praised—and I enjoyed every subject bar math, which I hated as a child because I saw no everyday application for things like differentiation. I didn't know or care what x equaled, and I resented being asked to figure it out. My teachers struggled with my need to know the why of things. There is no *why* in math, they'd tell me; things just are the way they are.

Biology, on the other hand, made sense. Everything could be explained by evolutionary or environmental factors. Even the organs we no longer need, even bad things like death, disease, and mental disorders, they all have a practical, reasonable why if you go back far enough.

English was Donal's favorite subject and it quickly became mine too. Prose and plays and poetry allowed me to escape my own mind and live momentarily in someone else's. Some of the writers we studied were dark and depressed—like poor old Sylvia Plath, whom I, of course, fell instantly in love with—but at least it was their depression and not mine; I could close the book whenever I wanted and leave it there between the pages.

Once a month, my English teacher tasked us with writing an essay based on a random phrase or theme. I would jump at the chance to write a story of my own, retreating to my room and scribbling furiously for hours, stopping only to shake off a cramp from my wrist. Donal noticed this and signed me up for creative writing classes at the library. Every Wednesday afternoon, he'd stay late after his shift to walk me home, and on the way he'd give me a new book of short stories to read that week.

Saturday nights were for me and my mother; when the others went out to discos or pubs, we'd go to Dunnes and get a pizza from the deli; then we'd come home and watch the same lineup of family-friendly game shows before switching off the telly and chatting for a while. I was sent to bed before midnight, but I'd stay awake until every one of my siblings was home safe, listening for the familiar sound of their key in the door and the late-night search for leftover pizza in the fridge. When the house was full and quiet once again, I could finally drift off. To this day I struggle to sleep when I'm expecting someone home; some part of me still won't accept that people who leave will eventually come back.

On Sundays we'd all pile into Donal's tiny, tinny excuse for a car, and he'd drive us to Xtra-vision to rent a movie. We could never agree on one, so inevitably we'd get an eclectic mix of movies—ranging from *Pretty Woman* to *The Terminator* to *Rear Window*—and watch them all back to back.

Rituals and routine became a safety blanket of sorts, something I could wrap around myself when things felt uncertain, which they so often did. Awful as my father was, I had adapted to his presence—my little brain growing around the problem like roots around a rock—and after he left I had to adapt all over again. New neural pathways were thrown up like scaffolding, protecting my mind from collapse, only the scaffolding never came down; it never had a chance to because my father's brand of loud, violent chaos was replaced by something quieter and more insidious; a mother who meant well, who tried to give me everything but failed to see that everything was too much. Boundaries fell away and the lines between parent and child blurred; things I'd been fortunate enough not to witness first-hand I was told about in the aftermath; and along with all her love and care and sacrifice I also got her grief, despair, and dread, along with a false belief that I was somehow responsible for fix-ing it all.

And so, having spent the best part of my childhood in sur-vival mode, what should have been a temporary measure to cope in a crisis became my way of dealing with everyday life—stay on high alert, push your feelings down, and always, always have a plan. To this day, I have a faulty security system running con-stantly in the background, sounding the alarm and sending me into fight or flight over every perceived threat. I live life with a proverbial tiger in the room, but I can somehow withstand its presence as long as everything else is in order.

Una understands. She knows why my wardrobe is color-coded and my kitchen is always clean. She knows why my books are arranged alphabetically, why I need to know the route before I start driving, why I panic when people don't come home on time, and why, if one domino falls, they all come crashing down. Ritu-als and routine. They keep the tiger at bay.

Una talks to me for the whole drive home, nattering on about her job and her family and their upcoming holiday to Greece. She's passing the time, keeping me company.

I turn the corner onto my street and drive past the field where I spent most of my childhood, kicking half-flattened footballs around or sitting cross-legged in circles talking nonsense with friends. We came of age awkwardly, navigating puberty together as best we could—a gaggle of gangly limbed, hormone-riddled kids with not a single clue between us. I had my first kiss in that field with a boy named Alan Murphy, all rigid tongues and teeth smashing noisily against one another. I shudder at the thought.

"Whatever happened to the Murphys from down the street?" I say, almost to myself.

"Dunno," says Una. "Didn't one of them get arrested for something?"

As I pull into the driveway, Una is listing all the things I might need—toothbrush, hair dryer, warm coat—and asking if I've packed them.

"I'm leaving the country, Una. I've packed everything."

"Oh yeah," she says, as though that's only now dawning on her. "Shit."

I pull the handbrake and sit for a few minutes, looking in at the house. I can hear Una thinking on the other end of the line.

"Listen," she says finally, "go easy on Mam, will you? I know she's a fucking basket case but . . ." She trails off.

"But what?"

"You're the baby," says Una. "You're all she has left."

"Fucking hell, Una!" I say, half laughing, trying to make a joke of it, but Una doesn't laugh this time.

"I mean it," she says. "She did her best."

I stare ahead at the house, at the front door that she painted blue last winter—it wasn't quite the shade she expected it to be—and the baskets of yellow flowers that she hung outside "to cheer the place up." The curtains are half-drawn in every room and the porch light is on. She always leaves it on till I get home. "I know," I say.

I step inside and sling my coat across the banister. I'm instantly met with the thick, sweet smell of stew on the boil, and a smile spreads across my face as I head straight to the kitchen, where, sure enough, I find a massive pot of bubbling brown liquid on the stove. Thick chunks of carrots and celery and potatoes bob busily about on the surface. Next to the pot, on the counter, a loaf of crusty bread stands cooling.

Steam wafts up from inside the pot, and sticking out of the top I see the shiny silver handle of a ladle. Suddenly, the words of some half-remembered Seamus Heaney poem come swimming up at me, where he'd compared love to a tinsmith's scoop discarded in a meal-bin. "Sunlight," I think it was called. The poem had always reminded me of my grandmother, standing in a floury apron at the window or sitting by the fireplace, "broad-lapped, with whitened nails and measling shins." And now it made me think of my mother too.

I loved that poem—I loved the sound of it, the way the rich, warm words seemed to slide across my tongue like syrup. I remember standing at the top of a muggy classroom in a dowdy gray uniform, reciting those words from a book of poetry clasped firmly between my hands. "There was a sunlit absence," it began, but I had never understood that opening line before. What could possibly be missing from this scene, I wondered, which seemed almost to overflow with light and love?

Standing here, now, I finally understand; the scene itself is absent. The moment has already come and gone and faded into memory. It exists outside of time, as though it's happening in the present but is already part of the past, and it's this awareness of a future absence that makes his love for the woman he's describing—who bakes him scones on hot summer afternoons—so bittersweet and beautiful.

"There you are," says my mother, appearing in the doorway behind me. "How was the beach?"

"It was nice, thanks."

But there's so much more I want to say.

I want to tell her that I'll miss it. I'll miss the seagulls and the sand. I'll miss Tayto crisps and Lyons tea and fish and chips from Macari's and chicken-fillet baguettes from Spar. I'll miss RTÉ and 2FM and hearing the accent everywhere I go. I'll miss strangers talking to one another like old friends. And I'll miss the DART—the Underground is too bloody reliable; it's unnerving. I'll miss places that mean something, like the Gaiety and the GPO. And that one Leaving Cert weekend in May when the weather is nice. I'll miss people knowing what the fucking Leaving Cert is. And all our other vernacular, for that matter. I don't want to call presses "cupboards" or explain what an immersion is or ask someone to "stall the ball" and have them look at me like I'm mad. I'll miss the odd *cúpla focal*, and the buskers on Grafton Street, and late-night sessions where someone suddenly gets a *bodhrán* out.

I'll miss my friends and my car and feeling like I belong. And I'll miss you, Mam, I really will.

But I don't say any of this. The words all stop and slip back down my throat, and before I can find them again she's scooping stew into two big bowls and ordering me to cut the bread into slices for dipping.

"You didn't have to go to all this trouble," I say as I smear butter on the bread I've cut.

"Of course I did!" she says, affronted. "I couldn't have my baby emigrating without one last bowl of her mammy's stew, could I?"

"Technically, it's *your* mammy's stew," I say, and she lets out an easy laugh. I place an arm around her shoulders and squeeze her into me. "But thanks all the same."

"Why don't you take some with you?" she asks.

"I don't think they allow that, Mam."

"Well, you'll have to learn how to make it yourself, then," she says.

It's business as usual tonight. We sit to the table together to eat, and we talk about everything and nothing at all. My mother tells me she has three funerals to go to next week, two of which fall on the same day, and she can't decide between them because she knew one of the deceased longer but she reckons the other one will be better *craic*. I tell her to go to the fun one.

After that I get filled in on the well-being of people I barely know, like Anne from Up the Way, whose bastard of a husband just left her, and Poor Pat Rooney—her official full name—who's "not long for this world now."

"That'll be another funeral I have to go to," she says. "God forgive me."

"I don't think God cares," I say, which is my standard response to any of her God-related comments now; rather than argue with her over God's existence, I've settled for reminding her that if God does exist, he probably has bigger fish to fry.

After dinner we retire to the living room to watch *The Late Late Show*, me stretched out on the sofa and her in her plush pink armchair. There's a tribute to Thin Lizzy at the top of the show, and my mam tells me, not for the first or final time, that she used to know Phil Lynott back in the day. After that, she pours us both some wine, while a panel of priests and politicians argue about abortion.

"Load of shite," says my mother. "What do a bunch of fucking men know about it?" She pauses briefly, then adds, "Nothing!" as though that wasn't implied.

She's snoring by the final interview and I have to take the wineglass out of her hand and shake her gently awake.

"Come on, now," I say, placing the glass back on the table and sliding a coaster underneath it. "Time for bed."

"What did I miss?" she asks, half opening her eyes.

"Nothing. Just some author flogging her latest crappy novel."

"Right you be," she says, and I help her up out of her chair.

As we climb the stairs she mutters something that I don't quite catch.

"What's that?" I ask.

"I said you'll be on there one day."

"On where?"

I assume this is just sleepy, drunken nonsense.

"*The Late Late!*" she says, and I laugh.

"Okay," I say.

"You will," she insists, stopping at the top of the stairs, "flogging your latest crappy novel." Then she winks at me the way my nana used to and a smile wrinkles the corners of her eyes. I smile back, but suddenly her expression changes. She's looking at something behind me and I turn to see the two suitcases just outside my bedroom door. "Well," she says, "good night so."

"Night," I say.

"See you in the morning."

"Yeah."

She hugs me, then goes quickly to her room.

I climb into bed, switch off the light, and stare up at my ceiling. It's covered in glow-in-the-dark stars; I stuck them there when I was twelve years old, and every time my mother asks about painting over them I tell her that I can't be bothered. The truth is I like the little constellations I created, and I'm scared that she'll get rid of them when I'm gone.

It's been a busy weekend. My college friends took me to Bray on Saturday—the same friends I told Niamh about—we sat on a cement wall by the strand, shouting and laughing over the loud, biting wind and ignoring the dark sky, which threatened rain all day. In the evening we ate soggy bags of salt-drenched chips, absolutely soaked in vinegar, then headed to a nearby pub, where round after round of drinks seemed to appear by magic on the table in front of me. The inevitable downpour came as we stumbled back to Bray station to catch the last DART home, and we spent the entire train journey damp and shivering but still laughing our heads off. At what, I haven't the foggiest.

I wouldn't mind, but I was already hungover from Friday night; my colleagues had thrown me an impromptu going-away party after my last day at work, and we ended up in Charlies Chinese restaurant at two a.m., each gobbling down a 4-in-1 (rice, chips, chicken balls, and curry sauce). It has recently come to my attention that the 4-in-1 is exclusive to Chinese restaurants in Ireland and that they in no way resemble real Chinese food. The whole night, my very drunk boss, Ciara, kept reminding me that there'd be a job here for me if I ever changed my mind and decided to come back. I think she means it too.

By yesterday, I was thankful for the low-key Sunday dinner my mother put together for the family. I guzzled water all day and helped myself to seconds of both the roast dinner and dessert, collapsing on the sofa afterward and unashamedly opening the top button on my jeans. All four of my nieces were there, and I spent the whole day pushing through the haze of my hangover, desperately trying to soak up every moment with them, like the last few rays of light before sunset.

As I hugged them good-bye, I held each child in my arms a fraction longer than usual, and I vowed to come back and see them soon, knowing on some level that time would trundle on without me, and I would miss entire chapters in their little lives.

• • •

There's nothing like saying good-bye to a place to make you want to stay. Everywhere I look I see memories I've made, good and bad, and it hurts. I feel as though I've been afflicted by some rare disease that renders me incapable of seeing an object, place, or person for what it is right now, and instead forces me to remember what it has been or wonder what it might become in my absence. It's like a kind of preemptive grief. I told my therapist, Nadia, about it and she said that it was perfectly normal.

I'm sad to be leaving her too; it's been almost a year since I first turned up at her office, crippled by anxiety and unable to imagine ever feeling calm again. That version of myself feels distant now, and I haven't had an episode in months.

I knew my time with Nadia was drawing to an end, but still, it was reassuring to know she was there if I needed her. Just like the horizon, I suppose. She's encouraged me to see another therapist in London if I need to—and maybe I will—but for now I feel strong and steady, like my feet are bolted to the floor.

I'm still staring up at my ceiling when I'm suddenly struck by the sense that this is all a terrible mistake. *I'm finally feeling good,* I think, *my body and brain are both well for once, and my family is here, and my friends, and career. So why uproot all that and move away? It's madness. This is madness.* I'm beginning to spiral when my phone rings loudly beside my head, snapping me out of it. I grab it as quickly as I can so as not to wake my mother.

"Hello?" I whisper.

"Hello, angel," whispers Theo in his lovely London accent.

"Why are *you* whispering?" I ask.

"I don't know." He laughs. "I can't wait to see you tomorrow!"

His excitement is palpable and I feel guilty for not feeling the same.

"Just called to check what time your flight gets in," says Theo.

"Two o'clock," I say. "But that's not really why you called, is it?"

"All right. You got me. I'm calling to make sure you haven't thrown a fit and talked yourself out of moving here."

"You know me so well."

"It helps that you're incredibly predictable."

We both laugh but there's an underlying nervousness in each one. I know he's afraid that I won't be able to leave. I'm afraid of the same thing.

"I'm scared," I say finally, as tears roll from the outer edges of my eyes and straight down into my ears. I turn onto my side so they can land on the pillow instead.

"I know, angel. But you got scared before our first date too, and that turned out okay."

"It was fine," I say, and he laughs again. Talking to him is so easy.

"Look, of course you're afraid. This is really big. You're leaving home."

"You weren't afraid when you moved here," I blubber.

"No, but that was different. I knew it wasn't permanent. And besides, I don't feel the same way you do about home. To be totally honest, I'm a little jealous of it sometimes."

"Of what?" I ask, wiping my face and sitting up to listen.

"You love being Irish. You love telling people you're Irish. When you're over here, and we go out, your ears prick up every time you hear an Irish accent. And you smile at them and they smile back. Like you're all automatically friends because you share this thing that nobody else gets. And the way you talk about . . . Wentford?"

"Wexford."

"That's the one. Where you used to go for the summer. It sounds like this magical, idyllic, made-up place. It's the same when you talk about the beach, or the Liffey, or Temple Bar, for fuck's sake. Which as we all know is a hive of scum and villainy."

This makes me laugh.

"You're just so proud of where you come from," he continues. "I have no idea what that's like. Most people don't."

There's a long silence, which is interrupted by me noisily blowing my nose.

"Oh shit," says Theo. "I'm not helping the case for you leaving home, am I?"

"Not really, no."

He inhales deeply and then lets it out in a soft sigh.

"I am excited to make a new home with you," I say, sniffling into a tissue. "It's just hard to let go of this one. I don't think I realized how hard it would be."

"That's okay. Look, all I can really say is thank you for even considering moving here to be with me. And if you don't like it and you want to go home, I will completely understand. But if you do stay, then I promise I will do everything in my power to make our life here really fucking lovely."

"Really fucking lovely? Wow."

"Yeah, I know."

I smile and close my eyes. A familiar ease settles between us in the silence. He knew this would all hit me. He knew before I did.

"Why don't you sleep on it?" offers Theo, but I've already made my decision.

After we say good-bye, I find myself lying in the dark, thinking about Wexford. I haven't been back there in almost a decade, and I didn't realize I spoke about it so often, or with quite so much fondness. My mother took us there every year when we were kids; as soon as we finished school for the summer, we'd migrate south for a month and stay in a caravan park in Kilmuckridge.

No wonder Theo thinks it's some magical place; I see it in my mind's eye through a warm pink filter, as though tinted by time itself. The memories are more like textures than pictures, and as I drift steadily toward sleep, floating in that space between thinking and dreaming, I feel like I'm hovering over them, looking down on them from above.

A field of memories . . . lush green and grainy. Freshly cut and yellowing at the edges. The orange glow of sunlight through closed eyelids. Blades of grass like broken bottles, sparkling in the afternoon sun. Moist soil between tiny toes, dirt paths made for two, the low hum of an electric fence, and a stripy beach ball echoing empty bounces on hot black tarmac; endless rings of yellow, red, and blue.

I sink. Lungs heavy with thick, salty air. The tinny roar of rainstorms on a corrugated roof. Bare gravel when the circus has moved on. Colored crayons in a row. Freckled shoulders white with sun cream. And a plump purple raspberry bursting between teeth, while sticky fingers reach to pick another.

My father doesn't exist in this place. I have no memory of him here. I try to place him between brightly colored windbreakers, or squeeze him into the small alcove that served as our breakfast table, but when he appears there—always in the act of raising a cigarette to his lips—he looks wrong somehow, like a stain on a watercolor.

Suddenly, I'm on Kilmuckridge beach with my feet planted firmly in the soft sand, looking out at a honey-colored horizon. The sound of geese drifts by on the breeze but I can't see them. I'm searching for them in the sky when I'm distracted by something floating in the sea in front of me; a huge, flat rectangle, dark and slick with water, is submerged just beneath the surface. I wade in for a closer look, but the tide is rising fast now and it pulls me under the murky water, dragging me toward the object, which rises toward me like a terrible fish. As my body slams into it, my head reeling from the impact, I realize it is in fact a car. It's my mother's car. Her old black Honda. And I can just about make out the shape of her inside. I press my face to the window, desperately trying to see inside; then suddenly her face thumps against the glass, her eyeballs bulging, and her pale flesh bloated and decayed. I scream. Water rushes in. I wake up.

I thought about it once. Suicide. Toward the end of my last relationship it crept into my consciousness and lodged there; a little seed that grew into a plan. He was a lot like my father, my ex. They so often are. We choose these men, I'm told, because the pain they cause is familiar and therefore comfortable. How sad is that?

For a long time, too long, I was reluctant to call his behavior abusive. Abuse, I thought, was bruises and broken ribs. Abuse left marks. But I've since learned that abuse can also be insults and isolation, veiled threats and accusations, a clawing, cloying control that stifles and suffocates till you forget what it was like to take a full, deep breath.

He wore me down until I was just a walking, talking shell. And one night, while he was out getting drunk somewhere, I lay in bed, shivering and sweating and giddy at the prospect of escape. I stared at my face in the bathroom mirror—stared and stared until all I saw were two black holes in a flat, white circle— then I opened the medicine cabinet behind the mirror and gathered together all the pills inside—I even arranged them in order of potency—before finally coming to the conclusion that they might not kill me. They might, in fact, leave me only half-dead, catatonic or comatose in some hospital bed somewhere. And what if it did work, and I left my family and friends behind, wondering if maybe this was their fault? I couldn't do that to them.

It had, of course, occurred to me to just leave him. But he kept me crazy to keep me around, because that's what they do. And so it took my options being whittled down to living without him or dying to finally make me leave. The next morning I worked up the courage to tell my doctor about him. I remember how she looked at me, and without a moment's hesitation she said, "Run. And never go back."

I left the doctor's surgery and went straight to my mother's house, where I planned to stay the night and wound up staying for more than a year. I saw him only twice after that—once to tell him it was over, and once more to move my things out of our house. I was wracked with a mixture of guilt and fear and relief.

I didn't sleep or eat for weeks. Then one night I stood in my bedroom and looked at my body in the mirror. My hipbones protruded, and my ribs rolled under my skin, just like my mother's had all those years ago.

I sometimes wonder if it's possible for a person to inherit a connection to a place, or a propensity toward loving bad men, like the ability to roll one's tongue. I wonder if we're born already knowing and feeling certain things, the same way those geese seem to just *know*, without ever being told, which way to fly and when. I wonder if my father made me the way I am, or if my mother did, or if he's to blame for how she is too. And if so, who's to blame for him? I wonder if we're all just the product of our parents' fears and failings, and their parents before them. I wonder how far back the cycle goes, whether I'm predisposed to being mentally ill, whether I have any choice in how my life unfolds or the person that I'm destined to be. You could go mad trying to figure it out.

My therapist says I do have a choice, not in how I'm programmed but in how I let that programming affect my behavior. In doing so, she says I can "break the cycle of abuse." I hope I can do it. I hope I can change. Because I'm still haunted by the ghost of what I almost did, and the knowledge that, given the right circumstances, it might one day seem like an option again.

I can't get back to sleep after my nightmare, and for the first time since I was a child, I decide to go sleep in my mother's bed. She opens her eyes when she hears me come in, and for a moment I think I'll have to explain myself, but without a word, she pulls back the covers and sleepily shuffles over to make room for me. I climb in beside her and go straight to sleep, and in the morning she asks if I slept okay and I tell her I did.

We have tea and toast in bed while she worries over a crossword; then we get ready in silence, as we always do, sometimes popping in or out of one another's room to borrow lipstick or some hairspray. My mother helps me drag my suitcases down the stairs and into the car; then she pretends to be busy in the front garden, idly picking at the hanging baskets, while I take a moment to say good-bye to the house.

This is the hardest part so far, and it threatens to be my undoing, so I tell myself, "It's not good-bye; it's just see you soon," and I stop myself from lingering too long.

I've made a lot of trips to London in the past few months. Usually my mother stops the car outside Departures; then I grab my bag from the back seat and off I go. It's all very quick and unceremonious, like she's dropping me off at a friend's house for a sleepover.

Today is different.

As she pulls into the short-stay car park, this simple deviation from the usual routine is enough to heighten emotions in the car. Once we've found a spot, I pull the suitcases out of the boot and we each take one and wheel it into the airport.

She doesn't usually come inside with me.

We walk in silence, save for the odd, sporadic piece of advice.

"It gets much colder there in the winter," she says.

"I've packed loads of jumpers."

She nods.

"Do you need to convert some euros to pounds?"

"I'll just pay by card for now," I say.

She nods again.

"What if you need to get a taxi? Do they take credit cards?"

"Yeah," I say, "all good."

A bedraggled-looking family of five, all wearing Mickey Mouse ears, pass by us going in the opposite direction. My mother throws me a sideways glance and I laugh.

"I can't think of anything worse than going to Disneyland," she says, then: "What kind of plugs do they have over there?"

"Same as ours."

"Right so."

I can hear the cogs turning in her head as she tries to foresee and resolve all possible problems before they arise—after all, this is what mothers, and anxious people, do—but before she can think of anything else, we're inside the main door and it's time for me to go.

People hurry past with trolleys full of luggage, a gaggle of girls in matching blue hoodies talk excitedly on their way to the check-in desk—they look like some kind of sports team—and a few feet away, a woman is trying frantically to dismantle a pram while her husband soothes their screaming baby. My mother and I look around quietly, both unsure of our next move.

"Right," I say, "I'd better go check these in."

"Do you want me to come with you?" she asks, and suddenly I'm nine years old again and about to attend my first (and last) ballet class. We're standing at the gates of a big redbrick building. She's got the car keys in her hand and a worried look on her face.

"No, no," I say, "I'll be grand."

"All right. Well, if you're sure?"

"Yeah."

"I can wait here for a bit, just in case."

"No, honestly," I say. "Get yourself home."

My voice catches on the word "home" and I almost break. I'm sure she can sense it. She's probably holding back her own deluge of tears.

"Okay," she says.

"Okay."

"Are you all right?" she asks.

"Yeah. Just . . ."

I trail off and she nods.

"You'll be back before you know it."

"Exactly," I say.

"Text me when you land, okay?"

"Of course."

We hug then, both letting go a little too quickly, both acting like this good-bye is the same as all the others. We're trying to be strong for one another, which is silly, really, since we know we're both about to go away and break by ourselves.

"I'll miss you," she says as she steps back.

"I'll miss you too," I say with a smile. "Talk to you in a couple of hours."

I walk away awkwardly, wheeling both suitcases together and turning around occasionally to smile at my mother, who waves and smiles in return. *Everything is fine*, our smiles say, *this is no big deal.* Eventually, I round a corner and lose sight of her.

The queue at the check-in desk feels interminably long. By

the time I reach the desk I have watched several dramas unfold, including an American man who appeared to have packed the entire contents of his house, and a frazzled Italian lady whose passport expired last year. Everything outside of me feels faraway and fake, like this is a film set and these people are all hired extras.

Finally, I arrive at the desk. A blond lady in a green uniform and fuchsia-pink lipstick asks me to lift my luggage onto the scales; then she shakes her head and smiles up at me condescendingly.

"You have too much baggage," she says.

"Lady, you have no idea!"

She doesn't laugh. She doesn't even blink. Maybe she hears that one a lot.

"Our baggage limit is twenty kilos," she says.

"I know," I say, "but I've paid for forty."

"Mmm-hmm," says the lady, checking her screen, "I can see that."

"So how much do they weigh?"

"Well, one is fifteen kilos and one is twenty-five kilos."

Even with my terrible math skills, I know that adds up to forty kilos. But how do I tell her that without sounding like a patronizing bitch?

"That adds up to forty kilos," I say. Turns out there was no other way.

"Right. But I'm afraid each individual bag can't exceed twenty kilos."

"You're joking."

She shakes her head.

"But it's the same amount of weight," I say, "going on the plane."

"Our policy is that each individual bag can't exceed twenty kilos."

"Yeah, you've said."

She just blinks at me.

"So if I move five kilos' worth of stuff from this bag to this bag," I say, pointing at the bags, "you'll put them on the plane?"

"Yes!" she chirps, like she's proud of me for figuring it out.

I want to scream at her. I don't want to say anything in particular. I just want to scream, very loudly, in her face. Instead, I drag my suitcases back off the scales and start walking, looking for a space where I can lay them down and open them up and not be in everybody's way.

The airport is teeming with people and I've wandered almost all the way back to the entrance by the time I find a suitable spot. I round the corner where I lost sight of my mother and there she is, sitting on a bench by the window.

"My bags are overweight," I say, and she nods like we didn't just say good-bye forever. Her face is fixed in a placid little smile. I don't think I've ever seen her so calm.

"But if I move some stuff from one bag to the other," I explain, "they'll let me check them in."

"That doesn't make any sense," she says.

I just nod, exasperated.

"All right, then," she says, standing as she rolls her sleeves up. Moments later, we're kneeling side by side on the cold, shiny floor with my suitcases open in front of us. People veer around us on either side, paying us no mind.

"What about this?" she asks, holding up my hair dryer.

"Yeah, that's heavy," I say, and she moves it to the other case.

"How come you were still here?" I ask finally.

"Just thought I'd wait till you took off. In case you changed your mind."

I feel as though a fist has seized my heart. I want to grab her and hold her and never let go.

"I'm sorry," I say, delicately, "but I can't come home now."

My mother laughs, a proper, hearty laugh, and all I can do is stare at her in confusion.

"Oh!" she says, still laughing. "No, I wasn't waiting to take you home; I was waiting to make sure you got on the plane."

"What?"

She places one soft hand on my cheek and looks knowingly into my eyes.

"I know what you're like, love. You're prone to getting cold feet, just like me."

Everything in me relaxes. Tears fill my eyes.

"Oh," I say, "so, you *want* me to leave?"

"Of course I don't! I'd keep you here forever if I could. But you have to go."

She resumes reshuffling my luggage, as though satisfied that we've reached an agreement; then without looking at me she adds, matter-of-factly, "This place is too small for you. It always has been."

My mother moves one last bundle of clothes between cases,

and when she's done, she sits back on her heels, places her hands on her knees, and says, "There, that should do it."

We zip up the cases and I stand up first, helping her to her feet.

"Thanks," I say, knowing that doesn't capture even a fraction of what I want to convey. There are countless things I could say, countless questions I could ask. Maybe I will one day, I decide, but now isn't the time.

"Of course," she says.

We hug again and this time we don't let go straightaway. We stay for a few minutes, holding one another, as my mother cradles my head in one hand and rubs my back with the other.

"It'll be okay," she says into my ear, "everything will be okay." I'm not sure who she's trying to convince, but she repeats it over and over again.

By the time we let go, our faces and shoulders are wet with tears.

"I'll call you when I land," I say.

"All right."

"I love you, Mam."

"I love you too," she says. "Bye, love."

"Bye."

I turn and walk away.

I don't look back. I can't.

On the plane I read a book of short stories by Anne Enright. Donal gave it to me after dinner on Sunday—it's still odd getting books from him that I don't have to return to the library. I delve into the first few pages and am instantly soothed by the familiarity of the form.

I think I like stories because they're simple and contained. You establish a status quo, create conflict, then resolve it. In life, nothing is ever really resolved. Your story never stops. How can it, when all our stories are woven together, part of some greater tapestry of tales that make up our lives and the lives of those around us?

Take that story about my mother, the day she drove to the beach. That story didn't end when she came home. Nor did it end years later, when she decided to tell me the story herself—a decision I won't ever fully understand—because that story is all over me now. It drips from me.

And this story doesn't end when I get on the plane, or when she gets home to an empty house and stands in doorways staring into silent rooms and wonders where the time has gone. For better or for worse, I am my mother's daughter, and her story is my story too. It's mine to carry, mine to hold—with love if I can manage it—and mine to weave into my own.

knowing: part i

ON A BRISK MONDAY morning in mid-September, Theo and I wake up together on the cold, filthy floor of a tent. We've spent the past three days at a music festival in Sussex, and yesterday we stood at the barrier for the whole day, drinking and dancing and screaming the lyrics to all our favorite songs. We're both nursing particularly horrid hangovers today, but we need to get an early train to London so that I can catch a flight back to Dublin this afternoon.

I don't want to go; this is the first time I've seen Theo since he left Dublin two months ago and I'm already preparing myself for how much I'll miss him between now and our next visit— whenever that will be. I'd give anything to be going home with Theo now, back to some lovely London flat we can call our own. But that will have to wait till I can find a job here.

We pack up our things quietly, so as not to wake the still-sleeping people all around us; then we make our way slowly toward the exit. Our breath fogs up the crisp morning air as we trudge through fields of grass, still glistening with dew, and the damp soaks straight through my muddy boots.

On the train we find our seats and fall asleep before we even leave the station. An hour later we wake up, groggy and cranky and desperate for a cup of tea, so Theo goes in search of the food carriage. Before he goes, he gets a blanket from his backpack and covers me with it; then he kisses me softly on the forehead.

I snooze again, and when I wake up, Theo has returned with only one cup of tea. I frown up at him in confusion.

"Slight problem," he says, sitting down beside me. "They only had one cup."

"They only had one cup," I repeat.

"Yes."

"On the whole train?"

"Yes," he says. "They have apparently run out of cups."

"Fair enough," I say with a sigh, then close my eyes and snuggle back into my blanket. "Enjoy your tea."

"Wait," says Theo, laughing in disbelief, "we can share this one."

We can't share this one, actually, because Theo doesn't take sugar in his tea, and I take an embarrassing amount—so much, in fact, that the idea of tea without sugar is repulsive to me. It's been a bone of contention between us since the night we met.

"There's no sugar in that," I say.

"Firstly," says Theo, "we need to address your sugar habit." I roll my eyes. I don't want to have this argument again. "And secondly," he adds, "I've got you covered."

Theo produces four sachets of sugar from his pocket, finishes his half of the tea, and then pours all four of them into the second half. He shakes his head as he hands me the cup.

"Enjoy," he says, and then he settles back into his seat.

This is the moment I know that Theo has fallen in love with me.

are you a banana?

"WHY ARE YOU HERE?" she asks.

"How long have you got?" I say.

She smiles politely.

"As long as it takes," she says; then she glances at the clock and adds, "Today we have one hour."

Her name is Nadia, she's fifty-two, she grew up in New Delhi, and she's been practicing psychiatry here in Dublin for more than a decade. That's what it said on her website, anyway. There wasn't much else on there, just her credentials and an old photograph. At least, I assume it's old; the woman in front of me has the same unruly, dark hair as the woman in the picture, but now it's peppered gray, and her wrinkles are far more pronounced. They suit her, though. I wonder if my face will age as gracefully as hers.

Nadia is sitting opposite me, legs crossed, with a notebook on one knee and a pen at the ready. The epitome of poise, she practically oozes calm through every pore.

I haven't felt calm in weeks.

"Are you waiting for me to speak?" I ask.

"Yes," she says.

"I'm not sure what to say."

I look around me. The room isn't quite what I'd expected. Not that I thought I'd be lying on a squeaky leather couch, pouring my heart out about my daddy issues; I just didn't expect it to be quite so homely. We're both sitting in comfy mint-green armchairs, there are fresh daisies on the window ledge to my left, and a soft April sun drifts lazily through a pair of white net curtains.

I notice her notice me scratching my arm so I stop scratching, but then my big toe starts tapping inside my shoe. I feel like a water balloon springing leaks; if I cover one up, another one pops somewhere else.

"Let's start with something simple," she says. "How are you today?"

"I'm good, thanks."

"Is that true?" she asks, her eyes narrowing on me.

"No. It's just what you say, isn't it?"

She smiles, and when she does, a pair of perfectly symmetrical dimples appear on either side of her mouth. I find this comforting. The rhythm of my tapping slows slightly.

"Fine. I'm awful."

"Good," she says, making a note on her notepad.

Did she just write "awful," or "honest," or "fidgety"? Has she noticed something about me that only her expert eye can see? Has she solved it already? Can she fix me? Or did she just remember that she needs to buy some milk on the way home?

I hate this.

"You told me on the phone that you're a writer," says Nadia.

"I am, yes."

"You tell stories." It's not a question.

"Yeah."

"Then tell me your story." I stare skeptically at her.

"I'll even give you the ending," she offers. "How about that?"

"All right," I say.

"All right," she says, "the story ends last week. When you picked up the phone to make this appointment."

Nadia kicks off her shoes and tucks her feet underneath her on the chair. I decide in this moment that I like her.

"Off you go," she adds.

I nod. Then I take my first proper breath of the day and let it out slowly.

"There's this theory," I begin, "that none of the events of the first *Star Wars* trilogy would have taken place if it weren't for the gunner on the Star Destroyer."

I pause, wondering if she's with me so far. She just smirks.

"Go on."

"Well, if he'd just blown up the escape pod with the droids on it, then Luke wouldn't have got Leia's message, and he never would have met Obi-Wan, or gone with him to Mos Eisley, or—"

She cuts me off with a wave of her hand.

"Rescued the princess," she says. "Got it. You're describing the butterfly effect."

"Right!" I say. "Exactly. And I feel like the reason I'm here started with this tiny little thing that if it just hadn't happened, I'd maybe be fine."

"And that thing was?" she asks.

"I was singing in the shower."

I moved back in with my mother after what I describe to Nadia as "a fairly horrendous breakup." She doesn't ask for the details; maybe she knows that's not the story I want to tell. "Suffice to say, I met Zak when I was seventeen and he was twenty-four. It took me eight years to realize he wasn't a very nice guy. And when it did finally dawn on me, I ran home to my mother's house with nothing but the clothes on my back and the ring on my finger."

"You were engaged?" asks Nadia, matter-of-factly.

"Yes."

She makes a note of this.

"I had a dress," I add, though I'm not sure why.

Ten months on, I'm still living at home with my mother, which sounds like a recipe for disaster, but I like it. I know my mam likes me being there too; after my brother left home she was alone for the first time, so having someone to cook and clean for, to eat dinner with and say good night to, is all she really wants. Even if I did want to move out, I still can't afford to; I lost all my savings when I left Zak. He convinced me to use his bank account for the wedding fund but never quite got around to adding my name to it. In the moment, this seemed lazy and forgetful, but in hindsight I can see it was very much intentional; by maintaining sole access to our savings account, Zak was effectively ensuring I would one day be financially dependent on him.

So, I live with my mother now, which is an altogether different prospect when you yourself are an adult. The trick with mothers and grown-up daughters, I've learned, is simply not to spend too much time together. I get the train to work every morning and I'm gone all day; Thursday evenings I take writing classes; on weekends I go out with friends; and then of course there's Theo, whom I've found myself spending more and more time with since we met at Christmas.

One night, a few weeks back, my mother popped her head around my bedroom door to say good night.

"By the way," she said, "it was nice to hear your voice again."

"You hear my voice every day," I said, confused.

"No." She laughed. "You were singing in the shower."

"Was I?"

Now, I'm not a singer by any means. But I do enjoy it. And along with other things I enjoy, like laughing or masturbating, singing is not something I do when I'm sad. I didn't sing for a long time after the breakup; in fact, I couldn't listen to music of any kind—too sad and it made me cry, too happy and it felt wrong somehow—so I commuted to and from work every day with my headphones in but no music playing. I knew this was a weird thing to do but I liked it; having silence piped directly into my brain created a kind of barrier between me and everything around me; it reduced the world to a manageable murmur. And so, my mother pointing out that I was singing again marked a milestone of sorts on my path to healing.

The next day, a friend from work convinced me to go to New York on a whim. One miserable Monday morning, Aoife and I were looking up flights on our lunch break and by that weekend, we were tumbling out of some filthy dive bar and into a tattoo parlor on Manhattan's Lower East Side. As a direct result of all the tequila I'd consumed, I could not for the life of me tell you the name of said tattoo parlor, or indeed find it on a map, but I know the chairs were covered in threadbare purple velvet and there was a white cat sleeping in the window. Although it might have been a dog. I was really very drunk.

Aoife squealed and writhed and winced her way through her tattoo—an extravagant peacock feather on her shoulder—so when it came my turn I wanted something small. I panicked and asked for a treble clef on my right foot.

"Why your foot?" asked Aoife, while a deathly thin Korean woman slathered gel on her freshly tattooed shoulder.

"I don't like my feet," I replied. "Plus they're all the way down there, so if the tattoo lady fucks up, it's okay."

The tattoo artist looked up from Aoife's shoulder and frowned at me.

"And why a treble clef?" asked Aoife.

"Can't remember," I said.

Drunk Me had forgotten why music was suddenly such a significant signpost of my happiness, but she knew it definitely meant something, and that was good enough for her.

I tell Nadia about the tattoos and the trip in general, struggling all the while to convey just how much it meant to me. I use words like "fun" and "free," but they don't even scratch the surface. I tell her about the day I wasn't feeling well, so I left Aoife shopping in Macy's and went back to the hotel to rest for a while. I was lying on the bed of our thirty-second-floor hotel room, looking out at the city skyline, when I was overcome with gratitude for my past self for having the courage to walk away from that wedding and, more important, from that marriage.

I had received an email from Zak that day—I'd long since blocked his number—accusing me of stealing a set of his mother's dishes when I moved out. I'd done nothing of the sort, of course. This was just another one of his desperate attempts to exert control over me, to make me feel crazy, and there was a time when it would have worked. But seeing Zak's behavior now, with a little time and distance, was like the difference between seeing an elephant in the zoo and turning a corner and bumping into one on the street; I was suddenly and unavoidably aware of the enormity, absurdity, and danger of the situation.

It had seemed completely normal to have a partner who knew my whereabouts at all times, who checked my text messages in front of me, who never let me see my male friends alone; and now here I was, bounding about New York City with my friend, while halfway across the world Theo was rooting for me, telling me to get out there and enjoy every second of it. He was capable of loving me and letting me live my life, and in that moment, lying on a hotel bed thinking about him, I felt freer and happier and more like "myself" than I had since I was a teenager.

"You weren't feeling well?" asks Nadia.

"What?"

"You said you weren't feeling well," she repeats.

That's what she got from all this?

"Yeah," I say, "I was shopping with Aoife in Macy's; then suddenly I felt woozy."

"Woozy?"

"Yeah, like the lights in the store were too bright and the music was too loud. It felt like maybe I was getting a migraine or something and I wanted to lie down somewhere dark and quiet."

She scribbles something on her notepad and as she does I feel compelled to go on. "But I was fine after I lay down for a bit."

She nods.

"Was this before or after you read the email from Zak?" she asks.

"I can't remember. It's a bit blurry now."

"That's fine," she says with her reassuring smile. "Go on."

When I got back from New York I went straight from the airport to Theo's apartment. He knew my flight wouldn't land until three a.m. but he insisted; he even promised he'd wait up for me. When he opened the door, half-dressed, with pillowcase creases on his face, he smiled sheepishly and told me that he'd tried to stay awake. I threw my arms around him and without saying another word, we stumbled to his bedroom, where he proceeded to slowly remove each item of clothing from my body, kissing every morsel of skin he revealed in the process. First he slipped one strap from my shoulder, then the other, kissing his way across them to my neck. Then he unzipped my dress, his lips moving gradually down my spine as he went. He playfully kissed my stomach and my hips, and by the time he reached my legs I was standing there shivering from the cold and the anticipation. Suddenly, the kissing stopped.

"What's that?" he asked, looking up at me from where he was kneeling on the floor.

"Oh!" I said, beaming. "I got a tattoo!"

"Yeah, I can see that."

I laughed, excited to tell him all about it. "So I was singing in the shower and—"

"When did you do this?" he asked, cutting me off, and right then I sensed something shift. The shift was practically imperceptible—most people wouldn't even have noticed—but when you spend enough time around volatile men, you get good at predicting changes in their mood, like a drop in air pressure before a storm. And just as a bird detects that drop and instinctively takes shelter, I noticed myself scanning the room for something to cover myself up with; I felt exposed and vulnerable, standing there half-naked as goose pimples silently crawled their way across my skin.

"What's wrong, honey?" I asked, my voice becoming a mousy little version of itself.

"Nothing," he said, mentally shaking something off and standing up to kiss me. I pulled away.

"Something's wrong," I said, but he just shook his head.

"It's fine," he said, and this time he did kiss me, but I was tense and he could tell. He stopped and stared at the floor for a few seconds before he spoke.

"You know I don't like tattoos."

I was expecting him to be upset that I'd done such a momentous thing without him, that I'd kept it from him, maybe. I was not expecting . . . that.

"Okay," I said, calmly and quietly, trying to avoid an argument at all costs. "I'm not sure I did know that."

"I told you. The night we met, I told you I don't like girls with tattoos."

He had told me that. I remembered now. And I had, of course, assumed he was joking.

"You were serious about that?"

"Yes," he shot back, "I hate them!"

"You hate them? A second ago you didn't like girls with tattoos; now you hate them?"

"Not girls with tattoos," he said, flustered, "just tattoos. I hate tattoos. Stop trying to mix my words!"

"Stop talking nonsense, then!" I said, aware we were now teetering on the edge of an argument, unable to stop ourselves going over. I started putting my clothes back on.

"Don't be like that," he said.

"Like what!? You just announced that you hate tattoos, and as far as I'm aware they're kind of permanent, so there's not much I can do about it."

"Then maybe you should have asked first!" he blurted.

ASKED?!

That was it. That was the moment I mentally checked out.

The next hour or so happened as though I was hovering a few feet outside my own body, watching the scene unfold. We fought a while longer—I'm not sure what either of us said—then I broke down in tears, sobbing to the point of convulsion, unable to catch my breath. Theo, to his credit, instantly stopped fighting with me, sat me down, wrapped me in a blanket, and tried to comfort me. I found his face suddenly frightening, though, and each time he got close I pushed him away. One time, he tried to hold me by the shoulders and I shoved him so hard in the chest that his eyes widened at me and I knew he was afraid. I couldn't speak to reassure him. I was completely frozen in fear.

• • •

When I was around nine years old, I saw a group of boys throwing cans of tomato soup at a skinny old dog in the alley behind my house. After they'd gone, I took a leg of chicken from the fridge and brought it outside to the dog. It backed itself into a corner the moment it saw me coming, not growling or even baring its teeth, just staring at me, shivering and scared. I remember the dog's paws still scrambling to reverse, but there was nowhere left to go; its hind legs were right up against the concrete wall. I held the chicken out in front of me and the dog just stared back, so I moved closer, my hand reaching out, inches from the dog's face. The dog snapped, sank its teeth into my arm, and bolted.

My mother heard my screams and came charging out, only to find me stood in the middle of what looked like a complete bloodbath; there were puddles of red soup all around me and the walls were splattered with it too. The poor woman shrieked when she saw me.

"I still have a scar," I say, holding out my right forearm so Nadia can see. She leans forward to take a look.

"What made you think of that dog?" she asks, even though she already knows the answer. Therapists do that a lot.

"The way I was with Theo that night," I tell her. "It just reminded me."

"I see."

She frowns, considering something, then asks, "Have you ever been angry with that dog for lashing out at you?"

"No," I say, "it was just scared."

"But you are angry with yourself for lashing out at Theo," she says.

"I didn't say that."

"Well, are you?" she asks.

"Yes," I say.

"Why?"

"Because I should know better. I'm not a dog."

She smiles, then says, "We're not that dissimilar, you know, especially when we're scared."

Nadia asks what happened next with Theo, and the thing I remember most clearly was an overwhelming desire to go home. I wanted to be back in my own bed. I wanted to hear my mother snoring through the wall. I wanted my duvet, my toothpaste, my glow-in-the-dark stars above me, and the familiar sound of the creaky floorboards below me. But Theo wouldn't let me go home alone in such a state; he told me afterward that I was so exhausted, my eyes were practically rolling back in my head. So he put me in his bed and stroked my hair until I fell asleep, and apparently I apologized over and over as I drifted off. Theo made a bed on the floor next to me and in the morning he brought me a cup of tea. Then I went home, completely mortified and convinced he'd never want to see me again.

I didn't talk to him for a few days. I couldn't. I physically couldn't. Every time I so much as pictured his face, or thought of his name, everything got suddenly too bright and too loud, my chest tightened, my stomach turned, and a wave of heat burned across the back of my neck, like someone was holding a hot iron just an inch away from my skin. I kept myself distracted as best I could, but I knew I had to see him. And when I did, I knew I had to end it.

He couldn't understand why I was breaking up with him. As far as he was concerned it was just a silly fight; he didn't care about the tattoo, he didn't mean to say those things, and he was sorry he upset me. And maybe that's what I looked like on the outside, just a very upset woman, but on the inside I felt like I was fighting for my life.

The urge to run away was all I could focus on. Thoughts swam around in my head and they all seemed logical . . . It was too soon. I shouldn't have rushed into another relationship. We were getting too serious too fast. I wasn't ready. I didn't need another man in my life. I didn't need the hassle. So I should just end it, I decided. I should just end it and take care of myself for a while.

I lasted a week.

As soon as I removed the pressure of being with Theo, all of my symptoms went away: the tight chest, the nausea, the hot neck. I felt absolutely fine. And suddenly, breaking up with him seemed drastic and entirely unnecessary. I missed him. I wanted to be with him. So I called him to explain.

Cold feet, I said. Nerves, I said. A little anxiety maybe. It might even have been PMS!

We arranged to meet up that weekend, see a movie, and go for a drink. Theo understood completely that it had all been too much too soon, and before we hung up he said he wanted to take things slow. He told me there was no rush, that he was just happy to be with me, and he would wait for me if I needed more time.

WAIT FOR ME?

In an instant all those horrid feelings came flooding back. I was right back in it, and this time I had a guarantee that he wasn't going anywhere!

No.

I didn't want that.

Did I?

I wanted to be with him.

But I didn't want to feel like this. For fuck's sake!

It wasn't supposed to be this way.

I should be happy.

Why can't I be happy!?

"And that's when I picked up the phone to make this appointment," I say.

Nadia takes a long breath, then stares out the window for a few moments, tapping her pen against her lower lip. She asks when I first began to feel this way—the tight chest and so on—and I tell her it was when I was still with Zak. It's difficult to pinpoint exactly when it started; there are moments I remember vividly, and entire segments of our relationship that feel blurry and dislodged. It's like my brain is a messy filing cabinet with some memories in the wrong drawer, some with smudged ink, and some missing completely.

But as Nadia carefully presses me for information, I am forced to open up those drawers and look at things I'd never really looked at before. And as we trawl further and further back through my relationship with Zak, I start to see all the warning signs with a stinging sort of clarity. There were countless incidents that should have rung big, booming alarm bells in my head, and suddenly I'm furious with myself for being so blind, and for staying so long.

I was just going through the motions like some broken automaton with a plastered-on smile. I would see friends and family enough that they didn't worry, but behind the scenes I was spending days, sometimes weeks, unable to get out of bed, go to work, or live my life at all. I would convince myself I was ill, a viral infection perhaps, and tell myself, and Zak, that all I needed was rest. *I'll just stay here in the dark until I'm better, dear.* And he'd go off to work and come back in the evening none the wiser. Sometimes I made myself sick; I'd have big meals, then feel immediately nauseous, so I'd ram my fingers down my throat until I vomited. Afterward I'd tell myself it was something I ate. I saw numerous doctors but they couldn't find anything physically wrong. They'd ask if things were all right at home and I'd lie and say everything was fine.

I've tried to tell people what it was like—I've even tried to tell Theo—but the first thing they all ask is, "Why didn't you just leave?" Good question.

Why didn't I?

I ask myself this a lot. It plagues me. Especially late at night. It is the theme of most of my nightmares, where I'm trapped in a house with Zak and I can't get out, and I know the real world exists somewhere, but I can't quite remember what it looks like or where it is or who's there waiting for me, and he won't stop shouting long enough for me to figure it out.

Even when I was still with him I would ask myself why. I'd lie awake at night, the harsh blue glare of my phone screen lighting up my face as I trawled through forums and articles and advice columns, searching for answers. I'd take quizzes and tick off checklists.

Does your partner ever belittle or humiliate you?

Does your partner blame his bad behavior on his mental health or family history?

Does your partner ever shout or act out violently?

Does your partner make you do things you don't want to do?

Are you ever afraid of your partner?

I'd score too high and then I'd retake the tests so I could answer more conservatively. Maybe I was being too harsh, I'd tell myself. But whichever way you sliced it, all signs pointed to abuse. Zak's methods looked so different from my father's that somehow they had slipped under the radar until it was too late.

So, why didn't I leave? If he was so awful. And I knew he was abusing me. Why didn't I leave?

I tried to, but every time I did, Zak convinced me to stay. He told me he'd die without me. Threatened to hurt himself. Even threatened to make my life hell. As if it wasn't already. I'd tell him I wasn't happy, and he'd promise me things would get better. But they never did. He'd behave himself for a few weeks and then he'd get drunk, lash out, scream and shout and say the cruelest things. After every episode like this he'd break down, clutch at me and cry on me and beg for me to stay. He said that he'd get help, that he was only like this because of the things his father did to him, and he'd question what kind of person I was for even considering leaving him in such a time of need. He'd describe in grotesque detail how his father would hurt him as a child. And because I was never left to starve or beaten with a hammer, I told myself Zak had had it worse than me. That he needed me. That I had to help him.

By the end I was focusing all my attention on the stupid minutiae of the wedding, because maybe if I had the right dress and the right flowers and the perfect fucking three-tiered cupcake tower, it wouldn't matter that I was terrified of the groom.

I've done enough research to know that people get stuck in these relationships all the time—strong, successful, seemingly happy people. I know that it takes women, on average, seven attempts before they finally leave an abusive partner. I know that I was young when I met him, practically a child, and still highly impressionable. I know my history of abuse made me an easy target. I know some part of him knew this too and that's why he chose me. I know the seven-year age gap meant he could tell me how things were "supposed to be" and I believed him. I know my only model of a relationship growing up was an unhealthy one. And I know now that he did this to other girls too.

I know that staying with him doesn't mean I'm weak. I know it wasn't my fault. I know all this. But knowing something and believing something are two very different things. And part of me still blames myself for staying.

My fists are clenched. Nadia asks if I'm all right.

"I'm pissed off," I say.

"With?"

"Myself," I spit back. "I'm so fucking angry with myself. I should know better. I know about mental illness. I have friends with depression and eating disorders. I knew a guy who got so bad he killed himself. But I let myself unravel. I just stood back and watched it happen."

Nadia looks out the window again and thinks a moment. "Are you still making yourself sick?" she asks.

"No," I say, "that stopped as soon as I left him."

"Good," she says; then her gaze shifts from the window back to me.

"There was a study, a long time ago, with three groups of puppies," she says finally. "The first group was always treated with love and affection. The second group was beaten and mistreated all the time. And the third group received a mixture of both love and punishment, with no particular rhyme or reason for either. Now, which group of puppies do you think showed the most loyalty and obedience to their handlers?"

"The first one?" I ask.

"No," she says. "The third group of puppies became the most loyal, subservient dogs, because while they were sometimes mistreated, there was always the hope that this time, maybe, they'd receive love instead. And so they kept coming back for more."

"That's the saddest fucking thing I've ever heard," I say.

Nadia tells me about another study they did where they put three groups of dogs in harnesses. Nothing happened to the first group, the second group received electric shocks that they could stop by pushing a lever, and the third group were shocked too, but they had no way of stopping it. Later, they put all the dogs in cages, which they could easily escape from, and administered electric shocks again. The first and second group just walked out, but the third lay down and took it.

"They had learned that there was nothing they could do to stop the pain," says Nadia. "They believed they had no control, and so they allowed themselves to suffer. It's called learned helplessness."

"People really need to ease up on dogs," I say.

"They don't do those studies anymore," she replies, "but the findings are fascinating. Like I said, we're not all that different from dogs, or any animal, for that matter. When we're afraid, in danger, or suffering, logic goes out the window; our primary goal is survival. You were afraid, and you felt you had no control, so you did what you believed you had to in order to survive."

"But why do I feel this way now?" I ask. "I left him. He's gone."

"I wouldn't want to guess at a diagnosis based solely on what you've told me today," says Nadia, "but it sounds like you have an acute anxiety disorder. The panic, depression, and sickness you felt were all physical manifestations of the suffering and conflict in your mind. Your body was trying to warn you that something was wrong, but Zak's erratic behavior confused you into thinking there wasn't a problem, or indeed, that you were the problem, not him. So you ignored all the warnings and pushed through. Now, the new relationship, the fight, Theo being a bit controlling, have all triggered those old feelings."

"So I'm allergic to love?" I ask.

"I wouldn't put it quite like that," she says, "but in a way, yes."

"Brilliant."

"You were wrong about your butterfly effect, though. Singing in the shower, getting that tattoo . . . that's not where it started. It goes back much further, and you would have ended up here eventually, I think."

She's right. There are more files stashed away down the back of my messy filing cabinet, all gathering dust in the dark.

"You talk about your mother a lot but you haven't mentioned your father once," says Nadia. Her voice has softened a little.

"There's not much to say," I reply matter-of-factly. "He was an abusive, alcoholic asshole who occasionally beat my mother, made all our lives hell, and finally fucked off when I was eight years old."

"Did he ever hit you?" she asks.

"No," I say, "he'd just tickle us until we puked, and dangle us over the staircase by our ankles, and throw cold water on us in our beds sometimes. You know, fun stuff. Stuff that doesn't leave any visible marks."

Nadia seems surprisingly unfazed.

"What about Zak?"

"No," I say, "he kicked things a lot. And punched holes in the walls. But he never hit me."

Nadia nods. She's stopped making notes.

"Were either of them sexually abusive toward you?"

I stare at her for a moment. I want to tell her but the words won't come out. All I can do is nod; then I look away immediately.

"Both of them?" she asks.

I nod again, staring at the floor.

"Until I met Theo," I say, tears in my eyes, "I didn't know what sex was supposed to be."

"I'm sorry," she says. "And for what it's worth, I understand."

She does too. I can tell by the way she's looking at me now.

We're like mirrors, silently reflecting one another's sad truth. Our quiet nods speaking volumes. Our soundless stories shared.

Nadia hands me a tissue and waits for me to compose myself. Then she does something I never knew I would need when this moment came: she thanks me for trusting her enough to share this with her, she acknowledges how hard it must have been for me, and she promises that the information will stay between us.

"Am I the first person you've told?" she asks.

I nod again.

"And what are you afraid will happen if you tell someone?"

"That they'll want to know the details," I say.

Nadia nods. She gets it.

"It's like when someone commits suicide," I say. "The first question everyone asks is, 'How?' Like it matters how they ended their life. Like knowing the gory details might somehow change what happened.

"I don't want to be the subject of someone's morbid curiosity. I don't want them to imagine me that way. I don't want people to think about me like that every time they hug me or touch me. I'd rather they just didn't know. I'd rather carry it myself."

My voice cracks under the weight of these last words. Nadia hands me another tissue and says nothing until I'm ready to speak again.

"Can you fix me?" I ask finally.

"No," she says, "but you can."

"Nice. Very *Karate Kid*."

"Do you always deflect difficult emotions with humor?" asks Nadia, deadpan.

"Not always," I say, still dabbing my eyes. "Sometimes I light small fires."

I smile at her. She doesn't smile back.

"I don't do that."

"I know," she says. Then: "Yes, you can get better. And I can help. But it's going to take a lot of hard work and dedication. This won't be easy."

"Nothing is," I say.

Nadia glances at the clock and realizes we only have five minutes left, so she suggests we use the remaining time on something that will help tide me over until my next session. My next session, she says, and I flash back to this morning when I naively thought I might only need one, like all those people who go to the gym one time and wonder why they're not buff yet.

I ask how many sessions we'll need. I like plans, strategies, certainties, and I want her to tell me on exactly which future date I will be fixed. She, of course, can't tell me that—all she can say is that we'll need a few months, at least—so we schedule another appointment for the following week and she writes it down in her diary. Then she closes the little notebook in her lap, looks up at me, and asks what my biggest concern is in this moment.

I tell Nadia that I'm afraid what happened with Theo will happen again. I confess that sometimes I feel like someone else is behind the wheel, some other version of me, my fear, perhaps, and I'm just cowering in the back seat, watching my fear drive me around. I can see everything happening through the windscreen, but I can't do anything about it. Then this "other me" looks back over her shoulder and tells me it's better this way.

"She tells me I'm broken and I can't be trusted to make the right choice. She says I can't be fixed. And I'm afraid she might be right."

Nadia regards me a moment before speaking.

"Are you a banana?" she asks.

"I'm sorry?"

"Are you a banana?" she asks again, with no hesitation and not a hint of a smile.

"No," I say, "I am not a banana."

"Right," she says, "good. That's good."

She pauses a moment, as though deep in thought.

"What if you thought you were a banana? Would that make you a banana?"

"No," I say, "I would be a human who thinks she's a banana."

"Okay, good to know," says Nadia, like I've just given her the answer to a puzzle that's been bothering her for ages.

"I'm not sure what the point is," I say, a little frustrated now.

"Well, I'm just wondering, if your brain were to tell you all the time, rather loudly and emphatically, that you were a banana, would you be a banana then?"

And suddenly it clicks, and I smile and say, "No. Because thinking something doesn't make it real."

Nadia flashes me a playful smile. Her dimples reappear.

"Exactly!" she says. "So until next week, whatever your brain tells you—that you're useless, that you're broken, that you're unfixable—just hear it, acknowledge it, and try to let it pass. You are not broken just because your brain says so."

"Okay, I'll try," I say, and she sees me out.

I stand on the steps outside and I turn my face up to the sun for a moment. For the first time in a long time I feel calm.

Nadia and I will work together for almost a year, by which time I'll have discussed all this with Theo, and things will be going well with him. I'll have my anxiety under control by then and I'll be feeling much more positive about myself and my future. Nadia's area of expertise is cognitive behavioral therapy and, being such a diligent student, I'll take easily to this structured, scientific approach to bettering my mental health. Together we'll regulate my emotions, rewire my thought patterns, and practically put a stop to my panic attacks. Ostensibly, I will be better, but while CBT will help me function day to day and cope better with whatever life throws at me, it won't address the past events that led to me being unwell in the first place. My anxiety and depression are actually symptoms of a much deeper issue, caused by a lifetime of trauma, but I won't even begin to understand that until long after Theo and I have parted ways.

One day, years from now, a therapist in London will diagnose me with borderline personality disorder, stemming from complex post-traumatic stress disorder. But for now, unfortunately, Nadia fails to figure all this out—partly because her training hasn't prepared her for it and partly because psychiatry itself is still catching up with me and my plethora of problems.

What I fail to figure out is that Theo has issues of his own, maybe not as severe as mine, but enough to make him unstable and ill-equipped to cope with life. We are both wounded in our own way and, like a pair of tectonic plates shifting over time, our wounds will gradually grate against one another's, causing damage at a glacial pace. Neither one of us will notice until it's too late.

I leave this first session feeling hopeful, and blissfully unaware that Theo and I are playing with a losing hand.

this charming man

I ARRIVE AT THEO'S apartment at exactly eight p.m., carrying a bottle of wine and the coat I borrowed from him last night. I actually got here fifteen minutes ago, but I've been sitting in my car, watching the snow falling and gearing myself up to go inside.

I'm nervous, bordering on terrified. We only met yesterday and Theo's already invited me over for dinner, which seemed exciting on the way here but now seems insane. I haven't been on a date in almost a decade. Is this a date? I think it's a date. I've shaved my legs and I'm wearing red lipstick and a pretty dress, so it must be a date. But I'm not ready to date! What am I doing? I'll just give Theo the coat and go, I decide, but then he opens the door and takes one look at me, and that irresistible grin spreads instantly across his face.

"My coat!"

"Your coat," I say, handing it to him.

"And I suppose it's nice to see you too," he says playfully.

He's wearing jeans and a white shirt, with the top two

buttons open. His dark blond hair falls in cute little waves around his face and his brown eyes are practically sparkling at me. I need to get out of here.

"Listen," I say, and I'm about to explain that he's very lovely but I'm not ready for any of this, when I'm cut off by a deafeningly loud alarm coming from inside his apartment.

"Shit," says Theo, and he rushes off down the hallway.

Unsure what to do at first, I eventually follow the sound to the kitchen, where I find Theo desperately trying to turn off the grill. On the ceiling above him, a smoke alarm is wailing incessantly.

"Where are your towels?" I shout. Theo is clambering over the dining table to open a window but manages to point to a tea towel by the sink. I grab it and climb up on the counter to waft fresh air around the alarm. After thirty seconds of frantic fanning, the screeching stops and blissful silence is restored. I look down from where I'm kneeling on Theo's kitchen counter and I see what he's just rescued from the grill—a tray of fat, crispy sausages. There's a pot of onion gravy bubbling on the hob too, next to a much larger pot of thick, creamy mash.

"Holy shit, that looks amazing!"

Theo told me he was making mash, but given he's a twenty-three-year-old man, I was expecting the dry, lumpy student equivalent.

"You weren't joking about the mash," I say.

Theo looks up at me, deadpan, and says, "I never joke about potatoes."

My laughter quickly dissipates when I become aware of my predicament: perched on his counter in a rather short dress with no obvious way to get down. He notices me considering my options and steps in to help.

"If you could just, sort of, not look," I say, tugging at the hem of my skirt with one hand and leaning on his shoulder with the other. Theo turns his face away but laughs at my utterly ungraceful attempt to climb down, which ends up with me stepping on one of his feet and landing with a thump against his chest.

"Whoa," he says, catching me by the waist before I can fall any farther.

It's in these moments that I wish I were one of those waifish little Thumbelina types—the kind that men can just pick up and pop back down wherever they like. Alas, I am five foot eight with gangly limbs and a penchant for clumsiness.

"Thanks," I say, still pressed up against him. "You can let go now."

"I know," he says, smiling down at me. I smile back in spite of myself and we stay this way a moment longer, his face just inches away from mine, before he steps away and returns to the food.

"Wine?" he asks over his shoulder.

"None for me, thanks. I have to drive home."

"Sorry. Of course," he says. "I didn't mean to assume . . ." His cheeks flush red. This only adds to his charm.

"No problem. Can I help you with anything?" I ask.

"All good. Go ahead and take a seat."

We eat at the table by the window, which Theo promptly closes when an icy wind picks up outside. He's put jazzy Christmas music on and lit some candles. This is definitely a date.

Theo's apartment is simple but cozy—one bedroom, one bathroom, and a small living room with a kitchen at one end. It's a bog-standard box with magnolia walls, but he's clearly made an effort to make this space his own; there are framed posters of movies and musicians he likes, and shelves full of well-trodden books, and in the kitchen pots of fresh herbs grow in neat rows along the window ledge.

"What were you about to say earlier?" asks Theo as we tuck into our food.

"When?"

"Before the alarm went off, I thought you were about to tell me something."

"Oh," I say through a mouthful of mash, "I was about to tell you that you're very nice but I'm not ready for this. And then I was going to run away."

"Right," says Theo, his expression unchanging. "So why didn't you?"

"Well, you made me bangers and mash, for a start."

"Fair," he says. "I appreciate your honesty."

"Also, I like you."

Theo tries and fails to conceal a smile.

"But . . ." I continue, "I'm scared."

"Of bangers and mash?" he asks. I laugh and roll my eyes at his awful joke.

"Of dating."

"Dating!" says Theo, in mock horror. "Who said anything about dating?"

I just stare back at him with a look that says, *Come on.*

"All right," he says, suddenly sincere, "I get it."

"You do?"

"Sure. I mean, from what you said about your ex last night, he sounds like a real wanker."

"Oh God," I say, mortified by the memory of drunkenly ranting at Theo about how all men are essentially trash. "Sorry about that."

"Don't be," he says, "and I get why you'd be scared to date again after that. So, we don't have to date, if you don't want to."

I'm not sure what to say. I do want to date him. The thought of it just fills me with paralyzing dread is all.

"And as much as I'd like to kiss you right now," he adds casually, "we don't have to do that either. In fact, we don't have to do anything you don't want to do. I'm fairly certain that's how that works."

I giggle at this and he smiles reassuringly.

"Just so it's abundantly clear," he says, "it really would be great if you ever did want to kiss me too. But until then, there's no pressure. We can just be mates."

I let out an involuntary shriek of laughter.

"We can't be mates!"

"We bloody well can!" Theo sounds suddenly very defiant and very English. "If that's what it takes to keep spending time with you. I'll be the best goddamn mate you've ever had!"

I regard him for a few seconds, still laughing a little; then I offer him my hand across the table.

"Okay," I say, and he shakes my hand.

"Okay, then."

This whole time the TV has been on silently in the background. Neither of us was paying attention to it before, but now I notice a severe weather warning on the nine o'clock news.

"Oh shit, turn it up," I say, and Theo goes to find the remote. Some poor reporter is stood in the middle of a blizzard, clutching a microphone with both hands and screaming over the sound of the storm. She's urging people across the country to stay indoors and avoid unnecessary journeys.

"Well," I say, "we'd best open that bottle of wine."

We decide to watch *Star Wars* and wait it out, but the weather keeps getting worse. By three a.m. we've watched *A New Hope* and *The Empire Strikes Back*. We've just begun *Return of the Jedi* when we both pass out on the sofa.

I wake up with my legs on Theo's lap and his hands resting on my feet. I can hear the wind howling outside as it smacks fat flakes of snow against the window. I check the weather update—the DART is down, as are most bus routes, and the roads have all been deemed treacherous. I get up and put the kettle on, then go to the bathroom and try to salvage what's left of last night's makeup.

When Theo finally stirs, I hand him a cup of tea and give him the weather report.

"Oh no," he mumbles sleepily, "I guess you'll have to stay here a bit longer."

"Guess so," I say, settling back onto the sofa.

"What happened in the end of that movie last night?" asks Theo. "I fell asleep."

"Oh," I say, "the space bears all turn to the dark side and destroy the rebellion. It's pretty bleak, actually."

"Wow, I did not see that coming."

Theo notices me trying to get comfy in my too-short, too-tight dress.

"Would you like to borrow some clothes?" he asks.

"Christ yes!"

He finds me some pajama bottoms and a T-shirt to wear; then he pulls a pile of dusty board games off the shelf and we spend the day playing slightly less boring variations of them. These include a version of Monopoly where the objective is to go bankrupt—easier said than done—and several rounds of Rude Scrabble, featuring such semi-offensive gems as "tosspot," "wank-stain," and "arsebadger." I'm particularly delighted when I manage to turn "fuck" into "fucketybye," picking up a triple word score and winning the game in the process.

It's still too wild outside to walk to a shop, so in the evening Theo throws together some pasta, tomatoes, mozzarella, and fresh basil he just happened to have in his kitchen. It's one of the tastiest meals I've ever had, and we eat it curled up on the sofa with another bottle of wine.

"Why the hell aren't you a chef?" I ask him, having practically licked my plate clean.

Theo laughs modestly.

"And give up the dizzying heights of accountancy? Are you crazy?"

He's joking but there's an undertone of sadness.

"Did you always want to be an accountant?" I ask.

"No. My mother wanted me to be an accountant." Then he smiles. "I wanted to be a rugby player."

"Oh? What happened?"

"She's very persuasive," he says. "Also, I'm not very good at rugby."

Another almost-joke tinged with resentment. I decide not to push it.

"I wanted to be an astronaut," I offer, "but I can't do math and I get sick on roller coasters." Theo laughs.

"So you became a writer instead."

"I wouldn't say I'm a writer," I say. "I just take writing classes and fabricate reviews for a travel magazine."

"You write. Therefore you're a writer. And you've had some stories published, haven't you?" I can feel my eyes widen.

"You've read those?"

"Yeah," he says, a little bashfully, "they're really good. I mean, I liked them. For what it's worth."

"That's worth a lot, thank you."

I feel an overwhelming urge to touch his leg, and I'm about to reach out when he stands up and starts collecting the dishes.

I follow Theo to the kitchen and insist on washing up, since he did all the cooking. After I'm done, I find him in his bedroom, tidying up. There's a record player belting out music in the corner and I stand in the doorway, watching him and listening to a song I half know but can't quite place. Theo's bedroom, like the living room, feels very him. He's got posters on every wall, and an impressive record collection for someone living here temporarily. One wardrobe door is covered from top to bottom in

Polaroid pictures of people I presume are Theo's friends and family. He doesn't feature in the photos himself; I suppose that's because he took them all.

"Thought you might like to sleep in a fresh bed tonight," says Theo when he spots me in the doorway. He's just started to change the sheets from a stripy blue set to ones with big green, red, and black disks. They're unusual-looking but they suit the room.

"Thanks," I say. "Sorry to put you out again, though." He shrugs it off as I nod toward the record player.

"Who's this?" I ask.

"Jeff Buckley."

"Never heard of him."

Theo looks genuinely affronted.

"Jeff Buckley," he repeats, like this might jog my memory. "He was only the most iconic musician of the twentieth century."

"Was?"

"He died," explains Theo, "before he could finish his second album. So he only made one complete studio album."

"Is this it?" I ask.

"No, this is a collection of his live sessions."

Theo puts down the sheets and hands me the record sleeve. I read the title out loud: "*Live at Sin-é*. That's that," I say.

"What's what?"

"*Sin-é*," I say. "It's Irish for 'that's that.'"

"Huh," says Theo, smirking to himself as I hand the sleeve back. "All this time I never knew that."

"Are you a big fan, then?"

Theo points to a framed poster above his bed, a sepia-toned

print of a very forlorn-looking man in a white T-shirt. I assume this is Jeff, with his long, drawn face and perfectly unkempt hair. He reminds me of Theo, actually.

"I'll bet you have heard of him," says Theo, as he sits cross-legged next to the record player. He changes the record with delicate precision and carefully lowers the needle onto a particular groove. I hear a crackle first, and then a quick intake of breath, before the first few bars of "Hallelujah" come floating into the room.

"I know this one," I exclaim, sitting down on the half-made bed. Theo smiles up at me.

"I knew you would."

Halfway through the song I lie down on my back and stare up at the ceiling. Theo lies next to me, propping his head up on one elbow.

"He didn't write this song," he says. "Leonard Cohen did. But it's one of those rare cases where the cover is better than the original."

"Like when the sequel is better than the first film?"

"Yeah," he says, smiling down at me.

"We are officially a cliché." I laugh.

"Are we?"

"Little bit," I say. "Lying here listening to pretentious vinyls. At least it's not the Smiths. Then we'd be just like every tacky rom-com couple."

I flinch at my use of the word "couple" and hope Theo didn't notice.

"Like in *500 Days*," I go on, trying to fill the silence.

"I haven't seen it."

My jaw literally drops.

"All right," I say, taking his hand in mine and dragging him to the living room. I plonk him on the sofa and find *500 Days of Summer* online and we watch the whole film in silence, except for the fantasy-versus-reality sequence, at the end of which Theo shouts, "Oh, for fuck's sake!" and I look over at him and smile.

"Well," he declares when it's over, "Summer's a bitch." I laugh.

"Everyone thinks that at first, but the more you watch it, the more you realize that Tom is in the wrong."

"Yeah," says Theo. "It's like how I used to watch *Die Hard* and think John McClane was the hero, but now I feel like maybe the terrorists had a point."

"I'm serious!" I say, throwing a cushion at him. "Tom is so blinded by who he wants Summer to be that he can't see who she really is. Watch it again in a few years and I guarantee your perspective will change."

"But the story won't change."

"It doesn't have to," I say, "because you will."

"Deep," says Theo, throwing the cushion back at me and accidentally knocking the glass of red wine in my hand. It spills all over me but thankfully misses the sofa.

"Shit, I'm sorry," says Theo, running to the kitchen.

"They're your clothes," I shout after him.

He returns with a wet cloth and stands in front of me, unsure what to do. I'm completely soaked. "Maybe I'll just jump in the shower." Theo takes a step back.

"Yes. Good idea," he says.

"That way we can avoid doing that thing where you help me get undressed and we accidentally end up having sex."

"We would never do that," says Theo with faux sincerity, "because we're mates."

"Ah yes," I say with a smile; then I head toward the bathroom, where Theo hands me a fresh towel and leaves me to it.

In the shower, I feel weirdly agitated, like my body is full of energy I need to expend. The sensation is odd and a little frustrating, and running my hands over my own skin as I wash only causes the energy to build further. Even the hot water trickling down my body is pleasurable to the point of being bothersome. So I turn the temperature down and try to literally cool myself off.

Afterward, I wipe steam off the mirror and stand staring at my naked body. I've started to regain all the weight I lost during my last relationship, and I look healthy for the first time since I was a teenager. I've been eating properly again—my mother's made sure of that—and my boss, Ciara, has even convinced me to take up yoga.

"It's not for your body; it's for your mind," she told me as she perched on the edge of my desk one morning. "It'll help with your anxiety."

"What anxiety?" I asked.

"Oh, sweetie," said Ciara, tilting her head to one side and touching my shoulder in an uncharacteristic display of compassion.

Looking at my reflection now, I imagine Theo standing behind me, wrapping his arms around me, and I feel frustration creep back in. I take my right foot, place it on my left thigh, and press my palms together in front of my chest. Then, rooting down through my standing foot, just like the instructor taught me, I raise my arms above my head and close my eyes. Tree pose is my favorite posture, because you can't think about anything else when you're standing on one foot. My breath slows, my mind clears, and my body steadies.

When I'm done, I wrap myself in the towel Theo gave me and go back to his room, where I find him sitting by the record player again, deciding which album to put on.

"Laura Marling or Johnny Flynn?" he asks.

"I don't know either of them."

"Right, we need to sort that out," says Theo, before putting on what I can only assume is Johnny Flynn, since a very solemn, soulful male voice comes booming from the speakers. The voice contrasts beautifully with the music, which is whimsical and light, like traditional folk with modern arrangements. I sit on the edge of the bed and listen to a song I later find out is called "The Wrote and the Writ," and I'm almost moved to tears by the words, which are more like poetry than lyrics.

"Wow," I say when the song is over.

"I know," says Theo, beaming from ear to ear. "I thought you'd like this, being a writer and all. Wait till you hear Laura. You'll love her."

I find it incredibly endearing how much pleasure he takes in sharing these songs, which clearly mean so much to him. Suddenly I feel an overwhelming urge to be let further into his world. I want to crack him open and look inside. I want to understand how he works. To know him better than anybody else knows him, even himself.

Theo's left some fresh clothes folded on the bed for me, but I stay in my towel for now, lying back down on the bed to listen to the music. After a few minutes, he changes the record again. I recognize the Smiths straightaway and I let out a little giggle.

"Now we're officially a cliché," says Theo as he lies down next to me.

"Is this okay?" he asks. "Me lying here?" I nod.

"How did he die?" I ask, gesturing to the Jeff Buckley poster.

"He drowned in the Mississippi. Decided to go for a swim one night. They found him the next day, fully clothed."

"That's so tragic," I say.

"All the best musicians have tragic backstories," says Theo.

"Oh yeah?" I ask. "What's Morrissey's, then?"

"Well, people say he was madly in love with Johnny Marr, the Smiths' guitarist. But it was unrequited. Largely because Johnny's not gay . . ."

"Yeah, that's pretty tragic all right."

Theo nods and places a hand on my stomach, absentmindedly tapping out the rhythm with his fingertips. A mixture of excitement and apprehension sweeps through me and I don't want him to stop.

"Have you ever liked guys?" I ask. I'm just making conversation, but Theo seems a bit thrown by the question. I wonder if he and his friends ever talk about this stuff.

"I kissed a bloke once at a party, but it didn't really do anything for me. What about you?"

"Yeah, I'm attracted to girls . . ."

"That's hot," interjects Theo, and I shove him lightly in the shoulder.

"But I never really got a chance to explore it, because I got into a relationship so young."

"Wait, how long were you with your ex?" asks Theo, and I'm almost embarrassed to admit it.

"Eight years."

"Eight years!" he repeats. "Holy shit."

"Yeah, I was only seventeen," and I already know what Theo is going to ask next.

"So, was he your only . . . ?"

"The only person I've slept with, yes."

"Whoa," says Theo, like I've just landed a massive bombshell on him. I wonder how many women he's slept with, and suddenly I'm hit by a flash of jealousy, not that they got to be with him, but that he got to have those experiences and I didn't. While everyone else was at college, exploring their sexuality the way you're supposed to, I spent every night sleeping next to a man who often wouldn't touch me for months, and when we did have sex it was rough and unromantic and rarely about pleasing me. In fact, I think the only reason he ever tried to make me come was so that he could feel good about himself.

"I can't count the amount of times I faked it just so it would be over."

I didn't really mean to say that out loud, but there it is.

"He'd bark orders at me. And tell me I was doing everything wrong. And he'd never hold me after; he'd go and wash his hands straightaway, every time, like I was . . . dirty . . . or something."

"Fucking hell. I'm sorry," says Theo. "I'm really sorry."

He touches my cheek softly and looks into my eyes.

"What a complete arsebadger," he says, and this catches me

so off guard that it sends me into a fit of laughter. When the laughter fades, another thought occurs to me.

"What if I'm shit at it?"

"At what? Sex?" I nod.

"I doubt that," is all he says, just as the music stops. Theo goes and turns the record over, then comes back to lie beside me again.

"Any awful life events you'd like to share with me?" I ask.

I'm half joking, trying to break the tension, but something clearly comes to mind straightaway. Theo thinks on it awhile, as though deciding whether or not he should tell me.

"My dad was a junkie," he says finally. "There were always needles lying around the house. And I'm pretty sure he beat up my mum. We don't talk about it, though."

"I'm so sorry," I say, reaching out to touch his arm, "and for what it's worth, my dad was the same. But with drink, not drugs." Theo nods solemnly.

I pull him into me and hold him there, stroking his hair, until the music stops again and we both drift off to sleep.

When I wake up it's dark and Theo's gone. There's a damp patch on the pillow from my hair. I feel dizzy from all the wine, so I decide to go and get myself some water, creeping quietly down the dark hallway so as not to wake Theo, who I presume is sleeping on the sofa. I'm almost at the kitchen when I bump into him and scream with fright.

"Sorry," he says. "I was just coming to get another blanket. It's fucking freezing in there."

I just stare back at him.

"Are you all right, angel?" he asks.

I nod but say nothing.

Theo reaches out and touches my face, his fingertips brushing the back of my ear. I lean forward and so does he. Our lips meet. I feel his tongue flick softly against mine, and in that moment, my body makes the decision for me; my hands grab at his neck and I start slowly walking backward as we kiss, leading him toward his bedroom and undressing him as we go. My towel comes undone and falls to the floor, but I barely notice. When we reach the bed, I fall back onto it with him on top of me, still kissing me and pressing his body close to mine so that I can feel how hard he is against me.

Suddenly Theo stops kissing me. He pulls his face back a few inches and gazes down into my eyes with a look of such intense lust and longing that I feel like a magnificent white light is radiating from me, so bright and beautiful that he can't bring himself to look away. He lifts my arms above my head and slides his hands down them, tracing the outer edges of my breasts, then running his fingertips across my waist and hips. His mouth works its way down my chest to my stomach, and then on, farther, till he's kissing my hipbones. Then the inside of my thighs. My body buzzes with anticipation, as though every single cell is humming softly in harmony.

Theo takes his time with me, savoring me, bringing me to the edge over and over before finally letting me slip into rapturous release. And then he does it again. The second time, the feeling is so overwhelming that I actually notice a tear run down the side of my face. *This is what it's supposed to feel like,* I think, and the thought brings with it equal parts sadness and joy.

When we make love, Theo takes his time with that too,

slowly sinking into me and allowing me to thoroughly experience every single sensation; every brush of his lips against my ear, every stroke of his fingertips on my skin. My legs wrap around him and my hands grasp at his back, pulling him farther into me, and the whole time, I feel like my body is an undiscovered land being explored for the first time. It's like he's committing every inch of me to memory, in case he never gets to see this place again.

Afterward, Theo holds me in his arms and we lie in silence, both breathing heavily.

"Shit," he says finally.

"Yeah."

"Do mates do that?"

"No," I say, "they do not."

We doze for a while, and I'm woken by a sudden flash of light. I had been lying on my stomach with the sheets wrapped around me, and I look behind me now to see Theo shaking off a Polaroid picture.

"Bit creepy," I mumble, as he adds it to the wall of photos.

"Just something to remember you by."

Theo sits on the edge of the bed next to me.

"Remember me?" I laugh. "Why? Am I going somewhere?"

"I hope not," he says, and I feel a flutter in my chest, like a flock of birds taking flight.

By now a full moon has risen in the sky, bathing the room in ghostly blue light. A flurry of snowflakes swirls outside the window and the branches of some unseen tree beat gently against the side of the building.

In the half-light, Theo is exquisite, almost luminous. His

strong, sinewy shoulders rise and fall with each slow breath, pulling his pale skin taut across them like a drum. His face is like a charcoal drawing, all strong lines and shades of gray. I have an urge to reach out with one fingertip and gently smudge the shadow that pools in the small dent above his top lip. When he looks at me, his dark eyes appear endless, and I worry that I might fall into them and never find my way back out. He touches my cheek and my whole body hums again.

"I won't ever hurt you," says Theo.

I stare silently up at him, unsure what to say. Then I sit up quickly, take his face in my hands, and kiss him. Moments later, we're making love again, wordlessly, almost soundlessly, while a storm rages outside.

And so the winter passes with little regard for us. It lashes at our windows and freezes our fingertips and toes each time they venture outside the covers, where we remain, nestled in one another, making love and promises in the dark.

twelve pubs and coppers

✦

THERE IS NOTHING NICE about an Irish winter. It remains the only part of our culture—including famine, foul language, and a collective drinking problem—that is entirely immune to romanticization. Not even the magic of Christmas can salvage this sorry excuse for a season, which arrives too early and lasts long after the lights have come down and the gifts have been regifted. Cold, wet days give way to colder, wetter nights, and endless months of dark, drawn-out mornings linger long into the afternoon, where a low-hanging sun makes empty threats of heat. Irish winter is a nuisance of a guest, forever outstaying its welcome as spring sputters to a sleepy start, too polite to tell it to fuck off.

And as for snow, you may forget it; we go years without the merest whiff of snow. When it does finally fall, the entire population develops a sort of meteorological precognitive ability, insisting on asserting—out loud and to anyone who'll listen—whether or not "it'll stick."

If it does stick, if even a few centimeters of snow somehow do manage to stay on the ground, we rejoice! Curtains are thrown open and siblings are dragged unceremoniously from their beds and out into a rare wonderland that was, only hours before, a muddy back garden. Entire families—dressed in all manner of strange but cozy garb—laugh as they scoop up snow to throw at one another, or slide down hills in makeshift bin-lid toboggans. The next day, with the populace unable to cope with the "extreme weather conditions," a national state of emergency is called and the whole country shuts down—save for the pubs, of course, which will remain open until the Four Horsemen themselves call closing time. Inevitably the snow melts, and with our streets and farms and gardens submerged under a thick, gray soup, we instantly forget our fleeting fairy tale and curse the snow for ever having fallen in the first place.

I am woken by the sound of the central heating chugging to life. The room is freezing; I can just about see my own breath. I'm facedown on my bed in a coat that doesn't belong to me, and under that I'm wearing a long white gown, the hem of which is filthy and damp against my bare ankles. A sparkly object next to my head slides slowly into focus: a homemade coat-hanger halo, crudely covered in silver tinsel and Scotch tape. I vaguely recall cobbling it together in the office yesterday. Beside that there's a packet of unopened face wipes. I touch my eyelashes—still caked in mascara—and congratulate my past self on her good intentions.

Rising gingerly, I am instantly hit by the severity of my

hangover; every muscle in my body aches—even my bones are tender—and it feels as though my scalp has shrunk around my skull. I guzzle down the pint of water by my bed, another of my past self's best-laid plans, then reach for my phone, which I left charging on the nightstand. *At least you managed that*, I think, picking it up to check the time; almost four p.m. There's a text message from an unknown number. I hope it's him.

"I had the strangest dream last night," it reads. "There was an angel in my bed."

I smile as I type my reply: "How odd . . . There's an angel in my bed too!"

Within seconds, three little dots appear at the bottom of my screen, before materializing into words.

"Ask her if she's seen my coat."

I giggle at this, nuzzling my face into the collar of the coat, which still smells like him.

"You can have it back in return for some potatoes."

"Funny you should say that," he replies. "I was just about to make some mash."

"Be there soon!" I say, before saving his number to my contacts as "Theo from Accounting" and hurrying straight to the bathroom.

It's even colder in here. I undress quickly, keeping the time between stripping down and stepping into the shower to an absolute minimum. The water is lukewarm—apparently my past self also failed to turn on the immersion last night—but still, I brave the Baltic conditions for a few extra minutes in order to shave my legs. *Just in case*, I think as I slide a razor over goose-pimpled shins. My thoughts instantly turn to Theo and, just like the makeshift halo on my bed, the past twenty-four hours float slowly into focus.

I was looking out my office window at the sea of black umbrellas undulating along O'Connell Street—one bright red brolly bobbing among them like a life buoy—and waiting for an archaic printer to cough out my last article of the year. December in Dublin is a sad, sludgy affair; people trudging through puddles on their way to work, or on desperate expeditions for some last-minute Christmas gifts. I stood there in a pristine white dress, watching busy shoppers bustle about, laden with bags and clutching their coats against the cold, and I smiled smugly at the thought of my gifts—sitting in a neat pile at the end of my bed, all wrapped and ready to go.

The printer stopped abruptly, choking on my fourth and final page. I kicked it hard and it practically spat the last page at me, the ink slightly smudged but legible. As I turned to grab the stapler from the window ledge, I saw them from the corner of my eye: the first few flakes of snow. Within seconds they went from floating to falling to hurtling downward with great purpose, where they landed on the smiling, upturned faces of people below.

"It'll never stick," came a voice from behind me.

"Ever the optimist, Brigid," I said without turning around.

"Well, it won't," she said, stopping to marvel at the snow with me a moment before adding, "Are you right?"

"Almost done. Harvey's being a complete dickhead."

"What's new?" she asked. Then: "Hurry up, will ya? I'm parched."

•   •   •

Brigid is the fashion and beauty girl who sits opposite me. Harvey is the printer. And the three of us were the last remaining employees at Farrelly Publications yesterday afternoon; everyone else had already left for the Christmas party.

I have no idea why they named the printer Harvey or, indeed, why Brigid was assigned the fashion and beauty desk—as far as I could tell she wore the same brown cardigan every day of her life, and her pink, iridescent lipstick did sweet fuck all for her pasty complexion—but having only joined the company five weeks ago, these were two of many things that I accepted without question, because understanding them wouldn't make me any better at my job or earn me any more money.

I'd been hired to help with Farrelly's travel magazine, *Taisteal*, which is Gaelic for "travel." Genius. They wanted me to write articles on luxury holiday destinations, which I knew absolutely nothing about, but I was desperate to quit my current job at a local Northside newspaper. At the interview, my now editor in chief—a surly blond woman named Ciara—told me that the previous travel and leisure girl had "unexpectedly pissed off to have a baby." Her exact words.

I remember clarifying for Ciara that I was actually a fiction writer and, without blinking, she told me that since they had no budget left to send me anywhere, that would work out just fine. I later found out that they had spent the entire travel budget sending what they assumed was an increasingly overweight travel and leisure girl to various five-star resorts, none of which got a write-up in the end. Fair play to her, I suppose. In the meantime, I was hired on the spot and paid to write about all the amazing holidays I never had.

The office Christmas party is actually a glorified pub crawl called the Twelve Pubs of Christmas, wherein the participants visit twelve pubs, drink a pint in each one, and, I'm told, never speak of it again; apparently, someone shat themselves outside the Foggy Dew last year, but nobody will tell me who.

The whole office piled out the door around midday, all dressed as characters from the Nativity—the chosen theme for this year's shenanigans—and although I'd actually finished my article that morning, I volunteered to stay with Brigid while she worked on an edit. I did this because I'm a complete lightweight and, truth be told, I hoped the rest of the team would be on pub four or five by the time we caught up with them.

While Brigid, who'd been assigned the role of Mary, hastily shoved a cushion up her pale blue robes, I stapled together the pages of my "Flirting with Yurting" article—I had suggested the title ironically and been forced to use it—and left it on Ciara's desk along with a note that said, "Now I have a machine gun. Ho. Ho. Ho." I knew that would give her a giggle when she rolled into work tomorrow, hungover as all holy hell.

"Come on!" whined Brigid, jigging like a child on the verge of wetting herself.

"Okay, okay!" I shouted back; then I grabbed my handbag and followed her to the door, where she stood, haughtily eyeing me up and down.

"What?" I asked.

"Where's your halo?"

"You're joking," I said. She looked from me to her cushion belly, then back to me, and raised one eyebrow.

"Fuck's sake, Brigid!" I shouted, running to the cupboard to grab a wire hanger, while she pilfered some tinsel from the office Christmas tree.

Ten minutes later, the Virgin Mary and I were crunching our way across O'Connell Bridge through what felt like inches of snow. We were headed to the Long Stone—the fourth pub on the list—where we found Joseph and two shepherds smoking outside. The part of Joseph was being played by a young woman in what appeared to be Jedi robes and a crudely-drawn-on beard. She filled us in on the expedition thus far, then escorted us inside. As we approached, a stocky ginger man in a suit and tie stepped in front of us and stuck a hand in Joseph's face. Brigid was about to kick off when he said, "Sorry, ladies, no room at the inn," then burst into wheezy laughter, which descended into a filthy smoker's cough.

"Good one," I said. "Can we go inside now, please?"

"Do as you like," he replied through fits of coughing. "I'm not the bouncer; I'm just here on me Christmas do." Then he gestured to a bunch of other men in black suits and ties.

"What's the theme?" asked Brigid, still annoyed she'd fallen for his joke. "Used-car salesmen?"

"It's Bond, actually," he said, "James Bond."

"Jesus Christ," said Joseph, eyeing up the group of flabby, balding Bonds.

"No, Jesus is inside," said the guy who wasn't a bouncer, before guffawing once more.

"Fuck this, I'm freezing," I said, pushing past them into the pub.

Jesus was indeed inside, in the form of Gary from our graphic design department. Gary, a wiry-looking Cork man, had braved the elements today in nothing but an adult nappy, a scraggly brown wig, and a pair of old battered Reeboks.

"Dad!" yelled Gary, throwing his arms around Joseph. She laughed and hugged him tightly, half her beard rubbing off on Gary's face as she did so.

I left them locked in an embrace and headed straight for the pub's fireplace, where I spotted Ciara and the rest of the team huddled around it, defrosting themselves. Ciara was dressed as a Wise Man, beard and all, and as I approached I heard her make a joke about the term "Wise Man" being an oxymoron, to which some inebriated staff member replied, "You're an oxymoron!"

There was a pregnant pause before Ciara cracked a smile and the employee breathed a sigh of relief.

Unfortunately, my "brilliant plan" didn't go quite as I'd expected; apparently the rules of Twelve Pubs state that you must make up for any pubs you miss. And so I found myself downing three shots of sambuca and a pint of Guinness while the team cheered me on. I silently put a hex on each and every one of them, then wobbled to the bar in search of water.

I was doing my very best impression of a sober person ordering a drink, when a guy in a stormtrooper costume appeared beside me and asked the barman for a Heineken.

"Aren't you a little short for a stormtrooper?" I asked.

"Aren't you a little drunk for an angel?" he replied. His voice was muffled inside the plastic helmet, but I detected an English accent.

"Touché," I slurred, as the barman placed a glass of water in front of me. I picked it up with both hands and began guzzling it down.

"I'm Theo from accounting," he said, offering me his hand. I held out a finger, indicating for him to wait while I emptied the glass; then I smacked it down unintentionally hard on the bar. When I finished, I wiped my mouth with the back of one hand and shook his with the other.

"Nice to meet you, Theo from accounting. I'm—"

"I know who you are," he said, cutting me off. Then, presumably realizing how odd that sounded, he added, "I write your paychecks."

"Oh," I said. "I've never met a guy who already knows how much money I make."

"Sorry," he said, his body shifting uncomfortably. "Bit of a weird opener."

"Nah, it's fine," I said. "But I guess now you owe me a private detail about yourself."

"That's fair," he replied. He took off his helmet and placed it on the bar, instantly disarming me; I hadn't expected him to be so good-looking.

While he decided which piece of top secret information to divulge, I became suddenly and painfully aware of my face. At the best of times, my face betrays my every thought, but when I'm drunk it might as well be a fifty-foot neon sign. Right then I imagined it read "YOU'RE VERY ATTRACTIVE" in letters the size of houses, so I focused really hard on presenting a completely neutral expression, one that would give nothing away.

Poker face, I thought, *pretend you're playing poker.*

I have never played poker.

"Are you all right?" asked Theo.

"Hmm?"

"It's just, you haven't blinked in a while," he said, concerned.

"Oh?"

Before I could figure out how often a human should blink, the barman appeared with Theo's pint. After he paid for it, he turned to me, having clearly reached a decision about what secret to tell me.

"You know how men sometimes get erections at inopportune moments?" he asked.

I enjoyed hearing the word "erections" in his posh British accent.

"I'm familiar with the concept, yes."

"Well," he said, "when I find myself in that . . . predicament, I think about Margaret Thatcher addressing the House of Commons."

I pictured it myself, lingering on the image awhile.

"Yeah," I said, nodding, "that makes sense."

"Works every time," said Theo, picking up his pint and lifting it toward me. "I've never told anyone that before."

"I'm honored," I said, clinking his glass with my mine.

"Slanty," he said.

"*Sláinte*," I corrected, laughing.

"That one," he agreed. Then he took a gulp of his drink, nodded toward the rest of our group, and said, "Shall we?"

As we made our way toward the fireplace, I looked back over my shoulder at him and, feigning genuine interest, I said, "I'm curious, Theo . . . exactly how many stormtroopers were there at the birth of our Lord Jesus Christ?"

I watched him try to formulate a joke before he gave up, smiled, and said, "I didn't read the email."

Despite numerous warnings not to mix my drinks, I had a glass of wine, a pint of cider, and a gin and tonic in Chaplin's, Doyle's, and Palace Bar, respectively. Suffice to say I was a little worse for wear by the time we headed to the eighth pub on our list, O'Neill's on Suffolk Street.

Thus far, Theo had been keeping just enough distance to keep me interested, flitting between the various Farrelly factions and reappearing just long enough to buy me a drink or join one of the many strange conversations I was having with colleagues I barely knew. They ranged from the benefits of electric toothbrushes, to the first dog in space, to how Joel Schumacher had ruined Batman.

"*Batman and Robin* is the best Batman movie ever!" announced Joseph, whose name I had by now learned was actually Aoife.

"You're wrong. You're just plain wrong," I said, turning to Theo for support. "Tell her she's wrong, please."

"You are," said Theo, stone-faced. "Everyone knows *The Dark Knight Rises* is the best Batman movie."

"*Rises!?*" I exclaimed. "*Rises?* Really?"

"Well, that's me off the hook," said Aoife.

"Absolutely," he said.

I stared at him, gobsmacked.

"And I suppose you think *Jedi* was better than *Empire* too?"

"Yes," said Theo, a wry little smirk creeping across his face, "but nowhere near as good as *Attack of the Clones*, obviously."

We were still laughing when Ciara announced it was time to go, and on the way out, Theo moved ahead to open the door for me. His chivalry felt sincere and unforced, and while, yes, I presumed there was also some agenda at play, I welcomed it. I even played up to it a little, making a point of always being in his eyeline, and hooking my arm in his as he escorted me between pubs. I had somehow neglected to bring a coat to work on this, the coldest day of the year, and so we trudged arm in arm down College Street, an angel and a stormtrooper, both blending in with the backdrop of snow. We watched as ever fatter flakes tumbled silently across Trinity College, caught all too fleetingly in the orange glow of passing streetlights.

Perhaps it was the crowds of drunken men in O'Neill's, or the fact that I could barely walk upright, but I noticed Theo taking on a somewhat protective role by my side. He marched me straight to the big mahogany bar, where I stood, swaying slightly, while he ordered us each a pint of water. A man in a Rudolph jumper sidled up next to me and I was distracted by the flashing red light in the reindeer's nose. The man caught me staring and smiled. I smiled back.

"Is that your boyfriend?" he asked.

Straight in.

"No," I said, not looking at Theo, but sensing a shift in his energy next to me.

"Good," said the man.

"Why's that?"

"Because I'd like to buy you a drink."

"That's very kind of you. But I'm all right, thanks." I looked away then, indicating that I wanted the conversation to be over.

"So you do have a boyfriend," he declared.

"No," I said, "I don't."

"Are you gay?" he asked—because as we all know, any woman who doesn't want to sleep with a man must be either gay or taken.

"Only sometimes," I said.

"Then what's your problem?" he spat, successfully going from polite to inquisitive to complete cunt in less than ten seconds. He might have just broken the world record.

I felt Theo tense up next to me, so I placed a hand on his forearm and silently willed him not to get involved; if this gobshite heard an English accent right now it would only make things worse.

"My problem," I said, smiling politely, "is dipshits in stupid jumpers who can't quite seem to grasp that I can be simultaneously single and not fucking interested."

"All right, all right," he said, raising his hands in the air like I was some kind of madwoman with a gun. "I was only offering to buy you a drink, sweetheart."

I wondered, in that moment, if all men were pulled aside in school and taught this shit. I imagined a drill sergeant shouting at a row of terrified young boys, urging them to never admit defeat, never take no for an answer, and never, ever, walk away without first convincing the target that you weren't even interested in the first place.

"MAKE THAT BITCH FEEL CRAZY!"

"SIR, YES, SIR!"

Just then, Theo slid my water toward me.

"Water!" exclaimed the dipshit in the stupid jumper. "What kind of pussy comes to a pub to drink water?"

He was grasping at straws and I shouldn't have risen to it. But knowing that didn't stop me. I smiled, leaned right in—my lips almost touching his ear—and whispered, "The kind of pussy you'll never get."

Then I stepped back and jerked my hand, pretending to throw my drink at him. I savored the look on his face as he flinched and, I shit you not, instinctively covered Rudolph's little lightbulb nose.

"Merry Christmas," I said, before turning on my heel and walking away.

Theo found me sitting on a step outside, shivering and crying. I could tell he was surprised, but he just sat down beside me and said nothing. We stayed there for a while before I finally broke the silence.

"First of all," I launched in, "I'm not angry with you. I'm really grateful that you let me fight my own battle, actually. I'm angry with him. I'm angry with men in general. No offense. I'm angry with myself for rising to it. No, I'm not. What I did was hilarious. But I'm angry that I even give a shit. I'm angry that I'm out here crying and he won't think twice about it. He's probably in there, right now harassing some other poor woman. And maybe this one won't have the balls to say no.

"And I know what he did wasn't *that bad*, you know, in the grand scheme. But it all adds up. It wears you down. And I'm tired. I'm tired of having to be tough, I'm tired of having to keep my bloody guard up all the time and never being able to trust anyone. And, yes, I realize this isn't actually about that guy. It's about an entirely different guy, in fact, who treated me so badly for so long that I literally lost the will to live. And probably it's about my father too. But you really don't need to hear about any of *that* right now.

"Christ, listen to me. I'm just sat here blubbering at you like a fucking eejit. And it's Christmas. And we should be having fun. You should go back inside. I'll follow you in a sec. I'm actually fine. Just a bit drunk. I'm fine. Go back inside."

Theo regarded me a moment; then he nodded and stood up. He folded his arms and squinted up into the snow, seeming to mull something over. *This is it*, I thought, *I've gone and fucked it completely.*

"So, just to be clear," he said finally, "you don't have a boyfriend?"

Pubs nine, ten, and eleven are a bit of a blur. I drank twice in pub nine to make up for O'Neill's, but Theo insisted I bend the rules slightly and have a pint of water in the next two—his dedication to rehydrating me was quite adorable, actually. There was definitely karaoke in the last pub; Gary and I gave a rousing rendition of "Fairytale of New York," the only song in the world that is actually improved by the singers being completely shit-faced. Much to everyone's surprise, Gary did a great impression of Shane MacGowan, and while my Kirsty MacColl left a lot to be desired, there wasn't a dry eye in the house as we belted out the final refrain. When the music stopped the pub kept going; rows of people stood, arms around one another's shoulders, gently rocking from side to side as they raised their glasses and their voices to repeat the chorus one last time, reaching peak volume as we sang of the boys of the NYPD choir and hit the concluding "Christmas Day" with gusto.

"I don't get it," said Theo, en route to the penultimate pub. We had stopped at the entrance to an alleyway, inside which Gary was carrying out a tactical chunder.

"Y'all right, Gazza?" I called out.

"Grand," shouted Gary from inside the alley.

"Don't get what?" I asked Theo.

"Why you all love that song so much," he said. "It's so sad."

"It's not sad!" Gary chimed in.

"It's not sad," I echoed.

Theo laughed derisively.

"He's in jail! On Christmas Eve! And he's lost the girl. The girl hates him!"

"She doesn't hate him. They're just . . . passionate."

"Yeah, they're passion—" Gary was cut off by another round of vomit. I heard it splatter against the wall and was thankful I couldn't see it as well.

"You just look after yourself there, Gary!" I shouted, then turned back to Theo.

"I think we like it because it's not a fairy tale," I said. "It's bittersweet. And it's real."

I watched him think this over for a few seconds.

"I dunno," he said, finally. "Maybe I'm just a sucker for a happy ending," and something in the way he smiled at me made my heart beat a bit faster.

"Happy endings are for cunts!" announced Gary, as he emerged, wiping his face with the back of his hand and ruining a perfectly lovely moment. "Now, come on, will yiz? I'm freezing me fucking balls off here."

Gary had inherited a wooly jumper from one of the sheep—a nice lady from HR who gave up and went home after O'Neill's—but he was still proudly sporting a nappy and a pair of skinny bare legs. We followed him all the way to the Stag's Head, where we realized we'd lost more than half our group; apparently Met Éireann had issued a weather warning and it was due to worsen over the next few hours. Anyone with any sense had headed home to avoid getting stranded in town, but Ciara was having none of it; by this point, she had literally let her hair down—the beard and crown stayed firmly in place, of course—and climbed up on a stool to give her version of the Saint Crispin's Day speech, only with much more swearing and the odd hiccup. She referred to those who'd left as "turncoats," "deserters," and "a shower of bastards," before praising the "surviving troops" and, finally, promising a two-hundred-euro "Christmas bonus" to the last person standing. A bold tactic, to be sure, but it worked; the remaining team members cheered raucously before making their way to the bar, guzzling their eleventh drink of the day and stumbling determinedly toward the twelfth and final pub. Or so they thought.

Despite the weather forecast, Dame Tavern was absolutely rammed—we literally couldn't fit inside the door—but not to be dissuaded, our fearless leader bought shots for everyone and carried trays of them outside herself.

"Never leave a man behind!" she declared, handing out drinks to everyone. Then she counted us down from three to one and we threw back our shots in unison.

"COPPERS!" she roared out of nowhere, raising an imaginary sword in one hand.

Nobody wanted to go to Coppers, but go we did—not for the potential reward but for fear of being labeled a turncoat. Descending those sticky steps, I heard the opening bars of "Maniac 2000" waft up toward me from the pungent pit of people below, and suddenly I regretted every decision that had led me to this moment.

Hordes of off-duty nurses, all dressed to the nines, jostled for space on a densely packed dance floor, while burly men in short-sleeved checked shirts stared at them, mouths open and eyes glazed. The DJ, an unkempt middle-aged man in a faded Led Zeppelin T-shirt, took to the mic to dedicate this one to "the four *gardaí* from County Leitrim," and a group of men down the back, presumably the famous four themselves, went wild.

"What . . . is this place?" shouted Theo over the thumping racket, and I realized the balance had shifted; I was no longer the one who needed protecting.

"This," I shouted back, "is a hive of scum and villainy." He smiled.

"Don't touch the walls," I added, and his smile dropped. He looked around at the walls, which appeared to sweat, giving the impression one was inside some enormous porous beast. His eyes widened in horror and I couldn't help but laugh. "Why on earth do people come here?"

"To get 'the shift,'" I replied.

"The what?" he asked. I pointed out all the couples kissing in the corners. Although kissing is probably too generous a term; most of them looked like they were each attempting to fit the other person's head inside their own mouth. Theo was, quite rightly, appalled.

"Would you like to add a third hand?" I asked. He cupped one ear.

"What?"

"The third hand," I yelled.

"No," he shouted back, his expression melting from horror to revulsion, "I don't think I do."

"It's an ancient Irish tradition," I said. "You can't leave without doing it. Come on, I'll show you!"

I grabbed him by the hand and led him toward the corner, all the while intensely aware of his hand in mine. I picked out a couple locked in a particularly busy embrace; she was up against a pillar, her frenzied hands feeling their way across the man's back as though searching for lost valuables. I approached them and, maintaining eye contact with Theo, I added a hand to the mix, touching the man's back in the same frantic fashion. Nobody noticed. They carried on regardless of the third hand.

Theo stared on, aghast. I stepped back and gestured for him to take his turn. He shook his head wildly but I folded my arms, indicating we would not be leaving until he had completed this rite of passage. He closed his eyes and sighed heavily; then he reached out and placed his hand on the man's back. I waved my hand by way of demonstration and he reluctantly copied me, moving his hand around in a hilariously tender fashion. After ten seconds I nodded my approval and he bolted for the stairs.

Back aboveground, we drank in fresh air, welcoming the cool, crisp night that came to rest on our clammy skin. Theo offered to walk me to the taxi rank by St. Stephen's Green and we ambled quietly in that direction, our reluctance to end the evening almost palpable in the silences between our idle chatter.

There were no cabs to be had, so we stood there awhile, both unconvincingly feigning disappointment. I suggested we try the quays instead, and so we walked on borrowed time down Grafton Street, past the brightly lit displays in the Brown Thomas windows, where mechanical characters lurched soundlessly this way and that. Temple Bar was practically deserted, its cobbled streets now coated in white. We made our way down stone alleyways and under snow-laden arches to the Ha'penny Bridge, where the sight of the Liffey flanked in a blanket of snow caught me off guard.

"She's lookin' well, all the same," I said, leaning against the cast-iron railing.

"She is indeed," agreed Theo, and I turned just in time to catch him taking a photo of me.

"It was a pretty picture!" he explained, smiling shyly.

On the other side we turned right and walked along the river, both so caught up in conversation that ten minutes passed before either of us noticed not a single car had driven by, let alone a taxi. The streets were ours. The city breathed softly all around us. And as we approached the Famine Memorial on Custom House Quay, we too fell silent, wandering in quiet reverence among the cluster of thin bronze statues, their features hollow and drawn, each one frozen in an endless journey toward some long-departed coffin ship.

"I've been here almost a year and I've never seen this," said Theo, breaking the silence.

I just nodded.

"I'm sorry," he said, staring at the figure of a young man carrying a child across his shoulders, his thin legs buckling under the weight.

"It wasn't your fault," I said, smiling at the sheer magnitude of the apology.

"But I thought the English were sort of to blame?"

"Oh," I said. "Yeah, they definitely were. But it's not your fault, you know, personally."

Theo smiled, nodded, and then looked me earnestly in the eyes and said, "I would never deprive you of potatoes."

I burst into laughter, suddenly aware how alien that happy sound must seem in this mournful place. Without thinking, I took Theo's hand and pulled him toward me. And there, on the banks of the river Liffey, amid a crowd of gaunt metal ghosts, we kissed for the very first time.

The kiss was deep but delicate, and when it reached a natural conclusion, we pulled apart slightly and regarded one another's face at a distance only lovers know.

"What are you thinking about?" I asked, blinking up at him through falling snowflakes.

"Honestly?" he said.

"Honestly." I smiled.

There was a brief pause before he smirked and said, "Maggie Thatcher addressing the House of Commons."

I don't know if I'd have stayed at Theo's under different circumstances, but as it stood, I couldn't get home and his apartment was only a ten-minute walk away. So I agreed, but I made it perfectly clear that there would be "no funny stuff." Theo found this hilarious for some reason—maybe he hadn't planned on anything happening—and he assured me I could have his bed and he would sleep on the sofa.

The first thing I noticed in his apartment were the three framed *Star Wars* posters, which I complimented him on.

"Oh, those," he said. "They're just temporary while I have my prequel posters cleaned."

"Funny," I said, as I perched on the edge of his bed, still visibly shaking from the cold.

"Would the angel like a cup of tea?" he asked.

"She'd love one," I said, kicking off my shoes and climbing under the duvet.

"How many sugars?"

"Four, please."

"You're joking," he said.

"Sadly, I am not."

Theo looked at me, half-bewildered, half-disgusted, then disappeared off to put the kettle on.

That's the last thing I remember before waking up this morning, with a full cup of cold tea beside me on the nightstand.

My hair reeked of cigarette smoke, and I could taste stale booze on my breath.

Theo was asleep on the sofa, as promised. I couldn't bring myself to wake him up, and, truth be told, I didn't really want him to see me—or smell me—in that state, so I took his coat from the back of the door and left a note with my phone number and a message that said, "Thanks for the tea. And the coat."

I took the DART home, snuggling up by the window and placing my feet on a heater underneath my seat. A cool winter sun was climbing in the sky, its pink light flashing quickly in the windows of houses as we passed. I hurried to catch glimpses of the lives inside those windows; here a woman making a bed, there a family sitting down to breakfast, and over here a couple getting ready for work. The images flickered like frames in a film reel and were gone.

I looked out across Dublin City, a blank page of snow, and I found myself thinking of him. Without really meaning to, I began imagining a life with Theo in it; the places we might go, the adventures we might share, the kisses and the laughter and the countless cups of tea. I pictured the couple we might someday become. And in my mind, in that moment at least, they lived happily ever after.

a c k n o w l e d g m e n t s

This book is for all the Theos in my life. You have inadvertently been my greatest teachers, and a constant source of inspiration.

For my Mayas, without whom I would be very sad and a bit dehydrated. Thank you for the endless emotional support, the advice, the hugs, and the tea. You sustain me in more ways than you know.

For the Darrens who support the Mayas who support me. The world needs more of you.

For the Ciaras who got my work out there and the Omars who made it better. And even for the Maureens, those talented cows.

For all the Jocelyns. Yours and mine. May they find peace.

For every Nadia I've had over the years, who helped me take down the scaffolding and rebuild anew.

For my family, who do their best, and can always find the funny side.

For Lena, wherever you may be.

And finally, this book is for my Angels, those past and future versions of myself who continue to love and to hope and to fall in spite of themselves. Keep falling, please. I will always be there to pick you back up.

about the author

H a z e l   H a y e s is an Irish-born, London-based writer and director who has until now been writing primarily for the screen. Having graduated from Dublin City University with a degree in journalism, she went on to study creative writing at the Irish Writers Centre before finally honing her craft as a screenwriter. Hazel's eight-part horror series, *Prank Me*, won the award for Excellence in Storytelling at Buffer Festival in Toronto, and her short film, *Dementia*, received high praise from master of horror Guillermo del Toro. When asked why she wanted to make the leap from horror to romance, Hazel said she can think of nothing more horrific than love.